SUMMER SALVO

Book One in the Thromance™ Series

OLIVIA M. CHARLES

Paper Airplanes LLC

This book is for all those who dream of doing something different. Whether in your personal life, in your professional life, in your current life, or in your future life.

Keep dreaming.

Stoke the fire.

Push the imposter syndrome out of your way. Shove it to the fringes of your being.

Acquire the target.

Adjust as needed for environmental factors.

Then take your shot.

Escape with a THROMANCE™ novel—
where hot flashes and sleepless nights are good things.

1

closer to fine

S KIRTING THE BRIGHT BLUE waters of the Tyrrhenian Sea that glistened in the distance on her left, Jenna turned up the music in her car and left the chaos of Rome behind her. Her flight from the United States had landed two hours ago, and her blood pressure slowly leveled out as she made her escape north. Her red Audi A1 zipped north along the E80, and she made every effort to keep her eyes on the road, although it proved to be a challenging task.

Intrigued by the landscape, she maneuvered her way up the west coast of Italy, passing charming old towns interspersed amid striped patches of farmland. Undeniably, some of the towns she spied from the road appeared forlorn, but others beckoned to her with the promise of sun, sea, food, and wine. Add an interesting Italian man to that menu, and she'd have willingly detoured.

Slowing only for the occasional toll, she made good time before turning west to take SP161 into Orbetello, a seaside town situated on a narrow spit of land shaped like a finger pointing her toward the sea. A narrow roadway perched over the water connected her destination to the mainland. Anticipation grew, as did the need to stretch her aching legs. She'd been sitting in the same position for the better part of twenty-four hours—the only change being the mode of transportation.

Crisp blue water in various hues lapped the rocky shores of the causeway. Jenna was so enthralled by the scenery she almost missed the road sign that listed her destination above an arrow that pointed to the left. Steering the spunky red car south to Porto Arezzo, she resisted the urge to pinch herself, tickled that this Mediterranean paradise would be her home for at least a few weeks.

The last stretch was the longest part of the drive, compounded by the two bottles of water she'd consumed on the way. The upside-down teardrop on her phone's map that marked the address of her temporary home doubled in size minutes before the GPS deposited her in front of a newly constructed seaside community. Jenna double-checked the address. She had expected a typical nondescript government-contracted apartment building, and the colorful two-story villa was a pleasant surprise.

One of the many things she loved about her job was the travel. But seldom were the locale and the assignment itself on equal footing. After some of the physically demanding and frenetic missions she had endured over the past six months, a less intense mission couldn't have come at a better time. Coupled with the resort-like atmosphere, assuming the role of personal assistant to a seventy-something-year-old woman would be a welcome change of pace.

The details of the mission had been scarce when she'd received the tasking call two weeks ago. Salvo Agency field agents rarely had the discretion to turn down their assignments, but even so, when Catherine described it as a low-key tasking in Europe with the simple goal of gathering intel, she had jumped at it. Without a firm start date for the assistant position, the decision to stage her seemed a bit premature, but she didn't argue. The luxury of downtime in Italy at the company's expense would never be refused.

Jenna expertly maneuvered her car into a tight spot along the low curb and sent a quick word of thanks skyward to her late father. Not only had he taught her how to fly, but he'd also insisted that she master the crucial life skill that was parallel parking. That, along with being able to drive a stick shift, had proven to be indispensable in her global travels.

A soft smile played across her lips as his ever-patient reinforcement echoed in her head. "Let's do it again. You're too far from the curb," he had said over and over with an undercurrent of humor in his voice at the eye-rolling and huffing from the teenage version of herself. Although her significantly older self was used to maneuvering her much larger SUV around the zoo that was the Washington, DC, metro area where she reluctantly lived, driving in Europe made her appreciate the compact car industry as well as her dad's life lessons.

The parking spot Jenna chose was one of the few that benefited from the shade of a nearby tree whose scrawny trunk was no thicker than the fattest part of a wine bottle. Not a water bottle. A wine bottle. She would be testing that comparison later, for certain.

The adolescent tree sprouted from a small patch of dirt surrounded by sun-bleached pavers that lined the uneven walkway. She had tall, fuzzy dandelions in her tiny back yard at home that cast larger shadows. While the respite from the cloudless Mediterranean sky would only be temporary, for the moment, this scrappy overgrown dandelion served a purpose.

After turning the engine off, Jenna opened the door and winced as she extended her left leg, flexing it until her knee popped satisfactorily. The level of physical fitness needed for her job was taking a toll on her fifty-year-old knees, and the extra twenty pounds—well, thirty, if she were honest—she couldn't seem to shake didn't help. Turning in the driver's seat, she repeated the motion with her right leg while a light beachy breeze wafted in through the open car door.

Stretching as she stood, Jenna lifted her face to the sun, closed her eyes, and breathed in the fresh, salt-laden air. She held the cleansing breath for a count of three before releasing it slowly. At the sound of the sea methodically crashing against the cliff on the opposite side of the complex, a smile from deep down made its way to the surface for the first time in several weeks. Invigorated by the possibility of beach time and rejuvenating strolls along the water, Jenna slung the handles of her leather tote over one shoulder, hefted her carry-on bag and medium-size suitcase from the back seat, and locked the car.

Assignment lengths and locations could vary greatly with little to no notice. Having grown up as a military brat and then serving on active duty for eleven years herself, Jenna had perfected the art of packing for the unknown over the years. "You pack it, you haul it" was one of many aircrew mottos in the Air Force. Even with her flying days behind her, some things still held true.

It was a beautiful Monday in early April, and a few weeks on the sunny west coast of Italy held promise to be the head-clearing reset she needed. She was looking forward to this assignment, relishing the opportunity for another new start, no matter how temporary it might turn out to be.

Every mission was, in its own way, a fresh start. Each one provided the cover of anonymity in a new location with the opportunity to reinvent herself. Mistakes and regrets could be left in the past, and heaven knew she had plenty of those.

enjoy the ride

Aﬀﬁ**FTER CLIMBING THE STAIRS** to the front door painted the perfect shade of coral, Jenna inserted the large metal key that had been tucked in her ops package, then pushed the door open with her suitcase and stepped inside. She dropped her bags in the entry, then tossed her keys on the bar-height counter that separated the kitchen from the main sitting area.

Her first priority was to ditch the shoes that had suffocated her feet for the last twenty-two-plus hours. A contented sigh escaped as the refreshing cool of the tile floor seeped into her bones while her practiced eye studied the decor and layout of her temporary home. The space was compact—efficient, though not tiny—but it was the patio straight ahead of her that grabbed her attention.

Tall, rough-hewn wooden doors with elongated wavy windowpanes separated the outdoors from the cool, crisp interior of the villa. The rustic vibe of the doors had her imagining they had been plucked from an ancient Italian villa that overlooked rolling Tuscan hills dotted with olive trees and vineyards. They added much-needed warmth and helped compensate for the unimaginative, minimalist style of the interior. With a nod of approval at the designer's choice to mount the doors on tracks, she slid one door open and stepped outside.

The afternoon sun split the outdoor space into halves—warmth to the left and a growing triangle of shade to the right. Solar-powered as she was, she ducked to the left, welcoming the sunshine on her skin, knowing this was where she would spend any and all downtime.

The common courtyard, not quite a full floor below, was green and inviting, and the hushed cadence of water gently lapping the sides of a pool lured her to the railing to take in the view. Sunlit ripples on the surface of the water danced in the soft breeze. Evenly spaced among white chaise lounges, adjustable blue umbrellas stood at attention, only one of which dared break formation to bend longingly toward the edge of the pool.

Her gaze followed strings of haphazardly crisscrossed patio lights to a covered gazebo, where a family snacked at a picnic table. She envisioned evening swims with the patio lights glowing like bright fireflies and playing bocce on the short-shorn lawn, wine glass expertly balanced in one hand.

Tucked into the shady corner of the patio, two comfy-looking chairs with orange cushions flanked a Mediterranean-inspired tiled side table. The only thing out of place was an empty drinking glass, its striped paper straw lolling against the rim of the thick green glass. While the cynic in her hoped the bedroom had been cleaned more thoroughly, the mom in her picked up the stray glass and swiped her palm across the tabletop in a habitual move before heading back inside.

Jenna deposited the abandoned glass in the sink. She hummed as she opened and closed the few cabinets and small refrigerator to gauge how much her first shopping trip should yield. She was surprised, albeit grateful, to find some fresh-looking staples already stocked in the sparse but modern kitchen. While not terribly spacious to an American, it was clean and well-appointed compared to many of the places she'd been assigned.

A muted snippet of "Everybody Wants to Rule the World" coming from the entry area derailed her exploration of the kitchen. Inwardly resenting the pull back to reality, she grabbed the ringing phone from the depths of her almost-designer tote that served as both purse and laptop bag. The call on her work phone was rudely interrupting what was starting to feel very much like a vacation.

The private, self-funded—at least on paper—organization who had financed this escape specialized in covert operations, intelligence gathering, and information technology, including cybersecurity. The U.S. government and its federal intelligence organizations relied on agencies such as the Salvo Agency to handle sensitive operations in theaters where a certain degree of plausible deniability was desired.

Being on the leading edge of the intelligence world, the Salvo Agency employed numerous security measures to protect its 150-ish employees. This meant she rarely recognized the phone number that showed up on the screen. But only two people outside the Agency knew her work number, so, as tempting as it was, she knew there was no option to ignore the call.

"Cameron," she said, the greeting tinged with a mild sigh of irritation.

"Hi, Jenna. It's me—just checking in. I thought I might hear from you after you landed," chided a friendly, almost motherly, voice. "Are you at the villa yet?"

Catherine Healey was the glue that held the Salvo Agency together and had been for almost thirty-five years. Her real age was one of the Agency's deepest mysteries, but with their friendship as tight as it was, Jenna had been the only person from the Agency invited to her recent seventieth birthday celebration. It had been planned as a surprise party, but there weren't many secrets that could be kept from Catherine Healey.

She ran the place with a household-like efficiency that would strike fear into the heart of bureaucracy-laden federal agencies. Young agents who initially cast her as an archaic secretary left over from the days of typewriters and carbon paper quickly realized she was no such relic.

From her small desk and aging computer, she graciously had allowed the revolving door of typically male Salvo Agency commanders to believe they were somehow in charge. Over the years, the two women had developed a close bond, despite their twenty-year age difference, and had made a powerful team working hand in hand when Jenna had supervised the mission planning group.

In her early employment with Salvo, Jenna, then a recently divorced single mom, had been content in her role of overseeing mission planning and logistics. The position had satisfied her need to be home most nights, but as her kids had gotten older and moved on to college, Jenna longed to be on the other side of the desk. Becoming a field agent was difficult for any candidate. It was especially daunting for someone in their mid-forties who had no practical experience in covert or special operations. But Jenna rarely shied away from a challenge.

It had been Catherine who had encouraged her to pursue a field agent slot, even knowing it meant her closest friend and confidante wouldn't be in the office daily. When Jenna finished near the top of her training class, it was Catherine who had helped privately celebrate this crowning achievement upon her return.

And after more than two decades of putting her own wants and needs on hold, Jenna discovered that the greatest reward was finding out success tasted remarkably like fulfillment.

Relieved to hear one of her closest friends on the other end of the phone, Jenna casually propped her hip against a bar stool at the counter and launched into an enthusiastic account of the rented accommodations.

"I'm glad to know the villa is all they promised when I made the reservation. It seemed a little too good to be true," Catherine said. "But the real reason I called was to let you know about the mission briefing tomorrow morning at eleven."

"You told me about the mission brief already." Jenna smiled and lightly laughed, knowing any duplicative information was due to Catherine juggling too much as opposed to age-related forgetfulness.

"Did I? Well, maybe so, but anyway...well, just make sure your roommate knows about it, too, please," Catherine said, dangling the request all too innocently.

"Roommate?" Jenna's shoulders sank as her voice rose. "Seriously?"

"Oh, heavens," Catherine said with fake sincerity. "Certainly Commander Dugan didn't forget to mention that little detail to you."

"He's such an ass. Probably did it on purpose. He always enjoys throwing curve balls my way," Jenna grumbled, referring to the current commander of the Agency. "Spill it, Catherine. Who's this roommate?"

Catherine was already mentally hanging up as she expertly dodged Jenna's line of inquiry.

"Your roommate should be there already. I did the best I could on short notice. We'll go over all the mission details on tomorrow's call, so don't be late. Listen, I gotta run to a meeting."

"Wait, before you go—at least give me a name," Jenna insisted.

"Sorry, hon, I've said all I can say on an unsecure line. Enjoy that villa for me. *Ciao!*"

The phone bleeped as the call disconnected.

"Unsecure line, my ass," Jenna muttered.

To verify the dubious reason for Catherine's call, Jenna double-checked her calendar app. Sure enough, it showed an invitation complete with meeting link that Catherine had sent four days ago.

Irritation warred with amusement.

Leave it to Catherine to find a way to give her at least a little advance warning.

The dread of an unknown roommate quickly mutated into resentment at having to share living quarters. *What the hell,* she fumed. At fifty years of age and on a business trip, the last thing she expected or needed was a damn roommate. The unwelcome news dampened her mood significantly. Jenna picked up her bags—which felt a tad heavier now—and went in search of a bedroom to begin unpacking.

A closed door at the top of the stairs told her in no uncertain terms that someone had claimed that particular room. Had it not been for Catherine's timing, she might have flung it open. She was fairly sure no one else was in the villa, but if she was mistaken, things could have gotten awkward.

The hallway hooked in a ninety-degree turn, leading her past a small full bath replete with sleek Carrara marble tile. A green toothbrush formed the hypotenuse of a triangle with the back corner of the sink.

Just beyond the bathroom, a door stood partially open. The room was about the size of her walk-in closet at home and contained two twin beds, one of which looked slept in. Looking back at the closed door at the top of the stairs, she wondered if it was really a bedroom. If it was—and if it was also occupied—Catherine would have some more explaining to do.

Jenna was starting to empathize with Goldilocks as she continued to the end of the hallway where an open door welcomed her into a seemingly unoccupied and charming room. The armoire and its drawers were empty, and a much larger bed with its well-loved but cheerful pink quilt was undisturbed. She placed her tote on the pale-green desk that sat underneath a large window, then tossed her suitcase with a heave onto the sea of pink.

Snatching a handful of clothes to hang up, she opened the door to what she assumed was a closet, only to find herself in a modest private bath. She twirled in a happy dance at the prospect of privacy. There was nothing quite like sharing a bathroom to add to the misery of living with a coworker.

Desperate to shed the invisible film of international travel that still clogged every pore, she didn't even finish unpacking before taking a restorative shower. Between that and the power nap that followed, she almost felt human again.

She tossed on a pair of jeans, then brushed the now limp layers of her travel-weary hair. Over the past several years, plentiful strands of silver had infiltrated her natural honeyed wheat tones to give her the ashy look that many women spent hundreds of dollars to get. It was one of the few genes that worked in her favor. So, if that was the poetic "silver lining," she'd take it.

The back of her index finger made a suitable eraser for the smudged remnants of the eyeliner she had applied before leaving the States. After adding a dab of tinted lip moisturizer and a simple pair of earrings, she fished her wallet and keys from the bottom of her tote.

Still contemplating the roommate situation, Jenna made her way downstairs, scrolling on her phone to locate the closest grocery store. Food was at the top of the list, but it wouldn't hurt to pick up a bottle or two of an affordable, but certainly not the cheapest, local wine they carried.

3

breaking the rules

A N HOUR AND A half and ninety-four euro later, Jenna scowled at the scrawny tree that now guarded a silver Peugeot. Groceries in hand, she repeated her climb up the stairs, hesitating for a moment at the top step. Anticipating the roommate, she steeled herself and cautiously opened the door.

A man with his back to her stood silhouetted against the patio doors in the late afternoon light. He was about five or six inches taller than she was—so, roughly six feet—with well-defined shoulders tapering to a trim waist. The backside wasn't too shabby either. In the seconds before he turned around to face her, recognition dawned.

The incredibly attractive figure standing in the living area of her Italian seaside villa was a legend in the intelligence world.

It had been almost a year since she had last seen Grant Lawton, but even backlit by the glare of the afternoon sun, there was no mistaking him. The gray in his military-style short hair was more prevalent now, especially at his temples, which gave him an almost sophisticated look. How some men made aging into an art form she would never understand. Or forgive.

Lawton's reputation stretched far and wide—well outside the Agency, beyond the borders of civilized countries, and deep into the heart of the world's nastiest environments. From her mission planning days, Jenna was intimately familiar with his skill set. Skills that had been forged and deeply ingrained during his days as a Navy

SEAL. Skills that, at one time, had earned him the toughest and most complicated missions.

In their chosen profession, death was ever-present—a risk that was accepted and often unleashed. Each mission was a responsibility. Each target a blight on the civilized world. Each trigger pull justified. A way of underscoring and enforcing the old adage of choosing your company wisely.

Most highly lethal assets in the intelligence world excelled at compartmentalizing. But no matter how legendary, no matter the professional skill set, there was no training scenario for how to react when that carefully cultivated compartmentalization fissured and crumbled under the weight of unimaginable personal catastrophe.

Had she not been there and seen it for herself, she would have doubted it could have happened to him. Doubted that the universe could succeed in pushing someone as resolute as Grant Lawton to teeter on the edge.

It was about three years ago, and she had stayed at work later than intended that night. Other than Catherine and Dugan, everyone else had left hours ago. She had only one more checklist to draft to set her replacement up for success. Then she would be finished—off to start her training for her hard-won field agent slot.

Out of the stillness, Agent Mitch Garner's insistent voice ricocheted down the sterile tiled hallway. His pace quickened as he tried to keep up with Grant.

"Don't do this, Lawton. You're only going to justify his decision," Mitch warned his best friend.

The bow wave of tension pulsed through the hallway, invading every room as Grant's footsteps approached. Jenna's office was one of two with a light still on. Only a hint of recognition showed on Grant's stony face when they made eye contact as he stalked by her open door.

Seconds later, the sound of the door to Dugan's office hitting the wall ruptured what had been a quiet late Tuesday evening at the Salvo Agency. Jenna was on her feet instantly and darted into the hallway behind Mitch in time to see a startled Catherine spin around and step away from where she had been standing in front of Commander Dugan's desk. Dugan shot to his feet at the two-man intrusion.

"Get out, Lawton. I told you not to step foot in this building again," Commander Dugan said, nailing a manila folder to the desk with his finger as he spoke. "You fucked up for the last time."

The tragedy that was Grant Lawton's life was common knowledge around the Agency. Three months earlier, his mother and younger brother, Paul, had been killed in a car accident. According to the police, Paul had lost control of the SUV that he had borrowed from Grant, veering into oncoming traffic on a dark, rain-slick, two-lane highway. But the scrape of white paint on the rear fender told a different truth. Although the police listed it as an accident, Grant couldn't stop questioning whether he had been the intended victim. He had, after all, made a living by making enemies of ruthless people.

In the weeks that followed their funerals, Grant insisted on taking mission after mission in a desperate attempt to regain some sense of normalcy. After too many close calls, lapses in judgment, and unwarranted risks, Dugan had finally issued the directive to remove Grant from all ops rotations and place him on involuntary leave.

Placing their most experienced agent on leave and mandating counseling was one thing. Demanding that Catherine file an official reprimand without a medical and psych evaluation was another.

Several days ago, Catherine had flatly refused to draft the paperwork that would serve as a prerequisite to permanently ending Grant's career. Just thirty minutes ago, she had stopped by Jenna's office to rehearse her reasoning after being summoned to Dugan's office. Catherine had been vigorously defending her stance when the subject of their disagreement made his unannounced entrance.

As Mitch tried to intervene in the ensuing argument, Dugan dealt the final blow.

"You're terminated, Lawton. Fired. Now get out. And if you step foot in this building again, you'll leave in handcuffs," Dugan threatened.

The final crack in the dam gave way, and had Mitch not been able to restrain his friend, Catherine's resistance to drafting Grant's reprimand would have held much less credibility.

Once the situation had been neutralized and Dugan had been convinced to rescind Grant's termination, Jenna returned to her desk.

Finally confident that the transition of duties to the newly promoted mission planning lead would go smoothly, she turned off all the lights and locked up the office. The lights of the fountain in front of Salvo's building had been on for a good hour, and the Lebanese food truck she loved so much was closing its serving window.

Jenna negotiated a mishmash of whatever they had left in exchange for a hefty tip and juggled the warm polystyrene container that oozed heavenly scents while she dug for her car keys. Just as she prepared to cross the street to the garage, a lone figure sitting on a granite bench along a rare strip of grass caught her attention.

Illuminated by a flickering streetlight, a shattered Grant Lawton leaned forward with elbows on knees and head in his hands, the ends of his fingers buried in his hairline. Not expecting or waiting for an invitation, she took a seat next to him on the bench facing the opposite direction with less than a shoulder's width between them. Jenna didn't know Grant all that well but had lived long enough to know that detail didn't matter right then. She set her tote down and placed the container of food between them before glancing up.

Resenting the invasion of his space, his head turned briefly to identify the intruder. Maybe even to shoo her away. His normally keen blue eyes were dull, red-rimmed, and bloodshot. They showed recognition, but he said nothing as he looked away.

For twenty minutes they sat in silence. Eventually Jenna pulled a business card out of her bag and jotted the name and phone number of the Agency's therapist on the back. She stood wordlessly and then gently rested a hand on his shoulder before walking away, leaving the container of her favorite Lebanese chicken, with the business card and plasticware on top, tucked against his leg.

By the time she'd returned from her training as a full-fledged field agent months later, Grant Lawton was back in the field.

Jenna recalled this shared history in the time it would have taken her to open the bottle of wine she had purchased in town. Still standing motionless in the entry of the Italian villa, she was suddenly apprehensive at the realization she would be living under the same roof as this man. A male roommate was awkward enough in its own right, much less this tortured, distractingly attractive coworker.

"Hi," they said at the same time before he took one of the bags from her and set it on the counter.

"By the look of all these groceries, Dugan must have approved my request for a personal chef after all." His wryly delivered statement held a hint of humor that didn't quite spread to the rest of his face.

The sound of light footsteps on the stairs curtailed her snarky response about Dugan. A small head covered in dark, thick waves peeked around the corner. Jenna turned slowly back to Grant and raised a manicured eyebrow at him.

"I take it no one mentioned to you that my nephew would be with us for a few days," Grant said. He finished unpacking the bag onto the counter and then looked over at her.

A curious and slightly accusatory tilt of Jenna's head now accompanied her raised eyebrow.

"I only found out I had a roommate about...oh, let's see...two and half hours ago," she said, pretending to study her watch. "And this little cutie wasn't mentioned. So, yeah, no."

"This is Evan, my nephew." Grant made the introductions as he unpacked the last of the groceries. "His late mother was Italian, and her parents live just north of here in Tuscany. It's a long story, but he's staying with his grandparents for the summer."

"Does he still live with his aunt in Philadelphia?"

Grant's head swiveled in her direction. "How'd you know that?"

"I handled all the travel arrangements and logistics."

Grant turned back to his task with an almost imperceptible shake of his head. "Anyway, since he's home-schooled, we were able to take advantage of the timing of this assignment for me to be the escort. That's why we got here a day early—only to learn that his grandmother's sister had to have emergency surgery the day we flew out. Since their guest room is now occupied, my grand-nanny arrangements fell through at the last minute." He delivered the explanation matter-of-factly with zero contrition evident. "And, yes, Dugan's aware," he added.

"Then it sounds like maybe you should have requested a nanny instead of a personal chef," Jenna quipped, earning a rare half grin from Grant. "Hang on. Just how long have you known about this assignment?"

"Not that long. I think I had about four days' notice. Just enough time to coordinate with Evan's family and pick him up. Why?"

"Just trying to figure out how you got here ahead of me, yet no one bothered to tell me I had a roommate until Catherine called earlier," she said, tapping her fingernails on the counter.

He shrugged. "I got the impression it was a last-minute decision to add me."

Jenna cocked her head at him, then turned to the adorable youngster who was standing in the living room, clearly intrigued by the newcomer.

"Hi, Evan. I'm Agent Cam—well, I'm Jenna. Do you remember me? You spent two weeks with me and my kids at the beach when you were about five."

"I remember." The boy nodded shyly, swinging the two action figures that dangled behind his back. "But I'm eight now."

"You're eight already? Wow!" Jenna said with feigned surprise as he nodded enthusiastically. "I thought you looked a lot taller. Hey, why don't we catch up while you get washed up for that dinner your uncle's gonna whip up for us."

Jenna winked over her shoulder at a bemused Grant and added, "Guess you're on dinner rotation tonight after all, Lawton. Gives a whole new meaning to personal chef, doesn't it? I bought fresh pasta, so help yourself to anything you find in those bags."

Desperate to wrap her head around this development and recognizing a gifted opportunity to collect her wits when she saw one, she practically ran up the stairs behind Evan, scooping up an escaped Transformer car as she went.

learn to be still

TWENTY-FIVE MINUTES LATER, SHE followed the path Evan had taken down to the kitchen ten minutes earlier. Between the savory aromas coming from the kitchen and the solitary glass of red wine that stood next to the open bottle she had purchased, her new roommate—the one well past legal drinking age—scored instant points.

She sampled the wine and peeked into the pot simmering on the stove, if only to take advantage of the solitude. The cast of action figures had reconvened in a tumbled pile on the couch. On the patio, Evan leaned against Grant's shoulder as they inspected the Transformer car, heads bent closely together.

Jenna watched them from her vantage point in the kitchen and clasped her wine glass like a life preserver. On the job, she was confident and decisive. In her personal life, not so much. Aside from a select few worthy and well-vetted individuals like Catherine, the boundaries of her work and her personal life rarely overlapped. Insecurities that simmered just under the surface of her psyche started to bubble up.

It wasn't simply that Grant was an icon at the Agency, he was also unassumingly handsome, smart, driven—and apparently the man could cook too. No wonder she was intimidated by this living arrangement. She rolled her eyes and shook her head. Of all people to be sharing her roof.

She took another sip.

When she considered the path she had traveled over the last twenty-five-plus years, she knew she'd lived a damned good life marked by a number of impressive accomplishments. Despite her professional successes, the fog of middle age had enveloped her as she faced the milestone of turning fifty. While she thrived in her job with its challenges, risks, and international travel, there was something just out of reach that she couldn't identify. With her daughter now a successful engineer in the aerospace industry and her son about to start his own Air Force flying career upon graduating from the U.S. Air Force Academy, she floundered in her personal life.

A close friend and nurse insisted it was the joy of menopause. Her doctor, however, had insisted she suffered from anxiety and depression and had foisted needless medications on her. Unwilling to give in, she'd let the antidepressant sit unopened on the bathroom counter. The small bottle had mocked her for weeks—a constant reminder that her world was off its axis and rotating entirely too fast.

She had always defined herself by what she did, and aside from motherhood and her work, Jenna wasn't sure she knew who she really was anymore. No one needed her any longer, as evidenced by the fact that most of the calls on her recent call log were tagged with the telltale outgoing icon. After twenty-plus years of focusing on the kids and trying to measure up to everyone else's expectations, she had lost herself somewhere along the way.

Now that she had time to focus solely on herself, what she saw scared her. She hardly remembered the vibrant woman she used to be. Even worse, she wasn't convinced she even liked the cynical, overweight person she'd become. Lecturing herself in the mirror didn't help one bit either, only reinforcing that her youth, and her once enviable figure along with it, had faded to the point of obscurity, only to be replaced by gray hair and cellulite.

Her fantastic physique and good looks had been taken for granted when she was younger. She wasn't the heaviest she'd ever been but certainly still qualified as full-figured. At some point in her early forties, she had allowed her appearance to bully her confidence, beating it into submission.

Mother Nature had pulled some fast ones on her during the not-so-slow slide into her fifties. With the flip of the calendar, there was hair where there should not be hair, her once perky boobs now required constant support, parts of her jiggled longer than they should when she moved, and...well, the list was lengthy.

It wasn't that she couldn't flaunt her curves and 36C-cup, underwire-supported cleavage and use them to her advantage in the field when necessary, but she would trade the world to be just a few sizes smaller and perhaps a little more memorable. She almost snickered out loud imagining that she just might be the first woman over a size fourteen that the universe ever permitted to be within arm's reach of Grant Lawton.

Evan waved at her through the patio door.

She needed to get her shit together.

Telling herself that none of those things were going to miraculously change the longer she stood rooted in place, she topped off her glass and set her anxiety aside.

Joining Grant and Evan on the patio, Jenna felt a smidge like an intruder in someone else's home. Lawton was known for his efficiency in the field. Some might even call it detached ruthlessness when called for, and it put her a little off balance seeing him in a softer environment.

She leaned her forearms on the railing, intent on absorbing what remained of the sunlight, and watched as a young family of four at the pool gathered their things and began to make their way home. She envied them to some degree, but it did her no good to dwell on how her master plan for life had unraveled all those years ago. Her mother had always told her that there was a reason God didn't let folks see around corners. While she understood the wisdom of the saying now, it had always been delivered at times when she didn't need or want her mother's positivity.

Jenna took a deep breath—and an even deeper sip of wine—before her thoughts were disrupted by Grant setting Evan to the side and rising from his chair to go inside. Determined to contribute something to dinner, she snagged his empty wine glass and followed.

On the opposite side of the counter, she perched on a stool and bit back the urge to apologize for leaving the dinner preparations to him, reminding herself that she was neither his nanny nor his personal chef.

"Want to open the balsamic?" Grant asked, setting a bottle on the counter in front of her.

She twisted the lid off, and the bottle slipped on the smooth surface, spilling a few drops on the countertop. Humor laced his expression as he handed her a towel and turned back to the stove.

"Something amusing?" Jenna asked, curious to see whether she might get a real smile out of him.

"I think the first time I met you there was food clean-up involved too."

Jenna grimaced. Of all the things for him to remember.

"In my defense, you're the one who made the mess with the coffee in the break room that time," she said. "I just cleaned up after you. Plus, I had just left a meeting with our illustrious commander."

"That's fair. I think you scrubbed the laminate off that counter, and you used a few colorful phrases that I'd never heard before too, which was impressive," Grant replied, pausing to turn the burner off. "I was just relieved you were angry at Dugan and not me. Never a good idea to piss off the person who's in charge of your travel arrangements and lodging."

"Damn straight. You're a smart man," Jenna replied, laughing. "Even for a Navy guy."

"Ah, the wittiness of Air Force humor." Grant stirred herbs into a shallow dish of olive oil. "How long were you in?"

"On active duty? Not long enough," Jenna said with a small sigh. "I got out when my commitment was up thinking it would save what was left of my marriage."

"I'm surprised you weren't snapped up by the airlines."

"I wish I had gone that route, but having kids put me behind on flight hours. And then 9/11 happened. The mission planning job at Salvo allowed me to be home at night anyway. I had two kids to raise and, to some degree, an ex-husband too. I started flying with a unit in New Jersey once the dust settled after my divorce. I needed that connection—that sense of purpose. Thankfully, my mom was able to help with the kids."

"Air refueling, right?"

Her eyes widened in surprise. "Yeah, I flew KC-135s. Everyone in the flying community looks down their noses at tankers, but I loved it. Mostly good locations. The right deployment lengths. Made me feel like I was doing something that mattered."

"So, why'd you stop flying?"

"I didn't really want to, but it got to be a lot to juggle. Salvo gave me the time I needed for my unit obligations, but after I moved into being a field agent a few years ago, it didn't seem right to hog a slot that the unit could give to someone who was more available," she said as she topped off their wine glasses. "How long were you a SEAL?"

"You should have been a lawyer," he said, slicing a crusty loaf of bread with a paring knife and making it look easy.

Her head tilted and one eye narrowed. "What do you mean by that?"

"Don't get your back up. It's just that lawyers never ask questions that they don't already know the answers to," he said.

"To which they don't already know the answers," Jenna corrected, flinging the lid of the balsamic at him. It bounced off his shoulder blade. "Okay, fine. You win. I was just trying to make conversation."

He bent over to pick up the lid, and her eyes followed his movements. Getting called a lawyer was worth that view.

Steam from the pasta floated between them as he drained the water into the sink, but it didn't disguise the amusement on his face. "Do you have everyone's backgrounds committed to memory?"

"As a matter of fact, yes," she said, trying to tamp down the defensiveness. "Well, most of them. I had to be able to assemble the right team for each assignment, often quickly, so don't go thinking you're special." Jenna grinned then sipped her wine, watching him over the rim of her glass. "And you somehow knew I flew tankers back in the day, so...."

He shrugged. "When you came on board at Salvo, your background wasn't exactly a secret. Female military pilots weren't all that common back then."

Her mouth quirked dismissively. "Well, believe me, it's not always easy knowing every little detail about the people you work with."

"With whom you work," he corrected.

She laughed. "Touché."

The silence that followed told her to change subjects. "Speaking of secrets, that sauce smells amazing. Real tomatoes too. I was feeling a little guilty about sticking you with dinner," Jenna said, immediately kicking herself for pseudo-apologizing after all. "But now I'm glad I did. Do you cook a lot?"

"I'm so rarely home that, when I am, the last thing I want to do is eat out. And being single, it was either learn to cook or eat a bunch of processed crap. There were a lot of things tossed in the garbage over the years, trust me. Tonight, it was a good trade for you taking Evan upstairs to wash up. He's a great kid but still an eight-year-old boy. I'll take all the breaks I can get."

Grant turned back to the burner and stirred the sauce. He glanced back at her, angling his shoulders slightly toward her, and swallowed visibly.

"I, uh, didn't realize you'd helped watch him back then—after Paul died—but I guess I wasn't aware of a lot of things at that point." His eyes didn't quite reach hers before shifting to the floor.

It was comforting to see him uncomfortable for whatever reason. She twirled her wine glass nervously and tried to lighten her response by adding a casual hitch of one shoulder.

"My kids and I had beach time scheduled before I went to training, so I offered to take him with us. We had a ball. At least I did; it was fun to be around a little one again. Especially one that I could give back," she admitted with a smile. "He and my kids hit it off well, even though they were quite a bit older—my daughter was finishing up college, and my son was finishing up high school. I can't lie; having a little one to keep track of helped underscore all those talks about the birds and the bees with my kids."

That earned a laugh from him. A real, audible one.

"Anyway, we slept late, played on the beach every day, and were regulars at the ice cream place on the boardwalk. I think Evan's favorite was cookies and cream, although he wore more than he ate."

She paused, shifting around to watch Evan mosey in from the patio and collapse on the couch, engrossed in a book that showed one of his action figures on the cover.

"The Agency's a job, for sure," she said. "But it's kind of a family in its own right, I suppose. We all just wanted to help however we could. I'm not sure if you know how many people were in your corner. We knew you'd bounce back." So much for keeping it light, she thought. "Anyway, it's nice to see him—and you—doing so well."

The silence from the other side of the counter made her glance up to find Grant contemplating her.

"Well, regardless...thanks," he said.

Their eyes locked for the briefest of moments without a word, and it was all she could do just to nod her acceptance. He took a deep breath then reached for the plates.

"You didn't mention the beach trip that night."

Her glass paused halfway to her mouth. "What night?"

"Lawyer." The right side of his mouth lifted slightly.

"No, really...when?"

His eyes met hers again.

"The night Dugan wanted to fire me."

"No," she acknowledged. "No, I guess it didn't come up then."

"Well, either way, I still owe you food," he said, handing her a plate. "Hopefully this will reduce my debt. C'mon, let's eat."

She bit the inside of her cheek to keep from smiling; just knowing he remembered the sacrificial Lebanese chicken was enough.

Dinner was amazing, though it could have been microwaved hot dogs on stale buns for all she cared. Whether it was the villa that overlooked the sea, Italy with all its charm, the company, or the food itself, she felt relaxed.

And she wanted that sauce recipe.

After the dishes had been washed and Grant had carried a sleeping Evan upstairs, one last refill of her wine glass was in order. Jenna flicked off the inside lights and made her way to one of the chairs on the patio. Not knowing if Grant would stay upstairs for the remainder of the evening, she left the door open and set her small but mighty Bluetooth speaker on the table. She tapped the music app on her phone and scrolled to a familiar playlist. Andrea Bocelli would be the perfect way to wind down a surprisingly delightful first day in Italy.

The courtyard, perfectly illuminated by the strings of patio lights, was quiet except for the occasional sound of a neighboring patio door opening and closing, momentarily spilling voices and music into the air. Eyes heavy, she leaned her head back to enjoy the night air, the music, and the peaceful feeling that had settled over her.

She felt more than heard Grant sit down in the chair next to her. Jenna peeked through her lashes as he put his wine glass down and his feet up before leaning back and closing his eyes.

They stayed on the patio simply enjoying the quiet until just before midnight when Jenna gathered up their empty glasses and whispered good night. Without turning the lights on inside, she rinsed the blood-red residue from their glasses and made her way up to the pink-quilted bed.

5

heaven help me

G RANT LAWTON WAS EXHAUSTED. He used to be able to go days with minimal sleep, but now he was convinced eight-year-old boys could take down entire countries without a shot being fired. His old SEAL buddies would have a freakin' field day if they could see him now.

Most of his former teammates had long ago thrown in the towel and married. Maybe he should take Evan and find a small town to settle down in. Give the boy a home and some long-overdue consistency. Despite losing both parents at an incredibly young age, Evan was a well-adjusted kid and, according to Evan's aunt, excelled in his schoolwork.

As seemingly well adjusted as the boy appeared, Grant couldn't ignore his own observations when he'd picked up Evan the other day. Their house had bustled with activity and was certainly not a model of cleanliness. But who was he to judge family life? The environment wasn't slovenly—just lived in.

What bothered him was how quiet Evan had been. The young boy had sat, withdrawn without being sullen, watching and observing his cousins. He'd stayed on the fringe as if unsure of his place in their household. When Evan's uncle came home, the man greeted his own kids with hugs and hellos but made little effort to interact with Evan. Grant couldn't judge them for that; after all, they had stepped up when he hadn't. Even so, the observation stuck in his mind.

Could he be happy with a regular life? Grant wasn't entirely sure what happy or regular even meant anymore; however, it wasn't the first time he'd thought about exiting the game lately. Ball players were washed up and over the hill at thirty-five, and there were no guns or bad guys in that line of work. He kept himself in great shape, but here he was pushing fifty-three and still in the field. Who did that to themselves?

He knew who.

And he knew why.

He just had never imagined he would be one of those people. The ones running just to keep moving forward. The ones not wanting to stand still long enough to think or feel.

What the hell kind of life was he living? More importantly, what the hell did he think he could offer Evan? He hadn't exactly been a model of stability over the past three years. Maybe he should abandon the adoption inquiry he had made with his lawyer. Other than the ridiculously high bar set by his own parents' examples, he knew not one thing about parenting.

Tattooed on his brain from SEAL training was that the only easy day was yesterday, and no one knew that better than Grant Lawton did.

When he came downstairs after putting Evan to bed, Grant reflected on the first day with Jenna in the house. He wasn't a hundred percent sure what the atmosphere in the villa would be like tonight, since it would be just the two of them without Evan as a buffer. Although he was curious about the assignment they were staging for, he was too damn tired to worry about it. He wasn't up for talking about work tonight; tomorrow would come soon enough.

Sinking silently into the patio chair next to Jenna's, he gratefully took his cue from her, relieved that she didn't seem to want to talk shop either. Setting his wine glass on the small tiled table between them, he assessed her briefly. Even though her eyes were closed, he knew she was awake. Oddly comfortable with her choice of music and the lack of obligatory conversation, he propped his feet up, leaned back, and closed his eyes.

Reflecting on the day, he replayed Jenna's expression as she'd come to grips with having not one, but two roommates. Some of her shock was also a likely result of realizing she had been stuck with the loose cannon of the Agency, he thought with some remorse. She had schooled her expression quickly, yet it wasn't lost on him that she had jumped at the chance to use Evan as an excuse to escape upstairs while he made dinner.

Even so, the afternoon and evening had been calm and enjoyable. Grant knew he had lucked out in terms of a female partner, even if his jaw ached from her continuous attempts at conversation. He hadn't talked so much in one day since his mother was alive.

Had it not been for the encounter on a granite bench one evening when his world had all but imploded, he would have described their work-centric relationship simply as casual acquaintances. Something about her offering silent support to someone she didn't know all that well had elevated her to some other status in his mind—undefined as it was.

In their line of work, her profile was unique. Being an attractive middle-aged female with a military background gave her certain advantages in the field. He stifled a grin as he thought about the stories of the many people, both male and female, who had underestimated her and ended up paying dearly for it.

Welcoming the companiable silence, he forced his mind to empty while Andrea Bocelli sang of dreams and love in the cooling Italian night. Grant barely registered that Jenna had stood up until she whispered good night and softly closed the patio door behind her.

If this was how normal people lived, maybe he could get used to it.

whisper to a scream

T HE NEXT MORNING CAME too soon, but Grant felt rested. Between fighting off the mental demons that haunted his nights and his subconscious staying alert at night listening for Evan, he hadn't slept that soundly in weeks. Having someone else responsible, and armed, in the house was a bonus in that regard.

Having someone else able to make coffee and breakfast was also a bonus, he thought, as the smell of fresh-brewed coffee and something baking wafted up from the kitchen. He dressed in workout gear and jogged down the stairs.

Like something out of a modern-day European Norman Rockwell drawing, Evan and Jenna were seated side by side on barstools with glasses of milk and slices of something fresh out of the oven. They both turned as he hit the bottom stair.

"I'm having coffee!" Evan said excitedly, causing Grant to cast two raised eyebrows at Jenna.

"Well, coffee cake," Jenna corrected, stifling a laugh.

"That's an important clarification. It's a little terrifying to think of you pumped full of caffeine," Grant said, ruffling Evan's hair.

Jenna felt that twinge of intruder syndrome again but busied herself by collecting the dirty dishes and plating a slice for Grant. She set it on the counter and was reaching for a coffee cup for him when he interceded.

"I don't mind getting my own. Least I can do since you handled breakfast."

"Sure, but I don't mind either. It was kinda nice having someone to cook for this morning for a change."

As soon as the words were out, she wished she could inhale them back into her mouth. He grinned widely at her embarrassment as the double meaning of her words sank in.

"In a drought lately?" he teased after Evan disappeared into the bathroom.

Having bantered rather skillfully with more than her share of male crewmembers and teammates over the years, she met his parry.

"If you must know, just last week I ran out of room for more notches on my bedpost. I'm debating whether to make smaller notches or get a bigger bed," she said, angling her head and raising her eyebrows in exaggeration. She was enjoying this version of him. "Size matters, you know."

Grant chuckled while he poured his coffee then joined her on the patio. For the better part of an hour, they relaxed in the morning sun. Jenna flipped through a magazine while Grant made a few phone calls, wandering in and out when he wanted privacy or was summoned by Evan, who was watching old cartoons dubbed over in Italian. As the morning wore on, Jenna reached for her phone and walked inside to the couch.

"Is the briefing still scheduled for eleven?" he asked between bites of a second helping of coffee cake.

"No indication otherwise. I'm anxious to hear what sort of assignment warrants these digs," she replied.

"Experience tells me you might not want to know," he warned as he sat down.

"Actually, experience tells me what this setup costs," she reminded him just as a knock at the door sounded.

Without exchanging a word, Jenna instinctively led Evan upstairs before returning to crouch down a few steps from the top in the hope of catching a glimpse of whoever waited outside. Grant walked slowly to the door, glancing over his shoulder once before opening it.

A younger woman wearing black cat-eye sunglasses stood on the other side. She removed them to reveal striking dark blue eyes. Their visitor appeared to be around twenty-seven—give or take a year or two—and was gorgeous. Italian, drop-dead gorgeous. From her partially hidden vantage point on the stairs, something that felt like envy welled up inside Jenna at the sight of her. The woman wore a figure-flattering sundress and expensive heeled sandals. Bright pink lipstick both complemented and contrasted with her flawless Mediterranean skin tone.

After a brief exchange in her broken English, the newcomer handed Grant a card.

"*Grazie*," he said, nodding to her politely as he closed the door. Tossing the cream-colored card on the counter, Grant gave Jenna the all-clear and called to Evan. The boy followed Jenna down the stairs but was caught by Grant on the second-to-last step.

"Hey, buddy, think you can go play in your room while Jenna and I talk to some people from work?" he asked. Evan nodded and wriggled away to run back upstairs.

"So, what was that about?" Jenna inquired innocently.

"From what I gathered, there's a party in a few weeks, and it seems the whole complex is invited," he said, looking at his watch. "It's almost eleven; we should get dialed in and see what this whole thing is all about."

With a bottle of water in hand, Grant settled on the couch to boot up the computer and connect to the secure network while Jenna picked up the invitation from the counter and studied it.

"Oooh, a formal party. This would be incredible, but I wonder if we'll even still be here," Jenna commented. She placed the invitation on the table, sat down next to Grant on the small couch, and waited for the electrons to zip across the Atlantic.

On the remarkably clear video feed of the secure conference call, Commander Dugan sat at the head of the oblong oak table that had been brand-spanking new in 1983. A new operations analyst cowered in a seat to his right, and Catherine reigned unassumingly on his left. Too bad Dugan would never realize who really ran the show, Jenna thought.

As they waited for the meeting to begin, no one spoke. It was very early morning in the United States, as indicated by the cups of steaming coffee that sat on the conference room table. Two of the three around the table poked and pecked at the keys of their open laptops—the one exception being Dugan, who routinely shunned technology and relied on the computer-literate to carry the water. He opened the meeting by barking instructions at the analyst to pull up a series of photos of the target while he launched into the scope of the assignment and rules of engagement.

The target of the operation was the patriarch of the Santori family, a notorious figurehead in the local organized crime industry. Although not the biggest fish in the crowded sea, he had started with drugs and prostitution early in his dubious career, which set him up with built-in clientele for later extortion attempts. About ten years ago, his organization had launched a smaller operation providing illegal arms to Italy's notorious criminal underbelly. The family's more recent foray into trafficking military-grade weapons to international terrorist groups had moved them onto the United States' radar, and the Salvo Agency had been tapped to take them down.

"The situation has been rather fluid over the last two weeks," Catherine said. "When we were originally called in on this last month, the intel was a little fuzzy on what types of weapons were involved. Just a week ago, the updated intel indicated the shipment contains U.S. Javelins. I put Lawton on it based on an investigation he handled less than two months ago in Kazakhstan that had similarities to this one. Same U.S. weapon system involved."

Grant scowled. "I'm still not sure why I got pulled off that assignment."

"I pulled you because I needed you on the German prime minister's situation," Dugan said. "You go where I need you to go."

A single muscle near Grant's jawbone twitched.

"It was short-sighted. We were close. Really fucking close."

"Then you should've moved on them sooner. As I said, I needed you in Europe," Dugan stated flatly.

"Hell, the team in Germany had everything wrapped up by the time I landed in Munich," Grant rebutted.

The color of Dugan's face darkened, as did his glare.

"Enough," Catherine interjected with a practiced slice of her hand. "If nothing else, Grant, it made you available for this assignment. Which worked out well for you personally, don't forget."

Jenna loved this side of Catherine. Why her good friend refused to take the position of Salvo commander, she would never understand.

"Now, if you don't mind, let's get back to the topic here," Catherine directed, yanking her glasses off and pointing them at the screen. "This is where you come in, Jenna. Lourdes Santori is the matriarch of the Santori family. They own one of the homes in the same villa complex you're staying in. Just after we were asked to step in, she posted a position through a staffing agency for another personal assistant."

"Another?" Jenna asked. "What happened to the last one?"

"No one seems to know. Just packed up and disappeared about eight months back. Mrs. Santori didn't backfill that position at the time. The staffing company's recruiter indicated her age necessitates the help now."

"Um, I hope they know I don't speak Italian very well."

Catherine smiled. "That's why I jumped on it. Mrs. Santori specifically requested someone who doesn't."

"For an Italian family, isn't that a little...well, odd?" Jenna asked.

"Not if you don't want someone understanding *everything* that's said. And she only wants someone for three months. See? It's perfect." Catherine leaned back in her chair, clearly satisfied with how the chess pieces were positioned.

"Three months? We're here all summer?" Jenna asked. "This is going to be an expensive operation."

"It doesn't matter," Dugan lectured. "We need to take this organization down before they get any more sophisticated. The sooner the better."

His disregard for the cost involved was highly unusual. Either the Santoris were a big catch for someone very high up in the U.S. government food chain, she thought, or Dugan was desperate to make a name for himself. Or both.

"By the way, you start work at the Santoris' villa on Thursday, Jenna," Catherine said. "You know the drill. Figure out how the household works. Who's who. Who goes where. All that. Slowly drop hints about your husband's experience with weapons, and—"

"Whoa, back up. My what?"

"Your husband." Dugan sighed audibly and rolled his eyes. "We needed someone believable. And with the right expertise."

"I'm sorry, what?" Better judgment clamped her mouth shut, but a muscle twitched in Jenna's jaw. *Asshole.* She couldn't bring herself to make eye contact with Grant.

"Look. Lawton wears his background for all to see, right?" Dugan's exasperation was obvious. "I know the weapons as well as he does, but a one-eyed opossum can pick him out of a line-up as former military. He's close to the right age—a little old—but he's got the right weapons knowledge and the right look to pull this off. And having the kid there doesn't hurt either."

Grant visibly stiffened at the mention of Evan.

"Ah," Jenna continued tersely. "I see. Secondary to gathering intel, I'm just the little wife playing secretary to an old woman?"

Catherine's head rocked side to side as if there was more to the story. "No, there's more—"

"As far as I'm concerned, your sole purpose is to get Lawton an introduction to either the father or the son—or both," Dugan declared.

"And exactly how is that supposed to work?" Jenna asked, not liking where this was heading.

"Improvise. That's what good field agents do," Dugan shot back. "Plus, the younger Santori has a bit of a reputation with women. Use it. While you're monitoring the family and the household, get his attention. Reel him in. Get him interested in what Lawton can do for him, and do whatever you need to do to keep him on the hook."

Catherine glared at Dugan before she turned back to face the camera.

"Anyway, Grant will assume the role of a U.S. military officer who was recently stationed there in Italy at Camp Darby just north of where you are. The story being that he's put in his retirement papers and is on terminal leave. And when you were offered this role, you rented the villa to be closer to your new job and get some R&R before moving back to the States.

"The whole idea was that a couple would integrate better and seem less suspicious. Especially at a villa overlooking the Med," Catherine explained, shaking her head again. "That was it."

Dugan shrugged dismissively. "Whatever. Either way, Jenna fits the right profile."

"And what profile is that?" Jenna, still bristling from his earlier dig, cocked her head at his comment.

"Apparently, the younger Santori prefers...well, let's call it mature...he prefers mature women," Dugan said. "Married ones are even better."

Catherine looked pointedly at Dugan over the top of her glasses. "That wasn't part of anything we discussed," the older woman said angrily, then pushed way from the table in preparation to leave the meeting. "Weekly progress reports, please, you two. Call me if you need anything."

Catherine collected her things and rose from her chair. She made a show of fumbling her folders, not-so-subtly spilling her coffee so that it poured directly into Dugan's lap.

Jenna was oblivious to the commotion that followed in the conference room thousands of miles away. All she heard was the rush of blood filling her ears, which she knew burned bright red. Whether from embarrassment or anger, it didn't matter. When Grant reached to close the computer, she got up from the couch without a word and went upstairs.

She had worked for and flown with a lot of assholes over the course of her career but had never expended time or energy taking offense at every little thing. Over the years, she'd learned to discern when off-color comments stemmed from humor or poor judgment as opposed to malintent. Being deliberate about her reaction was the key. Most of the time, she parried—often dishing it right back. If the repartee pushed her ever-generous boundaries, instead of crying foul, she just usually delivered a biting retort, considered the source, and moved on with her life.

Dugan's pointed comment about her expertise was insulting, and only well-honed restraint had kept her from getting into an argument with him. But then her direct supervisor had referred to her as 'mature' in front of her fellow agent and now partner. What the ever-loving fuck was that about? His comment had been way out of bounds and had her wishing her brain had turned her mouth loose.

The planning that went into building teams for missions leveraged each agent's unique talents and was often what made ops succeed or fail. Jenna knew that. She was the one who used to build those teams. Everyone brought different skill sets to the table, and she'd used her appearance more than once to her advantage. For centuries, women had often been able to infiltrate in half the time that it would take a man. That's all this was, she told herself.

In the privacy of her room, she tried to get a handle on her emotions and control her reaction. Taking a deep breath, she looked at the ceiling and reminded herself that Dugan had it out for her; always had and always would, ever since she had shut down his advances. More than once, in fact. The last time she'd forcibly removed his hand from where it had no business being. She'd never breathed a word of that to anyone—not even Catherine.

However, it didn't change the fact that he had called out her most vulnerable insecurity in front of a coworker who was supposed to play her husband. Dugan had aimed perfectly and scored a direct hit to what little self-confidence middle age had left her.

Humiliation slowly morphed into anger. She'd be damned if she would allow Dugan to drag her down. Nor would she let him occupy any more of her thoughts. She would play the role she'd been handed well enough to deserve an Emmy just to end this assignment as soon as possible.

The best way for her to hit the mental reset button was to go for a run and sweat it out. At some point, she and Grant would have to have a mature conversation about appearing to be a couple. But not now.

A splash of cold water on her face helped. She threw on her workout gear and shoved her feet into her neon pink running shoes.

When she stalked down the stairs, Grant was sitting in the same place on the couch with his elbows on his knees. He glanced up but didn't say a word as she tucked her key into the pocket of her leggings and slammed the door behind her a little harder than she'd really intended.

The first fifteen minutes of her run were spent beating herself up mentally by rewinding Dugan's comments over and over. The next ten minutes yielded all the perfect responses she wished she'd thought of at the time. The physical exertion finally pushed her mind to a better place, and a clearer head prevailed. Her self-therapy session concluded with several brutal sets of squats, crunches, push-ups, and burpees in the shade of the villa.

As much as she hated burpees, she cranked out two full sets once she gleefully realized that "Fuck you, Dugan" fit the cadence superbly.

everybody hurts

I T WAS APPROACHING ONE o'clock when Jenna opened the door to find the apartment quiet and empty. Silently thanking Grant for the space, she dragged herself up the stairs on trembling legs and headed for the shower.

Since being away from home for the entire summer looked probable, she spent the remainder of the afternoon making a few phone calls, reviewing her calendar, and scheduling bill payments. She was rummaging through the kitchen to start something for dinner when the door opened, and Evan burst in ahead of Grant.

"We went down to the water like we did at your beach!" Evan exclaimed, thrusting a fistful of gathered treasures in her direction.

Jenna couldn't help but smile at the memory and knelt to inspect his collection while Evan babbled about their adventures. She tried to stay focused on his story, ever aware of Grant standing in the hallway observing the exchange. After Evan completed the inventory of shells and rocks, Grant tapped him on the shoulder and gently suggested he take them upstairs to his room.

Feeling cornered and a trifle embarrassed, Jenna rose without meeting Grant's eyes and spun back to the cabinets to resume her meager dinner preparations. She reached for something—anything, really—on an upper shelf.

Grant remained where he stood.

"Did you get it all out?" he quietly asked.

Her arm stilled momentarily; her head nodded, but she couldn't bring herself to turn around to face him. When she finally got the nerve, he was gone.

Both boys were clean and hungry when they came back downstairs and helped get dinner on the plates. She toyed with her food while they wolfed down her favorite baked chicken. The conversation remained casual, light, and perhaps a little superficial. Both adults were happy to let Evan monopolize the meal with his boyish chatter about how they had followed the trail down the cliff to the beach and played in the rocky surf. Surmising that Grant had really been doing reconnaissance, she expected he would share his observations of the complex and its surroundings with her later.

Once Evan had given in to sleep and with the awkwardness of the day dissolved in the dirty dishwater, Jenna and Grant repeated the first night's routine. When he joined her on the darkening patio, she had already filled a wine glass for him as if expecting his return. He sighed as he took the other chair and thanked her for dinner and the wine. She met his eyes as he propped his glass on the arm of his chair.

"Hey, about this morning—" she started, conscious of her tendency to rehash the ugly.

He cut her off with a shake of his head. One finger raised to his lips gave her pause. She watched as he lifted a small black speaker from beside his chair and placed it on the table between them. After a flick of a switch, a tiny blue light blinked on the back of the device that was just a tad smaller than a brick. He pressed a button and then sat back in his chair.

"There. Now we can talk."

"New toy from Salvo?"

"Not terribly new, but Catherine sent it along. It's an audio jammer so our conversations can't be overheard or anything."

"Hopefully it won't jam our neighbors' phones or signals too," she said. "Or my music."

"It's got that capability, but I'm using the audio distortion instead of actual jamming. Anyone bothering to listen electronically will just be hearing—or recording—random and unintelligible garble. We should probably just leave it on out here all the time. But, no, it won't mess with your music."

Jenna studied the black brick for a moment before getting back to her point.

"About this morning—"

"Not necessary. It's in the past."

"I just appreciate the space you gave me today. That's all." Pleased that she was able to issue a thank you, as perfunctory as it was, while managing to curtail her tendency to apologize, she took a slow sip of wine to celebrate that small victory.

"Speaking of space, we should probably talk about how we're going to play this," he said.

Jenna sighed. "Yeah, I guess so. You've never been married before, right?"

Grant picked up his wine glass and took a sip. "Let's be clear. I've never been married, but I'm not a monk."

Her cheeks reddened. "I didn't mean to imply...I mean...I know you're not. I just meant—"

"Ah, the all-knowing mission planning advantage again." He looked out across the courtyard and then back to her. "Will any of my past relationships prove useful for the purposes of this assignment?"

"Please don't be snarky, Grant. This is awkward enough already," Jenna said.

His laugh was low and controlled. "It's going to be more so when we're out in public."

"Agreed. Especially around Evan. I mean, when we're out and about, no one will assume we're married unless—" A sudden snicker caused her wine to slosh in her glass.

"Unless what?"

"Well," Jenna said, raising her glass in a mock toast. "You know the car test, right?" Grant shook his head and looked amused as she continued. "If two people in a car are talking and laughing and leaning into each other, they're dating. If they're leaning away from each other, looking out the window, not talking, they're for sure married."

"Wow. You sure paint a rosy picture of marriage," he said with no hint of humor. He held his glass at the base of its bowl and raised it ever so slightly in her direction. "I think we'll need to be more convincing than that at times. Any reservations about that?"

"Not for me. I was an expert at pretending for the last several years of my marriage." Jenna grinned before taking another sip. "There is, however, the small, noticeable detail of rings."

"Yeah, I'll give you yours tomorrow."

Jenna sputtered, sitting up straighter in her chair. "What did you just say?"

"I said I'll give you yours tomorrow," Grant said, relenting enough to allow a smile to creep across his face. "The rings were in my ops package."

"Wait. You knew about this…this arrangement?" she asked with a flick of her wrist that had her index finger making a circle in the air. "And you didn't think to mention it yesterday?"

"I assumed you knew, given how close you and Catherine are. You said she called you. Besides, why else would we be living together? Weren't you the mission planning expert? It wasn't until the call this morning that I realized you hadn't put two and two together."

The ensuing silence allowed her to contemplate this new information. After a minute, Jenna smirked at him over the rim of her glass.

"What?" Grant asked.

"How big is it?"

It was Grant's turn to sputter the sip of wine he'd just taken. "I'm sorry?"

"Size matters, remember?" While she honestly had been curious about the ring, seeing him flustered was oddly entertaining. She pretended to be oblivious to his discomfort. "My diamond. How big is it?" Jenna teased. "It had better be a good one."

"Oh. That." A mix of humor and relief flitted across his face. "It's pretty good size. I think you'll be impressed."

Smothering another laugh with her wine, she was tempted to keep razzing him. Instead, she behaved and took the conversation back to safer footing. "Good. Then maybe we'll talk when we're in the car together after all."

The stars glittered like diamonds overhead, and she turned up the music volume a bit to dampen their voices. Grant described the layout of the rest of the complex and surrounding area, pointing across the courtyard to the largest of the villas. The perfectly timed invitation they had received earlier was indeed for a party hosted by the Santoris. It would be an opportune event to make their debut as a couple if they could find someone trustworthy to watch Evan.

At the mention of the little boy, the topic of conversation morphed from work to something more casual and personal. Three hours later, when the patio lights in the courtyard went dark, Jenna gathered the empty bottle plus their stained wine glasses and stood to go inside. Grant rose with her, but as she started to open the patio door, his hand on her arm stopped her. Feeling a warm current course through her, she looked up at him questioningly, meeting his softened expression.

His voice, calm and soothing, washed over her in the dark, smoothing the rough edges of the day.

"About earlier. For what it's worth, everyone knows Dugan's a prick. No one more than I. Believe me, you'll turn more heads than just Santori's."

Wanting to stay right there in that moment and have him repeat that exact sentiment a hundred times, she willed herself to move. Unsure of how to respond, Jenna swallowed visibly and nodded, the appreciation in her eyes visible but unspoken.

The current broke as he dropped his hand and followed her inside, wishing her a good night before disappearing upstairs.

inside out

S HE HAD ONE FREE day before work would rear its invasive head. Eager to explore, they spent Wednesday sampling several local towns and getting familiar with various routes to and from the villa. Their time together gave her a peek into the still-evolving relationship between Evan and his uncle, the insight valuable as she constructed her role as Grant's wife and Evan's mother.

Much to her surprise, Grant initiated another patio session before seeing Evan to bed. After studying the small collection of wine they had purchased that day, he selected a bottle and opened it. He placed it on the counter next to two glasses before going upstairs with Evan's latest book tucked under his arm.

The unspoken expectation delighted her. After only three nights in the villa, the patio seemed to be the place where they relaxed the most, shedding the expectations of work and parenting.

Grant remembered the wedding rings only after they'd gone upstairs for the night, delivering hers with a light knock on her bedroom door. The hallway was dark as he stood outside her door, a small drawstring pouch of fabric in his outstretched palm.

"Not exactly how I thought I'd present a wedding ring," he said softly in deference to Evan sleeping down the hall.

Maybe it was the lack of light. Maybe it was the bottle of wine they had shared. Maybe she imagined a glimpse of wistfulness in his usually stoic expression.

Jenna leaned against the doorjamb, suddenly needing to make the moment feel less like the end of a first date under a porch light on her parents' doorstep.

"Thanks," was all she could muster after taking the fabric pouch from his hand. Her fingertips grazed his palm, but she pretended not to notice.

"Sure. I meant to give them to you earlier."

"It's fine. Then we would have had to explain it all to Evan today," she said, mimicking his glance down the hall.

"I'll do that tomorrow while you're at work," he offered. "Explaining why our last name will be Nichols for a while might be interesting."

A moment of silence followed. Neither made a move to leave.

"Ever been close?" she asked softly.

A hushed scoff was his first response. "Thought about it once. Not seriously enough to buy the ring."

"When?"

"I was thirty. Maybe thirty-one. Young enough to believe in all that."

"Ah. Who was she?"

Grant scanned the dark hallway, rubbed his jaw that was shadowed by stubble older than five o'clock, then looked back to her. "Let's save that for the patio some night."

"Sorry," Jenna said. "I didn't mean to pry."

"I didn't take it that way. All good."

Even in the dim light, she could see that his eyes were a bright, burning blue. They glittered as she looked up at him and back to the square of fabric in her hand.

"Aren't you going to look at them?" he asked when her palm closed over the pouch. "You know—let me know if it's big enough?"

His soft delivery disguised the reference until she caught his rare smile.

"You should do that more often," she whispered.

His head tilted almost imperceptibly. "Propose?"

"No, I meant smile."

His smile melted slowly, and she wished she hadn't said anything.

Grant lightly cleared his throat. "I'll try, then."

"It was meant as a compliment. I just hope it feels as good as it looks on you."

"I...well, it's...."

With a light hand to his forearm, Jenna smiled softly. "We can save that for the patio some night."

"Probably best." He cleared his throat again and took a step back.

Jenna straightened. Her hand clutched the rings that in any other scenario would symbolize sacred bonds and promises of forever. Tonight, they were simply a prop.

"Thanks for bringing these to me. Oh, as a reminder, my hours with Mrs. Santori are nine until two, four days a week apparently. But I'm not sure what tomorrow will look like, being the first day and all."

"Sounds good. I'll get something in the works for dinner while you're gone. Good night, Jenna."

"'Night, Grant."

Throughout her life, Jenna's parents had been habitually late to every event she could remember. Ironically, when her mother passed away only ten months ago, even her service had started fifteen minutes late. Whether it was that, the rigid punctuality of the military, or the precision timing so critical to in-flight refueling, she didn't know, but somewhere along the path to adulthood, she had reversed her parents' trend.

Her alarm sounded at seven thirty Thursday morning, pulling her from the dream that featured a man who looked remarkably like her coworker down the hall.

The house was quiet as Jenna got ready for her first day of work. She perched on the side of the bed and glanced at the black jewelry pouch that lay on the desk. She hadn't been in the mood to look at the contents last night.

Opening the drawstring, she poured two rings into her palm and gasped. She held them together so that the horseshoe opening in the center of the wedding band hugged the diamond of the engagement ring, giving the impression the set was a single ring. The princess-cut diamond of the engagement ring had to be well over a carat. It was stunning on its own. Square sapphires perched on either side of the wedding band, flanking the large diamond. After slipping the rings on, she extended and flexed her left hand. The fit was perfect. She couldn't have chosen a more beautiful set. And heavens, it was certainly big enough.

Hyperaware of wearing a wedding ring again, she packed her work tote and, shoes in hand, tiptoed down the tile stairs.

Movement in the kitchen alarmed her at first, but the boyish giggle that followed rendered her speechless. Evan stood on a chair next to Grant, who was doing something on the small two-burner stove. Her next breath registered the heavenly scent of coffee.

Jenna set her things on the table in front of the couch and made her way to the counter. Leaning on it, she spoke, startling Evan enough that he grabbed Grant's shoulder for balance. Seeing her, he giggled again.

"You weren't supposed to be ready yet," the young boy said impishly.

"I wasn't? Can I go back upstairs and get back in bed?" she playfully responded. "Just what are y'all doing that I wasn't supposed to see?"

Grant turned and placed a stack of golden pancakes on the counter.

"It was Evan's idea to make breakfast for you on your first day." Grant said, winking at her. "He was teaching me how to make pancakes."

Jenna's hand pressed against the smile that played across her lips and helped suppress the swell of emotion that rolled through her.

"Thank you very much. This is incredibly sweet of you. Both of you."

Evan clutched a cup of coffee with two small hands and placed it in front of her. He carefully poured a dash of cream into it.

"Is that enough?"

"Yes, honey. Thank you. This is all so perfect. Grab a plate and sit with me while I eat," she said.

Evan plopped pancakes on two more plates while Grant slid her plate onto the counter in front of her. As she reached for the plate, her ring caught his eye. His glance shifted to hers, and he nodded once in what she took as an acknowledgment that the assignment was underway.

Subtly, she scanned his left hand and spied a plain but thick silver band on his ring finger. The bite of pancake stuck in her throat, necessitating a sip of coffee to force it down. Even though she knew that what the rings represented was fake, it was weird. A degree of weird that lay at the intersection of uncomfortable and stirring.

Unwilling to let the crack in her equilibrium show, she chatted superficially with Evan while the three of them ate breakfast together. Then, in a domestic moment as disconcerting as the rings they wore, Jenna gathered her things, kissed Evan on the head, and left for work.

9

forever young

L OURDES SANTORI HAD HOMES all over Europe, but the one in this small Italian courtyard community overlooking the sea was her recent favorite. Born into a barely middle-class family in Milan, she'd never imagined she would have six homes to choose from: three on Italy's mainland, one in France, one in Spain, plus her husband's inherited property in Sicily.

Half a century ago, the stars had aligned to put Matteo Santori in her line at the bank where she worked as a teller. The up-and-coming successful businessman swept her off her feet and upended the image of the mundane life her future held. Infatuated with his attention, she'd felt like a princess when he proposed only ten months later. In the early years of their marriage, she had marveled at her good fortune.

Her husband had his faults, as did she, but at one time she had loved him all the same. They had been married for fourteen years when she'd stopped trying to convince herself that he earned his money honestly; about that same time, she had also stopped asking questions. She'd debated whether to leave him and live on her own in fear or embrace the man and the life God had handed her. Too terrified to leave him, she'd chosen the latter and never looked back.

And after over fifty-one years of marriage, she had too much invested and too little time left to leave him. They were in their mid-seventies and had lived well. At times, they had loved well too.

Well enough to have five children who were scattered here and there around the world.

At twenty-seven, she had become a mother. Filippo, the eldest son and a doctor, lived in France with his wife and two children. Three years later, Aria was born. It was hard to believe her oldest daughter was now a solicitor employed by Spain's royal family. The middle child, Luca, joined the family when she was halfway through her thirties. He had never strayed far from home, splitting his time between his home in Sicily and that of his aging parents. Her twins, Paetta and Stefano, were a fortieth birthday surprise, which perhaps explained their free-spirited personalities. Stefano was somewhere in America, a nomad enjoying his youth, while Paetta flitted around Europe sampling the man du jour before she was forced to choose a direction.

Now the years were etched into her once flawless Italian complexion. Obvious though her age might be, those same years brought a level of self-awareness that she embraced. Acceptance had been difficult, especially in her fifties, but once she had made her peace with the passage of time, she appreciated the view. What a blind, doting wife she had been.

But no more.

In the past fifteen or so years, she had established her footing. With her husband. With her children. With herself.

It was as if the household had been signed over to her legally when she finally took a stand against her husband's business ventures. Once she'd insisted that he keep his dealings separate from the family, she'd begun to earn the respect she'd never given herself.

Though her influence had grown, her health was failing and her energy waning. She hated the idea of needing help. This was her household. But in order to maintain the structure she'd worked so hard to establish, the harsh reality was that she needed someone to do the legwork.

The woman the staffing agency had placed there a year ago had disappeared eight months ago. Lourdes knew she hadn't been a great fit but had thought they could find a way to be compatible. She often wondered if the forty-five-year-old woman's disappearance was a result of the time spent in the Santori household and shuddered at the thought.

Lourdes knew Luca carried on the family business, working for his father. A benefit of being Matteo's favorite son was the freedom to spend money lavishly on designer clothes and expensive cars, even though he was technically not formally employed that she knew of.

A heavy drinker with a short fuse, Luca flitted from woman to woman and never seemed content—always wanting what was just out of reach. Though women willingly passed through the continuously revolving door of his villa in Sicily, distasteful rumors circulated. For many years, Lourdes had opted to believe only what she witnessed with her own eyes. Lately, though, she couldn't ignore the hushed whispers from the household staff about his sordid relationship with her previous personal assistant who, one day, had just stopped coming to work.

The rumors that snaked through the grapevine were distasteful at best. Rumors of depravity, obsession, murder, and secrets. Secrets that, if publicized, would have been frightfully damaging to her family's reputation. Somehow, the vanished woman's link to the Santori family had been kept from the media.

For months, Lourdes had managed on her own, trying to balance the woman's disappearance against the rumors while also resisting the parallels. Matteo wasn't the only Santori with a wide range of intelligence sources.

Over the previous fall and winter, despite the absence of an assistant, Lourdes had enjoyed a marked improvement in her health, which she credited to resuming a schedule and staying busy. But in mid-January, the symptoms and exhaustion returned, forcing her to repost the position.

This new candidate had been presented by a recruiter in the U.S. and fit the requirements perfectly. At first, the staffing agency she'd retained had protested the lengthy list of skill sets Lourdes had dictated to him for the job posting. Then they had doubted the recruiter's credentials, describing the contact at the American placement firm as flighty and unfamiliar with how the international industry worked. Despite those misgivings, her agent couldn't deny that the American candidate seemed to be a perfect match.

After taking breakfast in her suite, Lourdes checked the Rolex Oyster watch that dangled loosely on her frail wrist. It was three minutes before nine o'clock. She had learned that the saying about first impressions was true more often than not and was curious what impression her new personal assistant would be trying to make.

Two minutes later she had her answer as the doorbell chime echoed throughout the villa. The front door opened, then closed, and voices carried up the stairs, although she couldn't discern the words. With hesitant steps and her cane tapping mutedly on the tile floor, Lourdes made her way to the elevator to welcome her newest employee.

Downstairs, Jenna introduced herself to the housemaid who answered the door. The woman's reaction was cordial but far from warm; an undercurrent of distrust ran through the insincere greeting. Jenna fidgeted with the collar of her bright pink blazer and wondered what Catherine had gotten her into with this whole personal assistant charade.

Resisting the sigh that threatened, Jenna stepped into the entry just as elevator doors slid open down the hall with a controlled mechanical whoosh.

An elderly woman wearing black crepe slacks and a light-green silk blouse stepped out and crossed the room. Despite her reliance on a wooden cane, the woman's elegant posture reeked of society. A stiff smile showed on thin lips outlined in warm rose lipstick.

"*Buongiorno*, Ms. Nichols. I'm Lourdes Santori," the matriarch began. Sharp brown eyes studied Jenna, moving subtly to her tote and down to her shoes and back up again.

Jenna smiled inwardly at the inspection. "*Buongiorno*, Signora Santori. Please call me Jenna."

"It's a pleasure to meet you. Welcome to my home. I hope you find it a comfortable place to work. I understand you were able to rent a villa across the way?"

"Yes, ma'am," Jenna replied. "The staffing agency actually recommended it. We were wanting to spend some time enjoying Italy before we move back to the States, so we were fortunate to find a place to live and work that also is a bit of a vacation spot. This job was a perfect fit, and I'm looking forward to working with you."

The older woman turned toward the sitting area and motioned for Jenna to follow. Mrs. Santori settled on the ivory damask settee and waved her cane at the upholstered chair next to her. Jenna followed the unspoken instruction and perched on the edge of the seat.

"If you need any recommendations for places to visit around Italy, I know several of the best areas. Especially when it comes to shopping or restaurants," Mrs. Santori said with a light sigh. "I used to love to get out and about. Unfortunately, this silly thing slows me down quite a bit."

Clearly vexed by her dependence on the cane, she rapped it on the floor once before leaning it against the arm of the settee.

"Are there particular days that you like to go out, signora?" Jenna asked, anxious to learn more about what her days would be like.

"No, my dear, not anymore," the older woman said with an air of disappointment. "I seem to be a nuisance with how slow I am now."

With a tilt of her head, Jenna gave a gentle smile. "Well, I, for one, would love to see some of your favorite shops. And a restaurant or two, if you wouldn't mind. I have yet to find the perfect bruschetta after living here for almost two years. We can take my car. Just pick the day and time, and we'll go. Just you and me."

The older woman studied the self-assured woman who continued to think out loud, verbalizing her musings. Even if Jenna was just being nice, it still was an offer no one else in the household had made recently.

A spiral notebook with a floral cover rested in her new assistant's lap while the middle-aged American woman fished for a pen in her peacock-blue tote bag. After placing a pair of blue reading glasses on her nose, Jenna opened the notebook and sat poised to take notes. As the questions began, Lourdes smiled to herself and wondered exactly who was interviewing whom. Jenna's easy nature and genuine interest in learning more about Lourdes's expectations of her duties shifted what should have been a formal introductory meeting into an effortless conversation.

Interrupted only once by the housemaid bringing an absurd number of pills and a glass of water to the elderly woman, they talked for two hours. The questions soon morphed from expectations and schedules to preferences and wishes. Lourdes couldn't recall the last time anyone had spoken to her like anything other than an employer or a batty old woman, or both.

After a cursory tour of the villa, they returned to the first floor and followed the dour housemaid to the patio. Lourdes pointed her cane at a small bistro table covered in a crisp white tablecloth. In the center, a small plate of olives sat next to a tall bottle of water and two glasses.

Welcoming the sunlight after hours indoors, Jenna poured some water for Lourdes before snagging an olive and turning to survey her surroundings. Above her, a canopy of purposely unruly bougainvillea trailed from the slatted pergola, providing a magenta curtain from the afternoon sun. The patio itself was a riot of late spring color punctuated by red geraniums clustered among leggy foliage that was just beginning to trail over the sides of heavy cobalt planters.

"This patio is spectacular. I would spend every moment out here tending the flowers and herbs or just enjoying a glass or two of wine in the evenings. This is by far the most beautiful part of the entire villa."

Lourdes's face lit up at the praise. "It is indeed my favorite place. Matteo, my husband, doesn't understand how I spend so much time alone with plants. This one, the rose over here, is as much a part of me as any of my children."

Enlivened by Jenna's interest, the older woman explained the process of propagating the heirloom rose that her great-grandmother had started more than a century ago. The two women strolled among the pots, laughing together as Jenna scored correct guesses on most of the plants.

They returned to sit at the picture-perfect table where, between bites of handmade pasta, Lourdes chatted amicably about her childhood and her children, eventually diverting to family recipes and favorite foods. Despite the newly established employment relationship, they bounced from topic to topic like lifelong friends, eventually landing on Jenna's marriage to Grant.

Seizing the opportunity, but guarding against appearing too eager or overly informative, Jenna vaguely described her husband's background. A subtle reference to his knowledge of military weapon systems snuck in when she explained his upcoming retirement from the military. When petite plates of cheese and fruit were served, they moved back to more domestic topics.

"In a few weeks, we will host our annual party," Lourdes said. "It began as a celebration of Labor Day here in Italy, but over the years, the invitation list has grown substantially, so we hold it a few weeks later now. You can imagine that with the date fast approaching, most of the arrangements have been made already—the music, the food—all planned. Everything must go perfectly, so next week, I would like you to review the preparations."

Jenna's eyes sparkled. "Absolutely, signora. Event planning is a secret passion of mine, and I'm sure between the two of us nothing will be overlooked."

The older woman dabbed at the remainder of her pink lipstick with her napkin. "I would be pleased if you would call me Lourdes. We will be spending a lot of time together, and it seems we are well suited, so I believe we can dispense with the formalities."

"Thank you, Lourdes. I confess I was a bit nervous and am quite relieved after spending time with you today," Jenna said. "And I'm really excited about the party. I think that must have been the invitation a young woman delivered on Tuesday morning."

"Ah, yes. That would have been my daughter, Paetta. She flits in and out like a bee around the flowers. You'll meet her soon enough."

"I noticed it's a black-tie party, so do you have a preference for staff attire?" Jenna asked.

Lourdes gave a dismissive huff and swatted an invisible insect with her small hand. "You should plan to attend as a guest, not staff," Lourdes said. "As I mentioned, most of the arrangements have been set. While I do request your presence in case some mishap occurs, I want you and your husband to enjoy the evening. I've asked my sister-in-law's granddaughter to watch another couple's child, so perhaps your son would be comfortable with them for the evening."

Jenna nodded appreciatively at her offer, amused by the delicate way Lourdes discouraged children from attending.

"Thank you for your kind offer. I'm sure my son will be excited to meet some other children his age too."

"Then it's settled. Now if you'll excuse me, it's almost time for my nap. I just don't have the energy I used to have," Lourdes said. "I think we are done for the day, so I will see you on Monday?"

"Yes, definitely," Jenna said, rising from the table.

After escorting her new employer to the elevator and with her tote over her shoulder, she left through the patio door. Ecstatic about the vibe she'd gotten from Lourdes, she closed her eyes and lifted her face to the sun, soaking in the warmth of a successful first day.

make someone happy

THE FIRST WEEK AS Lourdes's personal assistant went quickly. Each morning, they sat on the patio and reviewed the day's agenda, then discussed any tasks related to the upcoming party. Getting to review the invitation list was a perk that Jenna hadn't initially appreciated. She fed the names to both Catherine and Grant for screening and awareness, respectively. While it contained an impressive cross section of international politicians and businessmen, none of the names appeared to be cause for alarm.

The following Thursday when Jenna arrived for work, the housemaid indicated Lourdes was not feeling well. Jenna's concerned questions received only shrugs in response. Wanting to see Lourdes's condition for herself, Jenna climbed the stairs to her suite and knocked gently, entering when prompted by a weak voice.

Clothes lay over the back of a chair, and a tray of dirty dishes sat on the bedside table, making it painfully obvious that no one in the household had bothered to check on or care for Lourdes in some time. Jenna fumed silently while fussing around the room.

"Stop, Jenna. You are making me seasick with all your bustling around," Lourdes stated as firmly as she could.

"I'm sorry," Jenna said. "But it's unconscionable that no one has offered you anything to eat or drink since last night. Or helped you to the bathroom or anything."

"Jenna, dear. A woman doesn't get to my age without knowing how to care for herself. You learn very quickly that, as a mother and wife, no one else is going to do it. I will be fine with some rest."

"Well, that's a crock of shit," Jenna said angrily, covering her mouth with one hand after her outburst. The twinkle in Lourdes's eyes only encouraged Jenna to continue her rant. "You need to see a doctor. And someone needs to be attentive to your needs."

"See? My point is valid. You are a mother and a wife." Lourdes leaned back on the pillows and sighed. "One might even say a friend."

Jenna stopped in the middle of hanging up a blouse that had been cast aside and glanced over at the bed. The ghost of a smile played on Lourdes's face.

"Thank you," Jenna said softly.

"For what?"

"The compliment."

"I should be the one thanking you." Lourdes said. "For being here. Most of all, for caring."

Jenna lowered herself to the edge of the bed. "Here, drink this."

She helped Lourdes sit up to sip the honeyed herb tea that Jenna had demanded from the otherwise unconcerned kitchen staff. "You know I'm nearby. Why didn't you call? I wish I'd known you weren't well last night."

"So you could stay with an old woman all night? I get these bouts periodically. And don't even think about staying tonight. I'll be fine. Besides, Luca is here for a few days."

"And he's clearly doing a great job of taking care of you," Jenna muttered wryly. "Let me call your doctor, please."

"We've been over this. All he does is prescribe me pills."

Jenna chuckled. "But do those pills usually make you feel better?" Lourdes huffed.

"That's what I thought," Jenna said. "Tell me his number."

After much debate, Lourdes relented, and Jenna was able to arrange an appointment with the doctor. An hour later, Jenna deposited her friend on the settee downstairs and went in search of the matriarch's driver.

A tall man with a beefy chest filled the doorway into the kitchen, his back to her. He leaned against the doorframe as the housemaid spoke to him in halting but pleading Italian with tears streaming down her face. Obvious even to someone who didn't speak the language, the man's harsh tone denigrated the housemaid's protestations.

"*Mi scusi*," Jenna said, interrupting their discussion. "How might I find out where Lourdes's driver is?"

At the mention of Lourdes, the man turned around slowly. The housemaid capitalized on the intrusion and darted away. The annoyance in the man's hard brown eyes caused Jenna to unconsciously step back. He appeared amused by her reaction. Crossing his arms, he resumed his pose against the opposite door jamb.

"Usually drivers are with their cars," he said.

"Really? I would never have thought of that." She mirrored his humorless, hard tone.

Slowly, the left corner of his narrow lips turned up. "Ah, this one has spunk."

"Call it what you like. I take it you must be Luca?"

His nod was almost imperceptible. "I heard my mother hired a new assistant. You must be Signora Nichols?"

She returned his curt nod. "The driver?" Jenna repeated. "Your mother has a doctor's appointment in half an hour."

The raised corner of his mouth distorted into a smirk.

"If she weren't so old and frail, I would think she was having an affair with her doctor. She sees him more than she does my father."

"Seeing as neither you nor your father are around much to help her, I wonder how it is you know that."

The hard look in his eyes snapped back into place. He stared at her as he pulled a cell phone from his pocket. A thick index finger punched at the screen. Luca spoke tersely in Italian as his weighted glare moved from Jenna's head to her feet and back again, lingering in the typical places. His eyes never left her as he pocketed the phone.

"*È qua*," he said flatly, raising his arm to indicate the car that rolled to a stop outside the leaded-glass doors.

"*Grazie*, Luca," Jenna said with a conciliatory smile.

Luca grunted, and the corner of his mouth lifted as he watched her walk away.

The next several weeks passed uneventfully, at least as uneventfully as they could living with a coworker and his eight-year-old nephew. An increasingly restless Grant spent his days watching and waiting, trying to fill the hours at the villa while Jenna was working her way into the Santoris' circle.

In the afternoons, when she arrived back at the villa, Jenna made an effort to spend time with Evan to give Grant a break. He seemed more than willing for her to take an active role with Evan, and they fell into an easy routine. She didn't dare use the term in front of Grant, but it wasn't long before it occurred to her they were effectively, and somewhat unintentionally, co-parenting Evan.

Although the boy's presence enhanced their roles, she sensed that Grant resented having Evan so visible. It made him edgy, which translated into gruff at times, and it wasn't until Evan was snug in bed each night that Grant relaxed.

Evenings on the patio became their nighttime routine, and she confessed to herself that she looked forward to it every day. It was becoming easier to let her guard down and be herself around him, and he with her. The conversation and laughter flowed effortlessly, both content to enjoy the slower pace before they were reminded this was not reality.

Some evenings they spent settled in their chairs enjoying a good wine, lost in their own thoughts and not saying a word—no emails, texts, social media, or other electronics other than that magic Bluetooth speaker. Alternating playlists, they found music to be a bond. It served as a springboard to other topics and, on rare occasions, opened the door to talking about deeply personal subjects that both typically kept locked away.

On a cloudy Thursday night after Evan had fallen asleep on the couch, Grant handed her a glass of wine and sat down on his side of the darkened patio. Her sixth full week in the Santori household had not yielded any information about the suspected weapon smuggling. They both had accepted that this would be a drawn-out process compared to the usual toast-and-coast assignment, but Grant was growing increasingly restless all the same.

"Luca was there again today," Jenna said, stretching her legs out on the footrest and flexing her bare feet. "He cornered me in the kitchen when I went to get Lourdes a glass of water."

"Cornered?"

"That's how it feels. There's something about him...the way he talks to women...I don't know. The cat-and-mouse game is one he seems to enjoy." She shrugged and sipped her wine. "He asked if I was married—which I know he knew already. To build his interest, I told him that I probably shouldn't talk too much about what you did."

"Building his interest in me or you?"

Jenna shifted in her seat. "Both, I suppose."

"And?" Grant asked. "Did you dribble anything more to him?"

Jenna laughed softly, twirling the stem of her glass between her thumb and forefinger before sliding a playful glance in his direction.

"What? And reveal the mystery that is Grant Lawton? Sorry, I mean, Grant Nichols."

Grant lifted his glass to his mouth and met her eyes.

"Yes, Grant, I dribbled some teasers. It would've been a little obvious if I'd drowned him in details. I mentioned your weapons background and that you're retiring from the military to take a defense-related position in Washington."

"Did he bite?"

Jenna laughed guardedly. "I'm sure he does."

Not even a smile from Grant.

"Wow, no humor tonight, huh?" Jenna prodded.

"I'm just ready to not be stuck in this villa for another week, that's all."

"Mmmm. I'd be happy to be stuck in this villa for several more weeks. Best location I've had in a while."

"No one waiting for you to get home?" Grant inquired, pulling his footrest toward him with his heels so his knees formed a right angle. Jenna recognized his body language cues and relaxed at the shift in conversation.

"No. My kids are on their own, and my mother died ten months ago. My dad's been gone nine years."

"I'm sorry to hear that."

"Thanks. I know you've been through worse," Jenna acknowledged. "My mom was pushing ninety and was in assisted living. It had gotten to the point where she was falling a few times a week and being admitted to the hospital at least once every two weeks or so. She hated being reliant on other people. I was lucky to have had the time with her, so I'm grateful for that."

Grant didn't say anything and kept his focus on the courtyard while Jenna mused. "It feels a little like I'm reliving that with Lourdes."

"Meaning?" Grant's head swiveled back to Jenna's silhouette.

"Something's not right with her, but I haven't figured out what's going on. She's very private about her health. But equally discouraged about it too."

The number of doctor appointments that Lourdes had on the calendar was surprising. The older woman had at least one or two every week yet never volunteered any information about the nature of the appointments. Typically on her own with just a driver, Lourdes seemed appreciative that Jenna accompanied her without asking a lot of questions. Although Jenna's curiosity had turned into genuine concern for a woman who was becoming more friend than employer.

"What do you think?" Grant asked. "A chronic condition, or something more serious?"

Jenna pulled her feet into the chair, angling her bent legs to the side just a bit.

"I honestly don't know. I think one of the doctors is some sort of oncologist, so cancer maybe? She tires easily. Struggles with abdominal pain. I mean, that's not entirely uncommon at seventy-five. The older I get, the younger that seems."

Grant laughed lightly at the last comment. "Does she seem with-it most of the time? Mentally?"

"Yeah, but I'm only with her, what, six hours a day? When I'm there, she's sharp. I don't know what it is, but I'm worried about her."

"Jenna."

"Hmmm?" she answered absently. She rested the base of the wine glass on the arm of her chair and swirled the contents.

"Jenna," he repeated. "She's part of a crime family we're investigating for smuggling weapons."

"So? What are you getting at?" Jenna responded. "Sounds like you've deemed her complicit already."

"It's a little hard to believe she isn't aware of her family's business dealings." He cleared his throat. "You...well, you tend to...look, just don't get too worried about her," Grant finally said.

"What's that supposed to mean? I tend to what?" Her defensiveness elicited an unyielding tone from Grant.

"She's your target. Not a substitute for your mother. Not your friend." Grant leaned back in his chair and looked away. "And if she is complicit, you're going to be the one who'll have the information that takes her down. Don't go getting attached to her."

"I get all that, but she's a human being, for God's sake. And I'd like to think I am too. Furthermore, she's lonely and sick." Jenna bristled. "Probably sick of living among criminals. Or sick of being alone in a house full of people. Either way, I will not shun her kindness or her friendship. She didn't hire a personal assistant because the household was falling apart, that's for damn sure. You may have more experience as an agent compared to me, as Dugan so kindly pointed out, but I don't need you to tell me how to do my job."

"Well, considering it's connected to mine—" He thought better of finishing that thought and switched to a tone that ratcheted the tension down a few notches before continuing. "It's just that we're in this together, Jenna. You need to stay objective. Detached."

The low music from her Bluetooth speaker filled the next thirty seconds. She tried to keep the retort in her head but failed.

"Is that how you do it?" she asked pointedly. Even in the dark, she could tell his eyes narrowed briefly. "Is that straight out of the Grant Lawton survival manual?"

His gaze moved to the gazebo illuminated by the strings of patio lights before he gathered his glass and got up from his chair. Banking his irascibility, Grant pulled the door open.

"How I conduct my personal life isn't relevant to this discussion or this mission."

He had one foot inside when her voice stopped him.

"It is to that little boy asleep upstairs," she said in a hushed tone, staring blindly out at the courtyard. She knew he looked over his shoulder at her. Knew he was about to respond, so she beat him to it. "As you said earlier, we're in this together. So, for what it's worth, it is to me too."

He didn't move for several seconds. Neither did she.

"Good night, Grant," she offered softly in dismissal.

His footsteps faded as he headed up the stairs, and she leaned her head back and wondered if she should heed his admonition about Lourdes.

And maybe apply the same caution to him too.

do you believe in magic

T HE NEXT SATURDAY MORNING, as was their habit, Jenna and Evan were sitting on the patio with breakfast in hand when Grant made his way downstairs. He was on the phone and appeared to be engaged in a serious conversation from what she could tell. As she watched him through the glass, she allowed her thoughts to drift.

She thought of him as a geological formation—the visible surface layers, hard and uncompromising, exposed to the world, protecting the softer, more porous layers buried underneath. Some buried so deep no one would ever unearth them. Grant Lawton was certainly intriguing the more she saw beneath the surface, and she treasured what had become a close friendship.

As unmoored as she had felt over the past several years, she had never been desperate to have a man in her life. While she dated occasionally, she was perfectly content living her life on her terms, single as that was.

When it came to potential relationships, it was imperative that the person complement her life as opposed to complicating it. She wanted someone to laugh with. Someone who challenged her without being challenging. Someone who would dance unabashedly with her in the kitchen to a favorite song. Passion. Spontaneity. Travel. Someone who answered the call of the ocean and the mountains alike.

While the living conditions demanded some degree of familiarity, the things they had shared and the genuine ease of their relationship transcended mere roommate status. The more time they spent together, the more she had to force herself to ignore her growing attraction to him.

Her wistful trance was broken by Evan tugging at her arm. He pointed at her cup of coffee, which had spilled on the side table after she'd placed it precariously on a stack of magazines.

"I can get some napkins," Evan offered and started to get up when she gently placed her hand on his arm.

"No, it's ok. That was careless of me. I'll take care of it." She set the mug upright and rose to get a towel to clean up the mess. "You finish your breakfast."

Jenna caught the final fragment of Grant's call as she stepped into the villa.

"It'll be good to see you. 'Bye," he said and placed the phone down on the counter.

She knew him well enough to pick up on the soft tone in his voice and the distant look in his eyes. Girlfriend? Lover? One of many? *Ugh*. Whichever and whoever, it really was none of her business.

Shoving her curiosity aside, she grabbed some napkins from the counter.

"Not sure if I mentioned it, but Lourdes gave me a suggestion on where to get a dress for the party." Jenna said. "It's up in Livorno, so I'll probably be gone most of the day."

Grant didn't respond immediately but stared through the patio door at Evan. Concern lined his forehead, accenting the weathered creases.

Worry trumped her curiosity.

"Everything okay?" she asked just as he started to speak.

"Jenna, I—" He seemed uncharacteristically unsure of what to say or how to say it.

Instantly on guard, she mentally prepared herself for being pushed away. They were getting too close. Too comfortable. He wanted her back at arm's length, she was sure.

"I can't let Evan stay here," he said.

She breathed half a sigh of relief, holding the other half just in case.

"This...," he said, motioning to Evan on the patio. "This was supposed to be temporary while his grandmother was caring for her sister. I shouldn't have let him stay this long. Our...the family atmosphere has been...he likes being around you. I got complacent. He can't be part of this assignment any longer. I'm taking him to his grandparents today." Grant's thoughts tumbled out like he was in confession.

He turned away abruptly so she couldn't see his face, and she was equally glad he couldn't see the abject relief that crossed hers. She stifled a smile at how he'd stumbled in his attempt to describe their living arrangement.

Recalling the losses Grant had endured in the last few years, Jenna empathized with his anxiety. He would never use that word, but it had to be weighing heavily on him to imagine his nephew's safety being in jeopardy.

Grant wasn't asking for her input, but her first instinct was to offer comfort. Jenna gently laid her hand on the back of his arm and felt him tense.

"It's not up for discussion," he said sharply. There was a beat of silence, and he looked up at the ceiling. "I'd never forgive myself if something—"

"Hey," she said softly, leaning forward slightly to peer around his shoulder. "I had no intention of debating your decision. He's not my son, and it's certainly not my call, but I think that's wise. I was concerned about that, too, to be honest. What we're doing is not...well, it's not going to stay this calm. We both know that. He'll be safer with them. You'll be safer, too, if you aren't worrying about protecting him."

He turned to face her as quickly as he had turned away, and the hand that rested on his arm slipped to his chest before she could react. The creases on his forehead relaxed as his serious blue eyes searched her face. Before she could pull her hand away, he closed his hand over hers, saying nothing. He glanced toward the patio, then back to her.

She continued, buoyed by his acceptance of her touch. "I'll miss him, but you're making the right call on this."

"Am I?" His voice, low and raspy, tugged at her heart. "I never know if I'm doing right by him. I really have no idea how to be a father to him," he admitted. "He's lost so many people in his life, and I don't want him to feel passed around all the time."

"I get that. Evan's been through more than a lot of adults ever will. But he knows you love him, Grant. That alone is all that's required to be a father. And I certainly hope you realize how much he loves you." Grant studied her face as she continued. "What if you make it an adventure? Make it more about his grandparents wanting him. He knows he's here to spend the summer with them. Remind him they want him to come instead of you telling him he has to go. Be excited for him, and he'll adopt the same outlook. It's all in how you present it."

"Yeah, maybe you're right." Grant shook his head as if to clear it, then took a deep breath and released her hand. With another shake of his head, he looked down at her. "Look, thanks for your—"

She silenced him with two fingers to his lips. "You're welcome," she said, then froze at her bold and uninvited act.

"Sorry," she breathed.

Unable and unwilling to move away, her fingertips grazed his unshaven chin as her left hand drifted down to rest lightly on his chest. The steady beat of his heart thumped softly under her other palm.

They stood motionless as time wound to a stop. His hand moved to her shoulder, his eyes softened, and the back of his fingers brushed a wisp of hair from her cheek. His nearness overwhelmed her senses.

The sound of the patio door sliding open broke the spell, prompting her to take a sudden step back. She felt her face flush as Evan turned on the cartoons. Averting her gaze, Jenna excused herself from the room under the guise of giving Grant and Evan some privacy.

It wasn't until she was upstairs sitting on her bed trying to calm her racing pulse that it dawned on her that she had completely forgotten about the spilled coffee.

The contents of her suitcase were strewn across her bed as she tried to evaluate what she needed in town. The ever-growing shopping list she made was a crucial distraction but proved not terribly effective. The pen remained poised uselessly inches above the paper as her mind drifted to the downstairs encounter.

Her fingers on his mouth.

Her hands absorbing his heartbeat.

Lord, her head almost on his chest.

Instead of forcing the pen to write, she closed her eyes, replaying the warmth that had flowed through her when they'd touched. Jenna allowed herself, just for a moment, to imagine that he was just as intrigued as she was by what had transpired between them. Her overactive imagination had envisioned his head tilting down toward hers just before Evan had wandered inside.

If only.

A knock on her door brought her illusion to a halt. She opened it to find Grant leaning against the opposite wall with his hands in his back pockets. He rocked on his heels.

"Your approach worked, so thanks. I appreciate the advice. He's excited about seeing his grandparents, so he's starting to pack."

"Oh, good. I'm glad it helped." She smiled warmly at him. "So, I guess it's a table for one for me tonight, huh?" she added playfully, trying to keep things light.

"Actually, it occurred to me that I could use a few things in town myself. I didn't pack anything for a formal party either. I was thinking if we went up to Livorno, we could have lunch, get what we need, and then drop Evan off at his grandparents' place on the way back. That is, if you don't mind the company or a detour on the way home."

"Sounds like a great plan," she agreed readily, grateful not to be on her own for the entire day and left to her fantasies. "Meet you downstairs in thirty minutes?"

Feeling like a teenage girl heading to the mall knowing the captain of the football team would be there, she caught herself changing outfits at least three times and checking her make-up in the mirror at least as many times.

Her reflection in the mirror triggered a groan. Damn the person who invented mirrors. She much preferred the idea of looking the age she felt. Unwilling to relinquish the high she was riding, she was determined to enjoy the day shopping in Italy at Dugan's expense with her boys.

Thirty-five minutes later, their little simulated family of three buckled into Grant's rented Peugeot and set out to make good use of that Agency expense account.

shock to the system

HE HAD ACTUALLY THOUGHT about kissing her...not for the first time either. Evan's grand entrance had kept him from making an idiot of himself. The other day, he'd watched her apply lipstick, and he'd had to resist the temptation to see how it tasted. How she tasted. And now, the warmth lingered on his chest where her hands had come to rest earlier.

Stay detached.

That simple phrase was quickly becoming a theme. Although, with the assignment they'd been given, keeping his distance was going to be tough since they needed to appear to be a couple. Truth be told, it hadn't been a hardship to play that role thus far.

The woman had been a shock to his system. The wall he'd spent the past few years erecting was intentional, and he was extremely resistant to any attempted breach of his defenses. But damned if he could figure out at what point she had broken through.

At some point, she had unassumingly worked her way under his skin. It had been nothing dramatic, and there wasn't one particular thing about her that stuck out; it was just who she was. And to think she'd been right under his nose for years.

It occurred to him that he'd relaxed more in the last several weeks than he had in recent memory. For the first time in a long time, he'd let go of the weight he carried on his conscience. He had smiled and laughed to the point his face hurt, talked more, and genuinely been interested in her thoughts and opinions.

Jenna somehow drew him into conversations about things that he never thought he'd reveal to or discuss with another human being. Around her, he didn't have to hide, lie, or apologize for the life he had lived or for the lives he had taken. He found their quick and deep friendship shockingly restorative while also a little unsettling.

Grant was more than grateful for her quick and gracious acceptance of the situation with Evan. Far from the withdrawn little boy Grant had stewed about night after sleepless night, Evan was blooming, which could only be attributed to Jenna's influence.

It helped that Jenna spent a few hours each afternoon doing some sort of activity with him. She had expressed alarm that Evan had essentially started summer break in early April and had vowed to ensure he stayed on track scholastically. While some lessons were academic, others were all about creativity. On more than one occasion, he had waited anxiously for her to walk through the door in anticipation of whatever she had planned.

Evidently, Grant wasn't the only male in the house who had been captivated by her.

On the east side of Orbetello, he turned north for the drive up to Livorno and considered how they would do one on one without Evan as their common focus. It was curiosity more than concern. His top priority was Evan's safety; everything else was secondary. He had, however, been anxious about telling her Evan would be leaving. Her support had been unexpected but at the same time reassuring. Validation of sorts that maybe he could figure out this whole parenting thing. What made him uneasy was how much he valued her approval.

Grant stole a glance at his partner. Her elbow rested on the door frame, and her head rested on the headrest, shoulders angled toward the door ever so slightly. To anyone else, she was simply taking in the scenery, but her gaze was distant, and her brow furrowed. She was a million miles away.

The way the color of her eyes changed with her moods fascinated him. Usually a rich deep green, but with a hint of blue at times, they betrayed her with sharp gold flecks when she was angry or hurt. She rarely tried to hide her emotions, blaming her age for her lack of filter. The way she kept her make-up light and her hair styled but natural echoed her authenticity. What you saw was what you got, and the honesty in that was refreshing.

He had first noticed the gold flecks in her eyes when Dugan lobbed his thinly veiled insults at her during their initial briefing. It was clear the asshole enjoyed tearing her down, and Dugan was damned lucky Grant hadn't been in the same conference room. Even though it had stretched the limits of her control, she had maintained her professionalism despite the ferocious, yet wounded, look in her eyes.

He stole one final sideways glance, wondering who or what occupied her thoughts, disconcerted by how keenly he hoped he was the subject. As badly as he wanted to know, he decided it really would be much wiser to concentrate on the road.

The traffic naturally got heavier as they entered the city, though Grant navigated the narrow streets with confidence. The bustling shopping district Lourdes had recommended proved to be a welcome distraction.

He wasn't one hundred percent sure how many things Jenna had on her shopping list, but she seemed enthralled by the tiny shops lining the timeless, stone-paved thoroughfare. He grimaced. This had the potential of being an exceptionally long day.

Leading Evan over to a burbling fountain, he sat down on the edge and watched as Jenna popped into a shop with a happy gleam in her eye.

She exited the small shop after only a few minutes, followed seconds later by a petite, well-dressed shopkeeper. The lady chattered in Italian and led Jenna to a tall wooden door a few shops away. Belying her petite frame, the lady pounded relentlessly on the door, shouting for someone named Angelo. Grant watched the situation closely, slowly rising to his feet.

A sullen wisp of a young man opened the door. He wore form-fitting pants that were as jet black as his wavy, shoulder-length hair. The wraith circled Jenna repeatedly, carrying on a rapid-fire exchange in Italian with the lady from the other shop. Heeled boots covered in what appeared to be rhinestones cast shards of light in every direction, transforming him into a human disco ball.

The lady eventually gestured toward the fountain, and all three of them turned to look at Grant. Angelo's eyes widened, and he whisked Jenna inside before she could object.

As amused as Grant was, he was uncomfortable leaving her, and his fingers flew as he typed hastily into his phone.

You ok in there?

Sì, Angelo says we'll be
done by 4. That ok?

Her response took longer than he would have liked, but satisfied with the situation, he texted a quick acknowledgment in return, chuckling under his breath before shoving the phone in his pocket. He tousled Evan's hair, feeling traitorously grateful to be liberated from shopping and to have a gorgeous afternoon to spend with his nephew.

True to his background and his chromosomes, Grant was a target-type shopper. He knew what he needed, located it, and was finished in a matter of forty-five minutes.

It was just before the four o'clock hour when they made their way back to the marble fountain in the piazza. Grant looked around casually for Jenna but only saw a few lone window shoppers out and about. The trickle of the water in the central fountain soothed his impatience. He placed his bag down and took a seat next to Evan on the worn fountain wall that had been eroded over time by generations of men in his same predicament.

An eye-catching woman in dark Italian-style sunglasses wearing a white sundress and turquoise strappy heels meandered in his direction from across the way. The late afternoon sun glinted off chin-length hair that tapered higher in the back, accenting a graceful neck and well-defined bare shoulders. The woman was about twenty yards away when she smiled and gave him a reserved wave of her fingers.

Evan jumped up from the bench and started running toward her a good twenty seconds before Grant recognized Jenna. He liked the everyday version of her but had to admit the added layer of confidence was incredibly sexy.

She took Evan's hand and made her way over to Grant and twirled in front of him.

"So? What do you think?"

Not waiting for his response, she pushed her sunglasses up to perch on her head. Thankfully, Evan's usual chatter compensated for Grant's inability to form words. Her green eyes sparkled with humor, self-assurance, and a bit of mischief as she shifted her focus to the shop where she had disappeared hours ago.

Angelo stood in the shop's entryway, illuminated in the afternoon sunlight like a guardian angel. Arms crossed on his chest, he leaned with one shoulder against the door frame, watching as if measuring Grant's reaction.

Still holding Evan's hand, Jenna walked across to where Angelo waited. Grant had no choice but to follow in her wake. Angelo greeted Evan with a pat to his head, then turned his attention to Grant, nodding approvingly and wiggling his eyebrows as he looked from Jenna to Grant and back again. Laughing nervously, Jenna handed Grant a few overstuffed shopping bags, then fiercely hugged a surprised Angelo.

"*Molte grazie*," Jenna said.

Angelo brushed her cheeks with two air kisses, then disappeared into the shop. The now-quiet square seemed bereft at his departure.

"What an amazing day! Now I know how Julia Roberts felt," she said breathlessly as they got into the car.

Grant struggled for the right words but was smart enough to know he needed to choose them carefully. Openly marveling at a superficial transformation probably wasn't the best approach. As he started the car, he verbalized his thoughts the best he could.

"I'm glad you enjoyed your day. And you look fantastic." He looked over at her. "But it helps when the clay is good. All they did was put an expensive glaze on it," he stated, staring straight ahead as their car exited onto the street.

"Thank you, Grant," she said. "Just when I thought my day couldn't get any better."

He glanced quickly at her to find her sparkling green eyes studying him boldly. Grant winked, then turned his attention back to the road.

"Well, I guess that makes it official," she added, donning her sunglasses with a flourish. "Livorno just might be my new favorite place."

not just a woman

Afternoon mellowed into evening. Grant's silver Peugeot sped south out of the city center before turning east toward the town of Volterra, leaving the city and its lights behind. Knowing it would be the last dinner together for a while, they stopped for a leisurely dinner in a charming village before resuming the drive. Grant eventually pulled off the paved surface onto a dusty, unlit road, following a single pair of tire tracks that marked the way through tall weeds.

Cresting a small hill lined by abandoned vineyards, a lime-washed villa with a brownish-red tile roof graced the landscape. The fading Tuscan sunlight colored the uneven roof with a hundred melted burnt-orange crayons.

An older woman in a blue ankle-length skirt and tan thick-strapped sandals was emptying the clothesline when she heard the car approach. As they rolled to a stop, the woman set the last piece of clothing in a basket that sat on the ground and turned to greet them.

Evan was out of the car like a shot, throwing himself into his grandmother's arms, where he was wholly absorbed into her aproned skirt. With only his legs and head visible, the woman kissed his dark hair. An older man shuffled out of the house, waved, then stopped to brace himself for Evan's exuberant launch into his embrace.

Jenna stood quietly next to the car watching the boisterous reunion while Grant was welcomed by his late brother's in-laws just as warmly. Evan would be loved here, she reassured herself. Grateful tears filled her eyes but didn't spill over. She had treasured their afternoons together. His giggles, chatter, and goodnight hugs would stay with her. The hollow feeling in her chest reminded her of numbly driving away after dropping each of her kids off at college. The unexpected realization of how much she'd miss him hit her squarely.

Evening bathed the hilltop surroundings. Lights from neighboring properties flared randomly as if to comfort her with their presence and silent support. Grant called her over for introductions, shaking her from her reverie and requiring her to abandon the car door that had served as an impromptu illusory shield. She tried not to feel self-conscious as she walked toward them, especially when Evan's grandfather elbowed Grant, only to be shushed by his wife.

Introductions were made, and they were ushered through an arched wooden door that creaked on rusty hinges into a courtyard overflowing with rustic charm. Red and yellow flowers placed in the center of a cornflower-blue wooden table perfected the setting. Five upside-down glasses, a bottle of wine, and a thick green bottle of water sat next to the chipped pale-pink vase. The scene could have been plucked off the cover of an Italian-themed coffee-table book from Pottery Barn, reinforcing her belief that everything in Italy held a touch of ancient magic.

When the last shadows melted into the darkness, they said their goodbyes. Jenna hugged Evan tightly, kissed his cheeks, then made her way to the car to give the family some privacy. She heard Grant thank Evan's grandparents, heard them try to refuse the envelope Grant insisted they take, heard his voice choke on a rare admission of love as he crouched on bent knees in front of his nephew.

That simple fatherly act warmed her heart, and she made a mental note to reassure him that he filled those shoes perfectly.

After the farewells were done, Grant strode toward the car with purposeful steps, avoiding the temptation to fill Evan's head with nebulous promises of adoption and houses in the suburbs with white picket fences. Running footsteps sounded behind him, and he turned to swoop Evan up for a last hug, only to be mildly yet humorously disappointed when Evan ran right past him.

In the obscure light, he saw Evan's arms outstretched before Jenna bent to pull him into a hug. Clutching him to her, she rocked him gently, brushing dark waves of hair off his forehead with her fingers.

"What's your favorite animal, honey?" Jenna asked Evan.

Grant cocked his head at her question as he observed their exchange.

"His challenge phrase," Jenna explained.

Evan grinned at her and then at Grant. "A Grant's zebra," he replied with a giggle.

Grant cocked his head and raised one eyebrow. Amusement danced at one corner of his mouth. "A what? Is that a real thing?"

Ignoring Grant's question, Jenna tapped the boy's nose. "Other than the fact that we have our own Grant, what's so special about that one?"

"If someone says I have to go with them, they have to know that it's the smallest kind of zebra," Evan answered seriously.

"If they don't know that, don't go with them or trust them. Run away if you have to," Jenna instructed. "Don't be afraid to ask that question if a stranger approaches you."

"I won't." Dark curls bounced once with his singular, emphatic nod. "I'll be careful."

Evan gave her one last hug, and she lowered him to the ground, gently nudging him toward the house. He paused only long enough to high-five Grant before running back to his grandparents.

Grant waved once more and walked slowly around the car while Jenna buckled into her seat. When had Evan adopted this woman? He was astonished and appreciative of the things that, as a mom-turned-agent, she had wisely thought to teach Evan.

He slid into the driver's seat and surreptitiously glanced at Jenna. Her shoulders angled toward the door, and her chin was tucked low, elbow propped on the door. She could have been just looking out the window again, but he knew that wasn't the case. Her fingers massaged her temples and shielded her eyes from view. He flashed the headlights in a farewell salute and guided the car down the now-dark path. In the muted glow of the dashboard lights, dampness glistened on Jenna's cheeks.

Without hesitating, he reached for the fist that sat clenched in her lap. The hand that was more accustomed to the cold steel of weaponry gently pried hers open, and his fingers slipped between hers. He moved their joined hands to rest on the console between their seats and felt her fingers tighten around his.

It was going on midnight when they arrived back at the villa. The exhilaration of her afternoon shopping adventure had faded, deflated by her unexpected reaction to leaving Evan. Touched by Grant's empathetic gesture on the way home, Jenna was also a little unnerved by that side of him.

He'd held her hand even as he shifted gears, as if not wanting to let her go, or so she wanted to believe. His thumb lightly stroking the back of her hand had lulled her into thinking there was something between them. But she warned herself not to read too much into it.

They unloaded their purchases and climbed wearily into the house. It was dark and quiet. Neither talked—both lost in their own thoughts and overcome by emotional fatigue. She dumped her shopping bags on the couch while Grant took his upstairs without a word.

Jenna grabbed a bottle of red wine and two glasses and took them out to the patio, seeking the therapy of their routine despite her exhaustion and the late hour. Grant never joined her, so when the patio lights blinked off in the courtyard half the bottle later, she gave up waiting and went to bed.

14

wicked game

THE SUN HAD BEEN up for several hours when Grant decided he needed to get moving. Without Evan to care for, he lounged in bed thinking about everything that had transpired in the last almost two months. He found himself listening for Jenna shuffling around in the house after her usual morning workout. Certain that he'd been rude last night by not even saying goodnight, he thought apologizing would only make things worse in that a reason of some sort would need to be offered.

He had been uncharacteristically wrung out when they arrived home at the villa and had not trusted himself to withstand the temptation of her. His unbidden reaction to her when she'd walked from the car to meet Evan's grandparents scared him shitless. In that white sundress with the sun setting, he'd wanted to put his arm around her bare shoulders, tuck her against his side, and introduce her as something other than his coworker. So much so that he'd made no attempt to deny Evan's grandfather's assumptions.

Interlacing his fingers with hers in the car hadn't been the wisest move either. Initially, her hand had clutched his tightly. When it relaxed to something that just felt natural, it had roused a long-forgotten awareness. A disturbing sense of contentment. Had he joined her on the patio once they were back at the villa, he wasn't convinced he could have resisted pulling her into his arms. And from there, any residual attempt at staying detached would have been useless, assuming she would even have been receptive.

Hearing no movement upstairs or down, he reminded himself this was an assignment—a temporary situation—and rolled out of bed. Voices outside drew him to the window. Through the small space between the closed window shutters, he saw two people chatting near the large pot overflowing with white flowers that marked the line between their villa and the one next door.

Jenna wore her signature black cropped leggings and neon pink running shoes. The back of her long tank top was wet and stuck to her back as she stretched her limbs in a modest post-workout routine. Grant's gaze may have lingered on her longer than intended before shifting to study the other person.

The man she spoke with was a few inches over six feet with a beefy chest and bulky shoulders comprised not solely of muscle. Dressed in tan slacks and a pricey blue golf shirt, his look was completed by trendy sunglasses with clear frames that probably cost more than yesterday's entire shopping excursion. Not a single strand of his brown-black hair was out of place. Expensive leather shoes on his feet shuffled slightly as the man removed his sunglasses to reveal a classic Italian look with heavy eyebrows that matched his hair. Between the man's plastic smile and his overly white teeth, Grant was reminded of a wolf in some old fairy tale crossed with a Ken doll.

Luca.

The fact that the two men had never met didn't matter. Grant had a wealth of experience in recognizing threats. And this man was just that.

Their conversation ended, and Jenna waved a polite farewell. Luca ogled her a little too long when she turned to walk away. In an unconscious response, a snarl of disapproval escaped Grant's throat.

By the time he finished dressing for his own workout, the muffled sound of running water behind her closed door invited illusions of steam, soap, and water streaming down forbidden curves. A vigorous run would help deter his imagination.

An hour later he stood on the patio cooling off, watching her blurred figure swim in straight lines along the length of the pool. She had spent many hours at the pool with Evan, thinking she was giving Grant a break in the afternoons. Instead, it had given him the opportunity to study her intently from the security of the patio on more than one occasion.

From where he stood, he could see only about half of her chaise but recognized her striped towel crumpled next to her wide-brimmed straw hat. Shapely legs kicked as her arms parted the water forcefully until she touched the edge and climbed the stairs out of the pool.

Movement near her chaise diverted his attention. A tanned, masculine arm swiped low and picked up her towel. The arm was attached to a bare-chested, burly figure in red swim trunks who walked confidently toward her. Now fully focused, Grant recognized the overly polished man from Jenna's morning encounter.

Bent to the side sluicing water from her wet hair, Jenna started when she saw the man approaching. The smile she offered was friendly enough but didn't brighten up her face like when she laughed freely. Luca draped the towel around her shoulders, and she fisted the ends together across her chest. She pulled a gauzy coverup from her bag, expertly slipping it over her head and removing the towel in a continuous movement.

Whether intentional or not, her gaze glided up to the patio of their villa. Luca looked up at where Grant stood and nodded in tacit acknowledgment.

This was the opening they'd been working toward. Faster than Clark Kent in a phone booth, he changed and was out the door in under two minutes—his cape merely a faded red striped towel slung over his shoulder.

Neither Jenna nor her new acquaintance was terribly surprised or welcoming when he opened the gate, then dropped his towel on her chaise as if planting a territorial flag in battle.

"Sorry, honey. That phone call took longer than I expected. Miss me?" he asked Jenna with a smile and a wink before gently lifting her chin. Ignoring her guarded surprise, Grant leaned in to kiss her lightly on the lips, lingering longer than necessary for Luca's benefit. He casually slung his arm around her waist—his hand resting on the swell of her hip—and felt her stiffen.

Jenna inwardly rolled her eyes as the men eyed each other warily. Her foot tapped furiously while Luca introduced himself to Grant. It was clear Luca expected a reaction—at least a hint of recognition—from Grant and seemed a bit perturbed at getting none. Turning his attention back to Jenna, Luca continued their conversation, paying little heed to her husband's presence.

Five minutes later, a shrill shout across the open courtyard disrupted the attempted dalliance. Luca didn't even look in the direction of the interruption but raised an open palm above his head, brushing off the summons with obvious annoyance. Shielding her eyes with her hand, Jenna glimpsed a slim young woman standing with her hands on her hips on an upper terrace of the Santoris' villa. The woman who had delivered the party invitation was clearly not amused by Luca's dismissal. She shouted her command again.

"*Porca puttana,*" Luca muttered while shaking his head.

"Your girlfriend?" Jenna asked coyly.

"No," Luca said. "My little sister."

"Ah, Paetta?" Jenna asked.

"*Sì*, have you not met her?"

"No, but I hope to when I'm there tomorrow," Jenna said.

"Ah, yes, I will be sure to introduce you." His slippery smile oozed back into place as he intimately touched Jenna's arm and excused himself. "Tomorrow, then." The promise was just a whisper at her cheek.

Luca cut his eyes in Grant's direction, giving a curt nod before sauntering toward the sound of a slamming patio door that echoed across the courtyard. Grant dropped his arm once Luca had ambled away.

"I had him on the hook before you made your grand entrance," Jenna growled. "Seriously, what the hell was that all about?"

Instantly defensive at her reaction, Grant met her angry stare. "That's called doing our job."

Jenna bristled. "And precisely what do you think I've been doing for the last two months?"

"We need to move this along," he stated flatly. "That is, if you're done playing house."

Jenna started to remind him that Luca was her job, but the cutting comment he had tacked on left her speechless. Her eyebrows shot up before her brow furrowed and her jaw clenched.

Grant dropped coolly onto the chaise, reclining with one arm above his head despite the tense atmosphere. Her movements were stiff but controlled as she collected her things.

She calmly adjusted the wide-brimmed hat on her head, then set her bag on the ground before turning to him. Her grandmother had always said that wearing a hat made a statement without saying a word. And she had a statement to make.

Jenna placed a hand on each arm of his chaise and leaned over him seductively.

"Well then, my dear husband, I suppose we should make this more convincing," she declared with a purposeful and expertly delivered blend of a sneer and a disingenuous smile.

Sharp gold flecks glinted in her eyes. His narrowed as every muscle tensed, anticipating well-deserved pain when she nudged her left knee between his outstretched legs. The brim of her hat hid their faces from view as she bent over him, affording him a clear view down the front of her coverup. Grant swallowed hard.

"Since you're so eager to move this along, maybe we should make sure our audience has no reason to doubt our undying affection for each other," she said, feigning breathlessness as she spoke.

Jenna was determined to show him exactly how well she could do her job. Her right index finger trailed tantalizingly from the waistband of his swim trunks to just under his chin, gliding over the light sheen of sweat on his torso. She lowered her head until their faces were inches apart, not caring that her hat had slipped to one side.

The gauzy fabric of her coverup grazed the hair on his chest, and his breath hitched. His eyes locked on hers, daring her to do what he thought she might.

Jenna dropped her right hand to the tense muscle of his left thigh, slipping the tips of her fingers under the hem of his swim trunks. Making soft circles on the top of his leg with her thumb, she lightly brushed his mouth with hers, unintentionally closing her eyes. The breath he released was soft on her cheek. Unable to back out, even if she had wanted to, she interpreted his reaction as an invitation to take more. Besides, she still had a point to make.

The pressure on his mouth increased with each brush of her lips. The fabricated intent behind her actions left her completely unprepared for him to answer the kiss. Her thumb stopped making the circles on his leg when his left hand cupped the back of her head with gentle insistence. Grant's head tilted; the rigid line of his mouth softened, then opened slightly against hers. Emboldened and intrigued by the hint of citrus and salt on his lips, she dared to explore further, tentatively touching her tongue to his.

The unexpected delicate heat caught them both off guard, yet neither moved to end it. His fingers grazed her neck. His thumb traced the soft path from behind her ear to her jaw and back up again. Even in the warm sun, shivers raced down her spine as his tongue stroked hers lazily.

It was supposed to only be a teaser. Part dare. Part threat. It wasn't supposed to be spellbinding.

Feeling that the balance of power was shifting dangerously, Jenna broke the kiss by slowly pulling back and trying to regain the upper hand she had so quickly abandoned. Steely blue eyes bored into hers as she stood up and adjusted her hat once again.

"I guess that should do it," she said icily, slamming a stony expression into place. "A cold swim might take care of that."

The smug advice accompanied a glance at the front of his swim trunks before she snatched up her things and stalked away, the gate slamming behind her as she left the pool area.

you go to my head

T HIS WAS HER DOING. Even if it had been payback for his bitter comment. Even if he had kissed her first. His had been superficial and for Luca's benefit only, he rationalized. Regardless of the blame, they had crossed a line. One that had been gradually blurring over the past weeks.

Grant sat up, resting his forearms on bent knees. He stayed still, moving only to steeple his fingers against his forehead while collecting himself. It wouldn't be a good idea to stand up right now anyway. But Jesus H. Christ, what had they done?

The temptation to kiss her, as arduous as it had been to resist, was ten times safer than actually knowing how she tasted. He also knew he'd been an ass. The harsh words he had childishly thrown at her were purely a reflection of what he'd been telling himself all morning.

This couldn't be.

Couldn't happen.

Couldn't interfere with why they were here.

But somehow, despite his halfhearted internal protest, it had.

More composed, he stood up and seriously considered that cold swim. His senses still registered the scent of sunscreen and salt water from the pool warm on her skin. That kiss had affected both of them more than either had intended, and he chuckled at her valiant attempt to stay pissed off as she left. Still, he owed her a major apology.

For a moment, he wondered if she'd bail on the assignment. Taking the stairs two at time, he grinned in spite of himself. The Jenna he'd come to know wasn't so easily deterred.

The sound of running water from upstairs gave him time to rehearse his apology, but the opportunity to deliver it never materialized. He waited a full hour before heading to his own shower. She still had not emerged when he plopped down on the couch with his computer.

The remainder of the afternoon crept by. He finally knocked on her bedroom door a few hours later to offer an apology in the form of dinner in town.

"Jenna? Hey, I'd like to apologize for earlier. Dinner's on me. You pick the restaurant, and I'll buy." There was no answer. "I'm sorry I was a jerk."

A little stronger this time. "Jenna?"

Still no answer.

"Look, we need to talk. Answer me, please."

Apprehension grew.

"Jenna? Are you okay?" he asked. "In three seconds, I'm opening the door." At the count of four, he turned the knob.

Her room was still. The bathroom door stood open, and the bed was made. Clothes lying at its foot gave him a passing sense of relief that she hadn't packed before leaving. That would be a tough one to explain to Dugan. More so, it wouldn't take Catherine long to figure it out if Jenna insisted on reassignment midstream.

A slight niggle of worry tugged at his conscience. He couldn't exactly go chasing after her—not after what he'd said to her at the pool—but they had an unspoken habit of sharing their whereabouts. The apology he'd prepared still needed to be delivered too. He pulled out his phone and started a text message. Just before hitting Send, he deleted it and shoved the phone into his pocket.

Reading did nothing to assuage his curiosity. He tossed the book onto the table after reading the same sentence three times. The hours crawled past, and he ended up eating dinner in solitude. When the courtyard lights ticked on at dusk, unease began to creep in. He grabbed her speaker, a bottle of wine, and two glasses and sat stonily in his chair on the patio. Certainly, she'd be back any minute.

An hour and twenty-seven minutes later, two car doors slammed. Laughter followed. Three, maybe four people, he estimated. Based on the direction of the sound, they were headed into the courtyard. Sure enough, two men and two women walked in pairs to the pool.

Illuminated by the distorted underwater lights, the surface of the water swayed in the night breeze. Shoulders bumped occasionally as the women laughed at something one of the girls said in French.

Was that Jenna?

Grant leaned forward to get a better angle. The other girl answered over her shoulder in French while kicking off her shoes and peeling off her dress to reveal a skimpy bathing suit. One of the men shucked his shirt and jeans and chased her into the water, leaving Jenna standing poolside laughing with the other man.

Jenna turned to the man Grant now recognized as Luca. Not liking this development one bit, Grant retreated into the shadows of the patio to observe. Luca disappeared for no more than five minutes and returned with two bottles of wine and two glasses.

Jenna kicked off her sandals and dipped her foot into the pool with a wine glass in one hand and Luca's arm in the other to steady herself. She continued her conversation with the other woman while dodging Luca's attempt to slide an arm around her waist. Her carefree laugh drifted into the air while Luca led her by the wrist to the grassy area and picked up the bocce set.

With the courtyard lights casting shadows, Grant had a hard time seeing Luca and Jenna clearly, and the pair in the pool laughing like drunken sailors made hearing their conversation difficult at best. He shifted his position again.

Jenna placed three balls on the ground near her feet, keeping one as she tossed the small white one onto the marked field of play. She laughed, pointed at the target, and took her wine glass from Luca's outstretched hand. He refilled it before positioning Jenna in front of him. He then pressed up against her backside, placed one hand on her waist and guided her toss.

Their mutual flirtation lasted through both bottles of wine until Jenna finally gathered up her sandals and said goodnight to her new friends. Plainly disappointed by her departure, Luca tried to convince her to stay. Ever the rehearsed gentleman, he soon conceded, reluctantly kissing the back of her hand in farewell as she backed away.

Jenna waltzed in the front door singing under her breath, satisfied that Luca had taken the bait that had been dangled. She had no idea—nor did she give a rat's rear end—where Grant was.

She had darted from the house earlier when she'd heard Grant start his shower. Her escape had admittedly been immature and spiteful, but she'd resented his imprudent portrayal of the past several weeks. His comment had cut to the quick. But holy crap, that kiss.

A lengthy walk on the beach had brought the reason for their mission back into focus. Her renewed sense of purpose had prompted her to knock on the door to the Santoris' villa, eyeing the expensive car that was parked in front. Lourdes had not been feeling well again when Jenna left work on Thursday, and although she had checked in via text on Friday, avoiding Grant gave her the perfect excuse to check on Lourdes in person.

The housemaid, Carina, had Sunday off. In her stead, Luca answered the door and ushered her in with an exaggerated flourish that brought a mutual smile. The charming version of Luca stayed close by as Jenna prepared some fruit and tea for Lourdes.

Her visit concluded as evening set in, and she was jotting a few notes for work the next day when Luca invited her to join him, Paetta, and her boyfriend for dinner. Deciding it was time to find out more about his business dealings, she accepted. After all, venting about her husband would be a good opportunity to drip information to him.

Luca kept her wine glass full all evening, happy to capitalize on Jenna's marital strife. She'd gladly played along, using her simmering anger at her husband as cause to be receptive to Luca's charms.

Jenna had been in no hurry to return to their villa and hoped it was late enough that Grant would already be upstairs for the night, but just in case, she kept the lights off to further shroud her arrival. Her head was still a little fuzzy from too much wine, which was yet another reason to avoid a confrontation with Grant tonight.

Dropping her phone and keys on the table, she headed in the direction of the stairs. In the dark of the living room, her little toe caught the leg of a chair. Jenna swore under her breath and hopped forward two steps on one foot. It was only then that she noticed him.

Outlined by the lights from the courtyard, Grant stood with his feet shoulder width apart, arms crossed on his chest. She felt like a schoolgirl sneaking back into the house after a night out and getting caught by an overbearing father. An audible giggle escaped at the memory and the likeness.

"Must have been a hell of an evening," he said in a slightly judgmental tone.

"Yes, it was, actually. Most fun I've had since I've been here," she tossed back lightly, pretending that she hadn't spent the last two hours thinking of what she would say to him.

"Didn't feel like introducing your new friends, huh?"

Her back stiffened when he took a step forward to continue the interrogation.

"New? You met Luca already, remember?" The twitch in his jaw at hearing Luca's name only emboldened her.

"And the other couple in the pool?"

"Pae—" She started to reply but caught herself when her brain registered his admission. "You were watching us?"

"Kinda hard not to with all the commotion out there," he snapped back. "I didn't realize you were fluent in French."

"It's highly likely there's a lot you don't know about me," she snipped in return.

Her foot was poised above the first stair when he grabbed her arm.

"Wait a minute," he said. Frustration usurped the apology he had rehearsed.

"Take your hand off me. I'm done being pawed tonight." She glared down at his hand and looked back up at him. "Let. Go. Now."

He relaxed his grip a bit but turned her toward him before he released her arm.

"Where have you been all day? You can't—" he attempted.

"I can't what, Grant?" she hissed, cocking her head and spitting venom. The gold knives in her eyes slashed as she interrupted him. "I was merely out doing that job you so kindly reminded me of earlier. Moving it along like you want. Despite what you—and Dugan, for that matter—think of me, I'm very capable of doing my job without you watching my every move or reminding me why we're here."

The sheer curtains at the open patio door ballooned in the night breeze, drawing her attention to the unopened wine bottle and two glasses on the small patio table. The playlist they had started together drifted in with the night air.

He had been waiting for her.

Any other night, she would have relished that realization. Tonight, it made her furious that he'd expected her to simply set aside the derisive comment he had thrown at her at the pool earlier. With his harsh words, Grant had intentionally diminished what she thought they'd built together, making her resent how willingly he'd accepted her help with Evan. But she choked back the bitterness that wanted so badly to be verbalized.

Settling for a biting observation, she indicated the patio with a toss of her head before anger propelled her up the stairs.

"And for the record, it looks like you're the only one playing house now."

enemy

CARINA HAD CALLED OUT sick again, so the household's normal chores had made for a busy Monday. Luca was away the entire week, and Lourdes was feeling better. At four o'clock, Jenna heard the tap of her friend's cane stop behind her.

Lourdes tsked at Jenna. The admonition was a language every daughter on earth understood.

The older woman had picked up on Jenna's residual irritation at Grant almost immediately that morning. The reason behind their squabble had been amended a great deal to keep with the script.

"*Cara*," Lourdes began. "You cannot hide here all day like you did yesterday. Your shift ended two hours ago."

"I'm not hiding," Jenna fibbed, scribbling furiously in her planner. "With Carina out, I'm just behind on a few things that need to get done today."

"Liar," the older woman said to Jenna's back.

Despite the gentle tone of the delivery, Jenna flipped the notebook closed and spun to face her accuser.

Lourdes smiled knowingly. "Go home. Work it out."

Jenna sighed heavily before acknowledging the basket Lourdes held out to her.

"What's this?"

"This is my way of making sure you don't blow things out of proportion. Food is how Italians set the past aside," Lourdes said and pointed her cane to the back door that led to the courtyard. "*È meglio pace certa che vittoria sperata.*"

Jenna chewed her lip for a moment as she decoded the saying, then dutifully gathered her tote and hefted the basket of food. "*Grazie*, Lourdes," she said, kissing the older woman's papery cheeks.

"*Vai a fare la pace.*" With a light hand on Jenna's shoulder, Lourdes ushered Jenna to the door.

Despite her friend's wise words, Jenna fumed on the way home, reluctantly prepared to be the one to offer the olive branch. Curse the female compulsion to be the peacemaker. Like so many other women, it was a role she had played her entire life.

Grant was rifling through the refrigerator when she entered. She unpacked a cold bottle of white wine and the warm dishes from the basket Lourdes had given her.

"I, um, brought a peace offering." She stayed on the other side of the counter and just looked at his back, waiting for him to respond. "Well, Lourdes sent it." Jenna pushed Lourdes's suggestive comment out of her mind, determined to keep him at arm's length. "Once this whole thing is over, we can go back to being nothing more than acquaintances."

He closed the small refrigerator, straightened, and looked back at her. For a split second, she thought he was going to rebuff her offer to negotiate a reconciliation.

"Is that what you want?" he asked.

"Grant, this is new territory for me. I haven't lived in such close quarters with someone I work with since I shared a tent with my squadron commander on my first deployment to Saudi. This has been harder than really being married, I think. Not to mention, I hate unnecessary drama." She needed to stop talking. At least she hadn't apologized. Looking down, she picked at the ruined polish on a broken fingernail. "I'm sorry this has gotten overly complicated." *Well, shit.*

She raised her head, startled to find him standing in front of her. With a shake of her head, she murmured, "And I really hate it when people sneak up on me."

"Problem is…I think it's you who has snuck up on me," he said in a quiet voice.

Her pulse picked up. Afraid to meet his gaze, she looked down at her hands again only to feel that current strike when his knuckles traced her jawline. She fought the urge to close her eyes.

"Hey, about yesterday." He gently lifted her chin. "My comment was unfair and totally out of line. I'm sorry for what I said. You were an easy target for the blame."

She nodded, still avoiding eye contact. It would be too awkward—and not entirely true—to tell him she was sorry for kissing him the way she had. One of those "sorry, not sorry" things.

"Wait…blame for what?" Her head whipped up defensively when his comment registered.

"This." His hand waved back and forth between them. "Us."

Her head cocked in misunderstanding. "Us? Based on how you disappeared when we got back from dropping Evan off and then yesterday's 'playing house' comment, I figured I'd served my purpose now that you don't need help with Evan any longer."

"I deserve that, I suppose," he admitted. "But that's not the case." A stray lock of hair rested on her cheek, and he brushed it back. Jenna looked away until his hand gently turned her face back to his. "I apologize again for yesterday. I didn't mean what I said."

"Every comment has to be thought before it's said." She searched his eyes. "If I did something to irritate you, just—"

He shook his head and took a step back. "No. That's just it. You've been nothing but the ideal partner." He cleared his throat. "And wife." He offered a restrained grin when her eyebrows shot up. "Even though we're on the job, I'm having a hard time keeping my...well, never mind."

The curious tilt of her head prompted him to continue.

"I'm having a hard time staying—" He paused again and inhaled. He stuffed his hands in his pockets and looked away.

"Staying what?"

"Staying detached," he said in a low voice. Head bowed, his eyes flicked up at her.

"I see," Jenna said quietly, digesting his admission.

"Saturday night, when we got home, I had to get some distance. From you." He looked back down and took another step back, putting his words into action. "From us."

"Oh," she replied in a whisper.

He took a deep breath and ran a hand through his hair. "Look, I didn't mean to make this worse. I should have stopped with the apology."

"I'm really glad you didn't."

Jenna fought the urge to reach for him but resisted. She turned to unpack the rest of the food, using the task as the graceful exit they both needed. The ability to exude calm while her mind raced had always been a gift.

"Lourdes said food was how the Italians set the past aside. Based on the amount of food in here, she's covered a couple of decades," she offered with a light smile.

The corner of his mouth lifted, and he moved back into the kitchen to grab two plates. He set the plates on the counter and wrapped a towel around the bottle of wine. The cork gave a muffled pop, and she reached for the wine glass he held out to her. When he didn't relinquish it to her, she intentionally wrapped her fingers over his.

"I'm sorry I was an ass yesterday. Am I forgiven?" he asked, releasing the glass only after a single nod from her granted his acquittal.

Accepting his apology and her wine, she retreated to the patio with plate in hand.

They ate amid sparse conversation, each digesting the implication of the earlier conversation as much as the food.

"I think Luca's a dangerous character," Grant prompted, once the food had been devoured and their wine glasses refilled. "I don't like him. Or trust him."

"I didn't expect either of us to like him. He's slimy, self-important, and handsy, but I'm not sure he's actually dangerous," Jenna said with a half shrug. "And even if he is, we need that connection to his father."

They talked until the courtyard lights reminded them it was getting late. With peace in the villa restored, they moved to head inside for the night, rinsed the glasses in the sink, and climbed the stairs together. Almost hesitantly, he stopped at the door to his room, but she kept walking down the hall, slowing to look back at him only as she approached her own bedroom door.

"Good night, Grant."

"Good night, Jenna."

save the last dance for me

BEFORE SHE KNEW IT, Friday arrived, and the formal party that evening loomed in her mind. She desperately hoped the dress Angelo had chosen for her was appropriate, and more so, prayed it was flattering. It was much more daring than her usual style, and she was deeply doubting the purchase as she got ready. Pleading a headache wasn't out of the question.

The dress was a deep, rich plum color with a form-fitting bodice and plunging neckline. She prayed Angelo had been honest when he had allayed her concerns about her curves muffining with the open back. It had taken several minutes to translate the term, and another several for him to stop laughing.

She'd never worn anything that exposed the whole of her cleavage since a bra had forever been a necessity with her full figure. Her preferred sports bra resembled a bullet-proof vest, so the flimsy, dark purple lacey thing Angelo had selected didn't instill much confidence. There just wasn't a whole lot to it. She bent at the waist in front of the mirror then bounced a few times on her toes. Surprisingly, in addition to passing the support test, it not only enhanced her figure but also stayed hidden.

From the plunging V that dipped between her breasts, the neckline gracefully continued upward in two thick bands of silk. The halter-style neckline tapered to clasp behind her neck, which, she admitted to the mirror, did very nice things for her shoulders. Small pearls interspersed with rhinestones graced the upper bodice, then thinned out to fade away at the waist.

The flare of the skirt camouflaged her tummy and flowed elegantly to the floor. The side slit that rose well above her knee kept it sassy, as did the rhinestones on the back of her black, strappy heels that twinkled when she walked.

With her make-up done as Angelo had recommended, she questioned whether her usual sterling-silver wire ear wrap with its tiny Swarovski crystals was appropriate. She felt naked without it, though, so she moved it higher on her right ear and added a simple three-pearl dangle to both ears.

The mirror confirmed that Angelo deserved sainthood. She hardly recognized herself as she took a deep, cleansing breath. *Okay, here goes,* she thought.

Had she remembered deodorant? *Yes.*

Brushed her teeth? *Yes.*

Shaved? *Yes.*

And plucked? *Yes.*

Everywhere? *Yes.*

Checklist complete, she dabbed on the perfume Angelo had slipped into her bag as a good luck gift. Realizing she couldn't delay any longer, Jenna put her phone in her black evening clutch and threw caution and insecurity to the wind.

A soft evening breeze drifted in from the open patio door. The only light downstairs originated from over the small stove in the kitchen.

Grant stood on the patio waiting for her, his forearms on the railing, watching some of the other neighbors make their way across the courtyard to the villa illuminated by lights and music. Just a hint of the sunset remained. He desperately wanted a drink but knew he had to be alert tonight for a lot of reasons. They would be expected to dance and act the part of a married couple. That thought alone stretched his nerves.

Hearing Jenna on the stairs, he straightened his tie, grabbed his jacket, and turned to go into the house. Locking the patio door served as a stall tactic as he fought for control of his thoughts. Shoving his arms into the sleeves of the jacket and tugging at the cuffs bought him a few more seconds.

"Grant, your dinner jacket is...I mean, it's perfect," she stammered as she stood before him in the dimly lit room.

Placing one hand lightly on her waist, he took her hand in his and twirled her around once.

"You look absolutely beautiful," he said, sincere awe in his voice. Dipping his head to her conspiratorially, he added, "Really glad he's not here, but I sure wish Dugan could see you tonight."

She blushed at his compliment and turned in the direction of the front door.

"Not so fast." He pulled her back to him and tilted her face to his. "Promise me you won't encourage Luca any more than necessary," he implored. "Remember, you're supposed to be mine tonight." His voice was a little raspy and his blue eyes serious as he brushed a kiss on her cheek, his lips lingering too close to her ear. "Don't get too far away from me at the party."

The hint of possessiveness in his tone both surprised and warmed her. Not even her ex had elicited the deep-down desire that coursed so potently through her that the rhinestones on her heels likely glowed.

They took the paved walkway through the courtyard, but neither spoke. Her knees felt like jelly. His intoxicating words had to have been spoken just to set the stage. To help get them into character. For the job. That's all this was, she reminded herself.

Good Lord, she was making this assignment hell, he thought, consumed by her as they walked side by side with her hand lightly tucked around his forearm. The silver and crystal wire thing she routinely wore was clipped high on her ear and hypnotized him—just enough of a statement of her individuality while still being classy. He'd suffered many forms of torture in his life, but this professional obligation to keep her at arm's length was killing him. At least tonight he'd have an excuse to hold her close and make believe this woman was really his.

Lourdes offered her husband a rehearsed smile as Matteo adjusted the elegant pale-gray shawl around her shoulders, then handed her a glass of 1990 Cristal Brut Methuselah champagne. At over fifteen thousand dollars a bottle, she chose to not to dwell on how they afforded such luxuries.

This annual party, to which many of his business acquaintances were invited, was the only remaining affair that he insisted on holding at their home. Every year, she dreaded the event. It was exhausting to paste on the persona she had left in the past. Usually there wasn't a single individual on the invitation list who she trusted, including Matteo. She smiled, realizing that, this year at least, there would be one.

With the annual summer formal party underway, she watched Luca as he interacted with a group of influential politicians who had recently arrived. Her interest piqued when he stopped mid-sentence, did a double take, and stared unabashedly at the couple who had just entered through the courtyard entrance. Her eyes followed his mesmerized gaze.

The man Luca studied was certainly worth a second look, but when she realized it was Jenna on the man's arm and who clearly was the focus of Luca's attention, Lourdes scowled.

Absently sipping her champagne, Lourdes assessed her friend and her handsome husband openly.

The striking color of Jenna's dress was a statement in and of itself; it reflected the level of confidence Jenna applied to everything—except herself. Lourdes smiled at Angelo's handiwork. Attractive as she was, Jenna wasn't what one would consider classically stunning. However, the mature elegance with which she carried herself exuded class. Jenna shared an adoring look with her husband as he kissed their entwined fingers then tucked her hand into the crook of his arm.

Lourdes turned her attention to Luca again. She would need to have a word with Jenna if his interest persisted. Based on how entranced he appeared to be, she hoped with a sigh, another sip of champagne, and a brief prayer to the Virgin Mary that the evening would pass without incident.

18

sway

SET ACROSS THE COURTYARD at about a two o'clock position from their rental, the Santoris' villa was naturally larger than the other homes and boasted massive glass doors on both sides that showcased a breathtaking view of the sea just beyond. The courtyard entrance was open, and a server in a short black jacket greeted the guests and collected invitations. Grant gathered Jenna's hand possessively in his as they waited to be ushered into the party.

While Jenna talked with the couple behind them, Grant looked down at the captivating woman by his side. Her hair, glinting with streaks of burnished copper he hadn't noticed before, shone in the soft light. He brushed his lips over her sapphire and diamond wedding ring. They needed to mingle, but trying to focus on anyone else was exceedingly challenging.

The smooth gloss of the marble floor reflected the soft light of the room that tinkled with the sound of champagne glasses and conversation. Music from a string quartet flowed over the guests from a location high above the dance floor, barely visible on a walkway that spanned the room.

He grinned when she squeezed his hand, clearly enthralled by the effect of the plans she herself had overseen. She glanced from beneath her lashes at him and chewed her lip before breaking into a broad smile at the culmination of her efforts.

Grant scanned the room, taking in the exits and number of guests present, and spied Luca on the opposite side of the room. The younger Santori was standing in a group with four other men to whom he was oblivious. Grant didn't even need to guess what riveted Luca's attention in their direction; Luca was smitten with Jenna, husband or no husband, and made no attempt to hide it. Grant shifted his feet, hoping to catch Luca's eye, wanting to warn him off. He was, however, mindful that they were on Luca's turf tonight, and a confrontation would not be ideal.

Before he could make eye contact, a wealthy-looking elderly woman wearing a pale-gray shawl took Luca's arm. With maternal authority, the woman turned Luca to face her, but not before she looked over at Jenna and Grant.

"What's the matter?" Jenna asked quietly, unconsciously tugging his hand. Following the direction of Grant's focus, she saw Luca escorting Lourdes into the elevator. "Hmmm, I hope she's feeling all right."

Lourdes exited the elevator onto the upstairs landing and, noticing Jenna's attention, tapped her watch and raised one finger. Jenna smiled in acknowledgment and nodded. Luca's interest in the exchange was clear, though he pretended not to notice. After he had delivered Lourdes to her suite, Luca made his way down the curving staircase and rejoined his father on the other side of the room. Jenna's thoughts raced.

She guided Grant to the dance floor where other couples swayed to the quartet's music. Dancing in public wasn't her favorite thing; however, the dance floor was the perfect place to set herself up to be in Luca's line of sight. Somewhat hesitatingly, she folded herself against Grant, finding her hand already entwined with his. When he pulled her closer, she couldn't help but smile up at him.

The path they made together became smaller and smaller as the crowd around them melted into the background. She tried desperately to memorize the feeling of his hand on the bare skin of her back and the reassuring strength of his body pressed against hers. During the brief transition between songs, Jenna leaned back, the soft adoration in her eyes only partially simulated. Grant's smile gave way to a pensive, intense look as she tried not to drown in his arms.

After only three songs, her ploy to appear lost on the dance floor and deeply in love with her husband wasn't so much of an act. She rested her head on his shoulder, her forehead tucked against his neck. His head dipped slightly, pressing against hers just before she felt his lips on her temple. He didn't lift his head as he whispered, "Don't do this. You're playing with fire tonight."

His comment drew her back into character. At first, she thought he sensed her all-too-real attraction to him. But something off to her right commanded his attention. His hand tightened protectively on her back, and his whole body tensed when a large hand ornamented with a black onyx signet ring tapped his shoulder. Grant's irritation was plain as Luca stood still, his hand extended to Jenna in unspoken expectation. A mix of anger, comprehension, and resignation flitted briefly through Grant's eyes as he nodded rather curtly at her before backing away.

The pieces of her ploy had fallen into place for Grant when he saw Luca striding in their direction on the dance floor. He had to hand it to her;

she had manipulated the entire scene and the two men masterfully. All the while, he—typically master of the setup—had simply been a pawn in her game.

Jenna had played her part perfectly, appearing to be mildly surprised and flattered by Luca's attention. Several other guests had taken an interest in the exchange, so Grant could do nothing but relent and walk away like a good sport.

Point to you, Jenna.

Grant ordered a scotch at the bar before returning his attention to Jenna, not eager to watch her in Luca's arms but wanting to keep her in sight at the same time.

Luca had only to make eye contact with the quartet lead upstairs, raise one finger, and the music changed to one of Jenna's favorite songs. For whatever reason, Grant resented that she had shared that with Luca. She leaned in and said something in Luca's ear. Grant downed what remained in his glass. Increasingly agitated, he watched Jenna as Luca smoothly led her around the dance floor for the better part of an hour.

Pleading for a rest, Jenna placed her hand on Luca's arm, and he snagged two flutes of champagne before leading her off the floor to the section of the room farthest from Grant.

Bastard.

Luca's hand moved possessively to the bare skin of her back and ushered her to where Lourdes now stood with Matteo. Jenna tossed her head back in laughter at whatever Luca murmured in her ear and glanced purposefully in Grant's direction. Grant bristled, not caring if it was professional concern for her safety or something much more personal.

Minutes dragged like hours, and the music hummed endlessly. Between snippets of conversation, he monitored Jenna's progress. Determined to socialize so that he could catalog the partygoers in his head, he faked interest in a conversation with a French couple and a representative of a Saudi prince. Grant turned away to grab a drink from a proffered tray, and in that ten-second span of diverted attention, she vanished.

After circling the room twice and not locating her, he regretted not putting a stop to her plan. Concern mounted when Luca and his father briskly crossed the room from the other direction. The two Santoris spoke in hushed tones to the security team at the front door. Luca pulled a phone from his pocket and entered a concealed room to the right of the entry. Four minutes later, headlights flashed through the ornate glass of the double door as a car pulled up outside. The door to the room opened briefly, and, accompanied by security, the two men were whisked away into the night.

The need to find Jenna intensified. Images of all kinds of ghastly scenarios flashed in his head. Grant was stalking through the crowd, heading toward the private rooms in the back of the villa, when Jenna's laugh drifted into his consciousness from the walkway above. Their hostess leaned heavily on Jenna's arm as they slowly walked, stopping every few feet.

Relieved more than he should have been, he glared up at her with an exasperated shake of his head, then turned his focus to figuring out why the men had made such a hasty departure from their own party.

He mapped out the lower floor plan in his mind and took in as many details of the household as possible. His discrete attempt to explore was foiled by security guards and locked doors, forcing him to wander back to mingle with the other guests.

The crowd slowly thinned as the evening ticked by and night settled in. Strolling casually to the sitting area near the courtyard door they had entered several hours earlier, he played the impatient spouse and struck up a casual conversation with the security lead who stood nearby. Grant sensed Jenna's approach and turned to watch her edge around the few remaining couples on the dance floor. Her elderly companion held tightly to her arm as they moved in his direction.

"Ah, *buona sera*, signore," the older lady greeted in a shaky yet cultured voice.

"*Che piacere conoscervi*, Signora Santori." Grant's head dipped in a respectful nod. "*Grazie dell'ospitalità. È una bellissima serata.*"

"Aside from finally having the opportunity to finally meet you, Jenna is the only thing that made tonight bearable," Lourdes replied, switching to impeccable English. "I apologize for monopolizing your charming wife tonight." Motioning to the security lead, she reached out to take the uniformed man's arm while patting Jenna's. "Jenna, dear, that is enough for me tonight. Please do stay and dance more. You know well what that quartet costs."

"That I do. But with the catering staff in place to clean up, we'll be going home. I'll see you on Monday. Thank you for a lovely evening." Jenna kissed the older woman's cheeks before their hostess was escorted away.

dance me to the end of love

GRATEFUL FOR THE REPRIEVE, they headed home across the courtyard, now dark and deserted, with the muted music from the party the only sound. Jenna steered Grant to the gazebo near the pool and dropped her purse on the picnic table. She pulled out her phone and tapped the screen to stop the recording. As she dropped it back in her purse with a flick of her wrist, she grinned triumphantly up at an unsmiling Grant.

"Well, that worked out splendidly. Oh, come on, admit it," she goaded, only to be met with silence. "Seriously? You're not angry, are you? You're in!" she said in a hushed tone.

"Hmm. I must have a different definition of "in." The whole point was to get me an audience with Luca and his father, and that certainly didn't happen," Grant said in an irritated whisper, still chafed about being relegated to being used as a chess piece.

"Just so you know," she said, "I gave Matteo a lot of details about your background. Hope he doesn't play poker; he's interested, I'm sure. The glance he gave Luca gave him away."

"Well, I wouldn't know since you decided to fly solo tonight."

"Oh, for Christ's sake, Grant. You can hear it in his voice on the recording. Listen to it yourself if you don't believe me. I swear, between you and Du—"

"Shhhh, we've got company. Someone's over in the shadows. Ten o'clock," he advised, letting her know where the person was. "I think it's Luca. C'mon, let's go."

Her hand grabbed his forearm, halting his steps. "No, we should use this."

"Well then, make it good. Unless, of course, you'd rather dance with him."

Jenna shot a look of annoyance at Grant as she placed a steadying hand on the table and slipped off her shoes slowly, one at a time. As she pulled the second one off, she released an honest sigh of relief followed loudly by a disgusted huff.

"Oh, for the love of God, I wish you'd stop being so damn sensitive all the time. I swear...don't get all pissy just because I danced with someone else. Your pouting is getting really old."

In response to the simulated attack, he swung her around and threw his arms up in mock frustration. "Oh, and if I had done that with some other woman? You'd be furious! I really don't get what you want from me anymore, but I'm tired of playing your stupid games."

"Really? You want to know what I want from you? How about a little attention now and then? A little romance maybe?" She straightened and tossed her head. "And you know damn well you'll never get where you want to be without me."

She needed to stoke Luca's jealousy a bit. Just enough for Grant to get a foot in the door, so she changed tactics.

"Besides, I remember a time when you used to like the games we played," she purred, pursing her mouth into a sultry pout. "I certainly hope you're not too tired tonight," she added, tracing a finger down the deep V of her dress. "We can play that game you used to like."

The look on his face was one of surprise tainted with a healthy shot of intrigue. With her back against the gazebo's support column, Jenna beckoned to Grant with a seductive crook of her finger and reeled him in as if he was hooked on an invisible fishing line.

His attempt to keep an eye on the figure in the shadows failed miserably. The attempt was further derailed as her hands slipped under his lapels and up his chest before her arms encircled his neck. Dropping her head to his shoulder, she swayed to the muted music. He rested his cheek against her hair, the light scent of roses filling his head.

Jenna closed her eyes, grateful for the cooler night air but unnerved by the current that raced through her when he placed his hands on the curve of her waist. His body picked up the slow, seductive rhythm. This was dangerous.

She raised her face to his. "Is it clear yet?" It was the only question whose answer might end this insanity.

He shook his head in response, and the usual cool intensity in his eyes transformed to the blue heat of an intense flame. His index finger caught her bottom lip and began to trail the same path hers had minutes before. Their eyes locked as his finger slowly traced the bare skin of her throat and then down between the exposed swell of her breasts, stopping where the fabric joined to form a point at the base of her cleavage. Luca was momentarily forgotten as his finger reversed its path. It paused lightly at her throat, as if measuring her pounding pulse. His thumb brushed her chin.

Grant was lost in her, and he couldn't bring himself to break whatever spell she had cast over him. Five minutes ago, irritation had governed his words, but now he couldn't remember his own name.

Tipping her chin, his head dipped, hesitating only once to watch her eyes close in anticipation seconds before their mouths touched. Firm lips hovered over hers, then gently swept her mouth, testing before softly teasing her mouth open. As the kiss deepened, he tugged impatiently at his tie, willingly relinquishing the task to her.

With his tie loosened, Jenna worked at the top few buttons of his starched shirt and parted the crisp collar. His breath caught when her fingers made contact with his bare skin.

Fired by her touch, his kiss was insistent. All pretense of restraint disappeared as he pressed her up against the gazebo's column. She hummed against his lips when one of his hands moved to her hip. The other skimmed her bare shoulders and then traced a path up her neck to hold her head to his while he savored her mouth.

She lost all sense of decency and time, drunk on the scent of him and the taste of champagne overpowered by scotch on his tongue. The need for him intensified, but her all-too-sensible mind won.

This needed to stop.

Lighter kisses indicated her reluctant withdrawal, giving her drowsy eyes time to open and focus. Making a halfhearted attempt to still play the part, her hand slid down his arm to lace her fingers with his. Silently, with her shoes and purse swinging in one hand, she glided backward through the grass, pulling him by the hand toward their villa.

From where he leaned against a shadowy wall, Luca watched as Jenna disappeared with her husband up the stairs. Their door closed, and he was left alone in the dark shadows, free-falling into a fit of sexual frustration and jealousy. Incensed, yet undeterred by the apparent reconciliation he'd just witnessed, he wondered how tonight could get any worse.

"*Figlio di puttana*." Luca cursed Giovanni while simultaneously insulting Giovanni's mother.

First, the Italian government had impounded the shipment of weapons that had been intercepted only fifty kilometers from the border where his client's team waited to take possession of the goods. He couldn't believe Giovanni had been so careless in plotting the transportation routes.

He took a fiery swallow from the bottle of grappa he loosely carried. Half of a cigarette dangled from the fingers of his other hand.

Then he had been pulled away from the party and away from Jenna to deal with it.

Now this.

He took another swig.

It should have been his hands on her tonight.

One more swig almost emptied the bottle.

The only thing that improved his mood was thinking about how frantically Giovanni had begged just before Luca drove the eight-inch knife blade into his scrawny throat a mere ninety minutes ago. It would be a good lesson for the others.

Not only had the botched shipment of FGM-148 Javelin missile systems cost him political capital with his client, but it also had the potential to cost him a fortune, both in cash and in future business. His father was infuriated by the whole situation.

Bribes, along with a few direct threats, would be slapped on the table as soon as they could identify the officials whose units had taken possession of his shipment. Without knowing where the shipment was being held, he held out only a slim hope that he could recoup the cache. A very costly error by Giovanni, indeed.

Seeing that the blunder had cost Luca a precious opportunity to be with Jenna at the party, Giovanni's fate had been sealed before Luca and his father had even left the villa. Regardless of the missed opportunity tonight, Jenna Nichols would be his.

At first it was her appearance that caught his attention. Attractive, but not so much so that people would remember her face. And not thin. He hated skinny, scrawny women. He preferred curvy women, thanks to an affair with the neglected wife of one of his father's customers when he was only seventeen. Although she had taught him much about physical satisfaction over a two-year period, her thirst for his money had been her downfall. She had been the first to beg in vain for her life. The first to ignite a dark fire deep within that continued to smolder to this day.

He also preferred married. Single women could be so inconveniently clingy. There was something about the challenge of luring married women with the promise of greener, and more virulent, pastures. The women he chose usually also had husbands who brought something of value to the risk equation, be it influence, information, or power. Often their value was simply the sins they themselves had to hide, making any investigations into their wives' disappearances shallow and of limited duration. And, if need be, the husbands served as perfect scapegoats.

Jenna's position in the household was the other thing that made her useful. She would have unfettered access to his mother and, as her confidante, her secrets as well.

Yes, this American woman was something special. This one checked all his boxes. Plus, she came with connections just when he needed them. American ones. Weapon-savvy ones. It was like God had placed her in front of him for a reason. While the need to possess her burned from the inside like his bottle of cheap grappa, the multiplier in this new equation was her husband's value.

If he played his cards right, he might have a chance to recover the goods that the Italian government currently held. If not, with Grant Nichols's help, there might be a chance of replacing the seized cache of weapons with new inventory. Luca would be a hero—not only with his customer, but also in the eyes of his father. Finding a worthy new supplier who wasn't as fastidious as the current irate one would be an added bonus.

It had a been a long time since a woman he selected had anything at all to do with his business dealings. Mixing business and pleasure was normally too complicated. But this time, the combination could be doubly lucrative.

Luca flicked the cigarette away and turned to stagger back to his parents' villa, his mind filled with less savory images of Jenna. The chase was already proving to be entertaining, but nothing compared to the image of her face as her wrists were secured to his bedposts. He could almost smell her fear. She'd fight him when she realized her mistake. He doubted she would ever beg for mercy. Once all other avenues were exhausted, drugs would help extract whatever blackmail-eligible information he could get out of her.

The recorded proof of her infidelity, willing or not, would be the leverage he needed. He would control her then, and thereby her husband. He would need Nichols's cooperation to get his weapons back. Even if her husband didn't care about her indiscretions, he would care about preserving his reputation and his new job. A simple threat to disclose the information gleaned from Jenna or merely to publicize Nichols's involvement would be enough. Either way, they would both be his.

When he was done with Jenna—if he tired of her, or if she became a liability—he knew of a cartel who would assist with making her disappear. They had proven themselves last year when Jenna's predecessor threatened to expose the reason behind his mother's decline.

Luca mostly avoided the whole human-trafficking market, although in his line of work, a wide array of acquaintances came in handy. Mostly because the Santoris had little tolerance for leaving evidence alive. At this point, he also needed to recoup some of the cash they had lost. Furthermore, if her demise became public, he would have his choice of scapegoats.

He stumbled through the private entrance to the villa, avoiding lingering party guests, still deep in his alcohol-drenched fantasies. His approach had to be planned carefully, but first he needed sleep.

20

at last

SLEEP WAS NOWHERE NEAR Grant's mind as the lock on the coral-colored door snicked behind them. Jenna tossed her purse and shoes onto the kitchen counter and slumped against the wall with her head back laughing. Anything to distract from the insanity of the gazebo. Insanity or not, this still was the most enjoyable assignment she'd had in a long while.

Grant shed his jacket and pulled his phone from the inside pocket. His thumb scrolled and tapped as his eyes flicked between her and his phone. The glow from the small screen was the only light in the house as he walked out to the patio and picked up her speaker. Locking the door as he came back inside, he dragged the wispy curtains closed and set the speaker down next to his phone.

Her laughter trailed off when she recognized their playlist of soft standards. Grant held his hand out to her.

"For some odd reason, we didn't get to dance together much," he said with tilt of his head. A humorless tone fused with a slightly calculating look in his eye.

"Not this again." She shook her head and sighed. "We danced together a fair bit, if I recall. And it was just work, remember?"

His outstretched hand jerked insistently. "Luca qualifies as work too. Seems like I should get equal consideration."

She would have loved to dance with Grant in the privacy and darkness of their own living room, but his petulance was starting to grate. The high from the gazebo was fading quickly.

"Trust me, you got a lot more than Luca did," she said. "Even so, I was doing what we came here to do. Isn't that what you wanted? And I really didn't dance with him all that—" she started before refusing to defend the inroads she'd created for them tonight. She shook her head in disbelief. "And how did we go from that…" Her hand flung in the direction of the gazebo where she'd been close to using the picnic table for a feast of another kind. "…to this?"

"We had an agreement about Luca tonight." He paused. "And about not getting too far from me."

Barely registering that last part, she mounted a defense anyway, her spine fortified by a surge of annoyance. "I've worked my butt off for months making sure you'd get your foot in the door. The situation tonight was too perfect to pass up. And it worked beautifully, I might add, so I'm not exactly sure why you're ticked off. Not to mention, I didn't agree to anything about Luca; you just assumed that I had."

"Oh, I see." He dragged out the words and rolled his eyes.

The conversation had gone south quickly.

How to Ruin a Perfect Evening 101.

"Damn you." Her eyes closed briefly with exhausted irritation as she weakly shook her head. "Please don't do this."

A quirk of his eyebrow gave her pause. "I think that's the one thing I asked of you earlier too."

Frank Sinatra's "All My Tomorrows" cushioned the strained silence as she studied him guardedly in the dark. The request he had murmured in her ear just before relinquishing the dance to Luca floated through her head.

Looking back at the evening, she considered his point of view. They were supposed to be partners in this—to work together—and she had pretty much left him out of the planning process before going off on her own.

"Fine," she agreed quietly. "I get your point. Won't happen again." Jenna gathered her shoes and purse from the counter and avoided him on her way to the stairs.

"Wait."

She kept moving. "I'd really hoped to remember this dress and this evening fondly. Can we argue about this tomorrow?"

"Depends."

"Oh? On what?" she demanded. Her aching foot rested on the first step.

"Depends on what parts of the evening you want to remember fondly." His statement hung in the air between them on a very tight string.

Jenna looked away.

"Come on...dance with me, Jenna," he insisted. The intimate tone of his voice was less aggravating and more intriguing, melting her irritation. Grant's hand extended in her direction once more.

She should have walked upstairs right then, but she couldn't make her foot take the second stair. With no viable, or preferable, alternative, she set her things down on the coffee table and placed her trembling hand in his open palm. Harry Connick Jr. crooned soft and slow in the darkness as Grant placed his hand on her waist and gathered her to him. She rested her hand on his shoulder formally, if not a bit stiffly. It took two songs for the tension to ease.

"Satisfied now?" Her whispered question dangled unanswered when the second song faded into the third.

His only response was to tuck their clasped hands to his chest and dip his head lower to rest against hers. Her bare foot bumped against the side of his shoe.

"Maybe I should put my shoes back on?" she asked, a hesitant smile tainting her voice. Not daring to look up at him for fear of getting hypnotized by his blue eyes and graying temples, her eyes remained glued to a button on his shirt. The one just below the two others that she had freed only twenty minutes ago.

"Your toes are safe with me, I promise." He tugged her closer as if to prove it.

Seven seconds passed.

"But I'm not sure I am," she said with a whisper. "This isn't a good idea, Grant."

He stopped the dance but didn't release her; his chin still rested against the side of her head.

"Tell me this is all about the job. Tell me what happened out there was work. That you don't feel this," he demanded, a bit more roughly than he'd intended, while leaning away ever so slightly. "Look me in the eye and tell me I'm reading this wrong."

She looked up at him and opened her mouth to lie to him.

But the lie wouldn't come.

"I...you're not...," she breathed and watched the relief settle in his expression. "I want to, but I just can't go there with you." There. She had said it.

He knew the answer before he asked the question. They worked together; this violated the sanctity of professional boundaries. Not to mention good judgment. Getting involved with a coworker was inadvisable in every way possible. It was the craziest thing he'd done in a long while. But the last several weeks had him thinking maybe he needed a little crazy in his life. Nevertheless, he was powerless to stop this.

"Why? We're adults. Is it Evan?" he asked.

In the dim light, the gold flecks flashed for an instant. "That's not fair. You can't bring him into this. Don't forget, I have kids. You know it's not that."

"Then what?"

She tried to pull away, not wanting to divulge her insecurities. The doubts and the fear of him seeing what was concealed by the gorgeous evening dress. Her mind raced for a way to stop this conversation—this attraction. Neither her confidence nor her heart would survive his rejection.

"Talk to me. What's going on in your head?" A brush of his fingers swept a lock of hair from her forehead. "One-night stands aren't my thing. But hell, you probably knew that already. Besides we live together for now." He felt her tense and shifted to clasp his hands behind her back before she could push away. "That's it, isn't it? You think this is just roommates with benefits?"

"No. Yes. I mean, no...not really." She heard herself rambling. "Aside from the fact we work together? Like I said, I've had kids, had a life, and"—wishing she could stop the words even as they came tumbling out—"let myself go more than I'd like. Gravity and Father Time are formidable opponents. Let's be honest—Angelo worked a bit of magic for tonight. I'm not twenty-five anymore, Grant."

"Damn it. And here I thought you were twenty-five all along." He pretended to release her before pulling her back against him.

His humor lightened the mood, and she found herself smiling. A low chuckle escaped as he looked down at her.

"You think I'd be interested in a twenty-five-year-old? Jesus, can you imagine how much drama comes with a woman that age? No, thanks." He grinned at her eye roll and then went quiet for a minute before pressing his lips to her forehead. "Do you remember what I said about the clay being good?"

"Clay is squishy too." Jenna scoffed, flicking her eyes to his face.

"Is that what this is about? We all get older, Jenna." He paused. "Well, if we're lucky. We're fortunate to have made it this far. Especially in our line of work." The music filled the heavy silence that followed until the lighter banter returned. "Besides, I'm no spring chicken either, you know. I've got my share of gray hair."

"You wear your years much better than I do. And men don't get stretch marks in their hair," she countered as she pushed against his embrace.

"Let's see," he said, rocking her gently side to side in a cadence choreographed with his words. "I've seen you in the mornings, when you're tired or mad, when you've had a bit too much wine, during and after your workouts, at the pool...and guess what?"

"Mmm," she murmured. If he only knew how many self-lecturing pep talks it had taken before she'd put that bathing suit on the first time.

"I couldn't begin to describe any other woman at that party tonight." He lifted her chin, but she couldn't meet his eyes. Fearing the depth of her attraction to him, Jenna tried again to put some distance between them, only to feel his hands move up her back, holding her in place. His mouth was dangerously close to hers, stopping only once to whisper, "Stop analyzing. This thing between us—let's go with it."

21

save a prayer

GRANT'S MOUTH TOUCHED HERS gently, transforming the simmering current into something that consumed her. When he teased her mouth open, the scotch-laced champagne she tasted once more drowned her ability to think. His tongue resumed the dance from the gazebo.

She couldn't do it—couldn't resist the pull of him any longer. She'd lost her will to fight against this tonight.

It had been...So. Damn. Long.

Decades had passed since a man had captivated her like he did. He made her feel beautiful. Wanted. Made her feel things she'd forgotten about. The tingle that electrified every cell when his tongue touched hers. The feel of his fingertips as they warmed her skin. The comfort she felt in his arms. The sultry heat when he held her close as they danced in the dark.

Her fingers slid under his open collar, trailing over his collarbone before they wandered lower, making short work of the remaining buttons. She dragged his shirttail from his dress pants then ran her hands possessively under his snug white cotton t-shirt.

God, the scent of him. For weeks, she'd gotten accustomed to how he smelled, whether fresh out of the shower with that aftershave lingering or after a sweaty workout. Tonight, it was a mix. No drug could be more potent.

Her hands trailed over his back, tracing the scars they encountered. He momentarily released her to shrug out of both shirts, letting them fall to the floor. The intoxicating, shirtless man standing in front of her had her wondering if she was hallucinating.

Hostage to her own inability to stop touching him, she suddenly felt the cool wall against her back. She only vaguely registered the music, her senses attuned to the pounding of her heart, their uneven breathing, and the sound of fabric rustling.

The trance ended when the kisses became shorter and barely grazed her mouth, as if he were backing away. Intense blue eyes captured hers while he calmly pulled her arms from around his neck. His knuckles traced her chin and the side of her neck, his hand continuing down her bare arm. The assurance in his gaze kept her protests at bay as he gathered her wrists in one of his hands, raising them and pinning her arms to the wall above her head.

A little intimidated and more than a little intrigued, she waited. His eyes darted back and forth, studying hers, watching for signs that she wasn't comfortable with the pace. With their gazes still locked, his other hand skimmed the exposed skin of her side, tracing the line of the backless bodice that started low at her waist.

She couldn't think, couldn't move, couldn't form words.

What was left of her breath escaped in an audible sigh when he slipped his thumb inside the silk, finding the lace of her bra. With a low groan of satisfaction at his discovery, he rested his forehead against hers. Arching into his hand in silent encouragement, she lifted her mouth to his. The rhythm of his breathing increased with each devastating kiss she delivered. His fingers slipped further and further inside the silk with each stroke of her tongue. A soft whimper escaped as the firm length of him pressed against her, as if to warn her wordlessly where this was going.

Then his free hand was fingering the clasp of the dress at the nape of her neck. Aching to feel his hands on her, Jenna no longer cared if he ruined the dress she so treasured. The clasp finally gave way, and the silk bodice fell to her waist. She would forever remember how he looked at her before his head dipped to her throat, searing the sensitive skin as he moved lower. His touch awakened the long-forgotten burn of passion, and every last doubt vanished when the warmth of his mouth tugged and teased through the light fabric of her lace bra.

"Stop," she murmured breathlessly. "Please, stop."

Grant froze.

"Stop?" he asked, trying to catch his breath while releasing her wrists. "Sorry, if—"

"No, it's not that," she reassured him. "I...I just can't stand up any longer...when you do that."

Relieved, he started to move them to the couch, but her hand on his arm stopped him, hesitating for only a second.

"No, not there...I, um...." She hesitated, looked away, and then dared to look at him. "Upstairs. Take me to bed, Grant."

It cost her a lot to make that request.

He said nothing but gently pulled her dress back up and refastened the clasp behind her neck. Disappointment raged at the thought that her request had allowed rational thought to regain control. The cost of that statement might be more than she was willing to pay.

A flash of fear and regret made her heart falter, thinking she'd ruined the moment, before she saw the hunger in his expression.

"Go, then," he directed her, a little brusquely. "Now. I mean it. Or we're not going make it all the way up."

Grant slipped his tuxedo shirt back on and left it unbuttoned, then swiped his t-shirt off the floor. With the skirt of her dress gathered in one fist, she skittered anxiously up the stairs with him close behind her.

Rational thought was still trying to regain the upper hand. She hesitated at the top step, beating back the voices in her head telling her not to be a fool by sleeping with him. Did she dare go through with this? He seemed to sense her internal debate and gently but insistently guided her toward his room, following her in.

Thankful that the only source of light was the moonlight, she turned as she stood next to the bed. "Are you sure about this?"

"I haven't been more sure of anything in a very long time. I should be asking you the same," he admitted, blindly tossing his t-shirt and shoes onto a chair.

"I'm sure. I think. Just don't judge harshly in the morning, please," she pleaded under her breath, swallowing the last part.

She started to unzip the lower part of her dress but stopped at the sight of a wicked grin lifting the corner of his mouth.

"Nope," he said reaching for her hand. "That's for me to do."

His teeth grazed her throat while his hands on her bare back stirred barely restrained cravings in the pit of her stomach. He worked the clasp at her neck again, and after watching the bodice fall away, he reached around her to unzip the skirt. After stepping out of it, she leaned into him wearing only the dark-purple lace bra and underwear.

"Just when I thought you couldn't be more beautiful," he said and reached for the fastener on his pants. But she stilled his hand in return and winked.

"Uh-uh. My turn," she whispered before turning him away from her. She guided his hands to rest on the wall and lightly kicked his feet apart, then positioned herself behind him as if frisking him in a late-night traffic stop.

Jenna lifted the tail of his loose shirt, the lace of her lingerie brushing against the firm muscles of his back. She took her time exploring before peeling his open shirt off from behind. As she drew the cuffs over his wrists, she trailed soft kisses along his bare triceps, boldly meeting the hazy eyes that looked over his shoulder at her. After tossing the shirt aside, Jenna reached around his waist to loosen his slacks. Grant remained motionless except for the quickening rise and fall of his chest, interrupted only by an occasional shudder. Her fingers ran just inside the top of his boxers before nudging them down.

She ducked under his arm to stand between him and the wall. Wrapping one arm around his neck, she pressed up against his arousal.

He groaned, dropping his forearms against the wall, one on either side of her head, and kissed her. Two fingers on her shoulder slid her bra strap to hang listlessly on her upper arm; his mouth trailed the same path, stopping only to watch while she unfastened her bra. Another soft kiss as his fingers grazed the underside of her breast.

When his hands slid into the sides of her panties, she panicked silently, terrified to lose the last ounce of her armor, ridiculously small as it was.

"Please don't tell me to stop again," he whispered while pushing the lace down and over her full hips. With nothing more between them, the heat of his erection pressed against her bare skin. God, this man would be the death of her. When the edge of the bed bumped against the back of her knees, she pulled him down with her.

They took their time tenderly getting to know each other in the darkness. The passion she had missed in her life for so long flared potently between them. She knew that if she didn't wake in the morning she would die a very satisfied woman. Answering his every move and savoring the prolonged intimacy, they ultimately found their release together.

The ray of moonlight had shifted when she awoke. The clock read 3:19 a.m. Jenna listened to him snore, reassured by how deeply he slept with her in his bed. Aware that this very well might be her only night with him and encouraged by the anonymity of the dark, she let unbridled need and fascination trump her inhibitions.

Manicured nails faintly scraped the contours of his back down to his exceedingly well-maintained rear. He stirred, reaching for her as he rolled over. The drowsy look in his eyes as he was pulled from sleep was one of the sexiest things she'd ever seen.

Before he was even fully awake, she straddled him and pulled the sheet over them as if it could conceal the fact that her naked body was splayed across him in the most daring way.

Moving in a slow rhythm, she caressed his body. Wiry hair scattered across his pecs softened into a stream of light fuzz that flowed down the center of his stomach. Her tongue traced the path before missing the heat of his kiss.

Her thumbs stroked his cheekbones and the overnight growth of stubble. With her fingers in his hair, her mouth sampled his. Her teeth tugged at his lower lip, prolonging the slow pace, while her breasts skimmed that perfect chest.

Turning the tables from downstairs, she slowly and deliberately pinned his hands to the headboard, letting him know it was her turn to drive. Jenna silently kissed, nipped, and licked, tasting the faint sheen of sweat on his skin as desire flared between them. She shifted lower to take him in, and both stilled momentarily, overwhelmed by the intensity of their connection.

"Jesus, Jenna." His voice was a raspy low whisper, her name on his lips its own form of seduction.

The rhythm consumed her, and she moved over him until she heard him quietly but firmly tell her to stop. His eyes were still closed, and she feared for a moment that she had been too forward. He gripped her upper thighs, fixing her in place.

"Don't move," he hissed, every cord in his neck tensing as he fought for control.

She stilled, reveling silently at his response to her. Her nails sketched faint tracks on his abs. Mesmerized by the extraordinary man beneath her, she covered his chest in kisses and worked her way to his throat. His mouth found hers, and his hands on her backside gently encouraged her to continue as he handed control back to her.

His hands roamed as she arched back, eyes drifting shut, trying to make the sensations last. Jenna whispered his name. Breathlessly at first, then more distinctly as the heat coursed through her, unaware that his eyes were open and focused, watching as she found heaven seconds before his release. When she collapsed against him, he gathered her close, then shifted to his side. She had no words for the feelings that swamped her and was content to simply nestle against him in the dark until they gave in to sleep.

The morning sun peeking through the closed shutters had her briefly considering a threepeat. Loath to leave him, but equally loath to be seen in the reality of daylight without her armor of clothing, she slipped out from under the covers.

Her dress and lingerie were strewn across the floor. With an unrelenting grin, she gathered her things and glanced once more at his sleeping form before creeping to her room to shower.

An hour later, Grant rolled over in bed, knowing full well she would be gone. For a fleeting moment he wondered if it had all been a dream, but the almost imperceptible scent of roses that lingered on the other pillow confirmed that Jenna had indeed been in his bed. Still tangled in the sheets, he closed his eyes and recounted the evening and the events of last night.

The life he had imagined—for however many years he had left—didn't include a woman. That ship had sailed.

Nevertheless, the hint of roses swirling in his head had him thinking otherwise. She had him thinking otherwise. Sitting up on the edge of the bed, he stretched and headed to the shower.

The patio door was open when he made his way downstairs. Jenna dozed in the morning sun with the remnants of her coffee perched on the arm of the chair. Grant leaned over and brushed a kiss on her cheek.

"Good morning, Sleeping Beauty," he said softly, touching his mouth to hers.

"Mmmm. Good morning," she greeted before kissing him in return. "I always imagined Prince Charming wearing a shirt, but I think I like this version much better."

He chuckled against her lips. "You good?"

"Very. Just a little sleepy, I guess." Jenna grinned at the reason for her sleep deficit.

"Then maybe you should have stayed in bed," he said with a wink as he partially straightened. "Unless, of course, you have regrets?"

She studied his shirtless body in the morning sun, debating how to answer. She opted for a measured response. "No, none. You?"

"My only regret was finding you gone this morning. My shower was lonely." His grin was contagious. "But the day is young."

"It is that," Jenna said, contemplating but dismissing his suggestion. No way was she ready for daylight interludes with him. "But it's also a perfect day to spend exploring Tuscany. Go find a shirt, Prince Charming."

22

mack the knife

A FEW ERRANT CLOUDS dotted the perfectly blue sky Wednesday morning, and Jenna was not sorry that Luca was nowhere to be seen when she drove over to pick up Lourdes. She also was not sorry that she was about to put a sizable number of purchases on Dugan's tab for the second time as she tried to keep pace with Lourdes's shopping habits.

Despite the phony role Jenna played, a true friendship had bloomed, leaving her feeling more than a little guilty. Given any other phase of life, she could see them being close despite their age difference, reminiscent of her deep bond with Catherine.

About an hour after Jenna had left the villa, Grant opened his laptop to do some research on various weapon system configurations and had just settled on the patio when a heavy knock sounded at their door.

Grant stuffed his Glock in his waistband and cautiously opened the door to find Luca standing on his doorstep. Although the intrusion was unexpected, Grant had perfected slipping in and out of character at a moment's notice.

"Yes?" Grant said gruffly to the man who had monopolized his wife on the dance floor.

"I was hoping we could have a conversation." Luca gestured between the two of them, the large signet ring flashing as he signaled his preference for an indoor meeting. "Privately."

The sport coat and dress pants Luca wore suggested business attire, but a loose jacket could hide a number of things.

"About what?"

"A business opportunity."

"You sure you have the right villa?"

"*Sì*," Luca responded.

Grant's brow furrowed. "Outside. At the gazebo. Give me five minutes."

Without waiting for Luca's response, he closed the door. She'd done her job well, he conceded with a grin. Relieved to finally be taking a more active role, he rehearsed his staged background mentally before making his way outside.

The sun was bright, and a light breeze brushed through the courtyard. A young family of four at the pool turned his thoughts briefly to Evan and Jenna. The revelation that he missed them both made it harder to focus on the business at hand.

He sat opposite Luca at the table, intentionally exuding an air of skeptical indifference reserved only for an adversary who didn't bother to hide his desire for another man's wife. Luca made no attempt to pretend this was a social visit as he began his line of questioning, relying on the two children at the pool to provide enough noise to talk freely without worrying about being overheard.

"What is it you Americans say? Ah, yes. A little bird—is that right?—a little bird said you are U.S. military—"

"Was," Grant stated.

"—and have experience handling shipments of certain military assets."

"Then maybe my wife also mentioned that I'm retiring. My experience will be irrelevant in a few weeks."

Undeterred, Luca drummed his fingers on the table. "I can offer you an opportunity to maintain your skills. There is an open position in my organization that requires someone with your talents."

"I have a new job, thanks." Grant started to get up.

"Mine pays better."

Grant sat back down. "I won't be in Italy much longer."

"Your employment would be, shall we say, short-lived. The Italian authorities have complicated my customer relations by intercepting a valuable shipment. You would be well compensated if you were available to assist for a short time." Luca danced around an admission of illegal activity as gracefully as he had danced with Jenna at the party.

"What type of assets might this position be responsible for moving?"

"The kind that make loud noises." Luca's hands mimicked an explosion.

"Be more specific."

"Javelins," Luca stated, continuing as Grant's eyebrows shot up. "And the missiles."

"No. Absolutely no fucking way." With his hands up to ward off hearing more, Grant started to rise from the table again. "I don't know what you're into, but leave me out of it. This conversation never happened."

"Sit down, Mr. Nichols."

Pure curiosity—as well as Luca's tone—had Grant lowering himself back to the bench.

Luca's hard stare relaxed at the small win. "There would also be a confidentiality bonus included. Enough that you might not need that new job after all."

Grant glanced over to the pool. "You mentioned missiles. HEAT missiles?" he asked.

Luca nodded. "I am in a hurry to reclaim my property before the inventory is outdated. As you know, your country has begun producing a multipurpose version. My inventory consists of high-explosive anti-tank—or as you call them, HEAT—missiles. When my customer finds out his purchase is not state of the art any longer, and if the new Javelin missiles hit the black market before mine are recovered, he will insist on a lower price."

Grant played with the key to the villa, tapping it rhythmically on the table while he absorbed the information. He flipped it between his thumb and forefinger, continuing the motion as he pretended to deliberate. Luca was slick, but Grant had played this game a hundred times.

"I don't think so. I have too much to lose." Grant rose from the table, gambling with the opening they had been vying for.

There it was. The almost imperceptible tic in Luca's expression revealed his impatience. The pressure he was feeling from his client coupled with the oppressive expectation from his father to clean up the mess had to be a heavy weight.

"It must be difficult to keep a wife like yours satisfied. Little birds do not like cages," Luca taunted, satisfied by the fury that settled in Grant's eyes. "She has expensive tastes, yes? Perhaps in men too?"

With an air of false confidence, Luca pulled an envelope out of his sport coat and opened the flap. He thumbed the stack of euros that peeked out before extricating himself from the picnic table bench. Laying the stack of cash on the table alongside a mobile phone, he casually strolled across the grass, leaving the ball squarely in Grant's court.

In the hours that followed, Grant gathered details from all available sources. The information that the Santoris' shipment had been impounded was new and concerning. He would have expected that critical piece of intelligence to have been relayed to them by Salvo within hours of it happening. Using a secure line, he placed a call to Catherine.

"This happened Friday. Any idea why that information didn't make it to us before now?"

"No idea," Catherine replied. "But you can bet I'll be finding out. Maybe they had nothing concrete to tie the shipment directly to Santori?"

"Doubtful. But for the sake of argument, let's say that's the case. It doesn't change the fact that an impounded shipment of smuggled U.S. weapons should have been on someone's daily brief."

Catherine clacked away at her keyboard while she talked. "You can bet I'll be checking with the agency that tasked us. It is odd that we wouldn't have been briefed. The good news is that it sounds like you're on Luca's radar."

"More than on his radar. I have an offer of employment from him." He relayed the details of the morning's meeting to her. "He's the one in our crosshairs now. Papa Santori might be orchestrating all this, but he's probably got enough corrupt people in his pocket that he'd be like a Teflon pan even if we caught him with a Javelin under his pillow. Nothing will stick.

"But if we take down Luca, the old man loses his protégé. Then he'll have to rebuild and retrain—which, at his age, might not be time or energy he has to invest."

"All true. I'll let you know what I learn. Be careful, Grant. And tell Jenna to do the same. Give her a hug for me."

"I certainly will," Grant replied and hung up the call.

As vast, dark, and deep as the intel world was, Grant knew that the flow of information rarely happened as it should. Layers upon layers of bureaucracy compounded by personal aspirations and egos often limited cooperation among the various agencies. And when international borders were tossed into the mix, everyone and their dog wanted a say in what happened when. The more people who were involved, the more political the game became.

Grant had been in this business a long time and was as well connected as any politician. Many of his contacts owed him massive favors for past successes and often for saving their skins, figuratively and literally. The person Grant called next was not a friend but an acquaintance who openly disliked Grant but also recognized the self-preserving value of professional coordination.

Ilaria Giordano was a harsh woman with a chip on her shoulder for a number of imagined reasons. Her abrasive nature and tactless approach to relationships, both personal and professional, led others to keep her at arm's length. The males in her organization gave her a wide berth, since anyone who challenged her eventually faced some embellished charge of violating one of society's new -isms. The females she worked with simply did not want to be known for associating with her.

An abomination to the Italian sense of fashion, her clothing style was two decades behind, often defaulting to a white button-down and boxy blazer. Her dark hair was straight and blunt cut just above the shoulder and likewise across her forehead in harsh bangs. She wore no jewelry other than her identification badge on a tacky, shoelace-like lanyard around her neck. No one really knew what her qualifications were or how she'd gotten into the position she currently filled, but no one dared ask or attempt to find out for fear of being professionally castrated.

Grant had crossed paths with Ilaria Giordano five years ago. He had spent months tracking a lethal bioweapons shipment across the Eurasian continent only to have his team be apprehended at the Italian border by Ilaria herself, then a junior officer.

In a perfect storm of events, their weaponry had been confiscated and half the team detained. It was Ilaria who'd held the power to dismiss the charges. She'd knowingly risked several thousand lives for the sole purpose of obstructing an organization that deemed their mission more important than her regulations.

Instead of sitting back and waiting, Grant had uncovered and then exhumed a few of the skeletons in her closet. He'd placed all his bets on Ilaria being more interested in keeping her own ethically challenged secrets buried and shamelessly resorted to blackmail to ensure his team's release and her cooperation. He was likely the only person who knew her sketchy background, and she was committed to keeping it that way.

As is often the case with difficult employment situations in entrenched public bureaucracies, the easiest path for management to deal with toxic employees is to promote them out of their existing positions. In the years since the border incident, Ilaria had been promoted a number of times, her reputation preceding her with every move. Her accelerated advancement found her in a senior cabinet position in which she enjoyed uncontested access to a variety of domestic and international intelligence.

Grant's telephone call was answered by a low-level administrator who transferred Grant to Ilaria's desk with little hesitation. After superficial civilities were exchanged, Grant divulged just enough of the situation to entice her to assist in the effort to bring down one of the many Italian/Sicilian organized crime families. He needed to know everything there was to know about the Santori family. Confirmation of what Luca had shared about the shipment also would be important.

She hedged at first, worried about protecting the kingdom she had built. But Grant knew her type well.

Despite Ilaria ending the call abruptly, without even the tiniest hint of good manners, Grant was sure that if anyone knew where impounded weapons would be stored, it would be her. And if anyone was willing to trade information for credit, it would also be her.

make you feel my love

LUCA'S MATTE GRAY LAMBORGHINI Urus SUV was thankfully not parked in its usual spot when Jenna dropped a weary Lourdes off after their shopping trip. The older woman had started to droop by late morning, but a light lunch had re-energized her for another several hours. They had talked and laughed almost the entire time, and Jenna had to admit she was just as exhausted.

After seeing Lourdes upstairs and helping put away some of her purchases, Jenna lingered to handle a few household tasks. Spending the workday shopping felt a bit like cheating her employer.

By the time she arrived back at her own villa, it was all she could do but collapse in her chair on the patio while Grant finished up a phone call. With her feet up and a glass of white wine in her hand, she watched him. Assured and confident, he paced as he talked.

A light smile flitted across her face as she thought about Lourdes pulling a slinky nightie off the rack in a ridiculously expensive store. They'd giggled like schoolgirls as Lourdes held it up to Jenna with a wiggle of her penciled eyebrows. The scrap of silk had almost gone back on the rack once Jenna glanced at the price tag. Lourdes, however, snagged it from her and tossed it on the counter, telling the clerk to gift wrap it for her friend.

The insecurities she had dragged around for years hadn't plagued her as much recently. Since being in Italy, she'd gone from wondering who she was and hating the person looking back at her in the mirror to buying slinky lingerie.

How unlikely was it that she'd be the one who was able to break through the diffident exterior for which Agent Grant Lawton was known? Maybe this was his thing—hooking up with the most convenient person he could find on an assignment. Maybe it was how he kept from letting the ghosts consume him.

No, she would know. A reputation like that was a hard thing to hide in a team as tight-knit as Salvo.

Had she kept count, Jenna was sure she'd had more, and undoubtedly better, sex in the last few days than she'd had in all the years combined since her divorce. They had the evening patio routine that, for the last week, had led right into what was becoming the nighttime routine. Still in the early stages of their relationship, the nights were still exhilarating and sleep never a guarantee.

Perhaps it was the wisdom that supposedly came with age, but this felt different. Stumbling into this relationship with Grant had her heart and mind reeling. Jenna wasn't entirely sure what he saw in her, but she was desperately afraid she was falling in love with him.

Overthinking was her thing. Instead of getting mired in thought, she needed to get off her ass and pull something together for dinner. Grant was hunched over his laptop talking on the phone with someone from Salvo while she chopped and stirred. Just as she was piling pasta primavera onto their plates, he disconnected the call, stood, and stretched.

"It's been an eventful day, to say the least," he said.

"Oh?" She handed him a plate of food and a fork, receiving a light kiss in return before they sat down on the couch. "How so?"

Over dinner, he described his visit from Luca and his discussion with Catherine. Initially Luca's direct approach unnerved her, but this exact situation was what they'd been working toward all along.

Dusk had settled when Grant picked up the mobile phone Luca had left on the table along with the stack of currency. He leaned back on the couch and nudged her leg with his knee.

"I need to call him back."

"I know," she said quietly.

A single contact was programmed in the phone, and he looked up at her as the call connected. Jenna could feel her blood pressure rise. Satisfied that she'd successfully executed her role, she gave a mental middle finger to Dugan. From here on out, Grant would be walking a tightrope. While that was the norm in the course of their jobs, this time she had an intense personal interest in his well-being. Regardless of the risks involved, she vowed that Evan wouldn't suffer more loss than he'd already seen in his young life.

Luca met Grant at the gazebo at ten o'clock Thursday morning. A small beverage cooler sat on the table between them. After describing the scope of Grant's role, Luca nodded at the cooler.

"Half of the confidentiality bonus I mentioned is in there."

Grant appeared irritated. "If I only get half the money, do you only get half of my confidentiality?"

Luca's expression hardened. "Prove yourself first. Find where they are storing my merchandise. And get me names. Then you will get the remainder."

Pushing himself off the bench, Luca stood. As Grant reached for the cooler, Luca placed one hand on the table, and the other on the handle of the container.

"Do not forget how much you have to lose, my friend. We would not want to upset our little bird."

Grant's first official duty in his new role with Luca's organization was to determine the physical whereabouts of the impounded weapons. He thought it improbable that Luca would mount an immediate raid on the location to take possession. Instead, his suspicion was that, once the names of the unit supervisors were identified, a brutal campaign consisting of bribes, blackmail, and threats would commence.

Just after noon, Ilaria returned Grant's phone call from the day prior. In her typical surly manner, she informed him that the authorities had intercepted the cache of weapons on its way to the Slovenian border. She also confirmed that the seizure consisted of U.S. Javelins and HEAT missiles; both were currently secured by the Guardia di Finanza, or GdF, in a federal warehouse district of Vicenza. The scope of responsibility of the Italian Guardia included smuggling, and its officers were well trained and militarized.

After jotting down the names of the Guardia commanders and confirming the location, Grant hung up from that call and immediately dialed another. His afternoon phone call marathon was just ending when Jenna walked in the door from work, later than usual.

Jenna grabbed two bottles of water, handed him one, and curled into a corner of the couch after kicking off her sandals.

"You stayed late over there today. Everything okay? Was Luca around?" Grant asked.

"Just needed to get the kitchen order placed before the weekend. Everything's fine. Usual, but fine. And Luca left just before noon to go back to his estate in Sicily for the weekend." She took a long drink of water. "So, tell me about your day."

"For starters, Ilaria called me back after I met with Luca as planned. Gave me the names of the GdF commanders plus the location of the storage facility."

"Oh, I thought maybe you were talking with someone at Salvo."

"Yeah, I was reviewing satellite images of the location with Carl, the new analyst. He's really good with imagery technology. Anyway, Luca's weapons are on the other side of Italy. They were heading for Slovenia, apparently."

"Are you thinking we'll go after the customer across the border too?"

"No, not really. Priority is tying Santori to this. Second is figuring out who is supplying U.S. weapons to him. If we get the buyer, that'll be icing on the cake."

"So, where are they holding the weapons? Did she confirm they're Javelins?"

"Yeah, they're Javelins." Grant crushed his empty water bottle and dismissed the screensaver on the laptop. "They are in a GdF warehouse over in Vicenza. Here's the map. Feel free to take a look while I get dinner together."

Jenna leaned forward to study the screen and saw two map windows open. Touching the screen, one popped to the front. She cocked her head at what she saw. The search box showed her address back home in DC.

"Grant. Hate to tell you, but you're focusing on the wrong continent."

He glanced up from the kitchen as she turned the laptop screen in his direction. He smothered a grin and shrugged.

"Well?" she prompted. Optimism mixed with apprehension.

"Just seeing how far your place is from mine," he admitted. "Thought you might be interested in cooking lessons."

"Oh? Well, I guess that depends," she said flippantly.

"On what?"

"Whatever's on the menu for dessert."

crazy

Upstairs that night, she pulled out the silk nightgown. Could she really wander into his room in this barely there piece of silk, offering her body and soul to him? The realization that he wanted to see her when all this was over emboldened her. Hearing his bathroom door open, she slipped the lingerie over her head and dabbed some of Angelo's tea rose perfume where it mattered.

Jenna tiptoed to stand just inside his doorway as he stood looking out his window. The muscles of his upper body rippled when he tugged off his shirt and turned around. His eyes widened.

The simple but elegant cream silk highlighted her curves and fell to just above her knees in soft waves. Thin, inset straps showed off her shoulders; the back, crisscrossed with those thin strips of fabric, was completely open down to the top of her shapely hips.

"Now that's dessert," he said appreciatively. "I really must thank Angelo."

Her nervousness transitioned into a girlish grin. "Angelo gave me confidence. But this...," she corrected him, indicating the silk. "This is a gift from Lourdes. She thinks you're a keeper, and I tend to agree with her."

"I'll have to send her flowers. Tomorrow, though." He pulled the shutters closed and stripped to his boxer briefs. She could watch him undress a hundred times and never tire of it. He placed his folded clothes on the chair before walking over to stand behind her. Strong arms wrapped around her, and she leaned back against him and closed her eyes. She was crazy for this man.

His hands caressed her hips through the silk gown. Turning her head so that her forehead touched his chin, she hooked an arm up and around his neck and pulled his mouth to hers. His fingers brushed her throat as he met her lips in a tender kiss.

"Dance with me, love," he whispered against her mouth.

"Always," she whispered back and turned in his arms to answer the heady rhythm of his kisses. Her hands skimmed over his chest, one reaching up to cup the back of his head. She tugged him down to the bed and wrapped one leg around his hips.

In a moment of raw tenderness, his eyes captured hers, and his expression softened. His finger traced her brow and trailed down her jaw and neckline. His mouth followed one of the straps as he slid it off her shoulder.

With a reverence she'd only dreamed about, he touched and tasted, savoring her responses. He made her feel worshipped. Made her believe she was beautiful and convinced her to give herself over to his touch. He wanted her just as she was.

When need consumed her, he answered, moving over her with a steady tempo, slow and strong like the pulse of the ocean tide. The potent undercurrent of unspoken intimacy threatened to drown her, and she heard him breathe her name as the waves washed over them.

They lay entwined in the dark, neither making an effort to move. She toyed absently with his earlobe and fought to hold back the words she so badly wanted to share. Gathered in his arms, she tried to quiet her mind, all the time wondering how she'd ended up in bed—and in love—with Grant Lawton. And if he changed his mind about those cooking lessons, how she would ever be able to walk away.

The coffee was brewing, and Jenna had her back turned, putting dishes away, when he came downstairs later than usual. In full stealth mode, he was there before she had a chance to turn around. From behind, he wrapped an arm around her waist followed by a lingering kiss on the side of her neck.

"You got up too early again," he said suggestively.

Amusingly panicked, she squirmed away and reached around him for the phone propped on its long edge on the bar top.

"Well, it looks like you two have really embraced that cover story," said a familiar voice from the phone. Jenna hit the mute button and dropped the screen to lay flat on the counter.

"Hey!" the voice objected.

After greeting Grant with a deep morning kiss, she looked up at him, catching her bottom lip in her teeth. "Sorry, I didn't hear you in time to warn you."

He kissed her nose, winked his reassurance, then slid a controlled expression into place. Jenna reached to reposition and unmute the phone while Grant gratefully took a hit of the coffee that Jenna had thrust into his hand. She stifled a smile behind her coffee cup, knowing full well Catherine would interrogate her later.

"I, uh, didn't realize there was a conference call this morning—much less a video call. It's awfully early for you, isn't it?" Grant said to Catherine.

"Apparently, my timing couldn't have been better," Catherine quipped when she reappeared on the video screen. "Nice to see you this morning, too, Grant. As to your other question, I happen to be working out of a temporary UK office providing support for another operation. Carl updated me on what you found out yesterday. With that in mind, I need to let you know a few things."

Banking the smug gleam in her eyes, Catherine went on to fill them in on the newest information she'd obtained, starting with backgrounds of the Italian GdF officers in charge of the confiscated weapons.

Catherine had concocted their cover identities in a way that rationalized Grant's knowledge of munitions and logistics and also made their relocation to Porto Arezzo plausible. To do this, she had capitalized on the location of Camp Darby, a U.S. munitions depot just north of Livorno.

Although located on the western side of Italy, Camp Darby was a geographically separated unit under the command of the fighter wing that was headquartered out of Aviano Air Base, located in the northeast corner of Italy. Given that Aviano was only an hour and a half from Vicenza, it would serve as a secondary staging ground for their operation.

"You have a meeting with the base commander at Aviano Monday afternoon. It'll just be you going, since Jenna has to work. Plan accordingly since it's about a five-and-a-half-hour drive without traffic," Catherine said to Grant. "Sorry, not the base commander—the base liaison officer. Aviano's a joint base, so your contact is the liaison between the U.S. forces and the Italians. He's fully briefed on the situation and should be able to advise you on working with the GdF, and he'll be your primary source of logistical support."

"Got it," Grant acknowledged. "I'll be there."

"One more thing," Catherine said when Jenna reached to disconnect the video call. The older woman brushed a stray lock of frizzy gray hair to the side and slid her glasses down her nose, peering over the frames. "Don't think for a minute Dugan had anything to do with pairing the two of you up for this assignment."

25

hello friend

G RANT ARRIVED AT THE Aviano Air Base Visitor Center thirty minutes before his four o'clock meeting. Based on the instructions from Security Forces at the gate, he placed the pass in his windshield and followed the directions to the U.S. headquarters building.

With its history dating back to World War II, the joint Italian/U.S. base had that trademark military appearance, and many of the buildings showed their age in both the architecture and the upkeep. The base was popular among military personnel and served as one of the key U.S. installations in the region. Its airfield routinely welcomed a wide variety of military aircraft—from the small fighters based there to tankers and larger transport aircraft. As a result, Aviano was well equipped to assist with missions of any nature.

Grant parked in a visitor's spot and weaved his way on foot through the concrete jersey barriers to the front entrance. Four minutes later, the colonel's administrative assistant pressed a button on her ancient desk phone. The monotone buzz of an intercom system announced his arrival, and he was ushered into the base liaison's corner office.

Air Force Colonel Eric Tamanski stood at the tall window that overlooked Aviano's busy airfield less than half a mile away. The rumble of afterburners bled through the glass as two F-16s launched into the cloudless sky. Only then did he turn to greet his visitor, but not before clenching his jaw and glancing at the oversized timepiece on his wrist.

"My ass was supposed to be strapped into the lead aircraft of that two-ship that just took off. But instead, I get a meeting notice over the weekend about an intercepted cache of weapons from some...never mind."

Grant stood in front of the colonel's scuffed wooden desk, quickly adapting to the less-than-receptive vibe. "And you had to cancel a rare opportunity for a sortie at the last minute to meet with some intel prick. There. I finished it for you," Grant stated.

The resentful look on the colonel's face shifted to a partially amused grimace. "Something like that, yes. So, since today's flight is history, what is it I can do for the intel world this afternoon? I don't think I have a dog in this fight, so I'm not exactly sure what the goal of this meeting is." Colonel Tamanski moved to his desk chair and motioned Grant to a chair on the opposite side of the desk. "I get notified of incidents that either are close by or have the potential to impact operations here, so I was briefed on the weapons being confiscated when it happened. Javelins, if I recall."

"Yes, both Javelins and HEAT missiles. For what it's worth, I appreciate your time. I know it's late in the day," Grant offered. He took a seat in a worn burgundy leather chair with flaking armrests and proceeded to outline the situation as it stood, closing by explaining his dilemma.

"So, the bottom line is that I'm working undercover for the Santoris to locate their shipment while trying like hell to keep the weapons out of their hands and take down their operation. I've never worked directly with the GdF. I understand you have. I need options, and I need to know what level of support I can expect from you and your teams here at the base."

"Where are you staging out of right now?"

Grant leaned back in his chair and balanced an ankle on the opposite knee. "We're over on the west coast. Staging out of Porto Arezzo where the Santoris live. But the weapons are being stored closer to here."

"Porto Arezzo? That's right on the Med, isn't it? Sounds like you intel guys live a hard life compared to how the military does things," Colonel Tamanski said derisively.

The hackles on Grant's neck stood up at the colonel's barb. Just when he thought the ice had melted. He rarely, if ever, acknowledged his background publicly, but this playing field needed to be leveled.

"Yeah, seems like Aviano is a real hardship tour, even if you are flying a desk, Eric." He spat the colonel's name, leaning forward to rest his elbows on his knees. "Just so we understand each other, I know intimately how the military does things. That's one reason I got out. SEALs don't get cushy assignments in Italy with private offices at the foot of the Alps."

"Technically, the Dolomites," Eric interjected, with a nod in the direction of the mountains.

Grant glared at him and unconsciously shook his head. "Whatever. I don't have time to get sidetracked by a pissing contest. If you aren't willing to assist, you should have saved me a five-and-a-half-hour drive."

Silence fell over the office.

"A SEAL, huh?" Eric rocked back in his desk chair and steepled his fingers. Slowly, he began to laugh. "Touché. Okay, Agent Lawton—Grant," he said pointedly, swallowing a grin. "Tell me, what kind of support do you need from our cushy little base here at Aviano?"

With the conversation on different footing, Grant leaned back and paused a few seconds before continuing. "I'm fairly familiar with operating in Italy and have decent connections, but frankly, you're the one who deals with the Italian military daily. As I mentioned, I don't know how the GdF operates. I suspect you do. I need that insight. And I'll need manpower if the decision is made to take custody of the Javelins and missiles."

Eric nodded. "All right. Fine. I can help on both fronts, but in the interest of full disclosure, I need to know how long your time frame is. I'm retiring in three months and start terminal leave in two, so it would be best to move this along to avoid having to transition responsibility for support."

That explained a lot about his attitude. Especially if the good colonel had been passed over for promotion to general.

"Do you have a team in country?" Eric asked.

"Right now, just two of us. In fact, maybe my partner, Agent Cameron, should have had this meeting instead of me. You'd probably relate to her better since Jenna was an Air Force pilot in her previous life."

Eric started to laugh at the intended dig but caught himself and sat up straight in his chair.

"Wait. Did you say Jenna Cameron? Air Force pilot? Tankers, by chance? Same Jenna?"

It was Grant's turn to be surprised. Eyes narrowing, he cautiously nodded.

"Well now, that's an interesting turn of events," Eric said with a pensive yet amused expression. He leaned forward in his chair to rest his elbows on the desk. "Haven't seen Jenna in...shit, I guess it's been twenty-five years. How is she?"

Grant wasn't sure he wanted the details of whatever shared history Eric had with Jenna, but the hotshot pilot kept talking without waiting for an answer to his own question.

"We met in Saudi—in theater. She was the aircraft commander on one of the last tankers airborne when I needed fuel pretty desperately coming out of...well, anyway, I wasn't going to make it back with the little fuel I had. She'd already been given clearance to return to base, but she essentially told the controller she was turning around to pick me up. We met up after the debrief. Great pilot, and a hell of a woman too." Eric gazed at the paper clip he twirled in his fingers, but his focus was somewhere in the past. "Ach, never would have worked long term, but I've wondered about her over the years. Private intel ops, huh? Good for her. Heard she got married. What's her story these days?"

"Divorced. So, single. Two grown kids." Grant stated with no inflection. "But not on the market."

They held each other's stares before Eric's eyebrows rose, realization dawning before he leaned back in his chair, a smug grin on his face and the paper clip clamped between his teeth.

"Sounds like that cover story isn't so much of a story now, is it?" The mildly smart-ass comment was more professional than the infantile one that had first crossed his mind.

Grant didn't volunteer anything more on the subject and leaned back in his chair, satisfied that he had drawn the line clearly in the sand.

Eric laughed again and tossed the paper clip to the side. "Okay, Agent Lawton. Since this meeting has turned out to be much more fascinating than I anticipated, how about you and I head over to the club and have a drink? Can't say I've ever bought a round for a SEAL before. But if Jenna Cameron thinks you're worthy, I guess that's a damn good endorsement."

Grant couldn't help but smile and nod as he stood up. This might work out to be the start of a beautiful friendship after all.

As Grant invested in their new alliance at Aviano, Jenna sat on Lourdes's patio and painted her bountiful prized flowers. Painting was both a hobby and a stress reliever, and the basic supplies she had purchased to pass the time with Evan needed to be used as much as she needed to use them.

The women talked while Jenna's brush transplanted the flowers from the patio onto the canvas. Their chitchat took them late into the afternoon when Lourdes paused and indicated the beautiful floral arrangement on the table.

"Do you know where I got those flowers?" Lourdes asked with a wink.

Jenna turned, looking over her shoulder at a stunning bouquet of cut flowers in a gorgeous vase, and shook her head, puzzled by the question.

"Come now, my dear. Really?" Lourdes winked at her again. "Your dear husband sent those to me in appreciation for a little something I picked out when we were shopping."

Jenna's reaction showed her embarrassment, but the two women had grown quite close, and all she could do was join Lourdes in laughter.

"I'm glad I chose well," a genuinely pleased Lourdes said. "It appears to have been appreciated."

"You could say that. He originally thought it was from my day with Angelo. When I told him it was from you, he mentioned sending you flowers. But I never thought he actually would." Her cheeks reddened, and her head shook in disbelief.

"Enjoy it, my dear. And enjoy him for as long as you can." Lourdes looked intently at her then shakily rose from her chair. "Now it is time for my nap, so enjoy those flowers as long as you like too. I will see you tomorrow morning. *Ciao*, my dear."

Weighing Lourdes's comments about enjoying Grant for as long as she could, Jenna stayed only long enough to finish her amateur portrayal of the flower-strewn patio. When the sun dropped lower in the sky, she placed the painting on the table next to the bouquet from Grant, then jotted a short note thanking Lourdes for lunch and, most of all, for her friendship.

Luca watched from the study window as Jenna packed up her paints and stepped off the patio. Well aware that Grant was away, he contemplated making his move in broad daylight but decided nighttime would be better. Time was on his side. The man he had assigned to trail Grant would alert him when his newest employee headed west, back to Porto Arezzo.

A malicious expression distorted his fastidiously groomed features. Once the location of his weapons was known, Luca would be better able to ratchet up the pressure on the GdF leadership. Of comparable satisfaction was knowing Grant would have to choose between saving his marriage or saving his own reputation.

The more pressing concern was the deal itself. The buyer had threatened to cancel the transaction entirely and was insisting on a five-thousand-euro credit for every day that the shipment was delayed.

At the same time, the supplier of the American armaments was starting to make noise. The longer the shipment was in government custody, his risk of being identified grew exponentially. Luca knew he had to move quickly lest the teat run dry. Daily updates to the supplier were now required, and Luca knew there were only so many more times he could stall.

His phone rang at six-thirty. Grant had just left the main gate at Aviano AB. Unable to resist, Luca did the math. He had just over five hours to catch Jenna alone.

obsession

Dinner was a solo affair. While Jenna looked forward to a quiet evening to herself, Grant's text letting her know he was on his way back was comforting. She had just pulled together some olives and cheese when her plans were derailed by a knock at the door.

Assuming Lourdes had found the painting, she opened the door. Luca casually leaned against the door frame, holding a bottle of wine and two glasses. The only thing shinier was his charming smile.

He took a step forward, and a wary Jenna placed a hand on his chest. She couldn't afford to alienate him just yet, but hell if she would let him inside.

"Luca, no," she said, furtively peering around him as if expecting company.

He looked over his shoulder. "You are alone, no?"

"Um, yes. For now. But sometimes I think my husband has me watched. You can't come in. Sorry. If he found out, he'd kill me."

"Then I would kill him," Luca stated.

Jenna laughed. "Either way, I'd be dead. And then I wouldn't get my evening swim in."

"I don't understand your fascination with the pool," he said.

"That's because you live surrounded by the sea," explained Jenna. "You take it for granted."

The smile that formed on Luca's face made her wish Grant was home. "That may be, but I never take a beautiful woman for granted."

"I bet you say that to all the women," Jenna said, rolling her eyes at him. "Look, thank you for the offer, but I'm going for my swim."

The door was closing when the bottle of wine he held clunked against it.

"Your glass of wine and I will wait for you there," he said as he started down the stairs.

The night was warm and cloudless. And eerily quiet. She looked around as she opened the gate with one hand. There was no one else at the pool or on the bocce court; it seemed as if Luca had shooed everyone in the complex away.

In the ten minutes it had taken her to change, he had too. He sat straddling a chaise lounge watching her approach. A shiver ran up her back, adding to her sense of unease. She dragged a small table between their chairs and purposely set the plate of cheese and olives on it. It wasn't exactly the Great Wall of China, but it made her feel better. She glanced at her watch and doubted that Luca's timing was coincidental.

Her thoughts tumbled. Unsure if she should admit to knowing that Grant was working for Luca or not, she opted to stay away from that trap altogether. She tried to keep the conversation superficial but soon realized that it came off as flirtatious instead.

For an hour and a half, she parried with him. Luca's probing questions about her past and her life in the States were deflected with questions of her own. Needing an escape from the exhausting charade, she opted for a swim, never anticipating that Luca would join her in the water. She swam a few laps just to stay out of his reach. But when she paused to stand in the shallow end, his thick arms trapped her against the wall.

"Your son's name?" Luca inquired. "I saw you teaching him to swim."

"Uh, his name is Ethan." Jenna fibbed, caught off guard at his line of questioning. His breath was laced with the pungent smell of cigarettes.

"Ah, Ethan. I haven't seen him with you lately."

"We, ummm, needed some time to work through a few things, so we sent him on to the States with some friends. He'll stay with my sister until we get there."

"I see." Luca reached out and touched her cheek with a wet finger. "Marriage is a lot of work; the reward being more years of even harder work." He pulled her hand out of the water and twisted the ring she wore. "A beautiful ring on a beautiful woman should mean a beautiful marriage, no?" He shook his head at her silence, tsking condescendingly. "Your husband does not appreciate what he has. You should know you have...shall we say, alternatives. *Sì?*"

His hand moved to the back of her neck.

Jenna was way out of her comfort zone. How far was she supposed to let this go?

"I, uh...I'm not sure what to say. My husband is a good man deep down. Marriage isn't easy, as you said."

Luca's expression darkened at her defense of Grant. The underwater pool lights illuminating his face gave his glare a sinister aura. His grip on the back of her neck tightened. "Don't waste too much time on a lost cause. I can give you so much more. And, lucky for me, my mother already loves you."

Had it not been a work situation and had Grant really been her husband, a response would have come all too naturally. But as it was, the right words evaded her. She laughed lightly at the mention of Lourdes.

"Speaking of your mother, I would hate for her to get the wrong idea about us." Jenna pushed his arm aside and headed for the stairs, only to be pulled back.

"Did I offend you?" he asked while the waves smacked against the side of the once placid pool.

"No, I'm not offended, Luca. What woman wouldn't be flattered by a man's interest? Just a bit nervous, I suppose. You're an imposing man." Jenna really wanted to tell him to fuck off, but that wasn't her role in all this. Nor did she want to rouse his temper.

The distraction of a patio door slamming gave her an opening, and she reached for the railing. A low and menacing chuckle at her escape followed her out of the pool.

Usually not easily intimidated, she felt like a sheep in a pen being stalked by a wolf. Her confidence in her ability to defend herself from Luca waned, sheerly based on his size. She hoped it wouldn't come to that. She hated that her hands shook as she grabbed her towel and cinched it around her. The air grew heavy as he approached.

"Jenna," he said, lifting her chin. Something wicked flashed in his eyes when she recoiled from his touch, conflicting with the silky-smooth tone of his voice.

He held her chin in his grip and roughly grabbed her arm with his other hand. She pushed against his chest to no avail.

"Luca, please. You're hurting me."

"As you do me."

Just as he dipped his head to kiss her on the mouth, she jerked her face away and tried to step back, but he held her in place.

"Luca. I'm married."

His grip on her arm tightened. "You should not tempt me then," he said tersely. "And you should be very careful while your husband is away."

He towered over her, anger radiating.

"Do not dismiss my offer," he warned. "The day will soon come when you will beg for my assistance. Then it will be me in your bed, and you will beg for something else entirely. I promise you that."

He shook her once then leaned in and kissed both cheeks, lingering long enough that she felt his hot breath on her neck. Luca glared down at her before releasing her with a dismissive shove.

Snatching the glasses and what remained of the wine, he turned to leave but looked back at her.

"*Buona notte*, Jenna. I will see you in your dreams. Sleep well for now, *bella mia*."

Near the gazebo, he turned around once more, seemingly pleased to find her eyes following him. Jenna hastily gathered her things and hurried back to the villa. She shuddered as she climbed the stairs, still feeling his glare boring into her back.

Once inside Jenna collapsed against the locked door. Her hand still clutched the doorknob while she calmed her soul. Her assignments often had her tangling with all sorts of questionable men who had even more questionable goals. Intimidation wasn't something she gave in to, so she couldn't figure out why Luca unnerved her so much.

After checking the lock on the patio door, she kept the lights off and sat on the couch in the dark with her gun in her lap for what felt like hours.

A few minutes before midnight, a car door closed, footsteps sounded on the stairs, and a key grated in the lock.

Abject relief flooded through her, and she battled the temptation to throw herself into Grant's arms. Instead, she sandwiched her gun in the stack of magazines on the table and turned on a lamp just before the door opened. She pretended to be engrossed in an article as he entered.

"Hey, surprised you're still up," he said, leaning down for a kiss.

"Yeah, I was just about to go up," she said, hoping he didn't register her anxiety. "Feel like telling me about your day? What did you learn?"

He grabbed three bottles of water from the kitchen and handed one to her. He drank a full bottle in a continuous swig, then opened the second. Smiling, he leaned back on the couch next to her and closed his eyes.

"What did I learn? Hmmm, I learned that being associated with one Jenna Cameron opens a lot of doors."

His head rolled toward her, and he opened one eye to gauge her reaction.

"Huh? What do you mean?"

"Colonel Eric Tamanski?" He tossed the name out to her like a tennis ball lobbed innocently into her side of the net.

"Eric Tam—wait, what the hell? I don't know where you got that name, but I'm really not in the mood for games tonight." Her head shook in disbelief. "I haven't seen Eric Tamanski in damn near twenty years or more," she said, knowing full well this was not a path she wanted Grant going down.

"Yeah," Grant grinned at her, wanting to convey that he was amused by the development. "That's almost verbatim what he said about you."

"Oh, for the love of God." She couldn't believe what she was hearing. "Eric is the base liaison officer at Aviano?"

Could this night just end already?

"Yep, and my new best friend." Sensing that she was aggravated, he offered reassurance. "Jenna, relax. I'm just yanking your chain. He was very complimentary and might have even asked for your number had I not squashed that idea. Our final toast after dinner was to you, by the way."

Grant was enjoying this entirely too much.

She couldn't.

Not tonight.

With her water bottle and one of her magazines in hand, she headed for the stairs. "I think this is better saved for morning." She turned to look at him and softened her tone. "G'night. I'm heading up. I'm really glad you're back."

She was on the second stair when he spoke.

"I knew guns had magazines, but I didn't realize magazines had guns," Grant said. His empty water bottle pointed at the gun that peeked out from its hiding place between the layers of magazines that remained on the table.

She crossed the room, picked up her gun, and straightened the remaining magazines but offered no comment.

"Want to tell me why you felt the need to have your Sig within reach tonight?" he asked in a subdued tone.

"No, I really don't," she responded wearily. "Tomorrow, okay?"

Grant got up from the couch.

"Jenna, what happened?" His tone was more demanding than questioning.

Looking up at a spot on the ceiling in exasperation, she gave him a small opening.

"You were right." Even she heard her voice break.

"Right about what?" His eyes narrowed, and a hesitant curiosity laced his voice.

"Luca." Her frustration at her response to Luca threatened to spill over. "He's dangerous."

"What happened? Are you okay? He didn't...he didn't hurt you, did he?"

"I wouldn't have let him," she stated defensively, wishing she believed herself.

"Didn't mean to imply you would have," he said with his hands raised palms out, wary of her defensiveness.

"Sorry. No. He didn't hurt me. Not like that."

She took a deep breath, defeating the tears of frustration that always surfaced at the most inopportune times.

"He showed up right after you texted me letting me know you were headed home. The bastard knew you were gone. Showed up with a bottle of wine and wanted to come in. I told him he couldn't because I thought you had someone watching me. Ridiculous, I know, but it was all I could come up with. Like hell I'd let him in here when it was just me. Anyway, I met him down at the pool. Eventually, I got tired of deflecting all his questions and trying to keep straight what I had said, so I went for a swim. In hindsight, that wasn't the smartest move."

"And?" Grant prodded. His brow furrowed. The crow's feet at the corners of his hardened eyes intensified.

"He propositioned me. Told me I had alternatives...to you. He asked about Evan too. I told him we sent him ahead to the States to have time for just us—that we needed to work on us." She shrugged. "I didn't know what else to say. It got really uncomfortable, and I started to doubt how far I should let this go. I'm just really angry with myself. I let him get the upper hand."

He reached for her, but she stepped to the side.

"No, let me finish. When I got out of the pool, he followed me. He made a move on me. I wasn't sure if he'd stop with just a kiss."

"He kissed you?"

"Tried. I pulled away. And that pissed him off. That's when I saw it in his eyes. It was like someone flipped a switch. He's seriously unstable. He warned me not to dismiss his offer because someday I would need him...and beg for him," she added with a derisive snort. "Warned me not to tempt him and to be careful while you're away.

That was it. I'm sorry. Hearing it back, it sounds innocuous, but in the moment, I—"

Grant cut her off by wrapping his arms around her.

Muffled by his embrace, she timidly verbalized her concern. "I hope I didn't blow this whole thing tonight. I should have played along, I guess."

"Stop." A small jolt underscored the word. "You did nothing wrong, and who knows what he'd have done had you gone along with it." He pulled her back to him. "Jesus, you scared the shit out of me, Jenna."

"I'm fine. Really. It's just...well, tonight was the first time I've thought about finding another line of work," she admitted. "I don't know what it is about him."

Grant placed a brusque kiss on her forehead and grabbed the bag that he kept in the entryway. He pulled his gun out and stuck it in the back of his khakis.

"Wait, where are you going?"

"I'm your husband," he said tersely.

"Grant. Come now." Jenna stepped in front of him. "It's midnight. What are you going to do? Knock on the door and challenge him to a duel?"

"Would you rather I let him get away with this?"

Silence fell between them for a moment.

"I'd rather you come upstairs with me," she said softly then kissed his cheek, slipping his gun from his waistband. She added it to the stack of magazines she carried, took his hand, and started back upstairs.

It was approaching one in the morning when, drained from the day's events and agitated by Luca's impudence, he finally gave in to sleep with her curled safely against him.

circles

THE FOLLOWING MORNING FOUND Jenna on the patio engrossed in a report when Grant came down for coffee. Grant set his coffee on the patio table between their chairs, then lifted the sleeve of her shirt with his index finger. She didn't flinch but met his stare, confirming what he thought he'd seen as she dressed this morning. Light purple bruises ringed her upper arm. He didn't need to ask, but he wanted to hear her say it.

"Is that what I think it is?" he asked more harshly than he intended.

She nodded, looking away. "I didn't really feel it at the time. I was in flight mode, I guess. But yes, that's where Luca grabbed me before leaving. I didn't expect it to bruise like that."

Grant picked up his mug and let the topic drop.

"So, aside from meeting a ghost from my past, what progress did you make yesterday?" she asked.

Kicking his bare feet up, he detailed his discussions with Eric. "We can count on his insight and support to the extent we need it. He seems like a stand-up guy. Doesn't hurt he's retiring in a few months so has a bit of a cavalier attitude. And no one is micromanaging him. He's worked with the GdF contingent before and thinks he knows the part of town where the weapons are being kept. He'll be a reliable asset."

He'd be lying if he said he had liked Eric at the onset, but by the time they toasted Jenna over drinks and parted ways, Eric's churlish exterior had dissolved entirely.

The man loved to fly, figuratively and literally; his lifelong career in the military was coming to an end, and Grant knew from experience what a hard transition that is for many to make. Eric would never again have a meticulously maintained, fully funded aircraft with full fuel tanks and afterburner at his disposal, waiting for him to strap in and take it for a ride. Although he was a tad bitter about going from Deputy Wing Commander to getting pigeonholed—as he labeled it—into the base liaison officer role, he would never find a job or career as challenging and fulfilling in the civilian world. And he would forever mourn a lost sense of purpose and belonging.

Eric had admitted to being uncertain about what he wanted to do with the next stage of his life. In a few months, he would lose his identity and be just another single, civilian, middle-aged man trying to make it all make sense.

There were certain characteristics by which Grant ranked people. Over their drinks and food, traits of fierce loyalty and integrity emerged. Like a lottery scratch-off card, it just took a little work to reveal the character that lay underneath the surface of what the world saw as just another arrogant fighter pilot. Maybe Jenna had recognized all that in him years ago, or maybe she just had good taste in men. He smirked at that thought. Jenna or no Jenna, Eric would likely always be one of those people he could call on a moment's notice, no matter how long it had been since they last talked.

"For what it's worth, I think it's a good thing that Eric is the base liaison," Jenna said. "The Eric I remember can come across as an ass sometimes, but he has a good sense of right and wrong. And if he says he'll do something, you can bank on it."

"That's the impression I got too. Regardless of my ribbing you last night, I'm also glad for the connection." He nudged her leg with his toes to get a smile. "I need to call Luca and plant the seeds."

"Did you all talk about taking custody of the weapons to move them? I'd like us to be aligned so neither one of us gets compromised. Or inadvertently compromises the other."

"Don't worry, I'm not going rogue on you," he assured her. "We didn't get that far, actually. I was thinking that I would just call Luca and give him the location that Ilaria told me about. If he asks where I got the information, I'll be cagey and tell him I got him what he asked for and that I won't divulge the source. Besides, he knows where I was yesterday."

"How does he know where...ooh. I knew he timed his visit over here, but I didn't connect it to him having you followed all the way to Aviano."

"He needs to train his guys better, that's for sure. Haven't decided if I'm going to let him know that I know I was followed."

"And what if he goes after the weapons immediately?" she wondered out loud.

"Yeah, that's a risk, but I don't think he'll make a move before scoping it out. He acts tough, but I think he'd rather buy his way in and not get his hands too dirty. Could be wrong, but that's my take."

"So, then what? We have to think beyond that phone call before you make it," she prompted. "Think he'll tell you what his next move will be?"

"Depends on if he needs me for anything. I think he'll want to keep me on the hook; I'm a relatively cheap but valuable resource for him." Grant said, steepling his fingers against his mouth. "Wanna get out today and do something?"

She rose from her chair and shook her head. "Maybe later—dinner out? I'm headed to see Lourdes in just a bit."

"Think that's wise?" His question went unanswered. "We're in, Jenna. There's no need to put yourself in his line of sight anymore."

With her hand on the patio door handle, she paused and nodded, keeping her back to him as she went inside and upstairs to change.

Jenna glanced at the bed they had shared last night and picked up the pillow from his side and hugged it to her. What was she doing? Torn between wanting forever and fearing where this thing between them was going.... God, how did it come to this?

The truth was, she wanted more time with him—maybe even wanted a future with him. Straightening the bed needlessly, she tried to convince herself to make the most of whatever time remained in her little Italian fantasy. The one thing she did know for certain was that she would not back down from spending time with Lourdes out of fear of running into Luca. She refused to cede that power to him.

Downstairs, Grant dialed the sole number programmed in the burner phone, wondering if the call would be picked up. It rang three times, and just as he expected to hear the canned voicemail message, Luca answered.

"What do you have?" he asked, cutting to the chase.

Grant responded with the same brevity. "GdF has it secured in the warehouse district of Vicenza." He gave the specific address and the names of the people in charge, then waited for Luca's response.

"How do you know this? Can it be trusted?" Luca challenged.

"Look, you asked for the info, and I got it. Take it or leave it. I don't really care. My job here is done." Grant stated as if he were about to hang up.

"Wait," Luca stalled. "And if I need more?"

"More what?" Grant said indignantly. "You said that was it—location and names."

"Just keep the phone charged in case I need you."

"Need me? No. No, I'm done. Out. Finished." Grant said with emphasis.

"You'll be done when I have my goods back." Luca's reaction was exactly what Grant had counted on.

"Or what? I told you, no more." Grant insisted, interested to see where Luca would take this.

"Or you lose it all. Ask your very lonely bird about what happened in the pool last night." Luca expertly laid the trap.

Grant wasn't expecting him to address that so bluntly, and his tongue-tied silence encouraged Luca to continue.

"She didn't mention that to you, did she? She liked it when I had her against the wall in the water. Is she always that responsive?" Luca exaggerated. "She also told me all about your son, Ethan."

Less of a statement, the threat was not so veiled.

"I'll keep the phone charged," Grant said, exiting the conversation.

He disconnected the call as his mind spun. Was there more Jenna wasn't telling him? He threw the patio door open to find her gathering her purse together.

"I was just on the phone with Luca."

"How'd it go? Did he buy it?" she inquired while hunting for her reading glasses.

"Yeah, but he wants me to stay on the job." She looked at him questioningly, hearing something in his tone. "When I told him no—that I was done—he taunted me about you and him last night. And he also threatened Evan—even though he got his name wrong." Clearly agitated, Grant tossed the phone on the table in front of the couch. "What aren't you telling me, Jenna? Did something more happen between you two last night?"

"Whoa, wait a minute...first, how did he threaten Evan?"

"He said you told him all about our son...my...I mean...you know." He raked a hand through his hair. "That's all he said, but the underlying threat was on the table. I need to know the truth about what you told him about Evan."

"The truth?" Gold flecks shimmered in her eyes. "You think I didn't tell you the truth? What do you take me for, Grant? You honestly think I'm stupid enough to talk freely about Evan to Luca? I love that boy like he's mine." Disgusted, she shook her head. "Luca brought it up. Said he saw me teaching my son to swim and asked where he was lately. I already told you what I said. I told him we needed time to work on us and that we sent Evan ahead to the States to stay with my sister until we got there. I'm the one who told him his name was Ethan instead. It was the best I could come up with on the fly." She felt her anger rising at his insinuation. "That was the extent of it, I swear. And how did this become all about me?"

Silence filled the room. His doubting her truthfulness cut to the core.

"I have to go. I told Lourdes I'd be there at noon." She turned to leave.

"What about in the pool? What really happened between you and him?"

Jenna could hear the suspicion and insult in Grant's tone. Luca had played his cards well. She set her purse down and walked over to Grant, feeling the invisible wall that had materialized between them. She was close enough to touch him but didn't dare.

"I fucked him."

Every muscle in his body stiffened, hardened into granite by her statement.

She was stunned. "You honestly believe that, don't you?"

"I don't know what to believe."

"Well, that's a damn shame then. Because you should." She grabbed her bag and slammed it onto the table. "For God's sake, of course I didn't fuck him, Grant. You really think I would do that?"

The hunt for her reading glasses continued. She cursed under her breath as she pawed through her purse.

"I told you everything. Think about last night, Grant. Do you really think I was holding anything back?" She was sick of choking down tears of frustration lately, and her voice quivered as the anger kicked in. "I let you see the worst of me last night. That was as raw and honest as it gets. If you choose to let Luca get between us, that's on you."

She turned again to leave.

"Don't go," he half asked, half demanded. "We're not done yet."

"Actually, I think we are." Turning to face him, Jenna lifted her chin in defiance, shaking her head as she spoke. "I'm not going to stand here and take this from you. I'm not doing another relationship that's mired in doubt and mistrust."

She was furious and insulted and everything in between. The devastation would hit later. But first, she needed to make a few things crystal clear to him.

"After all we've shared these past couple of months, you should know me better than that. At the very least, you should trust me as an agent. And you should certainly trust me a hell of lot more than you trust that madman. The fact that you doubted me for an instant tells me all I need to know."

She was calmer than she thought she would be as thoughts of a relationship with him evaporated in a matter of seconds.

"If you doubt my honesty...my integrity, my reliability, how I feel about you...then we've got nothing. It's just really great sex at this point. Hell, maybe that's all it was for you all along. Maybe you don't even think it was all that great. But know this, Grant

Lawton...personally or professionally, I would never lie to you. There's too much at stake on both fronts."

"I'm sorry. I just...I didn't want to believe you'd held anything back, but I had to ask. Had to know."

She didn't know what to say next as her mind processed what had just transpired. She wasn't about to tell him she was hopelessly in love with him. Nope. Not now, and probably not ever. Back on the roller coaster. She sighed audibly, knowing this was exactly why she'd been content to be on her own for all those years.

Men. Damn them all.

"It's not your apology that I need," she verbalized, the hurt evident in her voice. The understanding that it was likely really over for them tore through her. "I hate that Luca won. I can't reconcile that you'd think I'd purposely deceive you. More so, I resent you believing him over me—even in the heat of the moment. How could you?" The glasses were clutched in her hand to the point of breaking as she shoved everything else back into her bag. "At this point, it's probably best that we just wrap this assignment up as quickly as possible." Jenna fastened her purse and turned on her heel. "I'm late to my visit with Lourdes."

Lourdes could tell something was amiss. Jenna had never been all that great at hiding her anger or her hurt.

"It wasn't really a fight—maybe it was. Just a harsh realization on both sides, I think. Trust is a big thing for me. It's not something I take lightly." She tried to put her thoughts into words without spilling her own secrets. Such a hypocrite she was. Blathering on about trust while, day in and day out, she pretended to be someone she wasn't. Deceiving a dear friend.

Lourdes sat quietly, letting Jenna talk. When Jenna fell silent, Lourdes looked her squarely in the eye and asked, "Jenna, my dear, was Luca involved in this?"

Jenna's head shot up.

Lourdes continued with a heavy sag of her tiny shoulders. "It's all true, isn't it? All the rumors that I refused to believe all these years. I saw him at the pool with you the other night. I watched him grab you and saw the anger in his movements. You refused his advances, yes?"

Stupefied, Jenna nodded.

Leaning back in her chair, defeated, Lourdes's eyes filled with tears. "I didn't know just how disturbed he was...or is. At least, I didn't want to believe what I heard. What a tangled web...I should have warned you. I'm sorry my silence has caused problems for you, but if half the rumors are true, you need to stay clear of him. You are so dear to me; I don't want you mixed up with him. I'll release you from this job if that's what it takes. Please work it out with Grant—promise me you will—so I can die without that on my conscience too."

Jenna's first inclination was to scoff at the comment about dying, but the look in her friend's eyes told her there was more to that comment. "Lourdes?"

The older woman's perfectly coifed head sagged against the chair, her face streaked with tears. Jenna moved to sit next to her on the antique settee and wrapped an arm around her. They sat in silence while Lourdes dabbed her face with a handkerchief in a useless effort to minimize smearing her make-up.

In a soft, wavering breath, Lourdes said, "I haven't told anyone. Not even Matteo. Only my lawyer and doctor know...and now you. I am dying. I don't have much longer on this earth. They think I have advanced cancer, but I refuse to spend my time with all those tests and treatments only to be weak in my last days—just to fight the inevitable. I tell you this because I want you to know how bright you've made my life lately. You gave this old lady something to look forward to, and most of all, a friend. I'm extremely grateful for the time we've spent together."

Tears slowly rolled down Jenna's face, and she gingerly pulled Lourdes tighter to her. The news was tough to digest. She had no words so didn't attempt to say anything. Eventually, she pulled herself together.

"Oh, Lourdes, I treasure our friendship too. I'm so glad I took this assignment. Whatever comes to pass, please know I will always remember our summer together with such happy memories." Their layered hands squeezed together. "Come outside with me. A walk will do us both some good."

They meandered among the flowers in the sunshine. Jenna led Lourdes over to the heirloom rose where they snapped a few selfies, laughing together. At Lourdes's nap time, Jenna hugged her friend once more and headed back to deal with life in her villa.

Mentally sapped by the day's events, she stopped at the pool, dropped her purse on the concrete by her side, and lifted her sundress to her upper thighs. For hours, she sat at the edge of the pool with her feet in the water, letting the Mediterranean sun restore her.

It was approaching five o'clock when she dragged her weary self away from the pool. Grant's car was gone, and she was relieved not to have to deal with him this evening. She'd lived with him for more than two months and slept with him by her side every night for almost two weeks. Tonight, she would sleep alone. It would take some adjustment, but she was ready to put the drama behind her.

When she turned out her light at eleven, Grant still hadn't returned. Was he with another woman? Was he safe? She tried not to worry, tried to keep the sadness at bay, finally concluding that he was a big boy and she a big girl. It was time to move on.

She slept soundly and dreamed of a different life for herself. One with an old farmhouse to restore on some land. Her kids nearby and grandkids running in and out. A bountiful garden and enough home-improvement projects to keep her restlessness occupied. At some point in the dream, she was tucked up against Grant on a white porch swing, but when she awoke, she was still very much alone.

28

from cloudy bay to malibu

G RANT HAD LEFT THE villa shortly after Jenna had gone to see Lourdes. Agitation, jealousy, and anger were never a good combination. He grabbed his gear bag and started driving.

No other woman had ever been able to render him speechless like Jenna could. Emotions warred between his head and his heart. The flames of jealousy that Luca had stoked in him had taken the form of accusations and doubt. Those, allied with his fear for Evan's safety, had hijacked his judgment. Deep down he knew if he could convince himself that he couldn't trust her he could walk away unscathed.

But not now.

Now she'd played her entire hand and laid her last card on the table. The fact that she was willing to walk away if there was no trust between them spoke volumes and almost broke him. He'd been waiting for someone like her most of his life, yet here he was, about to push her away.

As late afternoon arrived, he found himself outside the base at Aviano not really knowing how or why he'd ended up there. Since he was in the area, he shot a text to Eric. They agreed to meet at an old farmhouse turned restaurant and inn near the foothills of the mountains in an hour.

Casa Colonica—or The Farmhouse as it was known to locals and base personnel—and its surrounding vineyards had been purchased by a tight group of former U.S. military friends who had opted to remain in Europe after they retired. The property had quite a reputation with active-duty military personnel stationed all over Europe. In some respects, it was almost like an extension of the base. The owners—most former Special Operations—were particular about security in addition to customer experience, which made it the ideal spot for both work and play.

Grant arrived early and used the time to walk the vineyards, grateful to not only stretch his legs but also burn off some of his edginess. Climbing the hill back to the parking area, he saw Eric leaning against his car, focused on his phone. As the two men shook hands, Eric looked inquisitively at Grant. "To what do I owe the honor of a repeat visit?"

"Just need to work through some things and thought you might be a good sounding board."

Removing his worn Air Force–issue aviator sunglasses, Eric studied Grant.

"Is this personal or business?" he asked, catching on when Grant hesitated. "Both, huh? If there's trouble between you and Jenna, I'm afraid I'm not exactly an expert on doing right by her. Or any woman, for that matter. C'mon, let's get a table outside and talk," he proposed, clapping Grant on the shoulder.

Over dinner and several drinks, their fledgling alliance morphed into the established friendship that Grant had thought it might. The conversation began with business, and plans were made to check out the storage location in Vicenza the next morning.

By his third drink, Grant found himself divulging more than he'd intended about Luca and Jenna and the situation from earlier this morning. When he was finished unloading, he ordered round four. By the time they were ready to leave, Grant was well into his fifth or sixth drink and in no shape to drive. An experienced wingman, Eric arranged to leave Grant's car at The Farmhouse and booked a room for him back at Aviano's base lodging.

As Grant fell into bed fully clothed, the last three things Eric had said floated around in his soggy brain.

"Drink these," Eric had said as he shoved two bottles of water into Grant's bag.

He'd then fished three tablets from an opaque plastic bottle and placed the acetaminophen in Grant's hand. "Take these."

Eric had tossed Grant's room key onto the old laminate desk, pausing before stepping out into the hallway. "And if you let her go, you're a fool."

The next morning, when Jenna went downstairs, it was clear that Grant hadn't returned at all last night. The worry she had dismissed last night returned.

Setting her coffee next to her on the patio, Jenna picked up her phone to check in with Catherine when she noticed an unread text from him. It had been sent late last night, or in the wee hours, depending on where that line was. The message proved to indeed be from Grant's phone but was not from Grant.

> *Hey, this is Eric on Grant's phone. Borrowed*
> *his thumb to unlock it. He's not in any shape*
> *to drive. Booking him a room here on base.*
> *Will send him back to you tomorrow pm. Glad*
> *to hear you are doing well these days. I'll shoot*
> *you a text from my number so you have it. Hope*
> *to see you before this is done.*

She typed a response to Eric's number, editing her response three times to make sure it was worded exactly how she wanted it to be received.

> *Hi, Eric. Small world, isn't it? Sounds like you've done well for yourself. Appreciate the update and many thanks. Hope to see you too.*

Humored by the development and relieved to know Grant had a babysitter, she made another cup of coffee as she plotted her day.

Despite her resolve to move on from their relationship, the villa felt empty without him. Keeping busy would be best. Her feelings for him would be difficult to set aside, but she would never stay in another relationship without a solid foundation of trust. No matter how much she loved him.

An hour later, she gathered her paints and meager supplies and called Lourdes. An outing would be just the therapy they both needed.

Knocking on the front door of Lourdes's villa, she found herself unexpectedly face to face with Luca. She took a step back reflexively as his most charming smile greeted her.

"Ah, what a nice start to the day." The practiced line slid from his mouth as he kissed her stony cheeks.

"Luca," she greeted with a cool nod. "I'm taking your mother out this afternoon, so please let her know I've arrived."

Being cordial to him was difficult, but it was the only option to avoid derailing their progress thus far.

He welcomed her inside and instructed the housemaid to alert his mother to her guest. Once they were alone, he watched her like she was his next meal. She glanced at her watch.

"Would you care to meet Paetta and me for dinner in town tonight?" he asked.

"Thank you, but I have other obligations." She tried her best to make it come out gracefully.

His eyes glowered at the repeated rejection, and his head tilted to the side. "Oh? I thought you might be alone again tonight."

The implication of his statement hit her squarely. Thankful for Lourdes's appearance behind him, she ignored his comment and leaned around him to greet her friend.

"I'm so looking forward to our outing, dear. What a wonderful surprise!" Lourdes said, reaching for her arm.

Luca followed them out to Jenna's car, only to be rebuffed by his mother as he tried to assist. Ever the chameleon, he maintained his slick composure and curtly wished them a good day.

As if sensing the need to escape, the little red car scooted into the flow of traffic. After an impromptu shopping stop in a quaint little town followed by lunch at a local trattoria, Jenna navigated to her chosen spot.

Settling Lourdes in the foreground and the castle ruins in the background, she unloaded her paint supplies. After an hour, Lourdes began to wilt. Sensitive to her friend's health, Jenna packed up, and they headed home.

my favourite summer

After a greasy brunch at one of the base eateries to chase away the lingering hangover, Grant was eager to get to work. Under a gray sky, thick with heavy clouds that threatened rain, they drove back to The Farmhouse. Swapping vehicles would eliminate any possible tie to Eric or to the air base. With fresh cups of coffee in hand, they climbed into Grant's rental car and headed southwest to Vicenza.

"So," Eric started. "What's the plan here?"

"Winging it."

Eric grimaced. "Not sure I love that idea. I can't afford to be compromised. It wouldn't do for anyone to know I'm the base liaison officer at Aviano.

"What do you have in mind?" Grant asked.

"I'm thinking we say we're with Europol and doing an inspection under SOCTA."

"Sock what?"

"SOCTA. Serious and Organised Crime Threat Assessment."

"Honestly? Did you just make that up?"

Eric laughed. "No, it's a thing. Trust me." He dug into a plastic bag and began unloading a few accessories. "Just let me do the talking."

"Gladly." Grant glanced over at him. "What the hell is all that?"

"Anonymity insurance."

The rundown warehouse district of the city consisted of a number of vacant properties that served as industrial camouflage for the nondescript government storage facility. The bland, pitted concrete building with its fabricated metal roof and loading dock sat seemingly abandoned but for two cars parked at the foot of a short concrete staircase.

By the time Grant put the car in park, the person sitting in the passenger seat was unrecognizable. With a false Italian mustache, wire-rimmed glasses, and dark blue baseball-style hat, Eric nailed the image of a career desk jockey playing out his fantasy as an intel field agent.

"You have a flair for the dramatic. Anyone ever tell you that?" Grant ribbed.

"Oh, that's rich coming from a Navy SEAL. You guys perfected the art of wearing camo face paint and disguises." Eric fired back good-naturedly.

"Fair point. I guess camouflage is camouflage. But we also kill with our bare hands while you fighter pilots sit fat, dumb, and happy thirty thousand feet in the air."

Still ribbing each other, they got out of the car and approached the windowless metal entrance door. Eric knocked with authority three times. They waited. He was about to knock again when a heavyset, balding man opened the door.

A disheveled sixty-five-year-old body disguised the thirty-something-year-old GdF officer. Judging from his appearance, he hadn't showered in several days. His uniform was wrinkled as if he'd worn it to bed and just crawled out from under the covers. One gold star on his epaulettes indicated he was a major, which gave Eric his opening.

"*Buongiorno, Maggiore. Parla inglese?*" Eric greeted him in a random and unidentifiable foreign accent.

"*Sì*, I speak English. How can I help you?" the major responded with a bored expression.

Eric mumbled something unintelligible which blended into "…Europol on an operational action plan under SOCTA. I assume you are familiar with it, yes?" Without waiting for acknowledgment, Eric plowed ahead. "We are here to inspect the weapons you are holding. Your colonel is expecting us."

"The colonel is not on station today, signore," the GdF Major meekly informed him. The transformation from bored to focused was instantaneous at the mention of his commanding officer and the Europol reference.

Eric rolled his eyes and shook his head in disgust. "We were told he would meet us here. Our flight leaves in five hours from Florence, so we cannot return later."

The acting was stellar. Anger showed on Eric's face as he abruptly turned from the door and yanked out his cell phone as if to dial, muttering under his breath. Impressed with his command of the situation, Grant didn't interfere.

The Italian major, now panicked and intimidated, spoke hastily to prevent the tenuous situation from escalating further. "Signore, I would be happy to escort you, if you would come with me."

The hardest part was done. They were in.

They walked through the stale, abandoned concrete hallway and down a short flight of concrete stairs. The peeling reflective non-slip treads were more of a hazard than the stairs themselves. The handrail had been painted several times over with bright yellow paint that now resembled the textured skin of a lemon.

Taking in his surroundings, Grant committed the layout to memory. He was less than impressed with the manpower present and the security. The GdF normally had a stellar reputation, and Eric and Grant exchanged concerned expressions. As they rounded a corner, pallet upon pallet of plastic-wrapped containers lined the warehouse.

Six dark-green containers were stacked two across and three high on each pallet.

Two junior enlisted men seated on metal chairs stopped their card game and stood up quickly, tucking in uniform shirts and picking up their discarded firearms. Class act, here, Grant thought sarcastically. The security was equivalent to airport TSA agents guarding the U.S. nuclear arsenal. It was so abysmal, he wondered if Luca had already infiltrated the security detail.

Grant split off from Eric and wandered down an aisle of containers. He couldn't read the yellow-stamped lettering through the plastic but recognized the font as standard U.S. military. The blade of his small knife sliced through the plastic to expose a label that read "NAS Sigonella, Sicily; Port of Catania." After taking photos of the container and the text on the label, Grant nodded brusquely to Eric indicating he'd seen enough.

The disheveled GdF major handed them the requested inventory of the weapons and preened as Eric praised him for allowing them to complete their assignment.

They made their way to the car, anxious to be on their way. Not a word was said.

Once they pulled out of the parking area and onto the main road, both began talking at once. The lax security and staffing of the storage facility was shocking. The potential of millions of dollars' worth of U.S. weapons making their way into the wrong hands underscored the need to devise an immediate course of action.

Eric peeled off his disguise and pulled the inventory sheet out. "This is some serious shit," he said, reading down the list.

Lost in thought, Grant glanced over as Eric flipped pages. "Did you see the stamping and the labels on those containers?"

"Yes." Eric rubbed his face and groaned. "What the fucking hell have you gotten me into?"

"Sure looked like they came through Sig. Interesting development. How would illegal arms get shipped in and out of an active-duty U.S. naval base with no one noticing?"

"Wouldn't happen on my watch, that's for sure. I'm briefed every time live munitions are being transported on or off base. I know the commander at Sigonella well, and I'm having trouble thinking she's involved. Think we've got bigger problems with senior leadership at Sig?"

"I'm not sure. I need to mull this over. Luca lives in Sicily, not far from Sig and Catania. That can't be a coincidence." Grant winced inwardly when an image of Jenna flashed in his mind as he said Luca's name. Looking over at Eric, he continued. "I have to recommend we take custody of the entire haul. How long would the approval and paperwork take to make a transfer possible? Can we move it all to the depot at Camp Darby?"

"One question at time. I'm still processing the Sig connection. A transfer will take some serious coordinating, but I'll start the paperwork and approvals to take custody as soon as I get back to the office. Unfortunately, I've got to raise this up the proverbial flagpole. As soon as I do that, I can assign a Security Forces unit to the warehouse. That's first and foremost, given the half-assed security. Then we can decide how, when, and where to move it."

The contingency-planning conversation lasted until Grant pulled into The Farmhouse's parking area next to Eric's car. Over a late lunch, they relaxed only slightly, trying not to think of the security risks they had just witnessed. As they walked back to their cars, Eric asked the million-dollar question that Grant had been avoiding all morning.

"So, what are you going to do about Jenna?" Eric inquired.

Grant's response was too quick. "I haven't thought about it."

"Bullshit. You're in love with her. It's written all over your face whenever her name comes up. Either piss or get off the pot, lover boy.

And if you are fool enough to let her walk, let me know." Eric knew he'd get his point across by expressing interest. "I'd be happy to help her pick up the pieces."

"Fuck off, Colonel."

Eric laughed. "Tell her, you stupid shithead. Either that or give her my number. It's in your phone in case you forget it. I'll be in touch with an update tomorrow."

As he drove into the setting sun, Grant's thoughts drifted to his personal life; the last thirty-odd hours had proven his life was seriously fucked up. The fact that he was good friends and drinking buddies with his now-disenchanted lover's ex-boyfriend from twenty-five years ago was messed up. The fact that he had used that same guy as a sounding board for his own self-inflicted problems with the same woman took it from messed up to categorically disturbing. Someone up there had a sick sense of humor, for sure. His life would have any therapist drooling to study whatever it was that made Grant Lawton tick.

About halfway back to Porto Arezzo, Grant started to consider what in the hell he was going to say to Jenna. He couldn't ignore how they had left things.

He briefly wondered how Evan was doing. He had stopped calling Evan's grandparents' house for fear of exposing them to any danger. The last time they spoke, he'd told Evan he wouldn't be calling for a while due to work, but the guilt ate at him. Guilt over not being consistent with his check-in calls; guilt over bringing Evan with him; and guilt over second-guessing if he was cut out to be a single dad. The term alone terrified him.

He would welcome the day when the constant guilt abated. It wasn't remorse for killing those who walked on the opposite side of the line; instead, it was the deaths he hadn't directly caused that weighed so heavily. His relationship—or whatever it was—with Jenna had alleviated the incessant ache. When the guilt managed to seep into his consciousness, just the thought of her—or even her presence—pushed it to the periphery.

Despite knowing the good, the bad, and the ugly, Jenna was one of the few people who wouldn't consider him a monster.

That alone gave him hope.

A text notification dinged, and Jenna unlocked her phone after seeing Eric's name on the preview.

> *Lawton's ETA should be around 1930.*
> *May not have told him I gave you my*
> *number btw. Go easy on him.*

She wondered what the hell that last part meant. Certainly Eric didn't know the gory details of her relationship with Grant? It was probably best to keep her response short.

> *Drama's not my thing anymore.*
> *Thx for update.*

She started to set the phone down when it dinged again.

> *Never was. At least if you bail on him, you have*
> *my number now ;-). Remember, it's all about*
> *energy management and small corrections.*

She literally laughed out loud at his applying flying concepts to life in general.

Good one. When did you finally mature?

Ouch. Fighter pilots fly fast and mature slow.

LOL

Seriously, if you need anything, call. TTYL.

shameless

PPARENTLY, OLD FIGHTER PILOTS were also still good at estimating time on target. At precisely 7:30 that evening, Grant walked in the door. Jenna was curled in her patio chair, reading. He closed the front door with his foot, dropped his gear bag on the floor, and walked toward her purposefully.

She laid her book down and slowly got up, determined not to be childish or drag this out. They still had a job to do together.

Although she'd spent the last day and a half listing all the reasons they were done, her unbidden reaction to seeing him scrambled her thoughts and turned her rationale on its head. She stalled by slowly closing the patio door behind her. Turning, she found herself folded into his arms and felt his cheek pressing against her hair.

"I'm so sorry, Jenna," he whispered. "I keep fucking this up."

She laughed quietly at his unexpected apology and raised her head to look at him.

"There's nothing left to fuck up. I'm done, Grant. With you. With us."

She pushed out of his embrace hoping he didn't hear her voice waver. His expression was guarded as she looked away, searching for the right words. Her eyes closed for a moment as her head shook in frustration.

"But for some reason, I'm glad you're home," she said without pretext.

The wariness on his face turned to relief.

"I'm really glad you're glad," Grant said. His index finger reached out to touch her chin, and his thumb skimmed over her lower lip. "It was only one night, but I missed you."

Her heart skipped a beat.

"Good," she said, letting him wallow in his act of contrition. The idea that she'd made her peace with letting him go was fading like the setting sun.

"I didn't really intend to stay gone overnight, but I met up with Eric and ended up drowning my problems thoroughly," he admitted.

"So he told me."

She said nothing to his raised eyebrow.

"Might not have been the best way to handle it, but he was a respectable Dear Abby," he said.

"Bet that was interesting," she prompted, curious to know exactly how much Grant had shared. And how much Eric had shared in return.

"That's what you drove me to." His voice lowered as he played with her wire ear cuff. She brushed his fingers away at the same time she took a half step back. He stuffed his hand in his pocket. "Look, I don't want to lose you...lose this, but I'm getting the distinct impression that you want to end it."

She averted her eyes and tried to stick to her decision, but this wasn't going the way she'd anticipated.

"I should walk away; we both should. The odds are not in our favor," she added matter-of-factly. "I told myself I was done. This isn't reality, Grant."

"It can be," he said. Based on how she avoided looking at him, he didn't think he had a prayer for redemption.

"Can it?" she challenged. "In my head, I know this needs to stop, but I can't seem to control my addiction to you."

He took her hand and tugged her closer, pressing his lips to her forehead. "Thank you."

She huffed. "For what exactly?"

"Giving me...us...another chance," he answered.

"Am I? Is that what I'm doing?"

"I hope so. I'm asking you to give me another chance. A chance to show you I...that I..." he took a step away from her, swallowing the words he struggled to voice.

"That you what?" she asked. The hopeful part of her wanted to hear him say it first.

"Nothing," he replied. Still holding her hand, he reached back and closed the curtains to the patio. When he turned back to her, his eyes held a look she knew well. Nevertheless, Jenna pushed against his chest.

"No. I have to know. I have to hear you say it," her eyes searched his.

"Say what?"

Her eyebrows arched in surprise. "For the love of God, never mind." She pushed away and crossed her arms. "If you have to ask...I mean, this is ridiculous."

"Tell me what you want me to say, and I'll try."

"That's not how this works. I don't want or need empty words."

"But I need you," he said softly.

"Grant Lawton doesn't need anyone," Jenna scoffed.

"Everything's different now. With you." His voice was low. "Tell me. If I can't say the words honestly, I won't say them at all. I swear."

She wavered, unsure if she wanted to know that he couldn't utter the words.

"The whole trust factor," she finally stated. "Do you trust me? Implicitly? Me over Luca? Me over anyone, for that matter."

He locked her face in his hands. Looking directly into her eyes, he confirmed what she needed to hear. "Yes, I do. I trust you, Jenna. More than anyone. I don't know what came over me—maybe concern for Evan. Between Eric and then Luca—maybe jealousy, I guess. I didn't handle it well, I know."

"No," she whispered. "No, you didn't."

"I'm sorry. A hundred times over."

She nodded silently and relented when he pulled her into his arms. Tentatively, she wrapped her arms around him.

"I need to share my day with you. Luca knew you were gone again. There's more. But first, what did you and Eric find out about the weapons?"

"Later."

That was all he said before his mouth captured hers. His body shifted, and she felt her pulse quicken as the kiss turned intense but languid. It held her under, drowning her reservations and shattering her intent to resist. He sensed the instant she surrendered. His ferocity caught her off guard, but she responded in kind, tugging his shirt off as he stepped out of his shoes. She pulled his mouth back to hers and unzipped his jeans.

One hand held his head, keeping his mouth on hers, and the other moved to his shoulder, while his hands found the waistband of her leggings. As she kicked them off, he backed her against the wall.

His hand on the back of her thigh lifted in wordless suggestion, and she wrapped her legs around him, silently begging him to hurry. When he pushed into her, she wanted to cry out in ecstasy. God, this man.

He whispered her name, and his breathing quickened.

Clinging to him, her nails dug into his back. He seemed to sense her desperation and shifted them just slightly, taking them both over the edge. He trailed soft kisses down her neck to her shoulder while their breathing returned to normal. She rested her head against the wall and ran her hands through his hair.

"I love you, Grant."

Her declaration slipped from her mouth without any thought. Without any restraint, and without any regret.

Blue eyes studied her, softening with understanding. His mouth opened, then closed.

"Shhhh," she breathed, her finger light against his lips. "No empty words, remember?"

It was enough that he knew.

For now.

"Good morning, babe," Grant said, wrapping his arms around her from behind while she poured two cups of coffee at the kitchen counter.

Turning in his loose embrace, she kissed him lightly, handed him his coffee, and wandered over to the couch to tuck herself into a corner against a pillow. He joined her on the couch, pastry in hand, reminding her there was something she wanted to tell him about yesterday.

Everything that had transpired the day prior tumbled out. She swore him to silence about Lourdes's cancer. Luca's reaction to her refusing his invitation made Grant scowl, and he tacked on a request that she avoid the man at all costs. Happy to oblige, Jenna nodded in consent as she stretched her legs to put her sock-covered feet in his lap. She smiled against her coffee cup as he absently massaged her feet.

"Tell me what you and Eric talked about."

He didn't go into great detail about what he and Eric had discussed with regard to her, but she got the gist. His surprise was genuine when he found out that Eric had texted her from his own phone to let her know he was okay. He didn't object—just studied her thoughtfully until she offered reassurance.

"That was a long time ago. It's you I'm in love with, Grant." Her toes poked his stomach. "C'mon tell me about the weapons."

He explained what they had discovered at the warehouse and detailed their concerns and the plan they were considering.

"Any thoughts on our next steps? Do you agree we should move the stash ASAP?" he asked.

"Yes, I suppose. Luca's getting pretty desperate, I think. What's the best approach for investigating the connection to NAS Sigonella?" she asked, shaking her head in disbelief. "Maybe I'm naïve, but I just can't imagine anyone on active duty taking that risk. I mean, that's rather...well, stupid, for lack of a better word."

"I know. I can't quite wrap my head around that either," he said. "But if people did the right thing all the time, we'd both be out of a job."

While there were times recently that she'd wished she was in a different line of work, she clarified her train of thought. "But here's where the disconnect is for me. If a legit shipment of weapons was transported through Sig and disappeared from there, wouldn't that have been known and reported already? Why wasn't that part of our in-brief? Certainly, Salvo would have had that piece of info."

"I hadn't even thought about that aspect. Maybe Catherine would know why it was left out?" he rationalized.

"Maybe. I can call her later and see. But if that's the second piece that hasn't filtered down, we need to think about why. Makes me think it wasn't a legit shipment to begin with." She paused to take a sip of coffee. "Does Eric have any feel for how long the coordination on his end will take? And what will you report to Luca?"

"Eric thought a day or two. He agrees this is pretty high priority. We'll need to make Dugan and Catherine aware in case anyone in Eric's chain of command contacts Salvo. As far as what I tell the local slimeball across the way, I thought I'd just let him know I scoped out the warehouse."

Jenna nodded in agreement. "He knows you were gone that night. I just hope no one tailed you over to the warehouse and recognized Eric."

"We weren't followed. Those guys are not that sophisticated. One of us would've noticed them, and the owners of The Farmhouse would have for sure." Grant said assuredly.

"Tell me about this Farmhouse place. It sounds fascinating. Part resort and part safe house?"

"A little like that, yes. It's owned by a bunch of ex-pats. Mostly special ops guys who wanted to retire but still keep a foot in the game, if you will. They're not running operations or anything like that out of there, so it's not an official safe house. But I get the sense they provide support as needed. To everyone else, it's one of those agritourism places. Pretty interesting business model, really."

Early afternoon found Jenna and Grant in much the same positions on the couch but deep into the planning process, running through various scenarios and contingencies. Their approach was simple and played to Luca's desperation and subsequent increased risk tolerance.

"So," Jenna began. "Just getting the Javelins and missiles back into U.S. hands is a win. But it doesn't necessarily implicate the Santori organization. Dugan wants that proof."

"True. However, Luca won't be willing to let them go without a fight. He's got too much riding on the deal. He loses a shit-ton of money, his customer, his father's good graces, and most of all, his reputation."

Jenna gave Grant a dubious look. "You really think he'd try to take on the GdF and the U.S. military? I don't know about that. He's blind with ambition, but that's a death wish."

"I think he risks more if he doesn't make a run at them."

"Then we'll be putting military lives in jeopardy."

"We'd be putting even more in jeopardy by not taking custody of them. If the customer was on good terms with the U.S., he'd be buying the weapons direct."

"That's fair," Jenna conceded.

"What if we tell Luca the weapons are being transported to Camp Darby for storage during what will certainly be a long, drawn-out investigation. Then we split the shipment along two separate routes from Aviano to Camp Darby. One with the majority of the weapons and missiles; the other a decoy with minimal cargo. Leak that decoy route to him while moving the actual shipment on another less obvious route. What do you think?"

"Can Eric muster that much manpower? That doubles the security escort needed."

"Yeah, we'll have to wait and see what Eric can rustle up. Can you call Catherine? I'm going to go ahead and touch base with Luca. I'll keep it short and on topic. Make him need me. Then trust me."

Jenna got up from the couch and leaned down in front of Grant, balancing a hand on his knee. "Trust should always come before need, my love."

He ran his hand up her forearm, his eyes never wavering from hers. "And after that?"

Pausing a bit, she kept it light. "Cooking lessons, I suppose. And dessert most nights."

gold

FEELING MORE POWERFUL THAN perhaps was warranted, Luca's supplier leaned back in his desk chair and thought about the almost-two-million-dollar home he had just purchased in Bermuda. His offer had been accepted, and it would be his in about eight weeks. He planned to retire from this rat race and run his new "consulting" enterprise remotely from the island.

If he could clean up the mess with Luca in Italy, he'd be free to retire within four months. At the rate this was all going, that might be a bit ambitious, but goals are goals for a reason. On the last update call from Luca, he'd learned that Luca had come up with some actionable information about the location where the weapons were being stored. With those developments moving in the right direction, Luca would be granted another week or two to make good on the recovery effort. Once the cache was delivered to the original client and the funds transfer executed, he would announce his retirement.

The scenario he had envisioned would, in a perfect world, eliminate Luca. While it was complicated and could get messy, it was a necessary outcome. He sipped his cognac, hoping Luca's effort to recover the weapons would be successful.

Luca was cagey. A certain amount of caginess was required in this business. What Luca didn't appreciate, much less realize, was that someone even cagier was pulling the strings.

Manipulation was a talent the supplier had honed over the years. By threatening to defund the operation, he had cornered Luca into revealing that the asset he had recently hired was former U.S. military. The supplier knew damn well how expensive that hire would be, but Luca wouldn't understand the full cost until it was much too late. This new team member was doing all the legwork and feeding information to Luca. When pressed further, Luca bragged he was controlling the situation by using the man's family as leverage and eventually, had admitted that having an interest in the man's wife. And as long as she was unable to identify or otherwise finger either of them, the supplier didn't care. Nor did it matter what happened to her.

Regardless, he'd insisted on Luca having an insurance policy. Silence can be achieved in any number of ways, but the sure ticket to ensuring the man's cooperation was by threatening his family—and not just the wife. If the woman happened to disappear, they would need collateral in the form of the couple's son. Luca had mentioned that the boy's name was Ethan, but the boy's whereabouts were currently unknown.

A week was all he would give Luca to find the boy on his own. Going after a child was distasteful, but if that's what it took to preserve his own ass, so be it.

hit me with your best shot

ERIC'S CHAIN OF COMMAND had been informed of the situation in Vicenza, and within two days, Aviano's base liaison officer had a green light to provide the necessary support to the Salvo Agency at his discretion. Initially, one of the generals wanted approval rights for each action but had backed off after realizing it would be the end to his political aspirations if things went off the rails. Eric, on the other hand, was more interested in keeping the weapon systems out of the wrong hands, so he was happy to have been granted decision-making authority on both the logistics and the day-to-day movements.

The first phone call Eric made to Grant on the secure line was a quick update to convey the green light to relocate the weapons. Two hours later, Eric called again to discuss the number of security forces needed to provide coverage for the warehouse. Uniformed only in black tactical gear without U.S. government or unit insignia, the security detail would be in place the following morning, after the GdF leadership had been informed through the proper channels.

Lieutenant Colonel Henderson, the commander of the Security Forces at Aviano, had established a good rapport with Colonel Tamanski over the last year and thus was tasked to determine the routes to be used for both the decoy shipment and the one that would contain ninety percent of the weapons. His job also entailed assessing the expected threats to the convoys and ensuring his security teams were outfitted appropriately.

Air support in the form of HH-60G Pave Hawk helicopters working in coordination with the Operations Group's Command and Control unit would be critical to the mission's success. Eric thought they would be ready in three days, but further coordination was needed before the timing could be confirmed.

Jenna was responsible for all the interagency coordination and for communicating updates to the operational plan to Catherine, who would ensure all the diplomatic and military clearances were in order. Given her experience in logistics, Jenna also oversaw the pre-mission planning, to include arranging the return of rental cars, delicately exiting her job with Lourdes, and any lingering details, not the least of which was food.

While Grant and Eric reviewed Lieutenant Colonel Henderson's proposed routes, Jenna left to pick up some groceries for the next few days in light of the likelihood of not having access to cooking facilities.

It was getting dark as she pulled into a small store in the neighboring town. While she loved the simplicity of the European approach to shopping, another part of her missed the variety of goods at American stores. Evaluating options that were easy to pack and store took about an hour, and finally Jenna walked out to her car with her purchases.

She had just loaded the bags and closed the rear car door when she noticed two figures walking purposefully in her direction. Headlights from a parked vehicle facing her made it impossible to see anything but the silhouettes of two men. She was instantly on alert.

They split up on either side of her car as she drew her keys, blindly punching the remote for the panic button, hoping to make enough noise to deter what she knew was an impending attack.

Now within arms' reach, one of the men swung a police-style baton and knocked the keys from her grip. Her left wrist throbbed from the impact. He chuckled, obviously deeming her to be a minimal threat. That was his first mistake.

As he approached more confidently, Jenna waited until he was within range. A solid side kick to his abdomen caught him off guard. He stumbled backward as his partner rushed in from her left. Pivoting, she kicked out again, but having seen his partner take a hit, the second assailant dodged, and her kick fell short.

The man on her right had recovered and now held a taser, which would severely diminish her chances of escape if it found its mark. Distracted as she was by watching the man with the taser, the assailant on her left landed a blow on her jaw. She staggered backward but remained on her feet.

He charged at her again, but this time she anticipated his move and delivered a solid jab to his trachea. His hand clutched his throat as he reeled, giving her time to focus on the assailant with the taser.

Instead of retreating from the weapon that was pointed at her, she dropped low and delivered a devastating kick to his knee. The joint bent unnaturally as her foot made contact. The man fell to the ground writhing in pain, his taser clattering on the asphalt.

With only moments to flee, she spied her keys and purse next to the rear tire and scooped them up in a single motion before jumping into the driver's seat. The door had barely slammed shut when the car lurched into reverse. Tires squealing, Jenna shifted into drive and hit the gas—not caring if one of them got in the way. Her red Audi tore onto the main road and disappeared into traffic.

She drove aggressively, fueled by adrenaline, slowing to a reasonable speed only as it receded. Still fifteen minutes out from the villa, she dug for her phone, cross-checking her mirrors to confirm that she wasn't being followed. It took two attempts for the voice commands to complete the call to Grant's number. Agitated, she cut him off when he answered and relayed the highlights of the incident.

Chances were slim that another attempt would be made at the villa, but she rehearsed her arrival strategy just in case.

After maneuvering into a parking spot, Jenna lunged out of the car, grabbed the bags, and darted up the stairs. Grant covered her approach from a crouched position on the landing and kicked the door open for her when she hit the top step.

The coral-colored door thumped closed, signaling an end to flight mode. She had barely set the bags down before his arms encircled her. Assuring him that she was fine, she pushed away and allowed the anger to burst through.

Jenna told her story in fits and bursts as she cursed her attackers up and down. She was incensed, convinced that Luca was behind the attack. Cabinets slammed, and groceries were thrown into the fridge with little attempt at organization. Experience told him to simply stand back and stay out of the way.

Eventually, she ran out of food to unpack. He had wrapped what little ice they had in a dishcloth, and as she flung the empty bags into the trash, he caught her by the waist and warily turned her to face him, shifting her into the light to get a better look. Her face was bruised and slightly swollen, and she pulled away in pain when he took her wrist to guide her to the couch. The gold flecks in her eyes started to subside when he forced her to sit and gently pressed the improvised ice pack to her jaw.

"Let me see your wrist," he insisted, gathering her injured hand in his lap and gently prodding around the bruising on the back of her hand. "Hold this pack in place. I'll be right back with more."

Moving to sit in the corner of the couch, Grant tugged her to lean back against him, wedging one ice pack between her jaw and his chest while he placed a second one over her injured wrist.

"Tell me everything one more time, just as you remember it."

And so she did, relaying every detail. When the account was finished, his mouth pressed against her hair, and his arms tightened around her until the tension began to ebb and exhaustion took over.

The sunlight infusing the apartment conspired with Jenna's ringtone to rouse her from sleep. She tossed the blanket off and groggily pulled the ringing phone from where it sat on the table. Her stiff jaw slurred her greeting.

"Jenna? Is that you?" a voice asked.

"Yes, who's this?" she responded, working her jaw back and forth. "Eric?"

"Hey. Long time, yeah? Sorry to call your number, but I need to talk to Grant, and he's not picking up."

"Oh, hi," she said, dismissing the awkwardness that drifted like smoke around the edges of the conversation. "Umm, let me see. Hang on."

"Are you sick?" Eric asked while she climbed the stairs to find Grant.

If her face wasn't so sore, she would have smiled. "No, Luca's goons met me in the parking lot of a store in town last night. I won, by the way."

Eric whistled softly, then chuckled. "Poor guys."

"Luca doesn't know Grant very well if he thinks grabbing me would make him easier to control," Jenna said.

Eric didn't comment.

Upstairs, she heard water running. A sweaty workout shirt hung over the desk chair in Grant's room.

"He's in the shower. Need me to give him a message?"

"Tell you what...call me back when he's available. That way I don't have to go through this twice. And have a map up too" Eric instructed.

"Yeah, wilco," she said, unconsciously using military lingo for "will comply."

"It's nice to be on speaking terms after all these years," he said. "I wasn't entirely sure how you'd react."

"I'm willing to bet we both have grown up a bit. But, yeah, it's good to connect again. Maybe we can catch up after all this."

"I'd like that," he said. "Call me back soon. And watch your six."

Dropping her phone on Grant's bed, along with her clothes, she decided to personally deliver the message.

Forty-five satisfying minutes later, they were back on the couch with breakfast, coffee, and a map up on the computer waiting for Eric to pick up the call.

"Colonel Tamanski," he answered. Visualizing the cocky then-captain with the devil-may-care attitude she'd met in the desert, Jenna couldn't help but snicker at Eric's all-grown-up business voice.

"Hey, it's us. What's up?" Grant said, wishing he hadn't noticed Jenna's smile at hearing Eric's voice.

"Need to talk routes so air support can get some scheduling and flight planning going."

After discussing the possible options Henderson had drawn up, they decided on two routes. They would move in forty-eight hours.

Grant would stage ahead of the others at the warehouse in Vicenza to supervise the preparation of the weapons for transport while Eric and Jenna would ride with the convoy teams from Aviano. Once both convoys were loaded, Grant would ride along with the decoy team carrying only a small portion of the cache in case Luca made a move on the supposed cargo. Jenna would accompany the team escorting the larger shipment of Javelins and missiles while Eric monitored the situation from one of the two helicopters to maximize reaction time should either team run into trouble. In the best scenario where Luca didn't take the bait, both teams would rendezvous at Camp Darby late in the afternoon.

With the plan finalized, Eric switched gears. "Grant, need to get personal with you for a minute." Grant and Jenna exchanged confused glances as Eric continued. "Is there a small, nine-year-old detail you may have neglected to mention? A detail named Ethan that we need to be aware of?"

Instantly wary at the name Eric used, they were both silent as they processed the possibilities.

Jenna found her words first. "Eric?" she asked, the apprehension evident in the pace of her words. "Where did you get that information?"

"Came down the chain. Shit rolls downhill, remember? Someone mentioned the kid to the general as a potential complication," Eric explained. "Please tell me that Grant's kid is not in country. The general has requested to have his location in case diplomatic coordination for a civilian extraction and repatriation is necessary."

Grant remained quiet as he and Jenna read each other's thoughts and expressions. When Grant nodded, and with her eyes still locked with his, Jenna continued.

"We can confirm that Grant's son is in country, Eric, but we are not prepared to disclose his location at this time. I would ask that you stall for us on this, please. I'm sorry to ask that of you, but Grant and I need to discuss this development. Did the general give you any other information on him?"

Eric shuffled some papers on the other end of the phone. "Umm...oh, here it is. No, just gave me his first name as Ethan. Jesus, he's not with you two, is he? Jenna, is that why you didn't come to Aviano with Grant for our first meeting?"

"Eric, please," Jenna pleaded.

"What's going on? Seriously, Grant. Think you might have mentioned this minor detail to me before? Why do I get the feeling there's more to this?"

"I just need you to go with us on this, Eric. I promise I'll fill you in, but you can't relay what you don't know, right?" Grant assured him.

"Okay, but I also can't help if I don't have all the pieces. I'll sit tight, but he's got a point about extraction if things go south on this next phase."

"We'll make the arrangements on our side, Eric. Appreciate you letting us know. See you in a couple of days."

Jenna hung up the phone and looked at Grant, who sat deep in thinking mode with his fingers steepled on his forehead.

"What the fuck was I thinking bringing him here?" He closed his eyes and sighed.

Jenna put her arm around him. "That's water under the bridge, love. We have to deal with the facts and the situation as it stands right now. Certainly the name Ethan isn't a coincidence? How in the hell did that name make it from Luca to Eric's boss? Perhaps a simple misunderstanding on a bad cell connection?"

"In our line of work, rarely are there coincidences. I'm just not connecting the dots right now."

"Well get out your crayons. Because if we don't connect the dots ASAP, someone else will, and it'll lead them right to Evan."

bésame mucho

T HE CALL TO LUCA to leak the transportation routes for the weapons had to be flawlessly executed. The script was reviewed at least five times for possible errors or hints that would blow their cover. Luca answered on the second ring, and Grant sank into character, appearing hesitant to divulge the route. His reluctance to give specifics was at first met with Luca's trademark slick coercion, but when that didn't work, Luca recycled the threats to Jenna and the boy he called Ethan.

Wanting to be believable, Grant finally relented and revealed the route through Padua and Bologna and then turning west out of Florence to the coast. Luca didn't question the uncertain timing and seemed content with Grant's estimate of forty-eight hours.

With that call complete, they began packing up all their belongings. The plan was to store everything at Aviano in case they couldn't come back to the villa for some reason. As excited as Jenna was about staying at The Farmhouse the night before the mission, it would be a short stay. The following morning, they would go their separate ways. Grant would head to Vicenza, and Eric would pick up Jenna and take her and their things to Aviano.

After months in the villa together, it was bittersweet to pack and leave what they had considered home, and Jenna wondered if things would be the same between them once life in the villa was behind them.

Hesitant to send a text message for fear it somehow would be read by Luca, Jenna walked over to Lourdes's villa to let her know she would not be at work for the next few days. Depending on how things went in the next two days, she might not get another chance to see Lourdes.

Jenna lifted her hand to knock on the door of the Santoris' villa. Their intel said Luca was at his home in Sicily, but still her heart pounded. One of the evening staff opened the door, and Jenna's pulse calmed temporarily until she learned that Lourdes was not well and was absolutely not to be disturbed, on the doctor's orders. Jenna hesitated at the insincerity of the housemaid's promise to give Lourdes Jenna's message. She ultimately relented, but not being able to say a proper goodbye to her dear friend only added to the despondency that had settled over her.

They packed Grant's car under the cover of darkness so that when they left the following day it would look to any observers like they were off for just a day trip. That night, Lourdes occupied her thoughts once more, and Jenna couldn't shake the guilt. Without an explanation, Jenna's abandonment would devastate Lourdes. The last thing Jenna wanted was to leave her to believe she'd been used by yet another supposed close friend.

As they got into the car the next morning, Jenna wistfully looked back at the coral-colored door, behind which her life had unexpectedly changed for the better. Her doubts had settled, blown to dust by a new sense of purpose and clarity. Friendship and love had knitted together the frayed ends of her world into a blanket of self-acceptance.

When she turned around, she realized Grant was watching her with a soft look in his eyes, as if he could see into the depths of her soul. He leaned over and placed a finger under her chin.

"It's been a good few months, hasn't it?" he said.

She nodded. "I wish we could stay and forget all the ugliness of our jobs. Forever."

"Our jobs gave us this time together. Don't overthink it, Jenna. We knew this day would come. *Que será, será*, right?"

"I know," she sighed. "But Lourdes...oh, never mind."

"Hey, you need to set the personal stuff aside right now. We came here to do a job, and we need to be on our game. I need you focused."

"You mean detached."

"If that's what it takes to get this done."

She knew he was right. But his overly realistic approach didn't help her frame of mind. Something resembling melancholy wrapped itself around her shoulders.

Oblivious to the weight of his words, he kissed her lightly and started the car.

It was late afternoon when they arrived at The Farmhouse. The agritourism industry fascinated her. Grant's description had been on point, but the old stone farmhouse was even more enthralling in person. It called to her love of Italy and to her love of home design and remodeling. After a short tour while their room was being readied, she unpacked while Grant wandered out to the parking lot to call Evan.

The distance between them had increased with every mile during the drive from Porto Arezzo. The farther they got from their villa, the more they reverted to being coworkers instead of the couple they had been for months. Eric's mention of Evan the other day weighed heavily on Grant. While she understood the impact of that on him, the thought of losing him to reality crushed her.

Against her better judgment, she had allowed herself to fall in love with him. And she'd fallen hard. Harder than was advisable at her age. Harder than she should have with a man like Grant Lawton.

Fifteen minutes later, Grant came through the door and handed her the phone.

"Evan would like to talk with you," he said matter-of-factly. While she was still caught in a whirlpool of emotions, the man who had begun to emerge from the shadows over the past months was retreating. He would find out after dinner that she wasn't so easily deterred.

Pleasantly surprised, she took the phone and couldn't help but smile at Evan's chatter. They talked for twenty minutes about his time with his grandparents and the adventures with their dog that he very clearly adored. At the close of their conversation, she told him she loved him and would see him soon. Tears threatened when he unexpectedly returned the sentiment. Blurry-eyed, she said goodbye and handed the phone back to Grant.

They wandered The Farmhouse's grounds in the fading light after dinner. Tomorrow would be a turning point—one way or the other. There wasn't much conversation, but she knew she wanted to make the most of the night with him. The cream silk nightgown Lourdes had selected weeks ago was folded under her pillow, and when she slipped it on, his reaction was exactly what she'd wanted and needed.

The nightgown didn't last too long, and as desire flared, the intensity of her love for him threatened to overwhelm her.

"Look at me," Grant whispered in the dark, and she opened her eyes, searching his face as she absorbed his words. His eyes glistened more than usual, and his voice was tight, almost strained as he spoke. "The last few months, you've reminded me that there are things worth living for. Things that make me whole again. I can't ever repay that." He kissed her nose. "You have me thinking of a simpler life. With you. With Evan. Our trio."

She stilled, reading more into his words than she probably should. Emotion filled her.

"I wasn't looking for this, but god, I love you," she said in a hushed voice as he pulled her tightly into his arms.

"You're part of me now, Jenna," he whispered with his lips pressed to her forehead.

It wasn't the declaration she longed for, but it was the closest he'd come to saying it, and they had not been empty words.

In the quiet darkness of the wee hours of the morning, the heat flared again, taking them over the edge and into a peaceful sleep.

The sound of running water woke her, and she fought against time marching on. A few minutes later, Grant came out of the bathroom wearing only his boxer briefs. He rubbed a towel over his head and let it fall to his shoulders. Padding over to the side of the bed and saying nothing, he touched her cheek tenderly as his eyes darkened briefly. He smiled softly as he backed away and started to dress—that singular moment etched into the bank of memories she would hold of him as long as she lived.

34

all hands on deck

ERIC MET THEM IN the parking lot of The Farmhouse just after dawn. It was the first time in twenty-five years Jenna had seen him. She hugged him, laughing, relieved that the awkwardness she had expected never materialized.

They loaded their bags into his car before exchanging final details of the day's schedule. From the passenger-side floorboard of his nondescript sedan, Eric removed a large black duffel and handed it to Grant.

"Take inventory of the contents when you get where you're going. There's stuff in there even a former SEAL will know how to use. Set the frequencies as noted. If we get compromised, switch to the discrete freq; the choppers and the convoy commanders will be up on that one too. Good luck, my friend. First round tonight is on me."

Grant offered his hand to Eric, but as Eric took it, he pulled Grant closer and clapped him on the back. "Take care of yourself, you Navy schmuck."

"Same, you chickenshit fighter pilot," Grant's grin lessened as he turned his focus to Jenna. He reached out and pulled her to him, lifting her face to his with a gentle finger under her chin. "I may not see you in Vicenza. Be alert. Be safe."

She nodded. "You too. See you at Camp Darby tonight." As he released her and started to turn away, she caught his hand. "I love you."

With a wink, he simply said, "Tonight."

Eric shot Grant a hard look as he gathered the rest of Jenna's gear and placed it in the trunk of his car. Both cars drove out of the parking lot; Grant headed southwest, while Eric and Jenna turned toward Aviano.

Jenna studied Eric as he drove. He had aged well in the decades that had flown by since she'd last seen him. For a second, she was transported back to the warm Saudi night when they'd met for their first date at a picnic table outside the portable trailer that masqueraded as a Burger King.

She deliberated how to break the ice. "You certainly haven't changed much in twenty-five years. You wear your rank well, Eric."

Without looking at her, Eric replied, "Yeah, time flies when the Air Force tells you you're having fun. You seem like you're doing good too. It's nice to reconnect after all this time. Although, admittedly, this whole thing has been a bit of a whirlwind. How'd you go from drilling holes in the sky in a tanker to this?"

The Reader's Digest version of her life morphed into relaxed conversation as they drove back to Aviano Air Base. After parking in front of the Command and Control Center, Eric pulled a small black bag out of his trunk and tossed it to her.

"Nothing personal, but your bag is smaller than Grant's since you're not on the decoy convoy that Luca knows about. Lieutenant Colonel Henderson, your convoy's commander, has a vest for you though, just in case. Wear it. Lawton will have my very nice ass in a sling if anything happens to you." Indicating the bag, he continued. "There's an older 9mm Beretta and extra rounds in there. There will be additional firepower behind the driver's seat of each lead vehicle if you need it, which hopefully you won't." He paused to take a swig of water. "I'll be overhead in one of the choppers. My callsign is Zeus 16. The other chopper that will be with your convoy is Zeus 29. Lawton is Loki 57, and your convoy is Juno 34."

Jenna grinned at the reference. "You and your god complex."

He laughed. "In all seriousness, keep your head on a swivel—just like flying. If you see something, say something." He hesitated. "Let's have that drink tonight so we can laugh about this in another twenty-five years." With that, he led her over to introduce her to the convoy lead.

Twenty minutes later, eight empty transport vehicles in a single convoy drove to Vicenza to pick up their loads. Four of the eight vehicles were deuce-and-a-half military utility trucks with large, tarp covered cargo areas—affectionally known as deuces—so labeled for their load capacity of two and half short tons. They attracted some attention, but nothing overly concerning.

An hour later, they pulled into the parking lot of the Vicenza warehouse where the Javelins and missiles were housed. As the trucks rolled in single file, Grant emerged from the building to direct the load teams. A GdF officer checked off the inventory to ensure that every case was securely stacked in the cargo bed of one of the deuces.

Each convoy would consist of a pair of deuces flanked front and back by a Humvee, an armored High Mobility Multipurpose Wheeled Vehicle. The driver of each deuce would be one of Lieutenant Colonel Henderson's security team members; a GdF officer would also ride up front in the cab, which meant two other U.S. security personnel would ride in the back with the cargo.

Jenna rode in the rear passenger-side seat of the lead Humvee and stayed out of sight while the deuces were loaded. Regardless of the acceptance of women in military-type roles, being the sole female on the operation would be memorable to someone, and being memorable was not advisable right now, especially in the event they needed to reprise their undercover roles. The black tactical gear she wore was standard issue, and her vest and helmet rested on the seat beside her while she waited patiently in the back seat of the tan metal sauna.

Over the noise, she occasionally caught Grant's voice calling out orders and directing which of the weapons went to which convoy. According to the plan, all the Javelins would be on Jenna's non-decoy convoy, along with the majority of the HEAT missiles. That left only a small number of the missiles in the decoy convoy with the rest of its containers empty.

The loading process was almost complete when disgruntled load teams began offloading several containers and shuffled them onto deuces in the other convoy. Even from where she sat sweltering in the back of the lead Humvee, she could hear their gripes and groans of annoyance.

Grant's sweaty black t-shirt stuck to his chest as he approached her vehicle and leaned in the open passenger door to coordinate final instructions with Lieutenant Colonel Henderson, who sat in front of her.

"What gives with the reshuffle of the cargo?" Henderson asked Grant.

Grant shrugged. "My little voice is warning me not to transport the weapons and the munitions together, so I'm splitting them up. If Luca ends up with either load, at least the Santoris won't have both the launchers and the missiles."

Henderson nodded in agreement from the seat in front of her.

Grant removed his glasses to wipe sweat from his face as he wrapped up his conversation with the commander. Blue eyes shifted in her direction for a half second before he replaced his glasses. His open palm casually slapped the outside of her door before he turned away to join his convoy.

Two hours into the drive, Jenna's butt was numb from a combination of what passed for a seat cushion and the notorious rough suspension of the vehicle. She shifted in her seat and, as she did, caught a few words coming across on the convoy frequency from one of the two deuces behind her. If she concentrated, she could hear the faint whomp-whomp of a helicopter in the distance.

The driver of their Humvee checked his rearview mirror and began to slow, then nodded to an instruction from Lieutenant Colonel Henderson, who had been coordinating with the other vehicles. Jenna leaned forward to listen, noting Henderson's skeptical expression as he keyed the radio to alert Eric and Grant.

"Be advised Juno 34 has a deuce reporting mechanical trouble. Juno 34 is currently stationary. Stand by for updates."

The helicopter that provided cover to their convoy acknowledged the situation. "Zeus 29 copies."

Eric's voice followed. "Zeus 16 copies."

With no choice but to stay together, all the vehicles in Jenna's convoy prepared to pull over. Every member of the team was on alert. The full complement of Javelins in their convoy would be a handsome prize for any interested party, and they would essentially be sitting ducks until the deuce's mechanical issue was resolved.

Less than eighty miles away, Grant and the crew of Loki 57 listened intently. They eyed their own line of vehicles in the rearview mirror for any issues.

Jenna was conferring with Lieutenant Colonel Henderson on a plan when Eric's calm voice instructed everyone to switch over to the discrete frequency.

The two convoys and the other helicopter all acknowledged his instruction and reported in on the new frequency.

"Juno 34, this is Zeus 16. Report," Eric said to Jenna's convoy.

"Zeus 16, this is Juno 34. We are stationary on the side of the highway. Awaiting update from the disabled deuce," Henderson relayed with a glance at Jenna.

From his position hovering above Grant's convoy, Eric keyed his mike. "Loki 57, this is Zeus 16. Your route appears clear ahead. We're going to head north to check things out. I don't love that situation."

"Zeus 16, this is Loki 57. Roger that. All's quiet here," Grant responded. "Juno 34, state your position."

"Loki 57, Juno 34 is five kilometers east of waypoint Lima," Lieutenant Colonel Henderson said.

The helicopter monitoring Jenna's route chimed in. "Juno 34, be advised Zeus 29 has eyes on three vehicles approaching from the south at a good pace. They appear to be black SUVs. They will be crossing the intersection ahead of you in about four minutes."

A string of imaginative curses followed as Grant realized what the appearance of three black SUVs meant. His little voice was screaming at him for the second time that day, and he jumped on the radio. "This is Loki 57. Our convoy will continue to Camp Darby, but lead is breaking off to head north to assist Juno 34."

Grant pulled the map up on the GPS and plotted the course for the driver of his Humvee, knowing full well they were about an hour away from where Jenna's convoy sat. Maybe more. He sat helpless and tried to listen to the radio reports, but the squeaking of heavy machinery braking, shouting, and weapons being readied in the background made it hard to keep up with the activity.

It was obvious the Santoris were making a move—but on the wrong convoy. Well, the right one—just not the one Grant had counted on. Somehow, they knew entirely too much about the transportation arrangements and the dual routes, but he would figure out how Luca had gotten the intel on their plans later.

Right now, he needed to get to Jenna.

warriors

Having been in the lead, Jenna's Humvee was parked two hundred feet in front of the deuces that now sat on the side of the road. After coordinating an emergency response team with vehicle maintenance capability from Camp Darby, Lieutenant Colonel Henderson stepped out of the vehicle to check on the deuce's status. He was standing behind the open armored door of the Humvee as the three unidentified SUVs stopped in a line, blocking the intersection about a tenth of a mile ahead.

A figure balancing on a single crutch awkwardly exited the first vehicle.

"Oh, shit," Jenna said out loud, instantly recognizing the thug who had accosted her at the grocery store. She fervently wished she'd done damage to more than just his knee that night. Her hand reached over the seat, and her open palm insistently beckoned for the microphone.

The man on crutches casually lit a cigarette and leaned back against one of the black SUVs that blocked the road.

"*Ciao.* What are you hauling, my friends?" he yelled.

"This is a joint military convoy. I suggest you keep your vehicles moving, signore," Henderson instructed in Italian.

"Ah, I'm afraid that's not possible, my friend. What you are carrying belongs to my boss." His unexpected admission was direct and overly confident.

"Our cargo is property of the United States military in custody of the GdF. Move your vehicles," Lieutenant Colonel Henderson said with authority. He closed the door and took three steps toward the man.

Jenna keyed the mike and ordered security backup for the commander. Two U.S. Security Forces dismounted from the cargo area of the rear deuce, ran forward in a crouch, and got into position to provide cover. After slipping into her vest, she studied the convoy behind her, and the pieces started falling into place.

It was no coincidence that the lead command vehicle was caught between the intercepting vehicles and the trucks carrying the weapons. With the GdF teams riding in the cabs of the deuces, the U.S. Security Forces personnel had been forced to ride in the back with the cargo, which she knew now was also not a coincidence. The Santoris had a bigger reach than she had given them credit for, and this was about to get exceptionally ugly.

Just as she keyed the mike to alert the others to the probable infiltration of the GdF teams, the man with the crutch flicked his cigarette butt in the air and laughed. Immediately, two shots sounded from the direction of the trees lining the road and a spray of blood covered Jenna's window. The scene erupted with gunfire as the Security Forces behind her responded to the attack.

Shouting for her driver to tell the deuces to reverse course, Jenna donned her helmet then opened her door to use it for cover. Her priority was to get the convoy commander to safety.

Lieutenant Colonel Henderson lay on the ground but was trying to drag himself back to the cover of the Humvee. Abandoning the armored door, she sprinted the short distance to him and fisted both hands at the back of his uniform collar. The blood stain near his collarbone was about half the size of the one on his thigh. She hauled him backward, ignoring his cries of pain.

"Get your good leg under you. We've got to get you inside the Humvee. On three, push off with your good leg," Jenna yelled over the gunfire.

With one hand, she reached back to open the door and started to count. Squatting behind him with her arms under his. On three, she hoisted the man up in one fluid motion. Thanks to the adrenaline rush, she was able to shove him into the front seat while the others pulled him further in. Once his wounded leg was inside, she slammed his door, and jumped back into her seat behind him.

Jenna leaned forward over the seat to assess the damage. He was in rough shape and was starting to lose consciousness. She was no medical professional, but the wound on his collarbone didn't concern her as much as the one to his leg did. Prompt medical attention would be vital.

"Keep pressure on that leg," she instructed the driver.

Assuming command, she turned in her seat to assess the situation unfolding behind them.

The driver of the deuce was slumped over the steering wheel, and the compromised GdF agent was climbing over him into the driver's seat. If the same fate had befallen the driver of the second deuce, both truckloads of Javelins were now under Santori's control.

"Sergeant, how many of our guys are hurt back there?" she yelled to the driver, knowing he'd been coordinating with the teams that remained. "And where the hell is the other Humvee?"

His answer was terse and not what she wanted to hear. "Both our drivers in the deuces are down. The four others are injured; three critically."

Luca would pay for this, she vowed silently.

Jenna grabbed the handheld mike from him and made a conscious effort to calm her voice even as alarm coursed through her.

"Zeus 29, need medevac ASAP. Keep eyes on the Humvee that's going to break off to the north. I've got men down and need immediate medevac for four."

Jenna hastily explained her plan to have the rear Humvee pull forward to collect their wounded commander along with the three seriously injured who couldn't remain on station. To complete this handoff and extraction, they would have to cram Henderson into the other Humvee with the three injured soldiers. That vehicle would then retreat to rendezvous with Zeus 29, which would airlift the most seriously injured back to Aviano. The Humvee would also continue back to base. The one soldier with minor injuries would have to stay on station with Jenna, leaving her a team of four.

While she outlined the plan, the sergeant nodded in consent and began coordinating with the Humvee in the rear. The diesel chug of the deuces' engines starting spurred them into action. Jenna grabbed the M16 propped on the floorboard and pawed unapologetically through Henderson's vest from behind, securing his extra ammunition in her vest.

By this time, the second Humvee had collected the other injured U.S. service members and pulled alongside Jenna's vehicle. While Jenna provided cover from errant gunfire, Henderson was transferred to the waiting Humvee, and it then sped away.

"This is Juno 34. Humvee exiting the scene from the rear has wounded. They'll rendezvous with Zeus 29 for medevac." Jenna's voice was steady as she relayed the information.

"Juno 34, this is Zeus 16. Copy that. How many friendlies remain on station?" Eric asked, trying to make sense of the snippets of chaos happening on the ground.

"Four souls remain on station," she responded, relying on instinct even more than her training.

A few minutes later, confirmation of the successful medevac rendezvous came over the radio. "Zeus 29 is RTB with four injured on board."

At least one thing went right, Jenna thought as the sound of the helicopter carrying the injured faded into the distance. Now she could focus on getting her team out of this predicament.

The gunfire from Luca's men had subsided to an eerie silence, which made Jeanna even more anxious about what was coming next. She inventoried their remaining firepower while ordering her driver to block the path of the deuces.

"Zeus 16, this is Juno 34. Requesting surveillance and air support." She hoped Eric wouldn't hear the stress in her voice. "Would be a great time to scramble some of those fighter jets, flyboy," she added cynically.

"Roger. Zeus 16 is two minutes out." Eric ignored the jibe. One low pass by an F-16 would scatter Santori's men, but the reality was that this would likely be over before any jets could even get airborne.

Jenna watched as the driver of one of Santori's SUVs angrily gestured toward the deuces and then to the sky, and she picked up the faint rotor noise of Eric's helicopter approaching in the distance. The indistinguishable words the man shouted to his compatriots made her nervous. A desperate adversary was unpredictable at best.

The man who leaned heavily on the crutch made a short phone call and stuffed the phone back in his pocket. From behind the trees on the other side of the intersection, a black civilian Hummer moved onto the road and stopped abreast of Santori's smaller SUVs that blocked the road. A figure exited the newly arrived vehicle and leaned into the open tailgate before hefting something large and slightly unwieldy onto his shoulder.

"RPG!" Everyone in her vehicle yelled the warning simultaneously.

Not knowing if the rocket-propelled grenade was for them or the approaching helicopter, Jenna keyed her mike again.

"Zeus 16, RPGs in play. Stay well clear. Repeat, Zeus 16, RPGs in play on the ground." She didn't bother to hide the distress in her voice this time.

"Roger. Zeus copies the RPG. Get the hell out of there, Juno 34," Eric insisted. "Let them have the weapons."

If only it were that easy. To avoid the wrath of the RPG, they would need a distraction to egress successfully.

Jenna grabbed the M16, checked the chamber, and inserted a magazine. Quickly prepping it for burst fire, she checked the magazine again and chambered a round. The helicopter, even staying out of range, would hopefully provide a decent deterrent—at least long enough for her to execute her plan.

"We can move your vehicle out of the way if you need assistance," shouted Luca's spokesman with the crutch, indicating the RPG launcher.

"What are our chances against that thing?" she asked her team.

"It depends. We're armored...but our chances wouldn't be good...especially if it's a direct hit," replied the driver anxiously. "And I'd rather not find out. I got a kid on the way."

"Anyone in here a good enough shot to take the RPG guy out and buy us some time?" Jenna remained optimistic as her mind raced for options.

One of the new guys piped up, "I can take out the guy with the RPG; no problem. But there's more of them than us. What then?"

"Take as many out as you can. Then we get the hell out of Dodge," she responded, knowing it was time to act. "Just buy us some time. They won't risk firing an RPG at us if we can get behind the deuces."

The deuces with the weapons were already in enemy hands, but she'd for sure go out fighting for her team's lives.

Allowing her best shooter to dictate positions, three of them would step out as if surrendering. The activity would disguise her chosen sniper getting into position. The minute he opened fire on the RPG target, they would pile back in, make a sharp left turn and head back the way they came. If all went according to plan, they would all be in one piece.

On her count, they slowly opened the doors with their hands up to throw the enemy off guard. She saw the RPG lower slightly and gave the command.

In slow motion, she heard the shot and saw the man holding the RPG fall to the ground. The others around him dove for cover. Exploiting the planned momentary opening, she shouted for her team to retreat.

Her driver was the first one in and threw the Humvee into motion as the other two Security Forces members clambered into the back. The driver gunned the engine and started a sharp turn away from her position as planned. Jenna held on to the passenger door with her right hand with only one foot partially in the vehicle. The tires squealed and spun on the pavement.

A searing sensation tore through her upper arm, causing her grip to loosen on the door even as it started to swing closed. Her helmet flew off as her head slammed against the door frame, and she fought to hold on.

"RPG incoming!" one of her team screamed.

"GO, GO, GO!" she shouted as the Humvee accelerated.

Instantly realizing they would have to slow or stop completely for her to get in, Jenna issued her final order to retreat and let go. She tumbled roughly to the ground and watched as her team's Humvee disappeared around the lead deuce.

Her plan had succeeded.

Or so she thought.

The unmistakable whoosh of the RPG ordinance fired in their direction indicated her relief was premature. But instead of hitting the Humvee that had just escaped, the imprecision of the RPG worked in their favor. The deuce that held half the Javelins exploded in a deafening roar, and Jenna braced for the concussion of the explosion just before her world went black.

twilight zone

"JUNO 34, COME IN. Juno 34, what the hell was that?" Eric's voice came across on the discrete frequency. It was met with deafening silence.

Helpless in the front seat of his Humvee as it sped north, Grant ran his hands over his face. Blind to what Eric could see from the air, he tried to wrap his head around what had transpired.

Juno 34 didn't respond.

"Zeus 16, this is Loki 57, report." Grant said with as much calm as he could muster.

"Loki, one of the deuces just went up in flames. Our pilot thinks they fired the RPG and hit the deuce accidentally. Trying to raise Juno 34 now."

Inside the fleeing Humvee, the three remaining team members increased their distance from the fireball and debated heatedly whether to go back for Agent Cameron. Ultimately, they decided to follow her order to retreat, rationalizing that they didn't even know if she was alive. Hearing the repeated calls to them on the radio, they looked at each other as if to silently elect the person who would relay that they'd done the unthinkable and left a team member behind.

"Zeus 16, this is Juno 34. Uh, we, uh...Juno 34 is RTB. Repeat, we are headed back to base."

Grant slumped in his seat, but his relief was short-lived.

"Juno 34, how many souls on board?" Eric asked.

"Three," came the muted response. "Juno 34 has three souls on board. Agent Cameron was hit while she was trying to get back in the vehicle. She ordered us to retreat without her before she fell. Then the explosion—we don't know if—"

Grant couldn't breathe. Dropping his head into his hands, he rested his elbows on his knees, unable to comprehend how this had happened and wishing desperately they could rewind the entire clusterfuck. He leaned his head back and squeezed his eyes shut. How the fuck had Santori known?

They were still eighteen minutes out. Eighteen minutes to survive with this empty pit in his stomach. His voice sounded like someone else's a million miles away as he keyed his mike.

"Zeus 16, do you have eyes on the ground?" Eric understood the crux of Grant's question. The defeat in Grant's voice mirrored his own.

"Loki 57, smoke's still clearing, and there's a lot of activity around the vehicles at the intersection. The remaining deuce is moving forward to follow. Stand by."

After a pause, Grant heard Eric say, "Get us lower."

A muffled response followed. Apparently, he hadn't released the mike button.

"I don't give a flying fuck about the RPG. Get us lower," Eric repeated.

Another incoherent comment.

"Just fly the fucking chopper and try not to get us shot."

After a minute, Eric continued. "Loki 57, two guys are carrying someone between them. Could be Je—our friendly. I can't tell." He paused. "The vehicles are departing to the south and mixing in with civilian traffic. There's no place to set down to intercept with the active RPG threat, and we don't have fuel to pursue. We're setting down in a field to the north of the highway. We'll be off freq and will wait for you here."

It was the longest eighteen minutes of Grant's life. As they drove in silence, Grant tried to pull back and see the whole picture.

Who in the hell was the leak? How had Santori known the route of the actual weapons? Grant had only fed him the decoy route. Even if Luca had infiltrated the GdF, which it sounded like he had, they would have only been able to give him location updates once they were en route. So, how had they known where the convoy would pull off the main road? He was missing something, but he couldn't focus; images of Jenna injured or dead kept derailing his thought process.

Emergency vehicles of every variety were on scene when Grant's Humvee finally joined the chaos. The Camp Darby Emergency Reaction Team commander was huddled with Eric as the Italian carabinieri rerouted traffic. As Grant approached Eric's group, Eric noticed the hollow, yet deadly, look in Grant's eyes.

"What the fuck happened?" Grant demanded.

"Still trying to put the pieces together. I directed her three team members to be debriefed immediately upon their return. Before and after Medical checks them out. She has to be alive. Why else would they have taken her with them?" Eric held up a mangled M16. "We found this here," he said, leading Grant to a spot not far from where the shell of the deuce and a half still smoldered.

Balancing his weight on the balls of his feet, Grant crouched down to study the tire marks and noticed the reddish-brown hue of blood drying on the asphalt nearby.

Something glinted in the sun. Shaking fingers gathered the crushed wire ear cuff that Jenna was rarely without. His stomach lurched as his one percent of hope that it had been someone else vaporized. He brushed his thumb over it, and it shimmered in the afternoon sun.

Eric followed Grant's eyes as he assessed the area and quietly confirmed what Grant already knew.

"She was definitely hit. We just don't know how badly. But if it was anywhere close to fatal, they'd have left her here. We have to go on that." Pausing as Grant looked up with doubt etched on his face, Eric ruefully continued. "It was a good call, you know—getting the others clear. There will be three grateful families tonight because of her." Eric rubbed his face wearily. "I would like to think you and I would have had the balls to do the same damn thing."

As Grant stood, Eric put a hand on his shoulder and said, "We'll pull out all the stops to find her. I swear we will."

Stone-faced, Grant nodded numbly, tucked her jewelry in his pocket, and walked away.

Two and a half hours later at Aviano, in a conference room that smelled like stale coffee, the increasingly painful debriefs of the day's debacle soon became repetitive. Nonetheless, they continued late into the night. Finally, only Eric and Grant were left in the conference room. They sat on the same side of the table with a few empty chairs between them. Neither spoke. Stress and exhaustion had caught up to both men. Frustration with the local police not being willing or able to track Santori's men had added to the strain.

Eric was finished professionally; they both knew he'd take the fall for what had happened. It was just a matter of time before the political and military vultures came for him. The military brass always found their scapegoat and pinned as much blame as they could on them for the public flogging. In Grant's mind, Eric was yet another casualty of the operation, and he regretted dragging him into it.

Eric, on the other hand, knowing full well he was royally screwed, had a different take on it. There wasn't much else they could take away from him. He had no regrets about his participation and doubled down on his promise to help find Jenna. Rising from his chair and clearing off the table, he offered to drive Grant over to base lodging.

Grant accepted the offer, although he didn't want to give in to sleep, wary of the dreams and nightmares that, without Jenna beside him, he wouldn't be able to keep at bay.

live to tell

"WHAT THE FUCK DO you mean the Javelins were destroyed?" Luca was incensed at his inept men who had been sent to intercept the cache.

"We brought two crates back," the man with the crutch interjected.

Luca kicked the crutch, sending the man to the floor. "Only because they were in the truck that you didn't blow up." He was frightfully calm, and everyone knew that meant one of them would pay the price for the debacle. "And the U.S. government managed to get the missiles safely to Camp Darby. Idiots—all of you."

He had gotten a different version of the story from each of his men; now it was time to decide which one would be put in the ground. The last-minute information about the actual route of the U.S. transport convoy carrying the weapons had arrived by text message just in time. He almost hadn't acted on it since it contradicted what Grant had told him. There was a minuscule chance that Grant had been misinformed, but the theory that Grant had double-crossed him was becoming more fact than fiction.

When the first reports of the incident had made it to him, Luca had been irate at the loss of the shipment. More so, he was in denial when Luigi insisted that Jenna was involved. She was the reason for Luigi's reliance on his crutch, and Luca considered that his accusation might be payback of sorts. But after seeing the photo that Luigi had texted to him as they made their way back, there was no doubt.

Eight hours later, when his team arrived at the port of Catania on the east coast of Sicily, he barely recognized her. Shining a flashlight on the black-clad figure lying on the deck of his yacht in the dark, Luca's first reaction was one of concern on seeing her condition. Then rage kicked in, howling at him to toss her over the side to satisfy his sense of betrayal. He nudged her foot with his Ferragamo loafer to see if she was even still alive. Assured that she was, he ordered her to be moved to his family's southern estate and placed under guard.

As she was roughly hauled to a waiting van, he braced both hands against the yacht's railing and stared into the dark water of the harbor. At least his men had done something right by bringing back a trophy. His promise to her had been realized.

She would need him.

And she would beg.

Halfway across the world, Luca's supplier slammed the empty shot glass down on the glossy mahogany bar top. After staring at it for over a minute, he hurled it against the wall, momentarily soothed by the stark silence that followed it shattering and falling to the tile floor.

The phone call from Luca hadn't brought the news he had expected—or wanted. What kind of incompetence was he dealing with? To light off an RPG had been rash in and of itself. And to hit the one thing you were supposed to recover?

An RPG. Honestly. In the middle of rural Italy. Jesus. Employing something that heavy-handed had been completely unnecessary and was just someone flexing their muscles needlessly.

He glanced at the watch on his tanned wrist and contemplated his options, desperate to salvage what he could of this FUBAR situation and preserve his own ass.

Jenna's mind fought for clarity as consciousness battled to break through the fog. She hovered in oblivion. One minute sinking back into the void of black and the next fighting through the stupor to revel in the pain that told her she was alive. Eventually, she shook free of the void, eternally grateful to be conscious. Yet when the pain registered fully, she wished for the void again.

Determined to push through it, she tried to open her eyes. Her head throbbed. She moved it back and forth slowly and worked her way down, flexing and moving what she could to see what capabilities remained.

She didn't get too far, and the pain almost dragged her under again as she tried to move her right arm. Flashes of the firefight stabbed into her memory. Recalling her team's vehicle speeding away gave her some comfort that her team had escaped the inferno. Involuntarily smiling at the memory of the deuce and half full of weapons exploding brought a whole new bout of discomfort.

She gingerly licked her cracked lips and tasted fresh blood. Moving her legs slowly, she was relieved to feel only some stiffness. Her right knee was a bit sore, but she'd take that any day. Her combat boots were missing, her pants dirty and torn but intact, and at some point someone had removed her tactical blouse, leaving her in only a short-sleeved black undershirt. A roughly applied bandage covered her upper arm, which throbbed incessantly.

Jenna stayed mostly still while trying to determine where she was, moving only her eyes at first. If anyone was watching, she wasn't eager to attract their attention just yet.

If dungeons still existed, she'd found one. The walls and the floor were rough stone and cold. A tiny slit of a window about twelve to fifteen feet up on the wall was the only source of light. It appeared to be either dusk or dawn. She had no concept of how long she'd been there. Dizziness washed over her when she raised her head. She closed her eyes, gradually let her head fall back to the stone floor, and welcomed the slide back down the dark tunnel into the void.

Unsure of how long she'd been out, Jenna managed to push herself to a sitting position against the wall. Approaching footsteps sounded outside the door. A key turned in the lock, and the door opened just enough for a small hand to set a tray inside the door and then quickly disappear. The door closed again, and the snick of the lock echoed in her dungeon.

Devoid of strength, she crawled over to the tray and sighed with relief to find a bowl of warm, plain pasta and a plastic bottle of water. Food meant someone wanted her alive. She forced herself to eat slowly and take small sips of the water.

For hours Jenna stayed propped against the wall near the door, hoping to catch a glimpse of the person to whom the hand belonged. The hand had appeared petite; if it was a woman, perhaps there was a chance she could play to her sympathies.

With no measure of time other than the window, the hours were filled by dozing off and on. When she was awake, she replayed her trips around Italy with Grant, concentrating on every detail possible. As she drifted back into sleep, she imagined being curled up against him, snug and safe in his arms.

38

calling all angels

L ESS THAN TWENTY-FOUR HOURS after they had returned to Aviano, Grant paced in Eric's office with his third cup of black coffee as Eric recounted his story to some faceless bureaucrat for the umpteenth time. Eric loosely held the phone to his ear with one hand and rested his forehead on his thumb and forefinger. The fingers massaged his raging headache as he spoke. His tone was an odd mix of impatience and boredom. Finally, having had enough of yet another ass-chewing, Eric disconnected the call, sighing as he leaned back in his chair.

Grant walked over to the opposite side of the desk and leaned on it with both hands. "I'm heading back to the villa," he announced.

Eric rubbed his eyes with the heels of his hands as he returned to an upright position.

"You sure that's smart?" Eric sighed again, then continued. "For a lot of reasons, my friend. Not sure you're in a great place to deal with that right now."

"Are you telling me I can't leave base? Unless you have authority to keep me here—"

Eric planted his feet on the floor and stood, placing his hands on the desk to match Grant's stance.

"Hey, let's try to remember that I'm on your side," Eric said bluntly. "You wanna go? Go. I don't know what you think that will accomplish, but hey, be my guest."

Grant sank into a chair and ran his hands through his hair and down his face, scratching at the stubble of the last two days. "I didn't mean to—"

Eric cut him off. "Yes, you did, but it's fine. I get where you're at right now. Just don't lose sight of the fact that I'm not the enemy. Shit, in a month or so, I may be knocking on your door needing a place to stay after my court-martial." He gave a self-deprecating laugh as he sat back down.

"Luca will jump at the chance to get to me now. He has to know I double-crossed him," Grant started. "If I can draw him out, I can find out where he's got Jenna. Then kill him."

"To be honest, Grant, we don't even know for sure that he has her. But if he does, you're assuming he's more interested in you than her," Eric reminded him.

"Yeah, he has her. Of that, I am certain." With a piercing stare, Grant stood up and walked to the door. "I'll be in touch."

As Grant drove southwest to Porto Arezzo, he relived the last several months, occasionally allowing a half-smile to drift up from the depths when he remembered certain things she'd done or said. The sun sitting low on the horizon brought on a deep funk, and he rolled the window down just to feel the air on his face. He should have heeded Eric's warning.

On one hand, getting back to the villa would be a comfort. Just to be alone. And in their space. On the other hand, he wanted to avoid it like the plague. He didn't count on getting much sleep there tonight but kept driving anyway. It was, in a way, self-flagellation dovetailed neatly with a way to revert to being a lone operator.

Five-plus hours after leaving Aviano, he pulled up outside their villa. The engine pinged and popped while he stared at the coral door. What he wouldn't do to turn back time and have her greet him at the door in her pink paisley pajama pants and bare feet.

Slipping the key into the lock, he pushed the door open. The light in the living area was on, and his psyche tried to convince him she had left it on for him. Probably the cleaning crew, he figured. It was then that he heard a noise upstairs.

His Glock led the way up the stairs. A light from the pink bedroom spilled out of the doorway. As he started down the hall to her room, he heard a sniff and a muffled sob. He increased his pace and rounded the doorway, gun out in front of him but pointed downward, praying to God she'd be standing there.

A pudgy woman with dyed auburn-brown hair pulled into a frizzy loose bun was bent over the drawers, opening each one as she sobbed. Finding each one empty, the woman turned to close a suitcase that was splayed open on the pink-quilted bed. Catherine jumped when she noticed Grant standing in the doorway. Tears streamed down her face, tracing the wrinkles like rain on a windowpane.

Fear paralyzed Grant's movements, but his chest pounded and heaved with each forced inhalation. All kinds of possibilities swirled in his head.

Catherine. Here at the villa to pack Jenna's things.

It seemed so final. Had Jenna's body been found? Catherine knew about their relationship. Had she traveled all the way across Europe to tell him in person?

Catherine pushed his gun to the side, and he mechanically slid it back into its holster just before she wrapped her arms around him sobbing. Grant was still processing the implications of her being at the villa while he cautiously returned the hug. Once her tears abated, he set her away from him.

"Catherine, what are you doing here?" He couldn't bring himself to say the words. "Is she—" His knees almost buckled as he asked the question, deathly afraid of her response.

"I should ask you the same thing. Why are you here, sneaking up on me like that?" Catherine wiped her eyes and went into the small bathroom to blow her nose. "Oh, Grant. This is the hardest thing I think I've ever done. I'm sorry, I don't mean to be insensitive. I know you two were involv—had become close." Another wipe of her nose. "How are you doing?"

"Damn it, Catherine, answer me," he demanded quietly, hoping she wasn't stalling. "Is Jenna...dead?"

"What? Oh. God, no. Why would you think that? I don't know any more than you do. She was wounded and then taken hostage. I guess that's what we're considering it, although there's been no contact and no ransom demand."

Catherine's words had him slumping against the door frame in relief, even though he knew the harsh reality of the situation.

"Luca won't ransom her. He wants her to himself. Has since day one. He'll kill her before letting her go."

Catherine stared at him in disbelief. "I didn't know. I swear. I didn't know Luca was that depraved, or I would never have assigned her." A single tear teetered then fell down her cheek.

"I know," Grant said. "But she'd be pissed if you hadn't." He couldn't help but take another look at the bed where he'd slept beside her almost every night for the last several weeks. His words sounded harsher than he intended as his hand indicated the dresser drawers. "There's nothing left here. We took everything to Aviano. Eric has her things. When you're ready, come downstairs. We need to talk."

Light filtering through the tiny window told her she had slept. Jenna rolled her stiff neck, wondering when housekeeping would arrive and if breakfast would be served before or after her massage. Grant would be rolling his eyes at her poor sense of humor, but it was all she had to cling to for the moment. She closed her eyes and tried to conjure an image of his face.

A fever had crept in while she slept. The skin on her face felt tight and flushed, and the inside of her mouth and throat were hot. She gingerly touched the bandaged area; it was swollen and hot, even through the dressing. She knew she'd been shot but had no idea if the bullet had passed through. If not, had it been removed or just bandaged up? Prodding the wound wasn't an option. Fevers for someone in her predicament could be fatal if medical attention wasn't swift.

Footsteps approaching roused her—whether from sleep or unconsciousness, she didn't know. She had no concept of how much time had passed, which only added to her disorientation. The blue-gray light in the window told her evening was approaching, and she hoped for another tray to be delivered. Two people this time? She scooted farther away from the door as the key scraped in the lock. The door opened, and a figure she instantly recognized filled the frame.

Luca entered her dungeon-like cell, followed by a young boy who was maybe twelve years old. In French, Luca commanded him to set the tray down and leave. The brown-haired boy cast her a look with downcast eyes and left.

It was then that her fear became reality. She was Luca's captive. That would have been bad enough on its own; now it was compounded by being isolated and injured.

Luca crouched down in front of her, elbows on his knees. He reached out and touched her cheek causing her to flinch. The cloying odor of his cigarettes overpowered what little air was present.

"Ah, still pulling away from me, Jenna?" His silky tone only added to her apprehension. "I warned you that you would soon require my assistance, didn't I? To say I was surprised to find you a part of all this nasty business would be an understatement. You would have a great career in your Hollywood. I would hate for my mother—God rest her soul—to know you were playing her too."

Jenna's head snapped up as he mentioned his mother in that way. "Lourdes. Is she…she didn't die, did she? And my friendship with her wasn't part of this."

There was really no need to defend her relationship with Lourdes, any more than there was any sense denying her role at this point.

Luca rocked back to study her reaction. "Not dead yet, but any day now, I'm sure. Now let's talk about you. And your husband." A single black eyebrow arched. "He was not really your husband, was he?"

Jenna said nothing. Without warning, he backhanded her, causing her head to snap back against the wall. She felt blood run from the corner of her mouth and involuntarily licked the area. Eyeing her tongue, Luca leaned into her. With an iron grip on her chin, he licked the same spot while his other hand dropped to her breast. With his face so close to hers, it would be incredibly satisfying to give in to the nausea that roiled in her stomach, but Jenna held back the urge to retaliate.

For now.

"I would have given you the world, my dear Jenna. But you ignored me and let a man you merely work with fuck you just for your job." She inwardly cringed at the crass description of her relationship with Grant. Continuing to circle his thumb in the blood on her chin, Luca leered as he asked, "You know he's dead, yes?"

Ice flooded her veins. She stared into his hard eyes and tried to breathe.

"No," she managed. "You're lying."

He gripped her chin again, perversely delighted by her glazed expression as she searched his face for the truth.

"Am I? You should know that I'm the one who killed him," Luca sneered. "For you. For us. Promise me your loyalty, and you can leave all this behind." His eyes circled the barren cell.

"I refuse to believe anything you say." The quiver in her weak voice belied the confidence in her words.

"Are those tears for him? Are you relieved or sad? If you guess the words he said while he bled out, you win the prize." Luca's eyes glinted with maliciousness.

"You're demented."

"And I'm in charge." His eyebrow rose again. "So? Aren't you going to guess? It was very touching."

"What's the prize? If it's you, it's a hard pass."

He backhanded her again.

"Remember, your life is in my hands. The prize is your freedom."

Jenna stalled, doing her best to evaluate her options for how to satisfy this madman yet distracted by the idea that Grant was gone.

"I have a fever, Luca. I'm not thinking clearly right now."

She choked back the tears that would do nothing but complicate her situation.

"Tomorrow." With that single word, he shook her chin once firmly. "That's all the time you have." He stood, towering over her. "If you haven't chosen sides by then—"

The warning hung in the air, dissipating with his laughter as the door slammed shut.

Jenna sat motionless in crushing disbelief. Her heart couldn't process the idea that Grant was dead. The more she thought about it, there was no way that a second-rate thug like Luca could kill a man like Grant.

Despite telling herself to ignore Luca's taunts, she couldn't eat. Ignoring the food on the tray, she took a sip of the water, letting the liquid soothe her burning throat. Her belief in God had wavered over the past two decades, but, leaning her head back against the wall, she prayed.

two princes

T HE PATIO CALLED TO Grant as he leaned against the kitchen counter and sipped his coffee. He was in a stare-down with Jenna's chair that sat innocently abandoned in the morning sunlight. Lost in thought, he barely registered his phone ringing.

"I'm en route to Porto Arezzo. We need to talk face to face. Give me the address." Eric's anxiousness was evident.

"And a fine good morning to you too." Sarcasm gave way to curiosity. "Talk to me."

"Not on this line. That's what face to face means."

He gave Eric the address and tried one more time for information, but Eric wouldn't talk.

"I'm just under an hour out. Be there." With that, Eric disconnected.

Grant was just out of the shower after his run when Eric arrived. He smiled for the first time in days when he heard Catherine introduce herself. Eric wouldn't know what hit him.

"It's about damn time, Lawton. What part of 'be there' did you not understand? Glad this is such a priority," Eric looked at his watch with mock irritation as Grant appeared downstairs.

"Maybe you could use a run too. Does wonders for shitty attitudes," Grant shot back.

"Whatever." Eric's tone turned serious. "Just sit down. We need to compare some notes. Things are not adding up." He indicated

Catherine with a not-so-subtle tip of his head in her direction. "Not to be rude, but are we good to talk openly?"

Grant chuckled as he grabbed three bottles of water and passed them around.

"Catherine pretty much runs the Salvo Agency. There's not much you could say that she doesn't already know or that I wouldn't relay to her. Jenna and I trust her implicitly. Yes, we're more than good."

Catherine smothered a smile at the compliment.

Eric pulled out a small notebook and laid it on the table in front of the couch as he paged through it, outlining a sequence of phone calls, calling particular attention to the times and participants.

"Following?" he asked, looking up at them.

They both nodded, and he continued, "With this timeline of events, let's focus on what information was discussed by whom and when. Your guy, this Commander Dugan, calls the number two general up my chain at about ten o'clock in the morning the day after the clusterfuck. Sorry, Catherine," he said, clearing his throat. "Keep in mind this is the first call from him since the operation went down.

"If you recall, the exact details that I provided to our higher-ups before we left Aviano and headed to Vicenza that day involved two convoys—one decoy with a minimal load of missiles and one non-decoy carrying the Javelins and the majority of the missiles, right?"

Grant nodded, interested to see where this was going.

"And as you were loading the trucks in Vicenza, you switched that up at the last minute, correct?" Eric asked.

Grant nodded again, his eyes narrowing in concentration.

"You put the missiles on what was originally the decoy truck instead of on the truck that should have been secure. Why did you split the shipment?" Eric inquired, although he knew the answer from their debriefs.

"Over the years, I've learned to listen to the voice in my head. That's all it was," Grant confirmed.

"So, you were willing for Santori to get all the missiles in the event he went for the decoy." Eric posed his question as a statement.

"What I wasn't willing to do was let him have both the Javelins and the missiles. Without one, the other would be useless—at least, for a time. He'd only get one or the other, regardless. That was my thinking at the time."

Eric took a drink of water and leaned forward. "Did you get anyone's approval? And who did you tell that you had made the switch?"

"When?" Grant asked. "Before we pulled out of Vicenza? I didn't tell or ask anyone then. I guess I mentioned it to Henderson, and I suppose the load team knew because they moved the munitions twice." Grant paused. "After we got back to base, it was in the debrief. And since the missiles were transferred to the armory at Camp Darby, there will be chain-of-custody paperwork filed eventually."

"I'd bet my life that Henderson is trustworthy," Eric brushed that reference aside. "But get this...the full report—including the record of our debrief—wasn't released up the chain of command until three o'clock that next afternoon. A full five hours before that, guess what your Commander Dugan told General Number Two during their ten o'clock phone call?" Eric took another swig of water for emphasis. "Dugan somehow knew the missiles weren't in the convoy that Santori attacked and was up in the general's face about why no one at his level approved that. Yesterday, after you left, General Number Two called me and was all up my ass about who approved that switch."

Eric sat back, crunching the plastic water bottle as he let the implication sink in. "Do you see the problem in that timeline?" he asked. "There's only one way he knew what weaponry was, or wasn't, in each convoy."

Grant steepled his fingers against his forehead and was quiet as the puzzle pieces fell into place. "Luca."

"Dugan bought a two-million-dollar house in Bermuda last month and plans to put his papers in to retire," Catherine mused out loud. "I always wondered how he managed that financially. I mean, I know what his pay is. Furthermore, there's been no annual bonus or large deposits in his accounts that I know of." She cut off Eric's questioning look with a raised palm. "Yes, I would know, and no, I won't tell you how."

"Dugan is Luca's fucking supplier." Grant said quietly before looking up at the other two. "Why send us here in the first place? Why authorize the mission?"

Catherine responded, taking the sobering revelation a step further. "Probably so he could orchestrate getting Santori out of his way. Think about it. With Santori no longer in the picture, Dugan can swoop in and close the deal without having to split the money with the Santoris. Then, with the new contact, he can expand his business without a middleman. Jenna's intel-gathering mission changed when you were assigned." She snapped her fingers. "Remember? He pulled you off that other mission right when you got too close. Same weapons were involved. I bet he was the supplier on that one too."

"Then why send me here? To get Santori to eliminate me? That's a big risk he took," Grant said.

"He didn't assign you. I did," Catherine said. "And he was pissed at first, but I didn't think too much about it at the time. Between your history with him and his history with Jenna, it wasn't out of character."

"What history with Jenna?"

Catherine rolled her eyes. "He asked her out several times—persistent asshole that he is. It got ugly. Awkwardly so. He tried to get physical. I emphasize 'tried.' She doesn't think anyone knows."

Grant's eyes hardened and his jaw tensed.

"I get the sense you know pretty much everything that goes on there," Eric said.

She sighed. "Apparently not everything. I certainly didn't see this coming."

"So," Eric continued. "With Lawton on the mission, Dugan would have had to pivot. By putting Grant in Santori's circle, was he trying to take them both out at the same time? I guess he didn't care who got who as long as they were both eliminated. He was playing both sides—all the while counting on being the last one standing with both the weapons and the cash."

Grant added to his comments. "And that's how Santori knew which route to target. Dugan knew the planned routes. To your point, afterward, the only way Dugan could have known that the missiles weren't on the truck that Santori actually ended up with is by Luca telling him. There was no official communication or report that would have given him that intel so quickly."

Shaking her head in disgust, Catherine scoffed. "I've never trusted that fucking asshole."

Surprised by her directness, Eric burst out laughing. "I knew I liked you."

Catherine gave him an amused smile.

Grant brought the conversation back in focus. "What's our next move? Other than to find Jenna. And how much do you think Luca has figured out?"

They continued to surmise and speculate until it approached lunchtime, and with no groceries in the villa, Grant was outlining their food options when a knock at the door sounded. With a hand signal, Grant shooed them both upstairs and out of sight. He opened the door a crack to find Paetta standing there. The sense of déjà vu was all too real.

"Can Jenna come visit now? Mamma is very sick and wants to see her," Paetta explained.

Grant hadn't planned for this, and he wondered just how much the family knew.

"She's not here at the moment," Grant told Paetta.

"Then I am to bring you. Mama said so. She has a gift for your wife." The young woman's voice broke as she played with her hands nervously. "The doctor thinks Mama will be gone by morning."

With a nod of his head, he told Paetta to expect him in fifteen minutes and closed the door. Catherine and Eric appeared on the stairs like children on Christmas morning. Grant filled them in before Eric spoke.

"Smells like an ambush to me. I'm a pretty solid wingman, you know."

Grant held up one finger. "If it is an ambush, I'm that much closer to getting to Jenna." A second finger joined the first. "And Jenna would never forgive me if I shunned Lourdes's request. She loves that old lady. Thanks for the offer. If I'm not back in thirty minutes, come on over with whatever friends you find in my gear bag upstairs." He pointed at the Santoris' home across the courtyard. "It's that villa over there."

Eric looked out the patio door, taking in the courtyard, and whistled under his breath, "Damn, you guys hiring? Three-bedroom place on the Mediterranean, pool, bocce, rich folks...what else you got?" He whacked Grant in his upper arm with the back of his hand and shook his head.

Catherine observed the exchange, still smiling as Grant headed out to comply with Lourdes's summons.

it was a very good year

T HE GLASS DOOR OF the Santoris' villa opened at the exact moment he raised his hand to knock. The aloof housemaid ushered him in and escorted him to the first-floor library where a pallid Lourdes lay in a hospital bed. Two uncomfortable-looking chairs were lined up to the side of her bed. Leave it to Lourdes to dissuade anyone from staying too long. Lourdes's eyes fluttered open as he walked over and gently took her frail hand in both of his.

"Ah, your mother did well with you, son."

"Thank you, signora. And thank you for being such a light in Jenna's life while we were here."

Lourdes coughed a bit then responded in a shaky voice, "She is a dear friend. Is she out shopping without me?" Lourdes stared at Grant with a somewhat intense expression. He opened his mouth to respond but was interrupted. "Let me give you a hug for you to pass along to her. Come closer now."

Grant leaned in closer to her, too interested in what she wanted to tell him to care about the smell of sickness. Lourdes squeezed his hands.

"Cameras." A hoarse chuckle escaped. "I know all of it. Jenna lives but needs you," she whispered with great effort. "Promise me you'll get her to safety."

Papery hands patted his cheek. Lourdes smiled through teary eyes at the relief that showed on his face.

As he straightened, in a steadier voice, she said, "Thank you for coming to get the things I want Jenna to have. I love her like a daughter, but I am afraid I will not see her again. I want her to have the paintings that she did for me."

Lourdes stared intently at Grant. "Be sure to read the sweet note she tucked into the back of the flower painting. I want her to hang both on the wall of that farmhouse she wants." The old woman fell back on her pillow. Shaky hands adjusted the blanket. "Now go, son. Go find Jenna and give her my gift. A wedding gift, perhaps?" She patted his arm knowingly. "Most of all, give her my love."

A multitude of questions swirled in his head. But remembering her warning about the cameras and admiring her courage, he didn't dare ask any of them.

"I'm old and tired, and I need to sleep. Farewell, son, and may God be with you both." Eyes that brimmed with tears closed, and Lourdes released his hand.

He had been dismissed.

Two gifts wrapped in brown paper sat on a table by the door, and he picked them up. Turning to look at her once more, Grant now appreciated what Jenna had seen in her.

The entire walk back to his villa, he wanted nothing more than to rip the paper off and find out what Lourdes had been trying to convey to him. He took the stairs two at a time. Eric jumped to his feet when the door burst open and watched curiously as Grant crossed the room to the couch.

"Well?" Eric prodded.

Grant's hands stilled on the package that he was about to rip open. Over his shoulder, he looked at Catherine and then Eric.

"Lourdes knows everything. Knew damn well Jenna wasn't here and knows we're not who we said we were." His hands trembled. "But lying there in a hospice bed surrounded by cameras, she still cared enough to find a way to save her. She said Jenna is alive but in trouble."

Catherine sank slowly into a chair, her eyes welling with emotion at the news. Tamping down his own reaction as the news sank in, Grant turned back to the package, anxiously tearing it open.

"Isn't—I mean, wasn't—that for Jenna?" Eric asked.

"The whole gift thing was a ruse. She all but ordered me to read the note Jenna wrote to her that's tucked in the back of the flower picture. It must tell us—"

He pushed the paper off the first picture and lifted it up. It took his breath away, and he sat heavily on the couch. The painting captured a hazy image of Lourdes in front of castle ruins along a street flooded with colorful flowers. It was not professional or flawless, but it was perfectly Jenna. Reflecting on their excursions around Italy, the painting was everything he imagined he would see through her eyes. He set it down almost reverently and picked up the other one. The torn wrapping revealed a painting of vibrant flowers cascading from planters on Lourdes's patio.

He flipped the painting over and gently removed a bundle of papers that had been tucked inside the frame's support. One page appeared to be the actual note Jenna had written to Lourdes. The additional papers were folded together in quarters.

Setting the painting gently on the floor to lean against the couch, he cleared the table in front of him. Eric moved two chairs to the opposite side of the table and motioned for Catherine to take one.

Grant smoothed out the creases and recognized a photocopy of a map of Sicily on the first sheet of paper. In the southeastern part of the island, a shaky circle drawn in red ink stood out against the black and white of the photocopy. A black circle farther north was labeled "estate." The red circle could only be Jenna's location.

Grant handed the map to Eric, then studied the next page, which appeared to be an enlargement of the red circle from the other map. It was an aerial diagram of a cluster of buildings with circles drawn in the same manner as the map—a black circle labeled "main house" with another shaky red circle just below it.

The third and last piece of paper was a poor photocopy of an already grainy photo of a man's face. He was an older man, probably in his upper sixties, with thin wisps of white hair and crystal-clear blue eyes that seemed vaguely familiar. Underneath the picture, the same shaky handwriting labeled him "Antonio." The familiarity of the eyes clicked when he read the next line. "Stefano and Paetta's father. He manages the family farm where Jenna is held. He will help you. Do not allow him to be harmed."

Grant expelled the breath he had been holding and handed the photo to Catherine as he slumped back against the couch cushions. The extraordinary risks Lourdes had taken to ensure that Jenna would be found astounded him. He ran a hand through his hair.

"I'm going to get her. Are you in, Eric?"

"Absolutely," Eric answered without hesitation. "But help me out here...who are Stefano and Paetta?"

Leaning forward to pick up the map again, Grant explained the family tree. "Stefano and Paetta are twins, and the youngest of Lourdes's children. Paetta was the one at the door earlier. I wonder if the girl knows Matteo Santori isn't her father. Antonio must be Lourdes's lover."

"Sheesh, that rivals a daytime soap opera," Eric said and shook his head. "I guess if Luca was your kid, you might seriously consider an alternate donor for the next ones."

"No shit," Grant acknowledged. "Remarkable woman. She's essentially giving us permission to kill her son to save Jenna."

Quiet up until now, Catherine spoke in a hushed tone. "A decision no mother would make lightly. I can't even imagine. Either she loves Jenna more than Luca or she understands the monster that her son is. Either way, my heart bleeds for her tonight."

"My guess is it's both," Grant said. "Let's figure out dinner and get ready for a long night of planning."

He stood up from the couch and stretched, silently sending a prayer up for Lourdes and simultaneously making a promise to Jenna through the universe. "Hang on, love. I'm coming for you, I swear."

policy of truth

ANGER SMOTHERED HIS EVERY thought. Joe Dugan could feel the walls closing in on him. Being both irate and anxious had him contemplating things he'd never imagined he would.

With the majority of the Javelins incinerated and the entire cache of missiles now in the custody of the U.S. military, it wouldn't take long for the containers' origins to be uncovered. He needed to tread very carefully from here on out.

There were still strings he could pull.

Luca would need to be eliminated. He was the least of Dugan's concerns. It was the two Salvo agents who worried him, one more than the other. Only a limited number of options remained in order for Bermuda to become a reality. But he was prepared to silence all involved to make it happen.

The phone call Luca had been dreading, and therefore avoiding, came early that morning. His supplier was antsy, insisting that Jenna be permanently silenced, which interfered greatly with his plans for her. Once he hung up the phone, Luca opened a bottle of grappa and poured a healthy amount into a crystal glass. The risks to his own well-being would be considerable if he crossed his supplier.

He raised the glass to his lips while he thought.

It seemed a bit rash and wasteful to simply abandon the elaborate plans for her that had been in his head for months.

He drank some more. And the more he thought about it, the more he convinced himself that he knew exactly who to call so that he could still play the game and win.

never surrender

JENNA KNEW SHE WAS fading. There were moments during which she was very aware that she might not have more than a few hours left on this earth. Then there were moments of delirium where she was swimming at the beach with her kids and Evan again. When she was lucid, she hoped she would at least die before Luca returned. That would be the best alternative to whatever he had planned for her.

Her mind registered the light footsteps outside her door and the key in the lock. Too weak to make an aggressive move, it was all she could do to grab the small wrist that shoved the tray in her direction.

A frightened boy's face filled her vision.

"Evan?" she whispered.

The boy tried to loosen her grip as she tried to make him understand that she needed help. She weakly indicated her injured arm where angry, red streaks ran from underneath the filthy bandage. Her fever had spiked in the last hour, making it difficult to come up with the Italian word for doctor. The boy finally pulled free, and her hand fell limply to the cold floor. She imagined a light touch on her forehead. Then the door slammed, and the footsteps disappeared.

Realizing her last hope had vanished, Jenna prayed desperately. She tried to picture her kids in her mind, wishing she could hold them one more time. This was not how she'd imagined she'd die. There were still things that she wanted to do. Places she wanted to go.

Her fevered mind played games, taunting her with the sound of the door opening again and a light in her face. Panic filled her at the thought of dying, subsiding only when the void once again welcomed her with open arms.

The young boy who had entered Jenna's cell was more than terrified. Even at his young age, he knew the woman was close to death. He had seen plenty of it to know. Being of an impressionable age, he worried about what God would do to him if he didn't try to help. He hated the big man who lived here occasionally and gave the orders. The boy had endured more than he should at his young age and knew that, even though the big man had paid money for him, this place was better than the squalid compound where he'd been before. The young boy knew exactly who would help.

Old Antonio was reading a book in his chair on the porch, as was his practice every evening before dinner. The older man initially laughed at the boy's jumbled words, spoken in French mixed with an occasional Italian word, until he realized the gravity of the boy's story. It was about a prisoner, her condition, and the desperate look in her bloodshot eyes.

Antonio despised the man who gave the orders around the farm as well, but he stayed on out of a misguided sense of loyalty to the family who had taken him in sixty years ago, orphaned after a fire claimed the rest of his family. He stayed for the children like Philippe. But mostly, he stayed to be as close as possible to the love of his life.

Lourdes Santori had never been his to claim publicly. What began as a summer romance when they were in their mid-twenties had, by their early thirties, turned into a discrete affair. Lately, her failing health had limited their conversations, and it pained him to know he might never again be able to tell her how much he loved her.

The cryptic message from her had arrived the day prior, passed to him through one of the housemaids. The note advising him that Luca held a prisoner had also included a photo of a woman with a genuine smile and bright, intelligent green eyes.

Antonio had always marveled at Lourdes's strength. It was one of the many things that had attracted him to her all those years ago. She had always harbored a healthy respect for the evil that was Luca but typically avoided confronting or angering him. The rumors of Luca's depravity disgusted Antonio as much as they terrified Lourdes. The fact that Lourdes was willing to cross Luca to help this female prisoner implied the woman was someone very dear to her.

An increase in activity and personnel at the farm had confirmed Lourdes's warning, but it wasn't until the moment that a frantic Philippe tugged on his arm that Antonio knew where the woman was being held. His animosity toward Luca deepened upon learning that the woman was in dire need of medical help.

Having loved Lourdes for over forty years, Antonio rarely questioned what she asked of him. But this. This development was a difficult situation. If he attempted to get medical care for the woman and Luca found out, they, including young Philippe, risked being swiftly killed in a fit of Luca's legendary rage. His only alternative was to confront Luca with a lie about how he had learned of the woman and present it in such a way that Luca could be the hero for saving her. Saying a short prayer, he set his dog-eared book on the table and rose on creaking knees to find Luca.

Either despite or because of his age, the old man was persistent, and as he talked, Luca's twisted mind recognized he had been gifted an opportunity. Assuring old Antonio that medical care would be arranged, he summoned two of his security guards.

Outside the door of Jenna's cell, Luca lit the lantern that one of the guards carried. The flicker of light widened as the door opened to illuminate a form slumped against the wall. One of the guards impulsively stepped forward to help her, but Luca extended his arm blocking the guard's forward motion while he fished for his phone with the other hand.

Jenna's complexion was ghostly pale despite the fever that coursed through her. It was perfect; he couldn't have planned it any better. The image of her like this would serve multiple purposes. Unconscious and slouched over just so, her bandaged arm was visible in all its infected glory. Impatiently, he kicked the untouched food tray out of the way, adjusted the lantern to better illustrate his story, and snapped several photos.

After checking the quality of the pictures on his phone, he motioned for the two guards to collect her limp form. The lantern cast dizzying shadows in the narrow corridor while the two guards trailed behind him, suspending Jenna between them.

these arms of mine

G RANT, ERIC, AND CATHERINE spent the entire evening reviewing the maps Lourdes had provided. They were wary of sharing the information with anyone outside their defined circle of trust, and as such, the coordination and planning was more time-consuming.

Eric had just dialed a contact at Aviano, and Catherine was reviewing the Salvo ops schedule to see if any agents were close enough to be of assistance when Grant's burner phone from Luca dinged. It was late enough for the unexpected notification on that particular phone to be concerning, and they all shared a questioning look.

Grant approached the phone as if it might strike from its coiled and rattling position on the kitchen counter. With his back to the room and elbows on the counter, he unlocked the screen and tapped the notification for the new text messages. Two images appeared, and he flipped the phone sideways to enlarge each one.

His heart twisted as he recognized Jenna asleep on a pillow in a large, plush bed with her hand resting intimately on a bare-chested Luca. The second, much darker picture of a pale form slumped on the ground didn't register until he read the sordid text underneath it.

Just wanted you to know I was her last fuck.
I enjoyed her, and she begged for more. But
this is the price of double-crossing your employer.

Grant felt like he'd been punched. The air in his lungs was sucked from his body, and he dropped the phone on the counter as if it was on fire. He couldn't form words and could hardly breathe. His chin fell to his heaving chest. His hand clawed at the phone in the hope of crushing the images now seared in his mind. A raspy voice he hardly recognized as his own whispered "no" over and over.

Eric's hand gripped his shoulder then pried the phone from Grant's clutch.

"Jesus Christ," Eric muttered, reluctantly handing the phone to Catherine, who stood behind them, one hand covering her mouth in apprehension.

Cradling the phone in her palm, Catherine scrolled. Then, as she studied the second photo, she stumbled to a chair and dropped into it, devastated by the photo of a seemingly lifeless Jenna lying crumpled on a wet stone floor.

"Luca dies tonight," Grant said stonily to no one in particular.

His eyes were unfocused as he held his hand out for the phone that Catherine studied. Eric intercepted the phone before Grant could take it from her.

"Don't do this to yourself, Grant," Eric said. "We need to get this analyzed, and you are in no condition to handle this right now."

"What the fuck is that supposed to mean? My condition beats the hell out of hers." Even as he lashed out, on some level, he recognized the truth in Eric's words. "And you have no idea what I'm able to handle or what I'm capable of doing."

Eric calmly stared Grant down. "Not too long ago, you told me you weren't interested in a pissing contest. I'm not either. While I don't doubt that there's not much you can't or won't do, you need some distance on this. You can't possibly be objective right now."

"Objective? Are you fucking kidding me?" Grant spat the words. "How in the fucking hell can I be objective about what I just saw?" His breaking point was closer than he wanted to acknowledge. "Luca dies tonight. By my hands, and my hands only."

He stalked up the stairs, leaving Eric and Catherine staring after him, afraid of what his next move would be.

The distinct sounds of weapons being checked and loaded reverberated down the stairs before Grant appeared dressed in tactical gear with a black backpack slung on his left shoulder. His gear bag swung in his left hand while he searched for his keys on the counter where Eric now stood. Registering the quiet in the room, he stopped and glared at Eric.

"Give me my fucking keys," Grant demanded.

Eric shook his head. "Can't. You haven't thought anything through."

The years Eric had spent in flying squadrons and command jobs had provided entirely too much experience dealing with squadron mates, subordinates, and friends who, while deployed, saw their personal lives fall apart thousands of miles away. Poor judgment and rash actions often followed—neither of which contributed to positive outcomes. But tonight, the stakes were that much higher.

"Get out of my way," Grant growled as he stepped in front of Eric, who stood a good three inches taller.

When Eric calmly shook his head in refusal, Grant dropped his gear and took a swing in one fluid move. The shovel hook he threw at Eric was powered by fresh yet raw anguish layered on top of years of bottled pain and guilt and honed through a lifetime of operating to survive. It connected solidly.

Eric was prepared for the aggression and, frankly, had invited it. Although he had never voluntarily been anyone's punching bag, his willingness to take the blow as Grant's impromptu therapist was borne of understanding—both of the need to transfer the pain and the release that physical altercation afforded.

Grant took another swing. The glancing blow caught Eric on the jaw, but the power and resolve behind it had weakened. The halfhearted swing was truncated by Eric grabbing Grant's wrist. Grant tried unconvincingly to pull away. Eric instead pulled him closer and wrapped his other arm around Grant's upper shoulders.

When the pain ebbed, Grant stepped away and allowed Catherine to guide him to the couch. He leaned back on the cushions with his eyes squeezed shut, trying like hell to avoid spiraling into the abyss that was yawning in front of him. All he had to do was let it wash over him and drag him into the same unfeeling vacuum into which he'd fallen after Paul's murder. The pain wouldn't find him there.

The villa was quiet, aside from the sound of Eric wetting a towel to wipe the blood from his mouth and the sound of water being poured into glasses.

Eric set a glass of water down in front of Grant and placed a chair opposite the couch, sucking in a quick breath as his ribs protested the sitting position.

"Hey, drink the water," came the muffled instruction from Eric who held a towel to his face.

The sound dragged Grant back from the edge. Not moving or opening his eyes, Grant managed to corral his thoughts into words.

"So, what's next, Colonel?"

"You drink the damn water," Eric repeated. "Then we'll talk strategy."

A reluctant Grant capitulated, expending just enough effort to take the glass and empty it. A second full glass replaced it on the table. Grant glared at Eric.

Removing the towel from the corner of his mouth, Eric said, "Look, think about it. If we leave now, it'll be daylight by the time we get to Sicily. Not great for the element of surprise. Also not optimal would be insufficient manpower and firepower."

Holding up a hand in anticipation as Grant's eyes opened, he went on.

"I respect what you can do on your own, but you can do even better with a wee bit of support." He held Grant's stare. "He's yours. No one is going to argue that point." Eric's posture and tone relaxed a bit. "And no one's arguing that Luca needs to pay, but we have to do this wisely. It's late and has turned into a really shitty night. The best option would be for us all to get as much sleep as we can tonight and hit this hard in the morning. That's figuratively speaking, asshole. Don't fucking swing at me again."

Still fighting the pull of the downward spiral, Grant stared at Eric, finally giving a nod of acquiescence. He reached for the second glass of water.

The computer screen illuminated the creases and stress etched on Catherine's face as she typed, paused, and typed again. She looked up when she sensed Eric and Grant looking at her.

"I forwarded Luca's text message to one of Salvo's best IT techs," she said. "Carl's starting to analyze the photos. We need those pictures to talk to us so we can confirm a few things before we swallow Luca's message hook, line, and sinker."

Grant didn't nod, but his eyes showed acceptance of her comment. He sipped the water, looking again at Eric and the embarrassingly minor damage he had done as a result of his inability to control the helplessness and hopelessness. There was no animosity on Eric's face and no apology in Grant's. It was simply done and in the past.

Eric set an alarm on his phone, showed it to Grant, and flicked his head in the direction of the stairs, still holding the damp cloth to his face. Grant picked up the empty glass, walked into the kitchen, and placed it in the sink. Eric didn't say a word or turn in his chair as Grant paused at the foot of the stairs.

"He's mine," Grant repeated.

With his back still to Grant, Eric nodded silently. After hearing the door to Grant's bedroom close, he gathered up Grant's gear and stowed it in an empty kitchen cabinet. A metal kitchen knife served as a rudimentary alarm, inconspicuously balanced across the top of the doors. At least they would be alerted if Grant decided to try a one-man operation again.

Exhausted, Eric moved to the couch and kicked off his shoes. The back cushions huffed when he collapsed against them.

"What?" His head rolled to the side when he looked over at Catherine in response to her silent stare.

"I get why you did what you did, but even so, it was remarkable—what you did for him tonight." Pointing upstairs, Catherine sighed. "He's the best in the business. But there are a few things you should probably know about him. About what he's endured in the past several years. It might help you appreciate where his head is or isn't right now."

Eric leaned forward, elbows on his knees, and listened to Grant's story relayed through Catherine's eyes.

Once finished, she closed the computer and went upstairs to what had previously been Evan's room. Jenna's room would remain Jenna's.

Eric stretched out on the couch, closed his eyes, and tried like hell to get some sleep, conceding that his often lonely existence paled in comparison to Grant Lawton's definition of alone.

don't dream it's over

S MOOTH SHEETS AND A warm, cozy bed registered in Jenna's mind as she was dragged from the void in which she had lain for the better part of thirty-six hours. She rolled to her side and reached for Grant, her mind not being fully truthful about her whereabouts. When her hand didn't find him, she opened her eyes slowly. She didn't recognize the room or the bed in which she slept.

There was a plastic tube attached to an IV stand, the other end of which was taped to the back of her hand. Her hazy recollection of the past week became clearer as the minutes ticked by, and she closed her eyes again out of disappointment and frustration, compounded by a healthy dose of uncertainty. Her upper arm still throbbed but was freshly bandaged, and she didn't seem to have the raging fever anymore.

A voice outside the door increased the uncertainty. She lay still, not wanting to appear awake until she knew if it was safe. Much to her dismay, it was Luca's voice she recognized as the door opened a crack. She didn't dare look and hoped he couldn't hear her heart pounding.

He was speaking English on his cell phone with the speakerphone on, and the person on the other end was clearly American.

"Did you do as I ordered?" a terse voice asked.

"I sent you the photo." Luca said with irritation in his tone. "I don't know what more proof you need. I assure you she is dead."

The voices faded, and the door click closed. Apparently, she was a key player in some deranged game of his. But that voice on the other end—something about it teased unreachable memories in her head. His insistence that she was dead even as he looked at her lying in the bed was unsettling at best.

A cold shiver ran up her spine as she contemplated what he might be up to, but none of the possibilities gave her any comfort. As unstable as he was, the realization that someone else was calling the shots added another layer to her anxiety.

An escape plan was crucial, but she was in no condition to make a worthwhile attempt. A lack of rest and food would derail even the best of plans. Closing her eyes, she forced the chaotic thoughts to the side.

A rattling sound echoed in her dream, startling her awake before she remembered not to open her eyes. She found herself looking at the same little boy she'd seen in her cell as he juggled a metal tray of food and slid it onto the table beside the bed.

Pleased to see her awake, he grabbed the bread from the tray. Tearing off a small piece, he offered it to her. She pointed to the glass of water, and he reached for a straw. He held the glass while she sipped the cool water. He smiled again once the glass was empty.

"Do you speak English?" she asked, hardly recognizing her own croaky voice.

Her rescuer shook his head, set the glass down, and raced out the door.

Worried that he would return with Luca, she was relieved ten minutes later when a gaunt, white-haired man peered into the room and hesitantly entered with the boy on his heels.

"Ah, it is good to see you alive. I was afraid we were too late to help you," said the old man, ruffling the boy's hair. "You have Philippe to thank for saving you. He's a good boy."

Philippe grinned up at him, the compliment evident despite the language barrier.

The skin on her face felt dry and tight as she attempted a smile.

"*Grazie*, Philippe," she said before returning her attention to her new visitor.

"My name is Antonio." The older man glanced back at the closed door. "I understand we have a mutual admiration for Lourdes Santori."

At the mention of Lourdes's name, Jenna looked inquisitively at him. The man's face softened at her reaction.

"Is Lourdes...is she well?" Jenna asked hesitatingly, unsure of how much this man knew of Lourdes's illness.

Antonio's shoulders drooped, and his eyes held sadness as he slowly shook his head, "My dearest Lourdes is very sick. I expect every day to hear that she has gone to be with God."

"She is special to you?" Jenna asked, afraid to pry but curious about this man's attachment to her friend.

He walked over to her bed and rested his hand on hers. "Yes, more than anyone left in this world. I know you hold a place in her heart too. I must go now, but we will talk more once you are rested."

"Do you know what Luca plans to do with me?" asked Jenna, not sure if she wanted the answer.

Antonio hesitated. "I do not, but I will help you in any way I can. Luca is not respected here."

"Where exactly am I?" she inquired.

"This is the old Santori farm and vineyard in southern Sicily. I've worked on this farm since Matteo's father first bought it. Luca comes here often but is rarely welcomed."

The news that she was in Sicily wasn't surprising to her, although she had no recollection of the journey.

"It's hard to believe he is related to Lourdes," she mused as Antonio prepared to leave.

Smiling over his shoulder, he paused at the door.

"Ah, but he is not," Antonio said in a conspiratorial tone. "Luca is Matteo's son—but not by my Lourdes. Take comfort in that. He was the unfortunate result of Matteo's affair with a young, drug-addicted fashion model. As you can imagine, the child was hard for Lourdes to accept, no matter his personality, but she did her best. Do not repeat what I have shared but enjoy the fact that not even he knows." With a wink, he ushered Philippe out the door in front of him before closing the door quietly.

Smug in the knowledge gained, Jenna finished the tray of food and pulled the covers over herself. She forced the revelation about Luca aside, knowing her priority was to start figuring out how to get away from the farm and, more importantly, from her captor. The improved conditions would be critical to regaining her strength. She would only have one chance at escape.

Retirement in Bermuda seemed to be getting further and further away. Being the control freak Joe Dugan was, he didn't trust Luca Santori. The need to travel to Sicily to take care of the situation personally had been all-consuming, to the point he'd decided it was necessary to risk exposure despite his misgivings.

Years of planning had been invested in constructing a shadow identity in preparation for his new life in Bermuda. Only recently had he received the forged documents in his new name. And just last week he had shelled out a handsome bribe to his agent to ensure that the closing documents on the new house would be changed at the last minute to reflect his new identity. No one would be the wiser on either end; the paper trail of deception would lead to dead ends should anyone start looking for him.

As the flight attendant handed him the drink he'd ordered, he pondered the new name he had selected. By traveling to Sicily now, he was testing the validity of the new credentials well ahead of the planned timeline for his vanishing act. If he were somehow compromised, replacing them under yet another new name would take several months and be a very expensive exercise. He had weighed the pros and cons in excruciating detail prior to purchasing his airfare.

Dugan knew that he needed to be prepared to disappear into the wild blue yonder without coming back to the States if things didn't go as planned with Luca. As a result, he'd been up late making sure his affairs were in order knowing he could sleep decently on the flight in his comfortable first-class pod.

His empty glass hovered in the air expectantly as the flight attendant walked down the aisle performing final checks before the aircraft was pushed back from the gate. The sideways glare from the flight attendant who snatched it went unnoticed. Dugan glanced at his watch, marveling that Luca had followed through on the order to eliminate Jenna Cameron. He smiled ruefully. What he wouldn't do to be the one to tell Catherine that Agent Cameron was dead. Catherine Healey had been a thorn in his side since the day he started, and it was a pity he wouldn't be able to see her crumble.

But right now, with one of the three loose ends out of the way, his focus needed to be on the two that remained. With any luck, one would kill the other before he even stepped foot in Sicily.

fight song

T HE HALL OUTSIDE HER door was quiet and the sky dark when Jenna awoke. She gingerly swung her legs over the side of the bed and slowly attempted to stand. The nighttime air was cool on her skin as she took a tentative step on legs that wobbled from several consecutive days of non-use. After a few laps around the bed, waltzing with the IV stand, she ventured into the middle of the room.

She had just started to get some confidence when the door opened. "*Così,* the little bird tries her wings. Will it try to fly away from the nest?" Luca mocked.

Surprised by his sudden entry, she moved toward the relative safety of the bed. Luca intercepted her halfway, holding her upper arm with one hand while she struggled to break free. Meaty fingers toyed with the loose, sheer top she now wore over drawstring pants. She brushed his hand away before jerking from his grip, but he moved into her path again.

"Still pushing me away, my little bird? You are mine now."

"That will never be the case, Luca," she sneered.

"I will have you," he said with certainty. "And I'm not willing to wait much longer." His silky tone did nothing to disguise the revolting threat of rape.

Anger emerged where good judgment should have prevailed.

"Do what you will, but I will never, ever be yours in heart or mind," Jenna promised. "You are nothing more than a repulsive, sick excuse for a human being."

The shift in him was sudden, and she didn't see the threat in time. The back of his hand contacted the side of her face. She staggered backward. In her effort to dodge the IV stand, she fell hard to the cold tile floor and tasted blood on her tongue.

"The next time you hit me, you'd better kill me or learn to sleep with one eye open," she warned.

He seized her injured arm to yank her to her feet. Diluted blood spattered across his face and shirt as she spit the result of his actions back at him. Furious, Luca threw her to the floor and followed with a vicious kick that left her fighting for air. When she opened her eyes, he was unbuckling his belt.

She knew what was coming and summoned the strength and will to put up a fight. As he unbuttoned his pants, she rolled and kicked out, trying to make contact with either of his knees. A malevolent chuckle mocked her feeble attempt as he roughly hauled her up and tossed her against the side of the bed. She clutched her injured arm and tried not to cry out in pain.

He glanced down to unzip his pants and push them to his knees, his actions providing Jenna with a momentary opening. In a fluid motion, she pushed to her feet and kneed him, crushing his balls. Luca doubled over, and with his pants loosened, the contents of his pockets clattered to the tile floor as he cursed at her and gasped in agony.

She used the distraction to pull the IV from her arm and bolt for the door, only to have him drag her back. With his fist wrapped tightly in her hair, spittle sprayed her cheek as he launched a string of Italian curses in her ear.

Throwing her face-first against the bed, he spread her legs from behind and lifted her head by the hair. With his other hand, he pawed at her breasts through the thin top.

Fight, she told herself, but between the grip he had on her hair and his weight pinning her against the bed, her struggle was useless. And in his state of mind, fighting might get her killed. Jenna attempted to disengage her brain to avoid being present for what was about to happen.

Through the drawstring pants she wore, his seemingly recovered and now exposed erection pressed against her backside as he grunted crude comments in Italian. The clammy hand that had pawed her breast found its way under her shirt, and his panting increased. The hand that fisted her hair moved to the back of her neck, immobilizing her head while his other hand tore at her pants. She squeezed her eyes closed.

The door flew open just as a seam ripped. He paused long enough to look up and shout at his second-in-command to leave. The shocked man only managed a few words about the arrival of a visitor named Kolya before stammering an apology and backing out the door.

Luca attempted to resume the assault, but, distracted by the interruption and the inference that the guest he had summoned earlier had arrived, his focus was lost. His now limp dick wouldn't cooperate despite his hand's best attempts to revive it.

Infuriated, he grabbed her bandaged arm and pulled her off the bed, forcing her to her knees on the hard tile floor. His hand twisted a handful of her hair again. He thrust himself forward, implying he wanted her to use her mouth on him instead. She glared up at him with a maniacal snarl that bared her teeth.

"If you insist on putting that in my face—much less, my mouth—I promise you will need stitches at a minimum. As small as it is, I might even be able to bite the whole thing off at once."

His eyes narrowed and his hips thrust forward.

"Go ahead," she taunted. "I dare you."

The gold knives in her eyes gave him pause, and he opted not to risk it. He jerked her head by the fistful of hair he still held, then shoved her onto the floor.

"When they bring me Ethan, you may choose to be more cooperative. He surely will not fight me as you have," Luca snarled as he zipped up his pants.

With his belt still unfastened, Luca swiped the spilled contents of his pockets from the floor. Five seconds later, he was gone.

The stillness of the room was both deafening and blissful. Jenna sagged against the side of the bed while she fought to control her breathing and heartbeat. Tears of relief burned her eyes and clogged her throat. She stayed seated on the cold tile floor until she'd regained some ability to think clearly, then rolled onto her hip and placed one hand on the top of the mattress to push herself up. Only then did she notice something under the foot of the bed.

A tingle of excitement raced through her, and she let out a crazed laugh when her fingers closed over the cell phone that must have fallen out of Luca's pocket when she kneed him.

"Karma's a bitch, isn't it, Luca?" she muttered.

He'd be back for it once he realized it was missing. Of that there was no doubt. But for now, it was her lifeline. She held the phone in both hands as her brain debated what to do. If she placed any calls or sent any texts, he would eventually find out; the penalty would likely be a painful death. Luca's threat against Evan might have been a bluff, but she wouldn't risk the boy's safety by doing nothing.

Jenna closed her eyes and tried desperately to remember Grant's cell phone number; her heart lodged in her throat at the thought that Grant was dead. Maybe she should call Eric or the Agency's emergency line. But the harder she fought to remember any of the numbers, the fewer she could recall. Damn her reliance on her phone's contacts list.

The phone's home button activated the screen and immediately displayed menu options in Italian. Her French skills, coupled with the recent exposure to Italian, allowed her to readily interpret the labels. The icons on the screen were limited, as if the phone had not been personalized. Perhaps this was a secondary or burner phone, which would explain why a PIN had not been needed.

With a hesitant finger, she tapped the contacts icon. There were only two numbers with no names identified. She tapped the text message icon next, and what she saw both stunned and confused her.

The first text string was to a U.S. phone number with a familiar Washington, DC, area code and contained a picture of a figure slumped against a wall in her dungeon cell. The text accompanying the picture read "It's done. She's dead." Only then did she realize that figure had been her.

She opened the text string to the other number which appeared to be Italian. This message string had the same picture plus another showing Luca shirtless lying next to her in her hospital bed. Based on the date and time on the phone, the text string had been sent a few hours earlier. Her heart faltered with the fleeting fear that Luca had raped her while she was drugged or before she was even conscious.

She swallowed hard and concentrated on the opportunity at hand. Her mind raced as it sorted through what she was seeing on the phone. Despite the fact that the message that accompanied the two pictures was crude and insinuated that Luca had raped her, it sent a wave of relief from her fingers to her toes.

Grant was the only person Luca would bait with that message.

She leaned her head back absorbing the confirmation that Grant was alive. It was almost two a.m., but she didn't care. After pressing the green call icon, she raised the phone to her ear.

"Answer, please. Pick up the phone. Answer the phone, babe," she pleaded in a whisper.

The voice mail kicked in.

"C'mon, Grant, pick up if you're there. Please, please, answer the phone. Be there, love; please be there. Answer the phone, damn it," she said breathlessly, finally realizing he wasn't going to answer. "Grant, I...I have no idea if you're really alive. Luca said he killed you. If he finds out I called you, he'll kill me for sure, but I had to warn you...he said he's going after Evan. He still calls him Ethan, though, so I don't know if he's bluffing. Either way, you have to get to Evan. Move him. Remind him to use the challenge phrase."

Jenna talked as fast as possible, stammering in her haste.

"Luca dropped his phone under the bed when he tried to—he didn't though. But I saw the pictures he sent to you. Grant, the picture of me and him...I didn't...I wouldn't...it had to have been staged. Had to be. I would know somehow. I need you to know that. Anyway, there's someone else who Luca calls and texts from this phone, but the number is a Washington, DC, area code. He sent the dungeon picture to that person, too, and told them I was dead. I don't know if it's the same person, but the guy I heard him talking to the other day was American. I'm sure of that."

She rattled off the DC number for him to research and took a deep breath, knowing she needed to beat the voicemail timer from cutting her off.

"I'm at the old Santori farm in southern Sicily. I don't know exactly where it is; that's all Antonio told me. Lourdes will know, though."

As her exhaustion kicked in, the knowledge of the likely punishment for her making this call sank in.

"If I don't get out of this, know I love you. Promise me you'll tell my kids how proud of them I am and how much I love them. Please, I have to know you'll tell them."

She took a deep breath to ward off the overwhelming flood of emotion.

"God, Grant, I really wanted to hear your voice one more time. I love you. And Evan too. Know that I wanted you in my life. I wanted to be a part of yours. Stay strong for Evan; don't lose that focus. He needs you, Grant, as much as you need him. You are—"

The beep of the voicemail told her she'd run out of time.

Reluctant to hang up the call, she clutched the phone to her chest, knowing that if Luca discovered the call, it wouldn't be just the voicemail that had run out of time. Jenna did everything she could to delete the call record from the history before climbing back into the bed.

As she lay there, she made a promise to herself. She would escape tomorrow, regardless of the cost. Tears of frustration, longing, and fear soaked the pillow. For her kids, for Evan, and for Grant. Until the night rescued her.

salt

CATHERINE WAS POURING FRESHLY brewed coffee when a sweaty Grant returned to the apartment. Despite not sleeping much, if at all, his personal punishment routine had taken just over an hour, and he suspected he would be smelled before he was seen.

But the most brutal part of his workout had not been physical. About halfway through, Grant had realized how fortunate he was that Eric had stepped in last night. While Luca would certainly be dead just about now, others on his team may have also been unintended casualties had Grant's rash plans been permitted to play out. And Jenna might have been one of them—if she was still alive.

His mind was numb to the possibility that she was dead. He refused to accept that picture as proof. But if she was, he knew the demons would come for him every night for the rest of his life.

Eric stood on the patio talking on the phone, and Grant fleetingly greeted Catherine on his way upstairs to shower. When he was presentable, he jogged down the stairs in search of food, and, for the first time, felt his fifty-two years in his knees.

Catherine had a mug set out for him, and he joined them on the patio, still feeling Jenna's presence in the chair that sat in the sun.

"Have a seat, Grant," Catherine said, in full business mode. "We got some interesting news this morning from the analyst team. The most important is about Jenna. They are certain that the pictures Luca sent you were taken in a different sequence than shown. Meaning the photo of her in the bed was taken after the picture in which she appeared...well, the picture from the cell."

Catherine wanted Grant to cheer and celebrate, but knowing him as well as she did, she simply paused to give him time to process the news. She watched out of the corner of her eye as he lowered himself into the chair looking out over the courtyard, secretly gratified when he swallowed hard.

Eric stood against the railing and spoke. "The other thing is about those weapon containers we found at the warehouse in Vicenza. The Sigonella markings were fake. Those containers came from the U.S. storage facility at Blue Grass originally."

"That's a lot to digest this morning. You all have been busy." Grant stared down at the ripples on the surface of his coffee. "Jenna...you're sure she's alive?"

There was not an immediate response, and Grant flicked his gaze up expectantly at Eric.

"I'll be straight with you—we believe so, yes, but we can't guarantee that. What is certain is that she was in that stone-walled cell before she was in the bed where that photo with Luca was taken. We're confident that was the sequence, based on the electronic time stamps from the photos, but you know we can't say for sure that something hasn't changed in the meantime. One of the analysts—"

"Carl handled the analysis of the pictures himself, Grant," Catherine interjected. "You know how much he respected—respects—Jenna."

Grant nodded, and Eric continued.

"Carl noticed something on the edge of the later picture. There was a clear plastic tube running from the bed off the edge of the picture. Literally, it was like a quarter inch showing, so it's amazing he caught it at all. He identified it as an IV tube."

"While it's a positive sign, it's another indication that she's not in great shape," added Catherine.

Accepting the optimistic view that Jenna was alive, his intuition told him he would know if she were gone. He chose to cling to that for now.

"So, the source of the weapons is the Blue Grass Army Depot in Kentucky, huh?" he deflected.

Catherine picked up the new topic with relief. "Yes. Carl is tracing those, too, and looking at visitor logs and telephone logs as well. We're a bit closer but still a long way from figuring out who's really behind this or funding Dugan—if it really is him."

"It's got to be someone with a fair number of connections and good visibility who can shuffle large shipments of weapons around without raising eyebrows," Grant surmised out loud. "To be clear, my priority is Jenna. And, while the intervention was well deserved last night, I can't wait for everything to be wrapped up in a nice, tidy bow. I have to go get her; I need you both to understand that."

Pursed lips and nods indicated their concurrence. A hint of a smile played on Eric's face, but Catherine spoke first.

"Where's that burner phone that Luca gave you?"

"Upstairs on my dresser," Grant responded.

"Well, go get it, please. Carl wants to tap into it to see if he can get any other intel from it."

"Sure, but I'm curious what you have up your sleeve," Grant said, waving his coffee mug in Eric's direction as he disappeared into the villa.

He returned with the phone in hand and powered it on, tossing it to Catherine before disappearing inside once more to refill his mug before returning to his chair on the patio. Once he set his coffee down, Catherine tossed the burner phone back to Grant.

"Looks like there's a missed call and a voicemail from the wee hours of this morning. Anyone else call you on that?" she asked.

"No," Grant said while scrolling through the missed call log. "Looks like he left a voicemail. Not a very smart thing to do. Guess we should hear what he has to say."

Jenna's thready voice filled the morning air. The phone shook noticeably in Grant's hands as they all listened to her voicemail. As stunned as he was, hearing her voice again filled a small portion of the massive hole inside him.

Fury was quick to follow. He was incensed at himself for not having the phone on and nearby constantly. He'd turned it off last night after the texts and photos arrived, unsure of his ability to cope had Luca continued to send other images. But most of all, he berated himself for being so careless with the one possible connection he had to the man who held Jenna captive. He'd permitted emotion to trump reason, and that was a problem.

When the voicemail cut her message off, the silence on the patio was resounding. Eric finally spoke and moved to the door to go inside.

"Listen to it again, Grant. As many times as you need to." Eric motioned to Catherine to encourage her to go inside with him and put his hand on Grant's shoulder. "When you're ready, we need to get it to Carl. Take your time. We'll wait."

Eric had no idea how Grant would react to this latest development.

In the past, Eric had been accused of having no heart. Possibly even by Jenna back in the day. But right now, whatever heart he did have went out to his friend.

Knowing now what Grant had been through in the past several years, he wasn't sure how the man continued to function. Navy SEAL or not, every man had a breaking point. It seemed like the man upstairs kept kicking Grant's breaking point farther and farther down the road—littering the path with rusty nails for fun—just to see how much the guy could take.

Eric thought about the voicemail. Jenna's call had substantiated a myriad of things, both good and bad. Most notably, she'd put her own safety aside to protect those she loved and to further the mission. Just like she had the other day when all hell had broken loose in the convoy. And just like she had that day so long ago when she had bucked her clearance to make sure he and his jet made it back to base safely.

In the years since their brief relationship, he hadn't come across many women he respected more. A part of him envied Grant.

Sighing, Eric grabbed his phone, pressed a few buttons, and raised it to his ear. He glanced at Grant, who was grappling—and understandably so—with a resurgent whirlpool of raging emotions. When the other party answered, he gave the order.

"We move tonight. Tell me you have two crews in crew rest like we discussed." He listened then nodded. "We'll be there an hour and a half prior. Get everything in motion."

About thirty-five minutes later, after Grant had made a phone call to Evan's grandparents and asked them to be on alert and prepare to relocate, the patio door opened. Grant somberly handed the phone to Catherine without a word. Despite being on a call herself, she caught his hand and gave it a motherly squeeze. While she talked, she connected the burner phone to her computer to allow Carl to mine its contents.

Eric watched Grant pull a bottle of Laphroaig whisky from an upper kitchen cabinet and set a glass next to the bottle. He poured two fingers of liquid and tossed half of it back. The remaining liquid sloshed when he set the glass down heavily.

Meeting Eric's stare, Grant leaned over slightly and opened the cabinet containing his gear, intentionally allowing the knife that was balanced on the top to clatter to the floor.

"You hear that?" Grant challenged sullenly, letting Eric know he would be moving on Luca.

"Yeah, I heard it," Eric replied flatly. "But, Lieutenant Commander, I will need a hundred and ten percent of you for what comes next. And I swear on my mother's Bible, if you are even slightly inebriated—if I catch the faintest whiff of alcohol on you—I will personally kick your sorry Navy ass off the Air Force chopper that will be launching from Camp Darby at 2030 tonight. You hear me?"

Grant's eyebrows arched at the realization that Eric had been discreetly coordinating the logistics for a rescue mission. The cocky Air Force fighter jock impressed him more and more every day.

"Yeah, I heard." He tossed the remainder of the drink back, capped the bottle, rinsed the glass, and loudly dropped his gear bags back in the kitchen cabinet with a mock flourish.

Temporarily mollified, Eric nodded, and motioning to the couch area, he wordlessly invited Grant to join the mission planning effort. Maps were spread across the small table. A red pen and clear plastic plotter had been used to mark the route they would take to pay an unannounced visit to the Santori farm.

As Carl worked his magic remotely on her computer, Catherine worked some magic of her own. From memory, she knew which agents were within a reasonable travel distance from their location. Within the hour, two agents would be en route to station themselves at Evan's grandparents' property in the event Luca wasn't bluffing. Once the security detail had been coordinated, a superbly grateful Grant communicated the arrangement to Evan's grandparents.

Her tasks complete, Catherine sat back and considered the earlier exchange between the two men, and the wheels started turning in her head.

mad world

THE DRIVE FROM CATANIA to the Santori farm where Luca was currently staying was just under two hours, and Joe Dugan reviewed the route as he ordered his second macchiato at the highly rated bed and breakfast, while waiting for his room to be available for check-in.

He had landed at Catania's Fontanarossa Airport that morning and had bribed two of Luca's men to meet him there, at which time they'd provided him with a car that stored some additional benefits under the driver's seat. The two men were more loyal to him than to Luca at this point. Their loyalty was not cheap, but their assistance would be necessary should things go sideways with Luca.

His return flight to the U.S. was only two days out, and he had no intention of lingering in Sicily longer than planned. All he wanted to do was make sure all the loose ends were tied up neatly.

After an hour and a persuasive tip, his room was ready. Despite enjoying the benefits of flying first class, he was worn out following the overnight flight. Duty called, however, and sleep would have to wait until he returned from Luca's estate late tonight. Somewhat refreshed after a long shower, he headed southwest out of Catania.

Roughly two hours later, Dugan pulled onto the expansive property in southern Sicily and navigated the long dusty road that led to the main house. He'd met Luca here once before when they'd sealed their initial arrangement for the Javelins. The estate as a whole appeared overly rustic, as if repairs and upgrades had been purposefully neglected in an effort to maintain a certain aura about the place. The contrast between the five-star B&B and the estate of one of the wealthiest organized crime families in Italy was a bit shocking. Clearly, the Santori family was investing their profits elsewhere.

None of his business, he concluded. All that mattered was their ability to get this mess cleaned up and the shipment delivered so that what remained of the balance would be paid upon receipt. Dugan had intentionally not advised Luca that he was inbound. The role of playground bully was one he enjoyed, and catching Luca by surprise was worth any resulting inconvenience.

It was late afternoon as he caught sight of the main buildings of the farm. He was amazed at how close he got to the house itself before being intercepted by two men in a small utility vehicle that resembled a souped-up golf cart. It pulled onto the road in front of him and forced his vehicle to a stop.

One guard remained in the vehicle and brandished an automatic rifle while the other cautiously approached the driver's side of the trespassing car. Dugan identified himself and watched in amusement as the name was passed verbally from the man standing in the road to the man in the vehicle and then to the person on the other end of the radio. Envisioning Luca's panicked reaction to his arrival entertained him greatly.

The man who had questioned him climbed back into the passenger seat of the laughable utility vehicle. If not for the weapons they carried, he would have been tempted to bump the cart out of the way and increase the snail's pace to that of a more worthy reptile. The remainder of the drive to the main house was an exercise in restraint.

After Dugan was escorted into the residence, Luca greeted him with a superficial graciousness, but the irritation that simmered under the surface was almost palpable.

A man of average height with sharp features and small, darting black eyes stood a few feet behind Luca and stepped forward to speak to Luca in a hushed voice. Although he couldn't make out the words, Dugan sensed the stranger was of Eastern European descent—his suspicion confirmed when the man was reluctantly introduced as Kolya.

Luca ushered his guests from the entry into a sitting room decorated in heavy masculine colors and mismatched yet obviously expensive antique furniture. Drinks were poured almost immediately, as if to drown the awkwardness of an uninvited visitor.

From across the room, Dugan studied Kolya, whose eyes were cold and flat. Unsure of the man's position or reason for being in Luca's employ, Dugan lost some of his initial arrogance and, for a fleeting moment, doubted the wisdom of showing up unannounced on Luca's doorstep.

As afternoon blended into early evening, Jenna plotted her escape. She had slept on and off but had been awakened by a commotion outside the front of the house. Wary of attracting their attention, she'd peered out from the gap between the shutters of her window on the second floor. Luca's men motioned to a man who had just exited his vehicle and escorted him to the front entrance. A niggle of familiarity registered in her mind, but she wasn't able to get a good look at him from where she stood.

Her intuition told her that whatever meeting was taking place here was probably not a good thing for her situation, although a distracted household might be just the opening she needed.

It was time.

She disconnected the IV, wincing as she slid the needle out of the back of her hand. Her clothes had been cleaned and folded, and Philippe had placed them in a dresser that sat under the window, but she had no idea what had become of her boots.

Her intentions would be hard to deny to anyone she encountered once she changed into her own gear, so her timing had to be flawless. She decided to change after her evening meal was brought up and tucked her clothes into the pillowcase for later.

A good meal—she tried not to think of it as a last supper—would help just as much as the cover of darkness.

the whole of the moon

Eric and Grant left the villa for Camp Darby four hours prior to the helicopter's planned departure time of 2030 hours. Tasked with monitoring the operation from the villa, Catherine hugged both men goodbye and issued strict instructions to bring Jenna back safely.

The two HH-60G Pave Hawk helicopters that had been staged at Camp Darby were uniquely suited for this type of personnel extraction operation. On each chopper, an insertion team of four would provide cover and additional firepower. Not only were the crews trained for highly volatile combat rescue scenarios, but each helicopter was also outfitted with .50 caliber machine guns.

Grant introduced himself to the crews prior to Eric starting the briefing. Building rapport was essential; these were the guys who might be responsible for saving his ass by putting theirs on the line. Tonight, though, he cared more about them saving someone else's.

During the mission brief, they reviewed the necessary airborne rendezvous with a fixed-wing HC-130 tanker off the coast of Sicily. The air refueling would take time but would extend their range and ensure they had adequate fuel for the return leg of the mission.

Eric studied the flight plan while Grant reviewed the layout of the estate, describing the buildings that made up the farm and highlighting Jenna's probable location. They then divided up into individual teams to cover communications and expected objectives during the assault and egress phases.

At precisely 2030, their two-ship formation received takeoff clearance. As they lifted off, Grant fervently prayed they weren't too late.

An hour before Grant and Eric lifted off from Camp Darby, the door to Jenna's room opened. Philippe smiled at her as he set her tray on the table and walked over to help her sit up as he usually did. He gave her a questioning look when he noticed the IV had been removed, and Jenna raised a finger to her lips to ensure his silence.

The first time Jenna spoke to the boy in French had taken him by surprise, but since then they had spent hours talking and getting to know one another. She had no concerns that he would betray her confidence. Jenna knew he and Evan would be fast friends, given the opportunity. She hadn't pried into the dark details of his stolen childhood, instead letting their shared hatred of Luca be their common ground.

Philippe sat at the foot of her bed and told her about the newcomer while she ate. He had helped the kitchen staff serve drinks to Luca and two other men most of the evening. At first, he was confused by her interest in Luca's company, but once he understood that she planned to escape, he proceeded to describe the layout of the house and all the possible exits.

Tears swam in his eyes at the realization that, if she was successful in her escape, he wouldn't see her again. When it was time for him to go, he hugged her tightly. Jenna kissed the top of his head and promised that, somehow, she'd find a way to see him again.

When the door closed behind him, she hunkered down to wait for night to settle over the estate.

Dinner had been a disappointing and unremarkable affair, and Dugan was sorely missing the hospitality of his B&B from the previous night. He sipped his single malt scotch, content to observe and listen. His Italian was elementary at best, but Luca's facial expressions, gestures, and verbal inflections made it all too obvious that he and Kolya were discussing a woman. Hearing the term 'American,' he discreetly perked up.

Kolya was the one who gave it all away. Luca made a crude gesture, and a disturbing smile crept onto Kolya's face. His laugh made Dugan's skin crawl. The glass of grappa the man clutched lifted ever so slightly when his index finger extended upward. At the same time, his eyes flicked upward in an almost imperceptible glance at the ceiling. Luca laughed nervously at the man's actions and cast his eyes at Dugan as if to assess how much he was following the conversation.

Unbeknownst to Luca, reading people and exploiting their weaknesses was how Dugan had climbed the ladder to the position he now held and how he had been able to maintain his lucrative side hustle without getting killed. He was no stranger to manipulation. Just by scrolling through his phone, he had conveyed that he didn't care or didn't understand their conversation. Neither assumption would be accurate.

Their conversation flowed as freely as the alcohol, and he began to piece it together.

Agent Jenna Cameron wasn't dead at all.

Luca, however, might be before the night was over.

Just after eleven o'clock, Jenna dressed in her tactical gear and did her best to search the room once more in the dark for her boots. She was attempting to quietly close the squeaky door of the armoire when she heard the doorknob to her room start to turn.

Taking cover behind the open door of the armoire, she peeked through the hinged opening as a bulky figure stole into her room. The figure reacted more calmly than expected to her empty bed and paused to look around the room.

Prepared to fight her way out, she took a step forward when the shadow reached into his shirt. Fearing a gun, she ducked back behind the armoire door. Used as a shield, it wouldn't do much but delay the impact, but it gave her a small, albeit false, sense of protection for a split second.

When no shot was fired, Jenna peered around the edge of the door. The figure leaned over and placed something bulky on the floor near her bed. The breath she'd been holding was expelled in a huff as she recognized Antonio and her missing boots. Quietly, she crossed the room and hugged him tightly.

"Philippe told me; do not be angry with him," Antonio whispered. "I knew where the maid had stored your boots and thought you might have use for them." His eyes shone with hope as he continued. "You should also know that Lourdes is still with us and will be glad to know you didn't give up. We will be watching tonight and will help if you need us. Luca and his guests are all ruthless men. Kolya, the ugly one, sold Philippe to Luca; the new one is connected to the weapons Luca has stored in the barn. Be safe." With a quick kiss to her cheeks, Antonio disappeared as unobtrusively as he had entered.

Fifteen minutes would give Antonio time to return to wherever he was expected to be. While she waited, she said a heartfelt prayer of thanks for Lourdes and for her new guardian angel. Adding a small request for her own fortitude, she stepped into the dimly lit hallway, pulling the door to her room closed behind her.

After the air refueling rendezvous over the Mediterranean, the helicopters' estimated arrival time at the Santori farm was updated to eighteen minutes after midnight. The Sicilian coast was illuminated by the lights of Catania glowing off to the right of their flight path. As the helicopters maneuvered south of the city's airport, the pilots began a descent to a lower altitude while the teams checked their gear, prepped their weapons, and recapped their briefings.

It had been several years since Grant had operated as part of a military unit, but like riding a bike, he settled into the rhythm and fell into his zone. His ability to compartmentalize had shut out his emotional ties to the mission.

Just another day at the office.

she's gone

LUCA HAD REACHED THE bottom of the bottle of grappa when his weapons supplier stood, stretched, and indicated his need for a bathroom. Needing to go himself, Luca showed him the way, steadying himself on the back of a chair. Kolya remained seated and never took his beady eyes off the others. Trust was not—and had never been—part of the equation.

The main hallway was dimly lit by a few antique lamps and only got darker when they turned down a short hallway. Double swinging doors at the end of the service hallway muted the sounds of metal pots and pans clanking in the kitchen. Luca's footsteps slowed, and he grunted and pointed to a single solid wood door to the right.

In a single motion, Dugan took a step toward the door, grabbed an unsuspecting Luca by the shirt collar, and forced the mildly intoxicated Italian into the bathroom. Luca struggled to keep his footing and only kept himself from falling by leaning against the wall. His mouth opened in indignant anger but snapped shut when the weapons dealer locked the large mahogany door behind him.

"You told me she was dead." Dugan's lack of inflection permitted no argument. "You lied."

Normally cool and collected, Luca blanched visibly. The stuttering excuse he offered revealed his fear and adequately served as an admission of guilt.

"I thought she was," Luca attempted. "When I learned she lived, I called Kolya. She will disappear into his world of trafficking. You will see. She is as good as dead to anyone who knew her."

"You are as stupid as they come. The problem is that she's a hell of a lot smarter than you and Kolya combined." He scowled. "Take me to her. Now. I'll kill her myself."

Shoving Luca out of the bathroom ahead of him, Dugan followed at a safe distance as they started up the flight of white marble stairs. A dark mahogany rail spiraled into the space above but obscured the view to the upper floor landing. Once at the top, Luca led the way down the hall to a closed door, turned the key in the lock, and rotated the doorknob. His bluff had been called, and he was winging it from here.

The room where Jenna was being held was quiet and dark. The IV stand stood on the opposite side of the bed like a soldier keeping watch over a still form lying motionless under the covers.

Dugan yanked the gun from Luca's hand and aimed.

Across the hall, the door to a narrow supply closet cracked open just enough for one eye to peer around the edge of the opening. Jenna's hand flew to her mouth to muffle her shock at seeing Commander Dugan with Luca in the doorway to what had been her room. Her thoughts flew as she tried to sort out the jumbled pieces of the puzzle. Was Dugan there to rescue her? As a diversion for some other plot? She couldn't wrap her mind around his presence, but the gun he aimed at her bed reinforced that he was not there to save anyone but himself.

Dugan lowered the gun and stalked over to the bed. He looked down for only a second before ripping the sheets off, revealing the bundle of sheets and spare clothing she'd cobbled together into a sleeping form. His reaction confirmed to Jenna that he wasn't there on her behalf.

Dugan stalked over to Luca and shoved his gun under Luca's chin. He gestured to the bed, one arm flailing in the air.

"What the fuck kind of operation are you running, Santori?" Dugan hissed. "You assured me she was dead and out of the way. Where is she? If you lie to me again, I swear I'll feed her your dick before I shoot both of you."

Dugan was livid at the deception, but Luca's astonishment at the empty bed was genuine.

"I...I...she was just here a few hours ago," stammered Luca as he began to search available hiding places in the room.

Movement caught Jenna's attention as a shadow ran down the hallway toward the two men standing at the open door of her room.

The newcomer fired a flurry of Italian words at Luca. Then there was silence as they both stopped to listen. Dugan looked from one to the other, waiting for a translation. His mouth opened, but his question was cut off by Luca throwing his hand up with his palm in Dugan's face. Even Dugan recognized the international "shut the hell up" signal.

Dugan paused and listened with them. They all looked at each other as the *whump, whump* of rotors beating the air into submission became evident.

"You double-crossed me?! You fucking Americans!" Luca screamed. Daggers flew from his eyes toward Dugan. "How dare you bring your soldiers to attack me in my own country!"

Luca's shrill outburst reeked of panic as the Doppler effect indicated the helicopters were getting closer.

Dugan stiff-armed Luca's chest. "I did nothing of the sort! I came here to clean up your damn incompetence and get whatever we could out of the client, you moron. Where are the weapons? We're going to need them if we want to be alive in another hour."

Kolya had been quiet until now and spoke to Dugan with measured curiosity. "If they aren't your people, then who is coming in on the helicopters?"

Dugan and Luca stared at each other.

"Lawton. He's one of my agents and a royal pain in my ass. You know him as Grant Nichols," Dugan said before leaning threateningly toward Luca. "I was counting on you to take him out, but you failed spectacularly."

"There's still time for that. He's coming for his bitch, so we need to find her first," Luca said. "It's our only chance of getting out of this if they land."

"You don't know Lawton like I do. Forget about finding Jenna. Even if he was fucking her for entertainment, he's not here for her. Firepower is our only chance of getting out of this alive."

Kolya poked Luca in the arm. "You said she was mine to sell. That's the whole reason I'm here tonight," the man countered with a tone of warning to Luca. "My boss won't be happy if I return empty-handed."

"You won't be returning at all if we don't get to those weapons and take out those helicopters before they land," Dugan snarled as he moved to the stairs with the other men close behind.

Seeing the three men disappear, Jenna exited the closet and darted into her old room. They wouldn't look there again. She sat on the bed as she pieced it all together, dumbfounded that Dugan was behind the whole thing.

Balancing that knowledge with the new motivation to avoid being handed over to Kolya's human-trafficking ring, Jenna reached under the mattress. Luca's phone was still where she had stashed it. She powered it on as she rose to her feet.

Helos inbound at farm. Hoping for friendlies. Dugan with Luca and man named Kolya. Think Dugan is Luca's supplier? Weapons on site. Helos will be targeted.

She typed furiously, not caring about anything but relaying the information, then secured the phone in a cargo pocket on her pant leg and ran as quickly and quietly as she could toward the staircase.

The first priority was to find Antonio and Philippe and get them to safety before all hell broke loose. The hope simmering in the back of her mind that Grant was on one of those helicopters was a distraction, and there was a lot to overcome before she could focus on him.

Stealthily, she made her way downstairs where the kitchen staff still worked. The clank of pots and pans resonated through the closed doors. The noises stopped abruptly once the two kitchen workers spied her slipping through the swinging doors. She raised both hands to show she meant no harm and then lifted a finger to her lips using the other hand to mime that they should listen. One turned the water off and cocked his head, his eyes widening when he picked up on the sound of rotors.

"Antonio? Philippe?" she inquired hesitatingly.

The younger of the two smiled in understanding and waved her over to them.

She looked behind her into the shadowed hallway to make sure no one was following before joining the men who were moving toward the back exit.

The older man called out, causing Jenna to jump, startled by the noise in the quiet space. He motioned for her to wait as he ran to the knives hanging above a prep counter. He grabbed three of the largest knives and, shoving the handles toward her, gave her first choice. She pointed at one and clapped him on the shoulder in appreciation as he gave her a gap-toothed smile.

The younger worker grabbed her free hand and pulled her toward the door as he opened it slowly and peered into the darkness. He looped an arm around her shoulder and indicated a drinking motion. The older man stood on her opposite side and looped his arm around her as well. She placed her arms around their waists, and they stumbled into the open area between the buildings, staggering and swaying. Upon reaching the building across the way, one of the men flung the door open, and they stepped into a large open area surrounded by what appeared to be bunk rooms.

The older man proceeded to knock on each door to rouse the residents. Some rubbed sleep from their faces as others pulled on clothing. The younger man spoke in rapid Italian as he informed the gathering of the likely trouble headed their way.

From his place behind the crowd, Philippe spied Jenna. He let out a whoop of joy and ran to her, hugging her enthusiastically. A hush fell over the room as Antonio joined her, and she relayed what had transpired since she'd left her room and warned them about what was about to happen at their farm.

"Come on," Philippe said in broken Italian, tugging her hand. "Come with us."

She stood rooted in place, shook her head solemnly, and crouched down in front of him.

"You go on. I have to stay and fight with my team. My job is to make sure that Luca and Kolya are stopped. To make sure they can't hurt anyone else. To make sure they never buy or sell another child," she said in French. "But you. You need to lead the others now. Take the other children with you and keep them safe."

Philippe nodded in understanding before she gently pushed him toward Antonio, who in turn hustled him to the group of evacuating staff. Jenna surveyed the scene once more. Satisfied that they would know the safest place to hide, she slipped out the door into the dark.

Luca shouted orders at four men who casually guarded a stone structure that, in the daylight, would have resembled a dilapidated barn. The guards, visibly nervous at the sound of the approaching helicopters, pulled the wooden doors open, allowing the three men to storm inside.

Off to the right, inside the barn, the few remnants of the weapons cache had been stuffed into stalls still coated with the dust of straw and feed. Luca stalked to a stall farther down and hastily pulled the lids off several wooden crates to reveal RPGs. His expression transformed from nervous energy into crazed eagerness, his faith in their survivability renewed.

The rotor wash kicked up dust and debris from the fields as the two Pave Hawk helicopters made their approach in front of the main house. Through night-vision goggles, Grant's second-in-command called the team's attention to a large group of people running across the open field away from the main house, but Grant was more interested in the rhythmic flashing light that came from the side of the building. He squinted, his brain processing the rudimentary morse code.

She was alive.

don't pay the ferryman

Tucked into a corner of the house, camouflaged by landscaping, Jenna repeatedly covered and uncovered the screen of the phone she had pulled from her pocket.

Three dots, three dashes, three dots.

After four cycles of S.O.S., she wished for the simplicity of a single text message.

Her singular goal was to let them know she was not a combatant. It was important for them to know she was a friendly in a space that soon would be lit up like the Fourth of July.

The sound of an incoming Pave Hawk was impressive in any situation. But at night, and knowing it meant military—almost certainly U.S. military—and most likely carried the man she loved, it hit a little differently. Knowing they risked it all for her was sobering, humbling, and exhilarating all at the same time. The tingling chill of realization was a thousand electric currents that spread from the top of her skull to disperse through her extremities.

Jenna turned the phone's flashlight on, tucked it into the pocket of her t-shirt, and took a deep breath. There would be no going back after her next move. Certain that they would be night-vision equipped, the diffused light through her t-shirt pocket would help differentiate herself from Luca's security teams. She waved her arms above her head three times then jogged along the shadows in the direction of the barn. She gave no thought to the risks of being caught again or being caught in the crossfire. If Luca and Dugan got to the few Javelins or had a stash of RPGs in the barn, this would end very badly and very quickly. It was critical to deny the trio of men the opportunity to take out one or both helicopters. Interrupting their plans was worth any risk.

Weeds and dead grass hugged the stone foundation of the barn. The cavernous doors at the front of the barn yawned open, and the dim beam of flashlights crisscrossed like light sabers deep within. Anxious voices were barely audible over the noise of equipment being shuffled.

Carried on the night air, the scent of cigarette smoke wafted from around the side of the barn, alerting her to the presence of a nervous or at least distracted guard. She turned off the phone's light, then crept along in the shadows, following the scent as it grew stronger and mixed with the smell of ancient straw dust stirred up as Luca's men traipsed in and out of the barn. She was at a severe disadvantage with only a knife and with no knowledge of how many guards were inside or nearby.

Her best option for a distraction was to toss a rock beyond where she thought the guard stood. He pivoted in the direction of the noise and stilled. Hearing no voices, she poked her head around the corner and confirmed it was a solitary guard who smoked while watching the helicopters, as if savoring what he knew might be his last cigarette.

His rifle was propped against the side wall of the barn and sat only about four feet from her yet a good ten feet from him. She darted around the corner and snatched the rifle at the same time he turned and saw her. He lunged toward his weapon, then threw his hands into the air as she leveled the rifle at him. While Jenna wouldn't hesitate to pull the trigger, shooting him wasn't her first choice for a myriad of reasons. Relying on her very basic Italian vocabulary, she gave him a chance to run.

"*Correre,*" she stated, waving the rifle in the direction of the trees off to the west of the property. The guard didn't hesitate and took off at a sprint.

The helicopters touched down in the field in front of the main house, enhancing the chaos. Alarmed shouts from within the barn had Jenna crouching in the shadows with her newly acquired weapon. The desperation was evident in Luca's voice as he barked curses at one of his men, who was lugging an RPG through the barn doors.

Shadowy figures jumping off the helicopters distracted her. The churning rotor wash flattened the tall grass around the crouching figures. The second one off had undoubtedly been Grant, but she tamped down the urge to yell to him. He couldn't possibly hear her, and all it would accomplish would be to give away her position. Turning her attention back to the threat at hand, she needed a clear shot at the person in charge of launching the RPG or at the weapon itself.

The trafficker named Kolya stood to Luca's right outside the barn. He shifted his weight from one foot to another, all the while looking around furtively for an escape route. She'd start with him.

Just as she was about to pull the trigger, Dugan walked out of the barn toward where Luca stood berating the man handling the RPG. Stopping in the shadow just beyond the barn door, Dugan raised his pistol. The movement grabbed Kolya's attention, and he took a few steps away from the others, alerting Luca, who turned to assess the disturbance behind him.

Dugan fired, the shot catching Luca in the face. Jenna wasn't sure if she imagined the spray of blood or really could see it in the dark. Luca's body crumpled to the ground. Kolya raised his hands in surrender, terrified he was next. Dugan lowered the gun as he shouted instructions at the man who was preparing to launch the RPG at the helicopters. He then disappeared back into the barn.

Without hesitating, Jenna clipped off two shots, and the man fell to the ground beside Luca's body. The launcher bounced off Luca's body and came to rest a few feet away. She fired twice more at the launcher just for good measure.

She lowered the rifle to assess the remaining threats before revealing her position but delayed a moment too long. The crunch of the dead grass behind her registered seconds too late.

An arm snaked around her neck, and a hand clamped over her mouth and nose. The rifle fell from her grip. A sharp burning prick in her neck brought a wave of panic. But as she fought to break free, her vision started to blur, and her limbs refused to cooperate. Someone caught her by the waist when her legs gave out. Her mind screamed for Grant, but her tongue was thick and useless. She willed her mind to resist, even though her body couldn't help.

Though blurred, the smirk on Dugan's face was obvious. He leaned in closer, his breath hot and putrid.

"Always nice to see you again, Agent Cameron."

Someone else said something in a language she couldn't comprehend. Kolya? Their voices sounded like an old vinyl record on the wrong speed as she slipped under, and the dark abyss she'd escaped only days before greeted her once more.

Grant watched Jenna's abduction unfold from his position in the bushes that lined the side of the main house. He had taken advantage of the distraction of Dugan shooting Luca to take down an adversary who stood between him and the barn. The delay had cost him precious seconds. From his position, he witnessed the small group carry an unconscious Jenna into the barn. He had to get to her—but needed to do so discretely to eliminate the risk of Dugan shooting her too.

"Zeus, cover the west side of the house." He spoke quietly, allowing the throat mic to do the work of transmitting his request to Eric.

Eric rounded the corner of the main house with his rifle trained on one of Luca's men as Grant stepped out of the bushes to head for the barn.

"Down!" Eric's warning echoed in his earpiece just before a sledgehammer crushed his chest. Pain flared as he fought for air. He wondered who had been hit when Eric called over the comms for a medic and backup. The continuing firefight was the last thing that registered.

Minutes later, Grant's chest heaved as he rolled to his side and opened his eyes. His body armor had stopped the bullet from being a fatal hit, but the impact had nevertheless knocked him flat on his back. He didn't know if he'd been out seconds or minutes, but he knew he had been damned lucky. It took him several more precious seconds to get to his knees. He'd feel that for several days, but right now, Jenna needed him.

The uniform shirt of the unconscious guard would help disguise his identity, but to make it convincing, Grant was forced to sacrifice most of his gear. After grabbing the guy's hat and pulling it low, Grant helped himself to the man's AK-47, then cautiously moved out of the bushes when the firefight subsided. As he emerged from the shadows and entered the barn, he assumed a more confident gait to indicate he belonged there, and when a group of three of Luca's guards called out to him to hurry, he folded into the group.

Four identical vehicles were parked in a single-file line down the center of the barn. Kolya supported Jenna while Dugan opened the door to the second black Hummer in the line. They shoved her into the back seat and slammed the door, shouting instructions to the guards who remained.

Outnumbered as he was, there was no turning back. The opportunity to not only stay close to Jenna but also have a chance to bring down whoever was behind the trafficking operation wouldn't come around a second time. There was no way to relay his plans to Eric since he had abandoned his comm gear when he swapped uniforms. Casting a wistful glance at the helicopters, he and his new compatriots climbed into one of the vehicles.

He was on his own.

By the time Eric's team secured the area, he was afraid it would be too late to get the injured Grant to a chopper. Shouldering his weapon, he ran at a full sprint to where he'd seen Grant go down.

Trampled shrubbery, evidence that someone had been dragged into the bushes, led him deeper into the vegetation. A black shirt had been discarded next to an inert, shirtless form, along with a collection of U.S. military gear. Either Grant had changed clothes to infiltrate Luca's team, or he had been injured just badly enough to be taken hostage. If the former was true, there was a strong likelihood that Grant would be mistaken for one of Luca's men and taken out by friendly fire.

Eric keyed the radio to alert his teams to the possibility, only to be drowned out by a deafening crash as vehicles burst through the back wall of the old barn. Only a few futile shots were exchanged as three black Humvees sped away into the dark toward the woods.

"Hold your fire! Hold your positions until we clear the barn. It could be rigged," he cautioned his teams.

If one thing at all had gone right during the raid, that single decision was it.

The minute the third vehicle cleared the opening, the lead SUV fired a single RPG into the barn in a final effort to use what remained of the weapons cache to their advantage. The resulting explosion turned night into day, the blinding light erasing the last shadows of the battle and simultaneously incinerating the last Humvee that was just about to exit the barn.

The explosion was over in seconds, followed by an eerie stillness. The crackle of the flames, the final collapse of the wooden structure, and the keening wail of a young boy being comforted by an old man were the only sounds.

It was then that Eric was told that the boy cried for Jenna, having seen her dragged into the barn and placed into the Humvee before it exploded. At that moment, Eric knew exactly where Grant had been.

A number of the farm's legitimate employees slowly emerged from their hiding places and assisted Eric's team in securing those who had been complicit in crimes under Luca's employ.

For the better part of ten minutes, Eric sat alone in the open door of the helicopter watching the flames devour the ancient wood of the barn. For the first time in his career, he was unsure of his next move.

A hand on his shoulder roused him from his numb state of shock. Sirens could be heard in the distance. The teams reconvened and loaded their injured teammates and remaining gear, and the rotors began to turn. The sky to the east was getting lighter, and they needed to be well gone before the police arrived.

They flew home in respectful silence.

Replaying the mission in his head over and over and over, he couldn't identify the exact moment when it had all gone so horribly wrong. Eric's mind reeled over the loss of both Jenna and Grant. He had no concept of how he would tell Catherine. His stomach lurched, bile burned his throat. He leaned his head back, numbed by the vibration of the chopper. He thought of Jenna.

Her smile.

Her fearless dedication to doing the right thing.

Her kids.

God, her kids. He owned this failure, and he would be the one to knock on their doors—a chaplain by his side. He wouldn't shirk that responsibility.

Somewhere over the bright blue waters of the Tyrrhenian Sea, it occurred to him that Grant Lawton was now free from all that haunted him. Free from the guilt of the deaths that had weighed so heavily on him. Free from the pain.

But while that might be true, the gut-wrenching cost of the mission had bestowed fresh guilt at the feet of those who had survived.

russian roulette

COLONEL ERIC TAMANSKI TOSSED the game controller onto the ottoman and leaned back heavily into the couch cushions. Sick of playing video games to dull reality and pass the time, he rubbed his hands over his unshaven face for the hundredth time that day. It wasn't even nine o'clock in the morning.

His superiors had removed him from flying status and ordered him to remain in his quarters at Aviano Air Base until the U.S. Air Force decided his fate for his role in not one but two ill-fated operations of epic proportions.

The self-rebukes started again while he hunted for food in his refrigerator. He should have gone flying that day and refused the meeting with Salvo Agent Grant Lawton. He had lost count of how many times he wished he could go back to that fateful day and tell Lawton to pound sand. Jenna and Grant would both still be alive if he had.

From the kitchen, he wandered over to his computer and tried to log in. In a subtle dig at his ragged appearance, his personal computer refused to recognize his face, and he tapped the password in resentfully. A single unread email awaited, and for a minute he was excited to have something new, until he saw that the sender was Catherine Healey. Jesus, would the woman not leave him alone?

Deciding he had nothing better to do, he started reading.

Eric,

While I know well the circumstances in which you find yourself, I have no one else to turn to with this urgent assignment. None of our other players can stage in time to be useful.

I received a phone call at 0200 from an Italian cabinet member, Ilaria Giordano. Her office received an email with the attached picture, a time, a date, and a location. You will also note there is a price quoted. No other information was provided, and the sender used an anonymous and untraceable email account.

On the off chance this is reliable information, I have wired sufficient funds to a Credit Suisse bank account in your name. The money isn't important if this is actionable intel. Please look closely at the picture of the merchandise being sold. To be clear, you owe our organization nothing. You've sacrificed your hard-earned career for our mission already.

That being said, I alone am personally and selfishly begging you to not allow Grant Lawton's sacrifice to be in vain.

Whether or not you choose to purchase the merchandise on behalf of our agency, no response to this email is needed. I will be notified by the bank if/when the funds are withdrawn.

In desperation,
Catherine Healey

No.

Eric stood up and grabbed a beer from the fridge. He knew it was barely nine in the morning, so he didn't open it, comforted by the simple fact it was there if needed.

He read the message again.

Fuck, no.

He couldn't do this again. He refused to get involved again with whatever harebrained scheme Catherine Healey had cobbled together.

Hadn't he just been wishing he'd flown his scheduled sortie that day and never given Grant Lawton the time of day?

His conscience reminded him that Catherine was begging. And she called out Lawton's sacrifice. While the logical part of his brain was still emphasizing that he was confined to quarters and in deep shit already, his fingers scrolled the mouse cursor to the attachment and double-clicked.

He hardly recognized her.

But she was alive.

He sat heavily in his chair.

Jenna's face was bruised and sallow. Her eyes dull and unfocused, she squinted at the camera as if the light hurt. His eyes dropped to the information that Catherine had referenced.

16 July, 21h30

Café Liberté, Marseille

€3.200.000

Eric checked his watch. *Fuck*. It was 16 July.

Without considering the consequences, he frantically popped up a map online and typed in the name of the café in Marseille, France. Nine and a half hours' driving time. Wait, the funds. Typing in the name of the bank, he located a Credit Suisse branch in Milan along his route—well, sort of. That would make it at least a ten-hour trip, not counting the time at the bank. Not to mention, how would he carry over three million in cash?

He had no idea if he was being monitored or what would happen when he tried to cross into France, but he didn't much care. There was little left to lose. Regardless, if rescuing Jenna, or rather purchasing her, cost him what little was left of his reputation, retirement, and rank, it would be worth it.

From the top shelf of his closet, he snagged a bag that he'd last accessed when he and Grant had visited the warehouse together. Grabbing a change of clothes for himself, his passport, an empty large duffel bag, some clean sweats for her, a towel, and some toiletries, he was out the door in twenty-two minutes.

Jenna had no idea where she was other than that they spoke French. She could hear car horns and traffic and at one point smelled briny seawater and the dingy odor of a port. Still blindfolded, she was grateful to have been provided a shower and clean clothes, although her foggy brain worried a bit about why now and what was to follow. A young Middle Eastern girl had combed and styled her hair this morning but had not spoken a word.

It was evening when the car stopped and the blindfold was removed. She recognized Kolya as she blinked in the dim light. Looking around as she was pulled from the car, she realized they were in an alley. It reeked of festering garbage and stale cigarette smoke. Roughly, she was pushed through a filthy door that led into a commercial kitchen and then into a private dining room. Food hadn't crossed her mind until the aroma of cooking registered.

One of the men shoved her into a chair, and the other four men joked as they took their seats at the table. The way they ignored her both relieved and scared her. Her stomach growled even as nausea overwhelmed her.

About fifteen minutes later, the door to the dining room opened, quieting their crude banter. Not a word was uttered while a man with a thick mustache, beard, and wire-rimmed glasses was subjected to a cursory frisk and ushered into the room.

The newcomer carried a bulging duffel bag but otherwise appeared confident and somewhat wealthy. He remained standing and arrogantly tossed the duffel onto the wooden table.

The movement triggered a twinge of familiarity. She studied his features until it occurred to her that she was being sold. To him. Her panicked mind processed the implications of this development while the duffel was unzipped and the money counted. Still, not a word had been exchanged.

She glanced at the door. Could she make it out before being shot? Did she care at this point?

Terror rose in the form of bile in the back of her throat as the deal closed. Two of her captors propelled her to the buyer's side of the table. The buyer casually looked her up and down and turned her around twice as he inspected his merchandise. Nodding his acceptance, he took her by the arm and steered her toward the door.

Just as he was about to put his hand on the doorknob, this man—who had just purchased a human being—whirled around and, with a silenced pistol, fired five perfectly placed shots.

He grabbed the duffel, cinching the open zipper with an iron grip, and shoved her out the door ahead of him. Her thoughts tumbled. She looked for an escape route as they hastily exited through the kitchen that bustled with disinterested activity.

"Don't run from me, Jenna," the man whispered, reading her intentions. He tightened his grip on her arm to the point it hurt like everything else already did.

Caught off guard by the use of her name and the vague hint of recollection, she twisted again to break free.

"Jenna, it's Eric, damn it. Just keep walking. We're almost clear."

Shocked into acquiescence, she obeyed. Relief washed over her in such waves that she stumbled as he led her to a white Mercedes that idled in the filthy alley. The driver waited impatiently, smoking a cigarette that he flicked out the window as they approached.

"Hush. Not one word until we're alone," Eric coached her. The duffel bag was thrown into the back seat of the waiting sedan. He pushed her in next, shooing her across the seat so he could follow.

"*Allons-y*," he told the driver. The car pulled away and into traffic. Eric reached across the back seat without looking at her, took her hand, and squeezed. He didn't let go.

Against the curb outside a dark car park, he paid the driver with cash and led her through a purposeful maze of parked cars. Relatively assured of their freedom, he pointed wordlessly to his blue BMW sedan and opened the passenger door for her.

Eric collapsed behind the wheel. His forehead rested on hands that gripped the steering wheel so tightly he thought it might snap. He couldn't stop shaking as he stripped off the disguise. It took several deep breaths to quiet the storm in his blood. Give him a combat sortie with enemy fire any day. He'd never been that unnerved in all his years.

It wasn't just getting her back; it was the sobering and highly disturbing realization that he had literally just purchased someone. He knew this type of depraved activity happened throughout the world, but witnessing it—partaking in it—left him in shambles. It was inhuman. People with no hope, no champion, and no options other than to just be bought and sold.

Pulling himself together, Eric finally looked over at her and reached out to touch her cheek. She flinched involuntarily.

"It's me, Jenna. You're safe. I can't pretend to understand what you've been through, but I won't let anything happen to you from here on out. I swear that to you on my life." Eric choked the words out. "God, you're alive." His eyes burned and filled with unshed tears as he pulled her into an awkward embrace. Her whispered thanks were tendered between choked-back sobs. As he released her and buckled the seat belt around her, the question he dreaded was already in her eyes and made its way to her lips.

"Grant?" Her question was barely audible, but the look in her eyes screamed for answers. "He was there. With you. At the farm. I saw him egress the helicopter."

Eric blew out a soft breath and looked away. "Yes, he was there."

"Where—" The vacant, haunted look in her eyes turned to desperation. "Where is he? Is he okay?"

He couldn't meet her eyes.

"Where is Grant, Eric?" She swallowed, her eyes filling with tears. Her breaking voice managed to shout at him. "Damn it, Eric! Is he—tell me, goddammit. Is he—"

Eric had no idea how to tell her. All he could do was shake his head and whisper, "We don't know exactly. He followed you into the barn before they blew it up. We...we never found his body."

Her chin quivered again; one hand covered her mouth as if she might be sick. They needed to get moving, and he started the car without another word. Tears streamed down her face as she slumped against the door. Her state of mind demanded he offer comfort, but he was struggling to hold it together himself. So, he let her grieve without interfering, knowing that the pain of Grant's disappearance outweighed whatever relief she felt at her escape. As their car exited the garage, her shoulders shook in an emotional tsunami that lasted several minutes, eventually dissolving into an almost catatonic state.

The heavy traffic offered him a welcome diversion, and they drove the nine and a half hours back to Aviano in silence.

52

time after time

THE STEADY HUM OF the assorted monitors surrounding Jenna's hospital bed was both reassuring and irritating. Reassuring in that she was alive and safe; irritating in that she was still stuck in this room. There were things she needed to be doing and questions that needed answers.

Despite her protestations, Eric had escorted her into the emergency room at the Aviano hospital immediately upon their return from Marseille. He hadn't asked or forewarned her, and when he turned into the entrance of the hospital, her hoarse voice had objected vehemently. But to no avail.

The longer she stayed in the assigned bed, the more agitated she became. There was no need for medical attention; she was fine. For whatever reason—and for which she was eternally grateful—her captors had roughed her up a bit but otherwise hadn't touched her while she was a prisoner of Kolya's cartel. The doctors and investigators had delicately but doggedly worked that question into their repeated inquiries. The answer was always the same. No. She had been kept in isolation unless they were on the move.

When her patience with the well-intentioned therapist ran out, Eric played mediator, reminding her that she'd been damned fortunate to come out of the situation at all—much less unscathed.

After her ordeal, sleep should have been welcome. Instead, when she closed her eyes, her mind whirred. She could still picture Grant's smile and hear his laugh. She could almost feel him sitting on the edge of the bed next to her, proof, in her mind, that he was alive. There would be a yawning hole in the universe if not.

It was in those moments that her subconscious allowed the doubt to enter. At some point in the few short weeks of her captivity, she'd recalled Dugan's words as he had stood with Luca and Kolya while the helicopters were inbound.

"Even if he was fucking her for entertainment, he's not here for her," Dugan had said.

Nothing Dugan said had ever held any credibility, so she wasn't sure why that one comment kept replaying in her head. But it did. And it wouldn't dissipate.

Agent Grant Lawton had a mostly impeccable record of success, and his dedication to any mission to which he was assigned was unflappable. The possibility that she had merely been a means to an end bounced around in her head like a pinball.

Had Grant used her just to make sure their undercover roles were convincing enough to guarantee the mission would succeed? And in doing so, relegated their entire relationship to nothing more than a ruse? Or, as Dugan put it, maybe she had simply been summer entertainment for him.

She weighed the fact Grant despised Dugan more than anyone else at the Salvo Agency did. There was no question that, given the opportunity, Grant would have welcomed a reason to rid the world of the traitor. So, maybe it wasn't so far-fetched to think that Dugan had been his sole target during the supposed rescue mission at the estate in Sicily.

Grant hadn't been heard from since that night. Perhaps it had been part of his plan all along to kill Dugan and disappear.

Jenna found that level of deception difficult to swallow. Rationalization was a beautiful thing. It helped that Catherine dismissed the concept entirely, describing Grant as nearing his breaking point during her captivity. According to both Catherine and Eric, Grant had barely managed to maintain control, a feat credited to his steadfast goal of finding her.

Catherine insisted they had every Salvo antenna out and every ear to the ground, listening for indications of his existence. Of all the people Jenna trusted, Catherine topped the list. If Catherine learned anything at all, Jenna would know thirty seconds later. Even if the news confirmed her greatest fear.

Jenna glanced at the standard-issue military clock on the wall. Marseille seemed more distant with every twitch of the minute hand. She had focused on that same clock when Eric had planted a kiss on the top of her head—just after insisting they admit her for observation.

That was thirty-nine hours ago.

She wouldn't be there to see forty.

"What do you mean she's not here?" Eric demanded of the nurse at the desk on Jenna's floor after stalking down the hall from her now-vacated room.

"I'm sorry, sir. She requested her belongings and said she was checking herself out. That was about three and a half hours ago. There were no severe injuries, so we had no reason to restrict her from leaving."

"You had every reason to notify me, though. Why in God's name did no one call me?"

"Sir, we didn't even know if you were still in country."

Eric rolled his eyes. "I dropped her off, for Pete's sake."

"And you are neither her guardian nor her spouse," came the nurse's clipped reply.

"Whatever. She doesn't know anyone else on this base, so just exactly how did she leave, and where did she go?"

"Sir, I don't know what her plans were," the nurse said as she gathered clipboards together. "All I know is that she requested a phone number just before she signed the discharge statement."

"Whose?"

"Sir, I can't—"

He pinched the bridge of his nose, squeezed his eyes shut, and counted to ten. "Yes, you can. She's at the center of an investigation."

Eric drummed his fingers on the counter of the nurse's station while the nurse distributed paperwork into a plastic document divider.

The nurse sighed audibly. "She left of her own volition, you know."

Eric was beginning to think the nurse was enjoying this game.

"Look, I need to find her before she puts herself in harm's way again. Please. I'm asking nicely, only as a concerned friend, since you've so kindly reminded me that I have zero authority here any longer."

The nurse hesitated and looked at him over her reading glasses. "I still don't think—"

Eric hung his head and then looked her in the eye. "For the love of all things holy, just tell me."

"Lieutenant Colonel Henderson. That's who she called. He picked her up about ten minutes later."

And by the time Eric stood with his fists firmly planted on Lieutenant Colonel Henderson's desk, Jenna was more than halfway to Porto Arezzo.

i'll stand by you

Her departure from Porto Arezzo before the mission had been abrupt. Necessary at the time, but not necessary now.

By this point, Lourdes would know Jenna had deceived her. Lourdes might also believe that Jenna had used her for not only a false friendship, but also as a way to kill her son. Only it hadn't been a false friendship. And Luca had not been Lourdes's biological son.

The joy at hearing from Eric that Lourdes was still alive had quickly turned to trepidation, and as Jenna drove, she tried to lay out her approach. It wasn't outside the realm of possibility that Lourdes would slam the door in her face. Worst case, Matteo would have her killed for good this time, to finish what his son had started.

But she had to try. Had to make an attempt to put the truth out there and help Lourdes understand that their friendship had been the one honest thing in the entire summer. It didn't matter if she was shunned. If the attempt wasn't made, she would forever wonder if she had been forgiven.

The car that Lieutenant Colonel Henderson had let her borrow rolled to a stop outside the Santoris' villa. The man whose life she had saved had been surprised to hear from her but swore to help her in any way he could in return for all she had done during the firefight. A little late now, but maybe she should have asked him to send some backup with her as well.

Matteo's security team was normally stationed at the point where the road transitioned into driveway, but this time there had been no one to question her arrival. Her entire being trembled as she got out of the car. She lifted her face to the sun and looked out over the water, wordlessly vowing not to take the small things for granted anymore.

A deep breath helped, but her nerves were still frayed as her knuckles rapped on the leaded glass of the tall double door. Footsteps sounded. It took only a second or two for Paetta to recognize her. Jenna released a hesitant laugh when Lourdes's daughter squealed in delight.

"Jenna!" Paetta managed through the hand that covered her gaping mouth. The young woman then grabbed both of Jenna's hands and tugged her into the villa and into a hug before placing a repeated series of kisses on Jenna's cheeks.

"Oh, we were so worried. Mama is on the patio. Come!"

With Jenna's hand clutched in hers, Paetta led her to the glass doors that stood open to the patio.

Nothing had changed, it seemed. The flowers Jenna had once painted still bloomed, and the elderly woman she called a dear friend still lived.

"Mama, it's Jenna!" Paetta exclaimed.

Lourdes rose from the table where she sat with a man. She gasped, her eyes wide with surprise and joy.

"Jenna?" she said as she neared. "Is it really you?"

Jenna nodded, her voice breaking with emotion on seeing Lourdes.

"I was so afraid you would be furious with me that I almost didn't come." She pressed a hand to her throat. "But I had to see you, if only to try to talk things out. To justify—"

"*Basta*," the older woman shushed her in Italian.

The women embraced, their laughter and tears interrupted only by Paetta trying to lead them back to the table. It was then that Jenna recognized the man who stood with labored effort to greet her.

"Antonio?"

"Ah, *sì*, my dear," he said. "I'm relieved you are well. How we prayed for your safety."

Overwhelmed, Jenna looked from Lourdes to Antonio and then to Paetta. "I'm confused. Ecstatic, but a little confused. How is it that you are here in Porto Arezzo?"

Lourdes dabbed her eyes with a cloth napkin and took her seat, patting the chair next to her. Jenna lowered herself into it, accepting a glass of water from Paetta and taking a healthy sip.

"Lourdes, you look amazing," she said, patting her friend's knee gently. "And no cane?"

A smile crept across her face. "Oh, Jenna, I feel like my old self again. I feel sixty instead of ninety with one foot in the grave."

"But how...what...." Jenna laughed. "I don't even know where to begin."

A rueful expression replaced Lourdes's smile. "It was him all along."

"What do you mean? Who? Matteo?"

Lourdes shook her head. "No, *mia cara*. It was Luca. He was poisoning me." Her eyes filled.

"But why?"

"To get me out of his way? For him to think there would be some inheritance allocated to him is laughable." Lourdes gave a slight shrug. "I guess we'll never really know."

Antonio reached across the table and squeezed Lourdes's hand before looking over to Jenna. "She was very near death when you were captured. Luca had been blackmailing Carina into adding potassium to her food and drinks. Before he left the last time, he increased the dosage, which is why Lourdes failed so quickly then.

"With Luca gone, there was no more poison. She confessed the minute we got the news that he had been shot."

Jenna was stunned by the revelation.

"Carina was as relieved as we were that the nightmare was over," Paetta interjected. "I got my mother back and met my father for the first time the next week."

Antonio's other hand reached for Paetta.

"But Matteo," Jenna started, her brow furrowing then relaxing when Lourdes waved an absent hand.

"Matteo and I are divorcing. Suffice it to say that this is my villa now. He wouldn't dare cross me. I will live the rest of my days here with Antonio, happier than I've been in a long time." Lourdes flicked a glance across the courtyard. "The only thing I will not have is my closest friend in the villa across the way."

Jenna couldn't avoid looking over to the villa where so much of her life had changed. Someone else's yellow towel hung over the rail of the patio, drying in the sun. She wanted to rip it down and scream at them to leave her villa...their villa. Instead, she closed her eyes, envisioning the evenings they had shared, each in their usual chair, enjoying a bottle of wine as the sun gave way to nightfall.

Lourdes's hand on hers pulled her from the memory.

"Jenna, I'm so sorry about Grant," Lourdes offered. "I knew you weren't really married all along. But I also knew you came to love him. And he you."

Jenna blinked rapidly a few times before turning back to them. "I don't suppose you know anything. About what happened to him?"

Antonio shook his head sadly. "He was in the barn, we know. Philippe saw him go in."

Jenna's hands clenched in her lap. "But you thought I was dead, too, and I wasn't. Right?"

"We did at first. But Lourdes has her connections. We knew soon after that you had been taken by Kolya's group."

"Are you the ones who told Catherine about Marseille?" Jenna asked.

Lourdes cocked her head. "I alerted a close friend in the Italian government about the trafficking ring and where it was based. But no, I didn't hear about you being moved until he called to tell me you had been rescued. If he knew how that happened, he didn't tell me."

"Catherine told Eric," Jenna said in a distant voice. "He came for me."

"I'm relieved Luca and Kolya are no more," Lourdes said with a heavy sigh.

Jenna nodded her agreement. Her thoughts tumbled, trying to piece together the timeline.

"Thank you," she whispered. "I owe you my life. Even when you knew I wasn't who I said I was. Eric told me how you gave Grant my location...and your permission. I'm sorry your family paid the price for my freedom."

"And my freedom, too, yes?" Lourdes said with reassurance and patted Jenna's hand. "The old saying that wisdom comes with age? Well, it's true. You may be accomplished at playing someone else, but it's very hard to change who you are inside. And that's the woman I befriended." The elderly woman pursed her lips. "I'm ashamed that I didn't speak up sooner about Luca. I don't know how many women suffered because of him, but I wasn't about to let you be one of them. That's why I gave Grant the information."

Jenna's lips pressed together in an effort to keep another round of tears at bay.

"I have to find him," she breathed.

Lourdes tsked under her breath and raised Jenna's chin so their eyes met.

"This will be hard to hear, my dear, but it comes from a good place. Listen to an old woman. You need…well, I would encourage you to take some time. Let your friends and coworkers handle the search. That's their expertise."

"That's what Catherine said too." Jenna sighed with a small grimace.

"For what's it's worth," Lourdes continued in a gentle tone. "I don't think you should be the one who finds him." She took a measured breath. "For a number of reasons."

Jenna studied her friend, contemplating her statement. She slowly nodded in understanding before her chin quivered.

"I really need to hug my children."

"Then that's what you should do. Go home, Jenna. Give it some time. I will miss you, but you need some normalcy."

"Speaking of children, Philippe sends his love," Antonio said, waving a cell phone. "I texted the farm to let them know you were here and well."

Jenna smiled, grateful for the new direction the conversation was taking. "Please hug him for me. Will he stay there? At the estate in Sicily?" She didn't miss the glance exchanged between Lourdes and Antonio.

"No," Lourdes said. "We will bring him here. It's time for him to have as much of a childhood as he can—even though we are old. Paetta will help with him as long as she's here."

"I'm glad for that. He deserves you as much as you deserve him."

"And what of Evan?"

"He and his grandparents all went to Philadelphia when Luca threatened to go after him. That's where Evan lives with his late mother's sister. The Agency is providing some security for them until this all settles down. I'm not supposed to see or talk to him until...well, until I'm told it's safe."

Moments passed in silence.

"Will you visit us?" Lourdes asked gently.

Jenna swallowed, trying to ignore the trepidation in her soul that threatened to suffocate her. Tears filled her eyes as she looked at her friend. She bit the inside of her lip to stem the flow and nodded.

"I'll try."

"I hope you will."

Another minute of silence passed.

She swallowed again and squeezed Lourdes's hand.

"Yes," Jenna added, her resolve strengthening. "Yes, I'll come visit."

i knew you were waiting (for me)

E RIC WASN'T SURE WHY or how, but by the grace of God, he escaped being subjected to a court-martial. His chain of command hastened the timing of his planned retirement to underscore the fact that the military always got the last word. The ensuing officer grade determination reducing his rank to lieutenant colonel was a hundred times more lenient than he'd ever expected. He would never wear colonel rank again, but he gladly accepted the miraculous honorable discharge and retention of full retirement benefits.

Jenna had finally boarded one of the aircraft that often transited through Aviano, shuttling personnel to and from Europe. After seeing her off on the flight back to the States, he went home.

Guilt was his newest and constant companion. It was unconscionable to be so relieved with his light sentence when she and others had lost so much under his command.

The movers had come and gone the day before. He stood alone in the vacuum of his now empty quarters and opened his computer. A new message from Catherine waited in his email inbox. Not sure he was ready to read it yet, he reached under a kitchen cabinet and pulled out what remained of Grant's bottle of Laphroaig. Resigned, he set it firmly on the counter with a clunk.

"You hear that, Lawton?" he muttered under his breath. The challenge that Grant had issued to him not so many weeks ago echoed against the walls of his empty house. Against the emptiness in his soul.

His hands shook as he poured a glass. He stood motionless for a moment, leaning heavily on the counter, palms flat on the hard surface and eyes closed, until he came up with the right words. Toasting Grant and then Jenna, he poured the amber liquid down his throat. And another and another. Until the bottle was empty.

As his flight touched down in the U.S., newly retired Air Force Lieutenant Colonel Eric Tamanski took a cleansing breath, grateful to be on American soil again. During the flight, his mind had started working on some of the inconsistencies that bothered him about the last few months. He would sort through them as soon as he was settled in DC.

After deplaning, Eric reflected on this chance to start a new chapter—hell, a whole new book—while he rode the escalator down to the baggage claim area to gather his checked bags. It took what felt like forever, but after the long flight, he didn't mind standing. One of his bags finally tumbled onto the conveyor belt, and the other was spit out from the black hole of the baggage sorting area a few moments later. Weighed down with his belongings, he weaved through the crowd of limo drivers awaiting their passengers as they waved signs and called out names.

Just before he exited the doors with his luggage, he noticed someone off to the side holding a sign with a name and title he vaguely recognized.

Eric Tamanski
Commander, The Salvo Agency

He did a double take and read the sign again to be sure. At the same time, the placard lowered, and Catherine Healey smiled broadly up at him.

"Welcome to Washington, DC, Commander," she greeted. After a quick hug, she patted his arm. "Got your bags?"

He grinned and nodded at the silver-haired whirlwind standing in front of him.

"Then that's enough dilly-dallying," she announced. "Let's go. You and I have a lot of work to do."

G RANT LAWTON HAD NOT been seen or heard from in three months and thirteen days. And the more time that passed, the more she was reconstructing her life without him.

Jenna didn't believe he was dead; the Agency would know somehow. Catherine had been monitoring the entry alarm and cameras at his now-abandoned condo. His known email accounts had not been accessed, his cell phones had gone silent, and none of his Salvo-sanctioned aliases had been tagged by any of the agencies that monitored Europe's transportation systems.

Most telling of all, the numerous intelligence networks in the world were silent on the topic. Those networks, especially the illicit ones, would certainly be talking if anyone had taken down Grant Lawton.

If and when they talked, the Salvo Agency would be listening.

See next page to order Book Two!

Book Two in the THROMANCE™ series is available now! Use your phone's camera to scan the QR code to get your copy.

I HOPE YOU LOVED reading this book as much as I enjoyed writing it! Solid reviews and ratings are critical to self-published authors, so please take a moment to leave a review on your favorite site. The algorithms—and the author—will be very appreciative!

Follow me!

<u>Facebook page:</u> Olivia M Charles - Author
<u>Instagram</u>: @omcauthor
<u>Website</u>: www.oliviamcharles.com (Join my mailing list!)

In keeping with my goal of helping readers escape, the chapter names are songs! So, of course, a Spotify playlist was obligatory. Use your phone's camera to scan the QR code below. If all else fails, search Spotify for the *OliviaMCharles-Summer Salvo* playlist.

Olivia M. Charles grew up in an Air Force family, so packing up every few years, traveling overseas, and spending hundreds of hours in the car fostered a love of reading. Books were a way of traveling even when she wasn't, a way to pass the time when she was, and a source of inspiration and escape throughout.

She then served as an Air Force pilot herself, flying air refueling missions around the world. Following her military service, she worked full-time while raising two wildly amazing children with a very supportive husband.

Ten dogs and twenty-two moves later, she found herself trudging through the days mired in the corporate grind. One night—in dire need of a therapeutic outlet—she sat down at the computer and just started typing.

Olivia currently lives in the southeastern U.S. and is an empty nester with a bucket list larger than her paycheck. Whenever time and temperature permit, she can be found on the screened porch typing away on her laptop, hoping to help others set the realities of life aside for just a bit.

acknowledgements

I'M NOT EVEN SURE how this happened to be honest. I do know that I never would have come this far without the consistent support and encouragement from my family and a handful of close friends. I'm not sticking a toe in the water of the self-publishing world alone, but instead I feel as if I'm holding hands with all of you, raising them high, and preparing to jump from the side of the pool as the camera captures the moment.

It goes without saying that I owe so much to my parents who encouraged reading and traveling and stressed the importance of schoolwork—as unwelcome as that last one was at times. My mom, who perhaps unknowingly, exemplified what it meant to be a mom and also a woman capable of standing on her own two feet through all life's ups and downs. My dad was an incredible man whom I miss so much. I can still see the twinkle in his eyes and hear his laugh. He was one of the best pilots ever, but he was even a better dad. He taught me to fly in so many ways.

To my husband, thank you for the love, support, and for never once griping about the credit card charges that fund this latest venture-or any of the previous ones, for that matter.

I couldn't have imagined two more incredible children. Thank you to my daughter who was the first to know of my foray into writing, then my first editor and beta reader (be sure to check out her book blog, https://beccasbookshelves.com/. Thank you to my son who painted and sketched the inspiration for my book cover and never rolled his eyes when I changed my mind or asked for more of his artistic help. And thank you to my newest daughter who offered her creative writing expertise and contagious enthusiasm. Much love to all three of you, and thanks for still taking my calls and not sending me to voicemail.

To my sister—trying to keep this short-but, wow, what strength. I could brag on you for days, but thank you for the edits, the suggestions, but most of all, for encouraging this craziness. Looking forward to turning more pages with you.

To my niece—your suggestions, encouragement, and social media prowess are so appreciated. Thank you for helping me navigate this whole social media marketing thing.

To my friends who have listened to me go on and on about this effort for months and never told me to be quiet. Kelly and Briar, thank you for your time, patience, and insight!

It was my trademark attorney (who didn't laugh at the proposed mark-at least, not to me) who pointed me in the direction of the Atlanta Writers Club. Thank you, Keely, for your expertise and constant advice as I started down this road. http://kherricklaw.com/

A huge thank you to my eagle-eyed editor (Sandusky Editorial Services LLC) for all the guidance, edits, suggestions, and saves! I so enjoyed working with you on this project! https://www.sanduskyeditorial.com/

Without the resources and knowledge so willingly shared by the Atlanta Writers Club, I would never have realized that this step was possible. The webinars and conferences are fantastic, but it's the open sharing of information that is so incredible. Thanks, George and Jerry, for all you do.

I'm humbled by any reader who chose to read my book, so a heartfelt thank you for purchasing and/or downloading it, and I hope you'll stay tuned for the rest of the series!